DATE DUE

MAY 1 9 2000	

Sir John Soane, Architect

JOHN SOANE, a portrait by Sir Thomas Lawrence, 1829.

SIR JOHN SOANE
ARCHITECT

DOROTHY STROUD

faber and faber
LONDON · BOSTON

First published in 1984
by Faber and Faber Limited
3 Queen Square London WC1
Filmset and printed in Great Britain by
B AS Printers Limited
Over Wallop, Hampshire
All rights reserved

British Library Cataloguing in Publication Data

Stroud, Dorothy
Sir John Soane, architect.
1. Soane, Sir John   2. Architects—England
—Biography
I. Title
720′92′4   NA997.S7
ISBN 0-571-13050-X

Library of Congress Cataloging in Publication Data

Stroud, Dorothy.
Sir John Soane, architect.

Bibliography: p.
Includes index.
1. Soane, John, Sir, 1753–1837.   I. Soane, John, Sir, 1753–1837.
II. Title.
NA997.S7S76   1984   720′.92′4   83-11488
ISBN 0-571-13050-X (U.S.)

Preface

It is now twenty-five years since the publication of my first *catalogue raisonné* of Soane's architectural works, and nearly twenty since that went out of print. In the intervening years a good deal has been written on various aspects of his style and his buildings, but little that touches on his personal life. It therefore seems appropriate to begin a revised catalogue of his works with an account of the background against which was set his remarkable progress from a humble origin to a position of eminence both as an architect, and as the founder of the museum which bears his name.

Soane was not an easy character. His own early struggles led to the conviction that hard work was the only sure path to success, and he had little patience with idleness or incompetence. That his sons should have failed to reach his high standards was a constant source of regret, yet his private disappointments did not harden him to the genuine needs of others, and he was a generous benefactor both to worthy causes and to many unfortunate individuals. He was a ready subscriber to appeals for the widows and children of several of his contemporaries, and these were the forerunners of the many who were to benefit in years to come from the fund for 'Distressed Architects and their Dependents', which Soane endowed in 1833. The improvement of architectural education and the future of the profession were probably the objects nearest his heart— which he furthered not only by his own Royal Academy lectures, but by his participation in the founding of the Institute (now the Royal Institute) of British Architects. These aims were ultimately reflected in his decision to settle, under an Act of Parliament, his house and its priceless collections of works of art, books and architectural drawings for the benefit of the public in general and students in particular. Architecture never had a more dedicated follower or generous benefactor than John Soane.

In the preparation of this account I must gratefully acknowledge the permission of the Trustees of Sir John Soane's Museum to work on, and quote from, the private correspondence and office papers in their keeping. To the Curator, Sir John Summerson, my warmest thanks are due for his constant and invaluable help and advice. I am also indebted to Howard Colvin for much useful information, and especially for copies of the Soane entries from the transcripts of the Goring Registers in the Bodleian Library, Oxford. The owners of the various houses and other buildings with which Soane was concerned have been invariably helpful in answering my enquiries or allowing me access, and my thanks are also due to the staffs of the County Records Offices of Norfolk, Berkshire and Essex. To Charlotte Roberts I am grateful for her help in the compilation of the index and the arrangement of the illustrations.

Dorothy Stroud

1983

Contents

Preface   *page* 7
List of Illustrations   10
Abbreviations   14

Part One   THE SOANE STORY

1. 'A Good Boy Learns . . .'   17
2. A Travelling Student   29
3. Setting up a Practice   49
4. 'Form, if You Can, a Style of Your Own'   62
5. The Pitzhanger Dream   74
6. Family Troubles   88
7. The Last Decades   106

Part Two   THE ARCHITECTURAL WORKS
            OF SIR JOHN SOANE

Major Commissions   119
   Early Works 1781–1792   119
   The Middle Period 1792–1820   169
   Late Works 1820–1833   210
List of Works   239

Drawings Exhibited at the Royal Academy   280
Bibliography   288
Index   289

Illustrations

*Unless otherwise indicated, illustrations in the following list are reproduced
by courtesy of the Trustees of Sir John Soane's Museum*

	John Soane, portrait by Sir Thomas Lawrence	*frontispiece*
1.	John Soane, aged twenty-one, by George Dance	*page* 19
2.	Mrs Soane, mother of John Soane, water-colour portrait by John Downman	19
3.	Old Somerset House, drawn by Soane	23
4.	Banqueting House, Whitehall, drawn by Soane	23
5.	Design for a monument to James King	25
6.	Design for a pavilion	26
7.	The Pantheon in Rome, drawn by Soane	30
8.	The Colosseum in Rome, drawn by Soane	30
9.	The Temple of Vesta at Tivoli, drawn by Soane	30
10.	A design for a mausoleum	31
11.	The Temple of Ceres at Paestum, drawn by Soane	33
12.	The Temple of Isis, drawn by Soane	33
13.	Design for a classical dog-house	33
14.	The Corsini Chapel, S. Giovanni Laterno, Rome, drawn by Soane	39
15.	Soane letter to Thomas Pitt, with drawings	41
16.	Design for a triumphal bridge	43
17.	Design for lodges at Hamels	52
18.	Dairy at Hamels, engraving	52
19.	First design for Mr Adams' shop front	53
20.	Mr Adams' shop front.	53
21.	Anna Storace, artist unknown	55
22.	George Wyatt, by George Dance	55
23.	Bath house at Botleys	57
24.	Tomb designed for Miss Johnstone	57
25.	A ceiling design from Bartoli's *Gli Antichi Sepolchri*	63
26.	The dairy, Hamels	63
27.	No. 12 Lincoln's Inn Fields, the Old Breakfast Room, by J. M. Gandy	67
28.	No. 12 Lincoln's Inn Fields, chimneypiece detail	67
29–31.	Unexecuted designs for House of Lords	68–9
32–5, 37.	Pitzhanger Manor, Ealing	75–7
36.	Wall-painting in the Villa Negroni, engraved by A. Campanella	77

38. Mrs Soane and the boys, water-colour by Antonio B. Van Assen   *page* 79
39. No. 13 Lincoln's Inn Fields   90
40. No. 13 Lincoln's Inn Fields, design   91
41. No. 13 Lincoln's Inn Fields, plan   91
42. No. 13 Lincoln's Inn Fields, dining-room   92
43. No. 13 Lincoln's Inn Fields, breakfast-room   93
44. No. 13 Lincoln's Inn Fields, section through dome   93
45. No. 13 Lincoln's Inn Fields, drawing-room, By kind permission of
    Country Life   93
46. No. 13 Lincoln's Inn Fields, painting of views of the house   94
47. No. 13 Lincoln's Inn Fields, the Dome   95
48. No. 13 Lincoln's Inn Fields, Soane's bedroom   95
49. Mrs Soane, drawing by John Flaxman   101
50. Design for the Soane Tomb   103
51–2. The Soane tomb, and detail of panel inscribed to Soane   114
53. Caricature of Soane by Daniel Maclise   115
54. Bridge over the River Wensum, Norwich   117
55. Letton Hall, engraving   120
56. Letton Hall, plan   120
57. Letton Hall. National Monuments Record   120
58. Letton Hall, first-floor landing. National Monuments Record   121
59–60. Letton Hall, chimneypiece details. National Monuments Record   121
61. Doric barn at Solihull. Author's collection   122
62. Langley, gateway. National Monuments Record   123
63. Langley, entrance and lodges. National Monuments Record   123
64. Earsham, music-room. National Monuments Record   125
65. Earsham, music-room, section   125
66. Saxlingham, drawings   126
67. Saxlingham. National Monuments Record   126
68–9. Tendring Hall, section and plan   127
70. Shotesham, engraving of façade   128
71–2. Shotesham, façade and vestibule. National Monuments Record   128–9
73. Shotesham, plan   129
74. Lees Court, stables   131
75. Ryston Hall   131
76. Blundeston House   133
77–8. Fonthill, section through gallery and chimneypiece design   135
79. Bentley Priory, rear elevation as enlarged   136
80. Bentley Priory, plan   136
81. Bentley Priory   137
82–3. Bentley Priory, hall and music-room   137
84. Piercefield, in ruins. Author's collection   139
85. Norwich Gaol, drawing   139
86. Gunthorpe Hall   140
87. Sydney Lodge   141

88. Simonds Brewery, drawing   *page* 142
89. Simonds Brewery   142
90. Chilton Lodge   143
91. Buckingham House, Pall Mall   144
92–3. Buckingham House, staircase hall   145
94–5. Norwich, Surrey Street, chimneypieces. National Monuments Record   146
96. Wimpole Hall, drawing-room. By kind permission of *Country Life*   147
97. Wimpole Hall, design for drawing-room   148
98. Wimpole Hall, the *castello d'aqua*   148
99. Wimpole Hall, the ante-library. Photograph by A. F. Kersting   148
100. Wimpole Hall, lodges and entrance, drawing   149
101–2. Baronscourt, plan and drawing of entrance front   150–1
103. Bank of England, plan   152
104–5. Bank of England, Bank Stock Office, design and plan   153
106–7. Bank of England, Bank Stock Office as built, and detail   154
108–9. Bank of England, Rotunda, drawing and sketch   155
110–11. Bank of England, Consols Office, first design and in course of construction   156–7
112. Bank of England, Lothbury, east end   158
113–14. Bank of England, Lothbury arch, design and as executed   158–9
115. Bank of England, Lothbury Court with Residence Court   160
116. Bank of England, Waiting Room Court, loggia   160
117–18. Bank of England, Princes Street entrance, drawing, and vestibule   161
119. Bank of England, £5 Note Office   162
120–1. Bank of England, Tivoli Corner, drawing and as executed   162–3
122. Bank of England, passage to Rotunda   164
123. Bank of England, Old Dividend Office   164
124–5. Bank of England, Colonial Office, drawing, and detail   165
126. Bank of England, Views in various parts, water-colour drawing   166
127. Bank of England, Threadneedle Street front   167
128. Bank of England, Barrack Building   167
129. Tyringham, drawing   169
130–1. Tyringham, section through house and plan   170
132. Tyringham   171
133. Tyringham, drawing of hall   171
134. Tyringham, gateway and lodges   172
135. Tyringham, drawing of bridge   172
136–7. Tyringham, proposals for church   173
138. Winchester, Mr Richards' Academy, design   175
139. Winchester, Mr Richards' Academy. Author's collection   175
140. Cumberland Gate, Hyde Park, drawing   176
141. Bagshot Lodge entrance, drawing   177
142. Betchworth Castle, chimneypiece drawing   178
143. Betchworth Castle, stable design   178
144. Betchworth Castle, dairy   178

145. Aynho, south front. By kind permission of *Country Life*   *page* 179
146. Aynho, north front, arch on east. National Monuments Record   180
147. Aynho, west façade. By kind permission of *Country Life*   180
148. Aynho, library. By kind permission of *Country Life*   180
149. Praed's Bank, design for façade   183
150. Mr Robins' house at Norwood   184
151. Lord Bridport's library at Cricket   185
152. Mr Knight's hall, Grosvenor Square   186
153–4. Port Eliot, south front and stables. By kind permission of *Country Life*   187–8
155–6. Port Eliot, chimneypiece and ceiling. By kind permission of *Country Life*   188
157. Ramsey Abbey, drawing   189
158. Cedar Court, drawing   190
159. New Bank Buildings, drawing   191
160–1. Stowe, library and vestibule. By kind permission of *Country Life*   192–3
162. Moggerhanger. National Monuments Record   194
163. Moggerhanger, design   194
164–5. Charlotte Street, design and plan for mausoleum   195
166. Royal Hospital, Chelsea, drawing showing Soane's various works   196
167. Royal Hospital, Chelsea, the Infirmary   197
168–71. Royal Hospital, Chelsea, stables, Royal Hospital Road, East Road and Secretary's Offices. National Monuments Record   198–9
172–3. Dulwich Art Gallery, design and in course of construction   201
174. Dulwich Art Gallery, interior   201
175–6. Dulwich Art Gallery, Mausoleum, drawings   202
177. Dulwich Art Gallery, Mausoleum, roof lantern   202
178. Ringwould House, design   205
179. Lord Bridport's tomb at Cricket St Thomas   205
180. Butterton Farm House   206
181. National Debt Redemption Office, section   208
182–3. Marden Hill, porch and entrance to hall. By kind permission of *Country Life*   209
184. Wotton House. By kind permission of *Country Life*   211
185–6. Wotton House, designs   211–12
187–8. Regent Street, Mr Robins' houses, drawing and chimneypiece design   213
189. Pellwall, front entrance. National Monuments Record   214
190. Pellwall, design for triangular lodge   215
191–3. House of Lords, new Royal Entrance, drawings and plan   216–17
194. House of Lords, Scala Regia, drawing   217
195. House of Lords, Ante Room, engraving   218
196. House of Lords, Royal Gallery, drawing   218
197. Insolvent Debtors' Court, design   219
198. Insolvent Debtors' Court   220
199–200. Law Courts, plan and drawing   221–2
201–2. Law Courts, Views of Court of King's Bench and side gallery   223

203–5. Law Courts, Views of Court of Chancery, Vice Chancellor's Court, and Lord Chancellor's Robing-Room   *pages 224–5*
206. Privy Council Offices and Treasury, drawing   *page 226*
207. Privy Council Chamber, drawing of interior   227
208. No. 10 Downing Street, dining-room   229
209. No. 11 Downing Street, breakfast-room   229
210. No. 10 Downing Street, ceiling detail   230
211. St Peter, Walworth, drawing   231
212. St Peter, Walworth. Photograph by A. F. Kersting   231
213. Holy Trinity, Marylebone, drawing   232
214. Holy Trinity, Marylebone. National Monuments Record   232
215. St John, Bethnal Green. National Monuments Record   233
216. Freemasons' Council Chamber, drawing   234
217. New State Paper Office, drawing   235
218. New State Paper Office, view from St James's Park   236
219. New State Paper Office, entrance elevation, drawing   237
220. New State Paper Office, doorway, drawing   237
221. Composite painting of Soane's Works up to 1815   238

Abbreviations

SMC = Soane Museum Correspondence (General)
SNB = Soane Notebooks
SPC = Soane Private Correspondence

[Part One]

THE SOANE STORY

[1]

'A Good Boy Learns . . .'

Throughout his long life John Soane maintained an extreme reticence about his early years and family background, a reticence which becomes even more apparent when we consider his careful preservation of such papers as dealt with his practice, or with the troublesome behaviour of his two sons from their school days onwards. When in 1835 he wrote his privately printed *Memoirs of the Professional Life of an Architect*, his reminiscences went no further back than a decision, made when he was fifteen, to pursue an architectural career.[1] That leaves many questions unresolved, the first and most obvious being his place of birth, which is most likely to have been the village of Goring on the Oxfordshire–Berkshire border where his father, a local builder, had resided for a number of years. The elder Soan, as the name was originally spelt, was a son of Francis Soan of the Swan Inn at Goring who had married a widow, Elizabeth Toby, *circa* 1698. Francis Soan was drowned while fishing in the Thames, an accident which was witnessed by Lady Fane of The Grotto at Basildon.[2] His son John the builder is said to have carried out work on the west tower of Basildon Church, which was added in 1734. On 4 July 1738, John married Martha Marcy, then aged twenty-three, as is recorded on the flyleaf of her bible which is preserved in the Soane Museum. Nothing has come to light as to her background, but it is likely that the Revd Mr Marcy, who was vicar of Broughton in Oxfordshire at the end of the eighteenth century, was a nephew or second cousin.[3]

During the twelve years which followed the marriage of John and Martha Soan, the names of their first six children were duly recorded in the baptismal register of the Church of St Thomas of Canterbury, Goring.[4] Of these two boys, William and John, died shortly after birth, but the names were then given to two further sons, the elder being William who was born in 1741. The girls were Deborah (1743), Susanna (1745), and Martha (1748). For the seventh and last child, John, born on 10 September 1753, there is, however, no entry in the Goring register, which has led researchers in the past to look further afield, although unsuccessfully, in the neighbouring parishes of Basildon, Pangbourne and Whitchurch. In the latter an entry in the register of St Mary's Church resulted in a confusion which has persisted over the years, for the birth of a John Soane (spelt with an *e*) which is recorded in 1748 cannot refer to the architect for two reasons: firstly, it does not accord with the known year of his birth, and secondly, the baby John registered here was the child of John Soane and his wife Frances (née Hannington) who had been married in this church on the previous 3 February.

As to the first years of the architect's life, then, little is known. But many years later he obtained from his old friend Timothy Tyrrell, Remembrancer to the City of London, a copy of an entry in a rent book which had belonged to the latter's father, Timothy Tyrrell who died in 1766. The note reads: 'A House lett to Mr Soane at 4 Pounds and ten Shillings a Year to enter at Lady Day 1761.'[5] Although this does not prove that the house was in Reading, it would appear likely since in that year young John Soan was eight years old, which fits in with the tradition that he was, at about this time, sent to the school in Reading kept by William Baker, a man of 'great classical and mathematical learning'. From about the same time there also survive some school books in which are the names of John and his elder brother William from whom they had presumably been passed on. Young John's heavy scribblings in some of these show no great respect for books and he apparently did not go unreprimanded for he added such maxims as 'A Good Boy Learns', and 'John Soan is a Noddy for Sc[r]ibbling His Book and ought to have his Licking.' As he grew older, he settled down to serious study of which Latin, Greek and mathematics formed part. A copy of John Robertson's *Complete Treatise of Mensuration* is still in the Soane Library and is inscribed 'J. Soan 1765', while among other books by the mathematician Benjamin Martin is one in which Soane wrote his name followed by 'Philom[ath] 1767'.

By the latter date, however, his carefree school-days were coming to an end, and some time before 1768 his parents and sisters had apparently moved back to Goring-on-Thames, for John Soan senior died there at the age of fifty-four and was buried on 1 May of that year in the graveyard of St Thomas's Church. The elder son, William, following his father's trade, had already settled in Chertsey.

If a story recounted by Joseph Farington is to be believed, young John had joined his brother by the end of 1767, the diarist having been told this many years later by the artist Thomas Daniell, whose father had been keeper of the Swan Inn at Chertsey in the 1760s and 'knew Soane when a boy at Chertsey, where he assisted his Brother, who was a journeyman Bricklayer, as a hod boy'.[6] A rather more informative account is given by Edward Wedlake Brayley when describing, in his *History of Surrey*, the now-vanished Ongar Hill, near Chertsey. 'The house which is of brick, painted white, but with little embellishment, was erected about eighty years ago [that is, about 1770]; and the late celebrated architect, Sir John Soane, is known to have worked on it as a brick-layer's boy.' In a footnote Brayley goes on to say that Soane 'was then under the control of an illiterate and ill-conditioned elder brother who was employed here, and who plodded through life as a petty bricklayer. In his old age, a small annuity was allowed him by his more successful relation. A lady of Chertsey (lately deceased) used to speak of recollecting Sir John, when a boy, attending on his brother; and that, at every opportunity, he would sit at the foot of the ladder, engaged with a book.'[7]

It is evident that the boy was eager to escape from this lowly position and the opportunity came in the following year when, as he recorded in his *Memoirs*, 'through the kindness of a near relative I was introduced to Mr Peacock, an eminent surveyor, and from the friendship of that gentleman, in 1768, I became a pupil of Mr Dance'. Probably

1. (*left*) JOHN SOANE, aged twenty-one, a chalk drawing by Nathaniel Dance, RA.
2. (*right*) MRS SOANE, mother of John Soane, water-colour portrait by John Downman, 1798.

the 'relative' was his brother William who could have become acquainted with James Peacock in the course of his building work. Very little is known about the early life of the latter, who was born about 1732, but there is nothing to show that he was connected with the novelist Thomas Love Peacock who came to live at Chertsey a few years later.[8]

Soane's meeting with James Peacock was providential since the latter was then carrying out measuring work for the recently appointed Clerk of Works to the City of London, George Dance. In addition to a backlog of City works inherited from his deceased father, Dance was also making additions to a house at Ealing for his future father-in-law, Thomas Gurnell, and it was for this in particular that he and Peacock sought the help of a young assistant and decided to give John Soane the chance at which he leapt. Dance was then still living in the narrow house at the corner of Chiswell Street and Moorfields, on the fringe of the City, which had been his family's home for nearly half a century. Soane's copy of *The Young Mathematician's Guide* by John Ward is inscribed with his name and the date, March 1769. The additional words 'Corner of Moorfields' confirm that he was living in the Dance household for his first months in London. His later use of the word 'pupil' in recollecting his position here did not, of course, imply the formal training which the term was to denote later in the century, but there is no reason to think that his duties undertaken for George Dance were, as implied by Joseph Farington, in the kitchen rather than the office. Living with a family inevitably involves a helping hand in general, and this no doubt gave rise to two more of the stories which the diarist delighted to record if disparaging to Soane. One was a recollection by Dance's nephew, the naval commander Sir Nathaniel Dance, that he had seen young Soane in the kitchen of his uncle's house 'while he was cleaning shoes', a chore which does not necessarily imply servility whether the shoes were his own or those of his employer.[9] The second story was a misinterpretation of a remark by the artist Henry Fuseli. What the latter said to Farington, when disapproving of Soane's conduct over Royal Academy business on a particular occasion, was that he showed a 'peevish and little mind expressed in a manner which might only have been expected from a footman', an opinion which certainly did not mean that Soane had been employed by Dance as a footman.[10]

Much of Dance's official work in 1768 was for new projects, which included his first venture in urban planning when a decision was reached by the City Lands Committee to develop a tract of waste ground in the Minories on which a crescent, square and circus were soon to rise. Simultaneously a plan was sought for land beyond the southern end of London Bridge; but a far more demanding task than either of these was now beginning to materialise. It was the outcome of discussions which had continued over several years on the need for re-building the notorious Newgate Gaol. The elder Dance had drawn out a striking but abortive design for this shortly before his death, after which his son was instructed by the City Lands Committee to prepare a scheme embracing both the Gaol and the adjoining Sessions House. The result was laid before the Committee together with estimates which were approved, although the design had then to be submitted for the consent of the Court of Common Council. Throughout the year, and for several years to come, the Gaol and its adjoining building were to become Dance's major preoccupation and eventually produced two of the finest buildings ever to grace the city; but in the early stages the preparation of endless working drawings and costing, added to the routine maintenance of City property, must have imposed a somewhat monotonous daily round for an ambitious and impetuous young assistant. There is, however, no doubt as to the importance of this period in Soane's training. Both Dance and Peacock were dedicated to their profession and had little time for social distractions other than their shared love of music. From them Soane learnt that the discipline of hard work had its own rewards, and that accuracy and reliability were the sure foundation on which to build a practice. It was, moreover, from Dance's exquisite draughtsmanship that he gained the essential knowledge of how to set out plans and elevations in ink or pencil, and how to apply wash. At the same time it was Dance's recollecting of his days spent in Italy, and his wide knowledge of that country's buildings, which were to kindle Soane's enthusiasm for classical architecture.

It was no doubt from Dance that Soane first heard of the formation of an institution which was ultimately to be of the greatest value in pursuing his architectural progress. Towards the end of 1767 a group of artists, dissatisfied with the course taken by the

Incorporated Society of Artists, and by the Free Society of Artists which had broken away from it, took steps to found a new Academy of the Arts and successfully petitioned King George III for Royal Patronage. With a charter (generally referred to as *The Instrument*) signed by the king on 10 December 1768, the Royal Academy came into being, its first forty members representative of the arts and including George Dance and his elder brother Nathaniel.

The first Academy meetings were held in premises on the south side of Pall Mall, but in 1771, on the king's direction, accommodation was provided in what had been the royal apartments of Old Somerset House, that is, on the north side of the south-east range, overlooking an open court, and, beyond it, the Thames. Into that limited space were squeezed the library, lecture room and a residential suite for the Keeper, this sufficing until the new Somerset House was built to Sir William Chambers's designs. It was here that students were required to attend the lectures given by the professors of Anatomy, Perspective, Sculpture and Architecture, and to study in the library. Those who did so were entitled to enter the annual competitions, for which gold and silver medals were awarded. The most glittering prize, however, was the travelling studentship endowed by the king.

To Soane, with minimal financial resources behind him, this studentship offered the only possible way in which study abroad might ultimately be achieved; but to qualify entailed admission to the Academy School. That may well have been a factor in strengthening Soane's decision to gain wider experience than Dance's City work could offer, and with the latter's approval he made a successful application for a junior post in the office of Henry Holland where he was to be paid a salary of £60 a year. Holland was the son of a widely known and respected builder in whose firm he had gained his knowledge of architecture. In 1770 he embarked on a professional career in collaboration with the landscape gardener and architect, Lancelot ('Capability') Brown, who had recently designed the carcase of Claremont for the 1st Lord Clive, and required assistance for its internal decoration, as well as help over a number of other pending commissions. It was for Claremont that Soane was first set to work as a draughtsman, copying out decorative details of which a number of small sketches are preserved in a miscellaneous album in the Soane Museum.[11]

The Hollands were a close-knit family long resident in Fulham. From 1766, however, they also shared a small town house, No. 31 Half Moon Street, where the principal occupants in the 1770s were Richard Holland, who later took over the building firm after his cousin Henry had launched out as an architect, and Henry himself who continued to reside here for some time after his marriage to Lancelot Brown's daughter Bridget in 1773. Whether Soane actually lived *en famille* in this house is not absolutely certain, but it seems likely as his letters were addressed there for several years, and it was the address which he was to give on his early exhibition drawings. Richard Holland was, moreover, to become one of his closest and lifelong friends.

In seeking admission to the Academy School in the early autumn of 1771 Soane had to submit to the Keeper, George Michael Moser, evidence of his ability in drawing.

The subject is not known, but it satisfied the Council at a meeting on 25 October and his name was duly entered in the Register of Students as 'Soan John, 18 yrs. 10 Sep. Architect'. The first of the architectural lectures for the winter session of 1771–2 was given on 18 November by the professor, Thomas Sandby, and Soane would certainly have been present, probably in company with Richard Holland who had been admitted to the Academy in the previous year and had already won a silver medal for his drawing of the gateway of Burlington House. The subject set for the annual competition this year was the south front of Somerset House of which, by chance, Soane had already made a measured drawing some months before (Plate 3). He therefore decided to submit that drawing, only to find that by some aberration he had missed by one day the closing date of 1 November.[12] In the following year the subject was announced as the front of the Banqueting House, Whitehall, on which he set to work (Plate 4). This time his entry was successful in gaining one of the two silver medal awards. Thus encouraged, he prepared a design for *The Front of a Nobleman's Town House* which was accepted for the Academy's summer exhibition of 1772, and which initiated the almost unbroken run of drawings contributed annually throughout his life. In 1773 his unsuccessful competition drawing of the river front of Somerset House was hung in the exhibition together with *The Garden Front of a Gentleman's Villa*, and in the following year his *Design for A Garden Building* was accepted. His address for the first two years was given as 'at Mr Holland's, Half Moon Street', but in 1774, 1776 and 1777 it was 'at Mr Holland's' either in 'Hertford Street' (the house which Henry had then built for himself), or simply 'Mayfair'.

In the autumn of 1774, Soane competed unsuccessfully for the Academy's gold medal; but a further attempt in 1776 brought success with his design for *A Triumphal Bridge*, a composition which was substantially indebted to Thomas Sandby's *Bridge of Magnificence* which had been one of the drawings used by the professor to illustrate his sixth Academy lecture. Soane's bridge design, however, shows clearly that he had also been studying such works as Piranesi's *Le Antichita Romane* of 1748, and M. J. Peyre's *Oeuvres d'Architecture* of 1765, although neither is mentioned in the list which Soane kept of books consulted in the Library of the Royal Academy.

It was in connection with the preparation of his bridge drawing that Soane had a narrow escape from drowning for, still busily engaged in Henry Holland's office on weekdays, he had to work on his own drawings after office hours or on Sundays. In his anxiety to have his entry ready in ample time, he excused himself from accompanying two friends to Greenwich to celebrate the birthday of one of them. After dinner they had taken a boat on the river but ran into difficulties as a result of which James King was drowned. As Soane was unable to swim, he felt that his decision not to join the expedition had providentially saved his life.[13] The bridge design was submitted early in November (it bears the date 4 November), and he then had to endure five weeks of anxiety before Prize Day, on 10 December 1776, brought a declaration by the president, Sir Joshua Reynolds, that Soane's was the winning entry. An account of the occasion by an anonymous writer describes the presentation of the gold medal by the president who 'accompa-

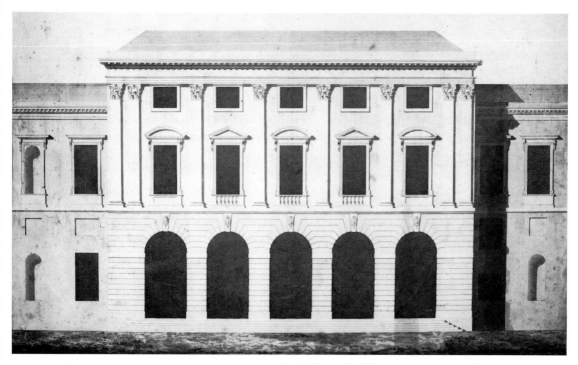

3. OLD SOMERSET HOUSE, drawn by Soane, 1770.

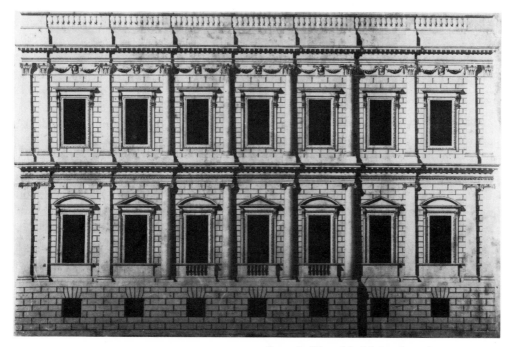

4. BANQUETING HOUSE, WHITEHALL. Soane's Silver Medal drawing of 1772.

nied the honor he bestowed on Mr Soane with such appropriate remarks upon his genius, such commendations of his performance, and such prophetic hopes of his perseverance, and consequent success, as were . . . far more valuable than even the medal itself'.[14]

Although Soane later recounted in his *Memoirs* that he owed to Sir William Chambers his recommendation to George III as a suitable recipient for the king's travelling studentship, Joseph Farington entered a somewhat different story in his Diary whereby 'Soane told me that before he applied to the Academy to be sent to Rome, He waited on Sir Wm. Chambers, who he prevailed upon to show some drawings which he had made to the King, which Sir William told Soane his Majesty approved, and directed that he shd. be sent to Rome by the Academy.' On hearing this from Chambers, Farington continued, Soane rashly assumed that the matter was settled and 'gave up the situation he was then placed in'.[15] Unfortunately, when Sir William made the announcement at an Academy meeting, it was challenged by Sir Joshua Reynolds who insisted that the final choice was to be by election of the Academicians. Soane was then informed that he must submit his drawings along with those of other candidates. In the event he received seventeen votes out of a total of twenty, but the loss of time—exactly a year—involved by this procedure was a set-back. However, on 31 December 1777 Soane was sent a letter confirming his election, and setting out the allowance and travelling expenses which he could expect to receive.[16]

In spite of having prematurely given notice to Henry Holland, and the fact that his place had been filled by John Jagger, it appears that some temporary work was found for Soane by his erstwhile employer in connection with measuring. One or two similar jobs were also forthcoming from other quarters. As was to become apparent later in his Italian notebooks, Soane had a confusing habit of writing at both ends of his notebooks, account books and even sketch books. A book marked 'Copies of Bills 1785' is a case in point, for inspection shows it to contain miscellaneous details of costing between 1772 and 1786, not arranged in any order, and referring not only to houses designed by Henry Holland and Lancelot Brown such as Claremont, Cadland and Benham, but to Busbridge in Surrey, attributed to John Crunden, and three houses in Park Street, London, built by the latter, as well as mason's work done at the house of Nicolas Kenny in St James's Street which Crunden is known to have built for the Savoir Vivre Club which later became Boodles Club. Several of the entries are initialled 'R.F.' with various dates in 1777 when they were settled. These particular accounts suggest that Soane and 'R.F.' were collaborating in that year over the checking of artisans' bills for work carried out for Holland, Crunden and other clients. As to the identity of 'R.F.', this is likely to have been Robert Furze, a nephew of the younger Matthew Brettingham who, on taking up an architectural career, added his uncle's name to his own in the hope that it would be professionally advantageous.[17] Robert Furze was already friendly with Soane, with whom he was soon to travel to Italy.

One of the entries in this account book, although slight, was of particular significance for Soane since it concerns accounts for masonry, brick-laying and carpentry carried out in the building of three houses in Hereford Street, Mayfair, for Thomas Pitt, later

Design for a Mausoleum to the Memory of James King Esq. drowned June 9,1776.

5. Design for a MONUMENT TO JAMES KING.

Lord Camelford. Pitt was already regarded as one of the outstanding amateur architects of his time, having embellished his own 'Palazzo Pitti' at Twickenham, and given advice to his friend Horace Walpole on the internal decoration of Strawberry Hill. A Palladian bridge at Hagley, a cottage and other garden features at Park Place, and the Corinthian Arch at Stowe, as well as additions to his family's seat at Boconnoc, were among his works carried out before 1771, the year in which he married and began building his own London house, or rather three houses, in Hereford Street—one being for his own use, and two intended for sale. To draw out designs is one thing, but to measure the completed buildings before settling the artisans' bills is another, and usually beyond the capabilities of even the most talented amateur. That Pitt himself made the designs for the houses is indisputable. But the entries in 'Copies of Bills' suggest that on completion he had the bills checked with measurements taken by Soane and his colleague. One of the bills copied in Soane's hand is for brickwork, including gauged arches, drains, and fixing seventeen chimney-pots and thirty window and door frames. It is headed 'Thomas Pitt Esqe. at his West house in Hereford Street'. Soane must, therefore, even if only in the humble capacity of checking work, have been known to Pitt a good while before they met again in Italy, and he may have owed his recommendation for this work to George Dance.[18]

The drawing submitted by Soane for the Royal Academy Exhibition in 1777 was his *Elevation of a Mausoleum, to the Memory of James King, Esq.*, his friend who had been drowned in the previous year (Plate 5). No doubt prompted by a surge of emotion, Soane's

6. Design for a PAVILION, from Soane's book of *Designs*, 1778.

design assumed a scale which might well have surprised the obscure recipient of this tribute by its domed temple set on a rusticated podium from which diagonal extensions supported pyramids, the whole offering accommodation for eighty-four coffins and twenty-four cinerary urns. Its real interest, however, lies in its being the forerunner of the architect's fascination with themes of a funerary character.[19] The King mausoleum design was in fact about to be engraved for inclusion in a modest book which Soane arranged to have published by Isaac Taylor of Holborn in 1778. According to the prospectus, the original intention was to include eighty copper plates of designs for bridges, mausolea, churches, a British senate house, town houses, country villas, furniture and garden seats; but probably on Taylor's advice the more ambitious projects were left out, while the rest were whittled down to thirty-six in a slim octavo volume (Plate 6). They presented a medley of somewhat immature essays, owing something to Chambers with a few touches from Piranesi's engravings, which are unlikely to have inspired much confidence among potential clients and it had no list of subscribers. There are, however, no grounds for the statement sometimes made that Soane attempted to suppress the edition. In fact some of the original plates were issued by the same publisher in a folio form in 1797 with a new title page on which Soane's name, now spelt with an *e*, is followed by 'Architect, Member of the Royal Academies of Parma and Florence'. As the plates are dated 1 July 1778, he must have passed the proofs of the original edition before leaving for Italy in that year.

Of the other preparations made by Soane before leaving there is no record other than some sound advice obtained from Sir William Chambers as to what he should study.

This Chambers provided in the form of a copy of the letter which he had written four years earlier to a former pupil, Edward Stevens, then in Rome. It was a long letter, not without jibes at some of the younger generation of architects of whom he did not approve; but the gist of it recommended the reader to study by

> drawing, measuring and observing everything upon the spot yourself. Always see with your own eyes, and though it is right to hear the judgment of others, yet never determine but by your own . . . Work in the same quarry with M. Angelo, Vignola, Peruzzi and Palladio, use their materials, search for more, and endeavour to unite the grand manner of the two first, with the elegance, simplicity, and purity of the last. Observe well the works of the celebrated Bernini, at once an able architect, painter and sculptor; see how well they are conducted, how artfully he took advantage of circumstances, and sometimes made even the defects of his situations contribute to the perfection of his work.

The works of Pietro da Cortona were among those also recommended by Chambers. But he warned the recipient of his letter that there would be little to find in the vicinity of Naples where there were some 'execrable performances' by Vanvitelli, Fuga 'and some blockheads of less note'. Borromini should be avoided, and all the later architects of Rome except for Salvi who 'sometimes fortunately hit upon the right, as appears by parts of his fountain of Trevi, and parts of his Dominican church at Viterbo. Form if you can a style of Your own in which endeavour to avoid the faults and blend the perfections of all.' In conclusion, he advised conversations 'with artists of all Countrys, particularly foreigners, that you may get rid of national prejudices. Seek for those who have most reputation, young or old, amongst which forget not Piranesi, who you may see in my name; he is full of matter, extravagant 'tis true, often absurd, but from his overflowings you may gather much information.'[20] This latter advice Soane, once he had mastered a few words of Italian, was eagerly to follow.

Notes

1. The opening sentence of Soane's *Memoirs* is in fact a translation of that with which Palladio began *I Quattro Libri dell' Architettura* (1570): 'Da naturale inclinatione guidato mi diedi ne i miei primi ani allo studio dell'architettura.'
2. Walter Money, *Stray Notes on the Parish of Basildon*, 1889, p. 12.
3. Between January and March 1806 Soane recorded in his notebook that several visits had been exchanged with a Mr and Mrs Marcy who were then staying for a few weeks in London, but no mention is made of their relationship to him, or from whence they came.
4. Bishop's Transcripts for Goring, Oxford Diocesan Papers, C. 539/1, Bodleian Library, Oxford.
5. SMC Div. 11 T (14).
6. British Museum, Prints and Drawings, Farington Diary Typescript, ix, p. 2250.
7. E. W. Brayley, *History of Surrey*, 1850, Vol. II, p. 231.
8. Thomas Love Peacock, born at Weymouth in 1785, later moved to Chertsey with his widowed mother and became attached to the surrounding countryside. He was probably the 'Mr Peacock of Chertsey' (so designated to distinguish him from James Peacock who lived in London), mentioned in Mrs Soane's notebook for 15 January 1806: 'Mr Peacock of Chertsey dined here, had a dance in the eve^g. Mr P. slept here.'

9. Farington Diary, op. cit., xii, p. 3496.

10. Ibid, xiv, p. 4017.

11. Soane Bookcase, Shelf C.

12. *Memoirs*, p. 11*. He gives the date as 1770 whereas it should be 1771.

13. Ibid, p. 13*.

14. *European Magazine*, Vol. 63, 1813, p. 5. It was probably in honour of this event that a small portrait of Soane was painted by a fellow student at the Royal Academy, Christopher Hunneman. This picture, which hangs in the Soane Museum, was later erroneously stated to have been painted in Rome, although Soane himself described it in his *Description* of 1830 as a 'Portrait of a young artist painted in 1776'.

15. Farington Diary, op. cit., i, p. 267.

16. Royal Academy, Council Minutes, 31 December 1777.

17. SPC Box 4, Envelope 8. In a note on Charlton House, Wiltshire, Soane refers to the 'taste and talents of the late Mr Brettingham, uncle of Mr Robert Furze, who accompanied me to Italy'.

18. Writing to his father from Rome on 7 October, 1761, George Dance described his introduction a week before to the Duke of Bridgewater, Sir George Lyttelton and Thomas Pitt. 'They received me very politely and Mr Pitt who is a great lover of architecture desired me to make him a drawing of the famous gallery at the Colonna Palace. . . . He is a young gentleman of an extraordinary fine character and fine sense. His friendship may be of great service to me in England.' Letters in the Royal Institute of British Architects.

19. Sir John Summerson, 'Sir John Soane and the Furniture of Death', *Architectural Review*, March 1978.

20. SMC Div. 1 C (7).

⌈2⌉

A Travelling Student

At five o'clock in the morning on 18 March 1788, Soane set out for Italy with the first quarterly payment of £30 from the Royal Academy and travelling expenses of a similar sum in his pocket. With him was Robert Furze Brettingham, also intent on study in Italy but not in receipt of any studentship and relying on an allowance from his father. For Soane the date was momentous, and an anniversary frequently to be recollected in his notebooks over the years. Deteriorating relations between England and France did not encourage the travellers to linger in Paris for more time than was necessary to obtain passports, Soane's being endorsed at Versailles on 28 March, after which they pushed on, probably, at this early time of year, by way of Lyons and the Rhône Valley so as to avoid the Alps. They reached Rome on 2 May.

There is no clue as to the whereabouts of Soane's lodgings during his first weeks in the city, but he followed the widely adopted practice of using the English Coffee House in the Piazza di Spagna as his *poste restante* address. The main room of this favourite meeting place for visitors from Britain had some years earlier been embellished with murals by Giovanni Battista Piranesi in the Egyptian manner.[1] The first essential for Soane was to familiarise himself with the Italian language, and he soon filled two small notebooks with verbs, grammar and phrases. However, larger sketch books[2] show that he also lost no time in beginning his architectural studies. From the outset his inseparable guidebook, whether in Rome or on his later Italian excursions, was Anna Miller's *Letters from Italy*, published in two small octavo volumes in 1777. In the margins of these he was to make copious notes of his own, and not always agreeing with her observations.[3] Thus equipped he set off to explore the city, and before May was out had measured and drawn the plan and section of S. Agnese Fuori le Mura. Brettingham was by now following his own course of study, and in June Soane became acquainted with another English architect, Thomas Hardwick, who had recently returned to Rome after travelling elsewhere in Italy. Their mutual interests prompted an arrangement whereby they would jointly undertake the measuring of various buildings beginning with S. Maria Maggiore and continuing with the Temple of Minerva Medica, S. Maria degli Angeli, and the Temple of Vesta. Drawings pasted into Soane's *Miscellaneous Sketches* suggest that he was also engaged at this time on some independent exercises such as measuring the Pantheon (Plate 7), various buildings in the Forum, the Arch of Titus, and that other Temple of Vesta which crowned the rocky gorge at Tivoli and which

7. THE PANTHEON in Rome, drawn by Soane in 1778.

8. (*left*) THE COLOSSEUM in Rome, part of external wall, from Soane's *Italian Sketches*.

9. (*right*) THE TEMPLE OF VESTA at Tivoli, from Soane's *Miscellaneous Sketches*.

was to become for him one of the most admired of ancient monuments (Plate 9). He also began work on designs for a projected mausoleum to the memory of William Pitt, Earl of Chatham (Plate 10), news of whose death on 11 May had recently reached Rome. This design duly emerged as a more sober and strictly classical variation of his 1777 project for the monument to James King, comprising a rotunda flanked by pyramids. The new elevation, together with a plan and elevation, was probably that which Soane submitted three years later to the Royal Academy exhibition, although the catalogue entry omitted the name of Chatham.

The only surviving letter from Soane at this period was written on 1 August to Henry Wood, the noted stone-carver extensively employed by Henry Holland and whom Soane would first have met when working at Claremont:

> I flatter myself you are so much my wellwisher as to receive pleasure in being informed of my safe arrival at this place (on the 2d. of May). I need not tell you my attention is entirely taken up in the seeing and examining the numerous and inestimable remains of Antiquity as you are no stranger to the zeal and attachment I have for them and with what impatience I have waited for the scenes I now enjoy, which has prevented my writing before . . . . I expect to hear from you very soon and a very long letter, how you go on at Knightsbridge and elsewhere, any news, ever so trifling, is acceptable.[4]

10. A design for a MAUSOLEUM, a water-colour by J. M. Gandy from sketches originally made by Soane when in Rome.

In spite of his still faltering Italian, Soane must by this time have followed Sir William Chamber's injunction to 'forget not Piranesi', and presented himself at the artist's studio in the Palazzo Tomati, in the Via Felici (now Sistina). It is evident that he was welcomed although Piranesi's rapidly deteriorating health was already apparent, and was to bring about his death on 9 November 1778. During the few weeks of their acquaintance, however, Soane had been given the four engraved plates of the Pantheon, the tomb of Cecilia Metalla, and the Arches of Constantine and Septimius Severus from the artist's *Veduta Romana* which he was to cherish and which still hang in his Museum.

In this autumn other eventful meetings were to take place. On 20 September Frederick Hervey, Bishop of Derry, had returned to Rome with his wife and one of his daughters after a lengthy stay at Castel Gondolfo. Born in 1730 at the family seat, Ickworth, in Suffolk, Hervey began his career as a clerk in the Privy Seal office, but was consecrated Bishop of Cloyne in 1768 through the influence of his brother, the 2nd Earl of Bristol, who had served as Lord Lieutenant of Ireland for a short period. In 1778 the bishop was translated from Cloyne to the see of Derry with an income then valued at £7,000 per annum which encouraged him to acquire the estate of Downhill, overlooking the northern reaches of the Irish Channel, and there to begin the building of a modest house to which he referred as his 'cabin'. At no point, though, did he allow his pastoral duties to interfere with his pursuit of the arts in general, but Roman antiquity and volcanic phenomena in particular. Much of his time was therefore spent in France and Italy where his undoubted personal charm and accomplishments made him the hub of social life in whichever city he chose to stay.

It is not known precisely when Soane's presentation to this celebrated patron of the arts took place; it was possibly brought about by Thomas Pitt who had left England for Rome at the beginning of September. A favourable impression was evidently made by the young architect who within a short time was in constant attendance, and had been presented with a handsomely bound facsimile of Palladio's *I Quattro Libri dell' Archi-tettura*, inscribed 'From the Bishop of Derry to J. Soan [an *e* was added later by the recipient] at Rome Oct.ʳ 1778'. This was followed by a copy of Galiani's translation of Vitruvius (1758), again inscribed 'From the Bishop of Derry to J. Soan'. Early in December the bishop, having decided to make 'a jaunt to Naples', suggested that Soane should accompany him, an invitation which was eagerly accepted.[5] The bishop also indicated—perhaps on a hint from Soane—that Brettingham would be welcome to accompany them, but the latter, although tempted, found difficulty in disengaging himself from a commitment to work for 'Mr Hamilton'—probably the artist Gavin Hamilton. As Brettingham regretfully wrote to Soane:

> . . . it was not in my power to persuade him that it was at all an eligible scheme. He would not come into it, and insinuated that, if I did so, he would have nothing to do with it; he even went so far as to say it would be imprudent. I signified to him the advantages, and the promise I had made. The former he did not think would be great, as there is so little to do for an architect there. The latter he was sure you would forgive, as you

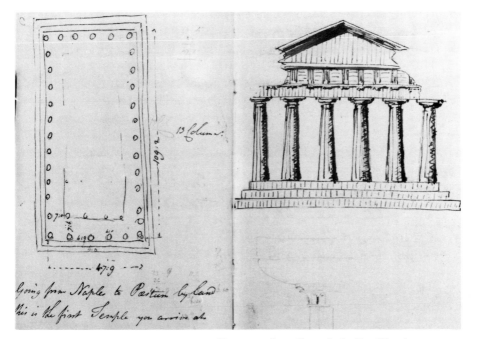

11. THE TEMPLE OF CERES at Paestum, from Soane's *Italian Sketches*.

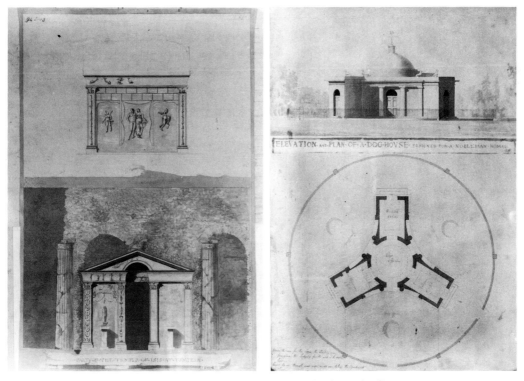

12. (*left*) THE TEMPLE OF ISIS, Pompeii, drawn by Soane.

13. (*right*) Soane's design for a classical DOG-HOUSE.

would find it rather inconvenient, considering the manner in which you go, and that you will of course be much with the Bishop, and other gentlemen. So my Dear Friend (for such still I will call You), you must not take it amiss. My will and inclination are with You most heartily, but as my friends disapprove, and the world would call me rash and foolish, I am sure there is no reason to apologize to you, who I think, at least hope, have yet more regard for me than to wish me to be guilty of temerity. So, though I can't have the pleasure of being with You, I hope to hear from You very often.[6]

It was arranged that patron and protégé would leave Rome on 22 December, accompanied by a servant, and make a leisurely journey across the Pontine Marshes with pauses to look at places of archaeological interest. Mrs Hervey and her daughter were to set out two days later and travel direct to Naples. Soane recorded that by Christmas Day he and the bishop had arrived at the so-called Villa of Lucullus, some twenty miles from Terracina, and there explored the extensive ruins, fragments of statues and fish ponds in a setting which he found 'exceedingly beautiful'.[7] Writing his *Memoirs* more than fifty years later, he retained the vivid impression of 'wandering over those monuments of departed greatness' where they had 'banqueted within the ruins on mullet fresh from the ancient reservoirs'.[8] While rambling over the ruins, and attempting to identify their original uses, the bishop had exclaimed 'Where is the *canile* and *tugurium*? I should like to form some idea of a classical dog-kennel as I intend to build one at the Downhill for the hounds of my eldest son', adding 'This will be a fine subject for the display of your creative talents.' Soane took the hint and, once they had reached Naples, produced designs with which his patron was delighted (Plate 13). 'They are admirably suited for my purpose', he declared, 'I have a large party to dinner to whom these drawings will be shewn, with your other designs in my possession, in order that the Monsignori may duly appreciate your classical taste and inventive faculties.'[9] In his reference to 'your other designs' the bishop was no doubt thinking of the design for a 'Summer dining room', proposed for Downhill, which Soane had already prepared in imitation of one of the rooms at Claremont on which he had worked while in Henry Holland's office. In his letter to Soane of 22 December 1778 Brettingham had asked if he might 'copy that Room You designed for Lord H.', and it was probably the first of his drawings made for the bishop.[10]

Although Soane does not mention where they stopped for the four nights following Christmas, Terracina would be a probable place, not only for the beauty of its situation overlooking the bay of Gaeta, but because it offered reasonable accommodation. By 29 December the travellers had reached Capua where a ruined amphitheatre of brick and marble had to be seen, and then rode on by Caserta to reach Naples by evening. There Soane took comfortable accommodation at the Albergo Reale Santa Lucia where he found already installed two Englishmen with whom he was to make lasting friendships, Richard Bosanquet and John Patteson. 'The situation is most desirable', he wrote of the hotel, 'we had each a room in the upper Story and paid for it 4 Carlines per day, and 7 Carlines for dinner, 2 for Breakfast &c.'[11]

Richard Bosanquet was a brother of Samuel Bosanquet, a City banker who was a director of the Bank of England in 1771, deputy governor in 1789, and governor from 1791 to 1793.[12] Later on Soane was to find the latter an influential and helpful client. Richard, however, had been less successful since the merchant banking firm in which he had been a partner with John Fatio failed in 1777 and he left England hurriedly in order to escape arrest. His exile seems to have been far from disagreeable, and early in 1779 he was staying in Naples where his meeting with Soane probably led to the latter's subsequent introduction to Samuel, and to their sister Mrs Brocas, who was also to become one of the architect's clients.

Although Soane was to make several expeditions with the Bishop of Derry from Naples, he seems to have been set free from continual attendance on his patron, and was able to explore the city and its surroundings by himself with the invaluable copy of Anna Miller's *Letters* as his guide, sometimes noting in its margins his own views on the various antiquities or natural curiosities encountered. These included the Grotto of Pausillipo, 'cut thr[ough] the rock', the Grotto del Cane, and the smoking mud of the Sulfaterra region. At the seaport of Pozzuoli he was sufficiently impressed by the remains of the Temple of Jupitor Serapis to make a number of sketches before moving on to Caligula's bridge and the amphitheatre. On 5 January he appears to have made his first visit to Pompeii as a sketch with this date shows the Temple of Isis (Plate 12). It is likely, however, that he waited till early evening before making the drawing, having been warned by a reference in Anna Miller's book to an official ban on sketching the ruins. In his Royal Academy lectures prepared many years later he stated that his illustration of this temple was redrawn from 'sketches made by stealth by moonlight'.[13] In a list of recommended sights which he prepared towards the end of his time in Italy he included the museum of paintings and other antiquities which he had presumably seen at Portici, and noted that for this a permit had to be obtained from the British Consul, Sir William Hamilton. By 13 January he had made his way to Cuma, where he found 'several ancient Temples' and a distant view of the islands of Ischia and Capri. His next expedition on 16 January took him to Liternum and Monte Nuovo, and three days later he set off from Naples to scale the slopes of Mount Vesuvius.

An entry in Soane's Italian Sketches on 22 January 1779 shows that he was then on his second visit to Pompeii, this time in company with Thomas Pitt. Also in the party was Sir William Molesworth, who, like Pitt, was a Cornishman. His estate Pencarrow, lay only a few miles from that of Pitt at Boconnoc. The third member was a 'Mr Pemberton' who may perhaps be identified with Robert Pemberton, the physician who in later years was to become Soane's close friend and consultant. If so, his travels with Thomas Pitt were probably in a medical capacity since the latter suffered from constant ill-health. On this particular visit Soane had presumably obtained permission to sketch for there are numerous notes and drawings made as the party wandered round the Porta Ercolano, the Surgeon's House, theatres and soldiers' quarters. Precisely how many days were occupied in this particular excursion is not clear; but on 30 January Soane was certainly back in Paestum where he encountered a party which included two other travellers who were friends of the Bishop of Derry, and who had recently arrived in Naples. They were Dr Thomas Bowdler[14] and the Hon. Philip Yorke, nephew of and heir to the 2nd Earl of Hardwicke. Writing to his uncle on 31 January, Yorke described the expedition to Paestum from which he had returned on the previous day. 'The three temples . . . are magnificent buildings and I was astonished to find how perfect they are. An English architect by name Soane who is an ingenious young man now studying at Rome accompanied us thither and measured the buildings.'[15] The meeting was also to prove of consequence for the 'ingenious young man' who was soon asked by Yorke to make a drawing of 'An ancient monument near Capua', mentioned in one of Soane's later account books[16] although the drawing itself has disappeared. It proved to be the first of a series of commissions undertaken for this client over some three decades. Much of Soane's time during this Paestum expedition was to be occupied with measuring and drawing the three temples (Plate 11), which involved him in climbing to dizzy heights.

After their stay here the travellers, that is Soane with the Bishop, Pitt and Molesworth, moved on slowly through Calabria, following the course of a river to Capaccio where they spent the night of 16 February. The following evening brought them to 'Supino' [Zuppino] and two days later they reached their objective, the monastery of San Lorenzo outside the hill town of Padula where the Anglican bishop had no qualms about enjoying the hospitality of the monks. As well as sketching a plan of the extensive ranges of buildings, Soane commented on the fountain in the great courtyard, the adjoining smaller courts, and the provision for each monk of two rooms and a little garden. The return journey was made through Pola, Zuppino, Eboli and Salerno which they reached by 22 February, and where Soane made notes on various features in the cathedral including the granite columns brought from Paestum, and several sarcophagi, before continuing to Naples.

The bishop's intention had been to take his family and Soane back to Rome early in March but this was frustrated by the illness of his daughter Louisa,[17] so the architect was able to make visits to the cathedral at Benevento and Vanvitelli's great palace at Caserta by which he was not greatly impressed. Random jottings in his notebooks at this time indicate that he was willing to undertake 'shopping' for small works of art such as 'two female Bustos to stand upon Therms' required by Thomas Pitt, and two views of Vesuvius erupting for which 'Mr Lumisdon'[18] had asked. By 12 March the bishop had grown impatient and decided to set off for Rome with Soane, leaving his wife and daughter to follow. Proceeding slowly so as to visit such places of interest as the Duomo at Gaeta, the new Canalone Portatore—constructed to drain the notorious Pontine marshes—and the Abbey of Fossanova, the travellers were nearing Rome by the 24 March when Soane's record of this particular excursion ended with a sketch of two 'old monuments' at the side of the Appian Way. On the following day they were back in the city, and in good time for Holy Week which began in 1779 with Palm Sunday on 28 March.

Once the Easter ceremonies were over, the English visitors in Rome gradually dispersed to other parts of Italy. The bishop and his family set off for Florence and were followed by Philip Yorke, but if Soane suffered a feeling of anticlimax at their departure, it was soon dispelled by the arrival during the first week in April of John Patteson who at once began to explore the possibility of a visit to Sicily in company with a few chosen friends. Soane, it was suggested, should join them as draughtsman. By the time Patteson wrote to his mother on 12 April he was able to tell her that 'Our party consists of 5 in which number is a very clever Physician and an Architect', these being Thomas Bowdler and Soane. John Stuart of Allanbank in Berwickshire and Rowland Burdon of Castle Eden near Durham made up the five, but there was ultimately to be a sixth in the person of Henry Greswold Lewis of Malvern Hall in Warwickshire.[19] In the same letter to his mother Patteson went on to tell her 'The architect whom I mentioned . . . is a young man whose Abilities twice gained him the Premium of the London Academy and who is now on his studies here with a Pension from our King. If ever you should see him you will like him I am certain, we have been talking over Plans for you viz: to give you two Rooms in Front 23 or 24 by 18 but in a few posts you shall have the Draughts in small.'[20] The rendezvous was to be Naples, and before setting out Soane made a list of such essentials as breeches, waistcoats, nightcaps and handkerchiefs. His packing completed he set off and arrived on 14 April, to be joined during the next few days by the rest of the party. A week later they boarded what proved to be a singularly ill-equipped Swedish boat in which only Patteson was fortunate in securing a hammock, while his friends had to sleep on the floor. In the morning they awoke to find that an unfavourable wind had delayed their departure. It was in fact to continue for two days, but eventually they sailed away and five days later were rewarded with a first sight of Mount Etna looming in the distance. Disembarking at Palermo on 29 April, they took rooms at a hostelry kept by a rumbustious French landlady where the rigours of their journey were soon forgotten as they breakfasted out of doors in hot sunshine, and revelled in 'Strawberries and Milk, Oranges, most delicious bread and such like Luxuries'.[21] Then began the first of seven days of sightseeing in and around the city under the guidance of Patrick Brydone's *A Tour Through Sicily and Malta* of which the two copies in the Soane library were probably acquired by him at this time.

One of their expeditions was to see the Villa Palagonia, belonging to the eccentric Principe Ferdinando Francesco Gravina, where the mirror-covered walls in some of the rooms made so deep an impression on Soane that more than half a century later he could recall the Prince's 'wonderful performances . . . in the decoration and furniture of his palace'.[22] At the end of a week, undeterred by the intense heat, the party decided to split into two groups and leave Palermo to explore the island. While Stuart and Bowdler departed for a visit to Etna, Patteson, Burdon, Lewis and Soane set off on 7 May for Trapani, accompanied by '7 horses 3 baggage mules with muleteers and a guard who cut a tremendous Figure, armed cap a pee his cap of crimson Velvet laced with Silver'.[23] Making for the west coast, and pausing briefly at the Greek Doric temple at Segesta, the cavalcade reached Trapani by nightfall and spent the following two days there before moving on in fierce heat to Marsala. Here they were given hospitality at a monastery for two nights and they then continued towards Agrigento, seeing on the way what

Patteson, whose appetite for ancient remains was less voracious than those of his companions, dismissed as 'some ruinous Ruins of old Temples'. At Agrigento their accommodation at the monastery of a Franciscan order was limited to one room for the five which proved 'rather too close a stowage', in spite of which they stayed for five days, exploring the ancient city on the outskirts. Although this proved something of an ordeal for Patteson, who found nothing to 'afford any Pleasure to any other than an Architect, except the Temple of Concord all the Pillars of which are standing', for Soane it was an experience to be remembered years later when writing his Royal Academy lectures in which he referred to the 'awful grandeur' of the temples at Segesta, Selinunte and Agrigento, particularly the Temple of Jupiter, 'which in its perfect state must have been the admiration of every beholder'.[24] Considering that he was the architectural draughtsman in the party Soane in fact contributed very little in the way of notes and drawings on this Sicilian visit, the record of the travellers' progress round the island being almost entirely contained in Patteson's correspondence with his mother. By 23 May, clad in their 'long trousers and white slouch hats lined with green silk', they had reached Licata (referred to by Patteson as Alicata), where they were 'very well lodged in a Convent of Carmelites'. It was while here that an extension of their itinerary was planned for, although Patteson had admitted to a surfeit of ruins, he was apparently still ready for further expeditions. Soane claimed in later years that while in Sicily there had been talk of continuing the tour to Athens but that 'to my great disappointment . . . from want of sufficient time' the idea had to be abandoned.[25] What did materialise was the alternative proposal for an excursion to Malta. Here again, precise details are missing but it seems from Patteson's letter written to his mother soon after the party had returned to Sicily that their short visit, made by the narrow boats called 'speronaros' over the rough sea, had been rewarding. 'I am sure Princes could not have had more attention shown them.' Their return journey landed them at Syracuse, which proved to be 'a miserable place' and they were glad to arrive back in Catania on or just before 10 June. In spite of the fatigue and no little discomfort encountered in the past six weeks, their good spirits remained and Patteson was able to tell his mother that:

> No four young Men could ever have stumbled upon each other more fortunately than our party, when we meet at Meals it is one continued Laugh from sitting down to getting up again; Mr Burdon is quite an Enthusiast after Antiquities, if he sees 4 Rows of Stones the Ruins of a Roman building it gives him infinite pleasure, Soan the Architect cannot help siding with him. Mr Lewis and Myself see these venerable ruins with less Passion and get many a good laugh against the others when they happen to admire a modern Arch for an antient one and such like.[26]

After a short rest Patteson and Soane set off for the two-day climb to the summit of Mount Etna which the former found 'the most noble object I ever beheld and well worth the trouble of seeing'.[27] From Catania they made their way along the coast road to Taormina, pausing to examine the ruined theatre, and then taking a 'speronaro' to Messina where they embarked for the return, by way of the Lipari Islands, to Naples.

14. CORSINI CHAPEL,
S. Giovanni Laterano, Rome,
drawn by Soane for Philip
Yorke.

On landing, Lewis, Burdon and Soane made for the Albergo Reale and a few days of relaxation during which the latter visited Thomas Pitt, now recovering from a serious illness.

The time had now come for Soane to set out for Rome, when he was probably accompanied by Burdon. Certainly they were both back in the city by 19 July when the artist Thomas Jones recorded that he went with Burdon and John Coxe Hippisley to the Villa Madama and St Peter's, and then on to the Villa Lanti where they were joined by the Abbé Bellew and John Soane for dinner 'in a pleasant Loggia overlooking the City of Rome'.[28] The meeting appears to have been the prelude to yet another excursion, this time organised by Burdon who suggested that Soane might join him on a visit to Venice, a proposal which the latter readily accepted since several of his friends had already left, or were about to leave Rome, and his only immediate commitment was to complete and dispatch to Philip Yorke a drawing of the Corsini Chapel, as added by Alessandro Galilei to the Church of S. Giovanni Laterano (Plate 14). This done, it remained only to pack up the nineteen volumes of Giannoni's *History of Naples* and six volumes of Sterne's

Sermons of Mr Yorick which Burdon had offered to include with some of his own luggage which was being shipped directly from Rome to England.[29]

The precise date on which the two left Rome is not recorded, and Soane's laconic reference in his *Memoirs* states only that 'I set out for Venice with Mr Burdon, from which City that gentleman returned to England; and I went on to Verona.' It must have been during the first week of August, for a letter by Burdon to John Strange in Venice[30] shows that they had already arrived in Bologna by 16 August. Their route continued through Modena and Parma to Milan where a short stay gave Soane time to write to Thomas Pitt about his latest project:

> Mr Burdon for whose friendship I can never be sufficiently grateful having brought me with him to Parma, I informed myself of the subject for the Premium in Architecture, to be given by the Royal Academy of this place in 1780 (May), for which I wish to become a candidate if it meet with your approbation.

The subject was a 'Castello d'acqua decorato d'una Pubblica Fontana' of which he made rough sketches in his letter (Plate 15).[31] Although Pitt's reply has not survived, he apparently advised against the proposal which was dropped, and Soane decided to wait until the following spring before attempting to gain a diploma. Travelling on from Milan, Soane and Burdon reached Brescia on or shortly before 27 August and there found John Patteson who was by then on his way back to England. 'Very agreeably we again passed 24 hours together', the latter subsequently wrote to his mother. Two years were to pass before he and Soane met again.

After a brief visit to Vicenza, where Soane's notes did not go beyond listing the more important buildings to be seen, he and Burdon moved on for a day in Padua before reaching Venice where they found accommodation in the house of Pietro Danna near the Rialto Bridge. Soane made the most of his time by visiting as many churches and palazzi as possible before Burdon was due to leave for England, and he had to make his own way back to Bologna. Here he obtained permission to spend a few days in copying various designs by Palladio and other masters in the archives of the Church of S. Petronio. As some of his copies bear the date 29 September, he had presumably arrived a day or two before, and there is no record of precisely how long he stayed, or how long he took in returning to Rome. It is, however, evident that on the way he must have stopped briefly at Florence to obtain details as to the procedure necessary for qualifying for its Academy's diploma, while the date 'Novr 4 1779' on a plan relating to Pompeii shows that he must have been back, and working on the material which he had left in Rome, by that date. Having duly submitted his application to the Florentine Academy, he settled down to a winter of study.

Meanwhile the Bishop of Derry and his family had been making their way slowly back to England where they arrived some time in November. A month later on 22 December he succeeded, on the death of his one remaining brother, to the title of 4th Earl of Bristol and inherited the family estate at Ickworth in Suffolk. The news must have reached Rome early in January and Soane may, indeed, have been the first to receive

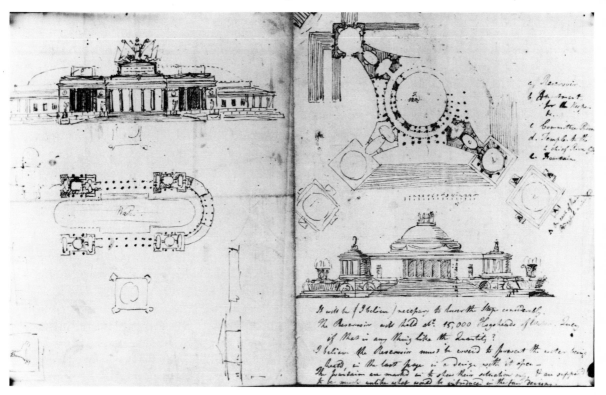

15. Soane's letter to Thomas Pitt, August 1779, with drawings for a *castello d'acqua*.

it for he stated in his *Memoirs* that 'On this occasion, I received a letter from his Lordship, requesting my immediate attendance, stating, that he had selected me for his Architect, to erect a mansion for the family, at Ichworth [*sic*] a subject which, under his Lordship's direction, had occupied much of my attention whilst in Rome. His Lordship also assured me, that several of his friends in Ireland had determined on erecting some considerable buildings as soon as they could procure designs from me. After repeated solicitations from his Lordship I left Italy, and returned to London in June 1780.' How many letters came, and at what intervals, is not known for on the journey home Soane had the misfortune to lose some of the contents of a trunk at the back of the coach in which he was travelling. In it were many of his personal belongings and all his letters from the earl bishop.[32] It is clear, though, that the latter were sufficiently persuasive for him to make the rash decision to forego eleven months of his studentship. On 19 April he left Rome in company with 'Messrs Holgate and Pepper'.[33] Making their way northward the travellers stopped at Caprarola to go through the Villa Farnese and then made for Florence where they arrived on 23 April, Soane noting that his share of the cost of the journey had amounted to six sequins and twenty-one paolini.[34] Here the party split up, Soane staying for five days during which he called on the English ambassador, Horace Mann, who persuaded him not to return through France, for which he already had a passport, but to take a route through Germany. Agreeing, though with reluctance for he had already planned a visit to Genoa, he was issued with a new document, signed by Mann and dated 28 April, in which he is described as 'Monsieur Soan[e] Architecte Anglois retour-nant en Angleterre par l'Allemagne'.

He left Florence on the following day but it seems that during his stay a chance encounter had filled his head with romantic notions. The object of his interest was Anna Selina Storace (Plate 21), the singer who, although still only fourteen, was then appearing in soprano roles at the Teatro della Pergola.[35] Carefully guarded by her father-manager Stephano Storace, it is unlikely that Anna would have had the chance of more than a few brief conversations with her admirer. But such was the effect of her charms, combined with the beauties of Florence and an Italian spring, that Soane was captivated and his usually prosaic notebook carries the admission that, on leaving the city, he had paused 'by Arno's delightful Vale' to reflect on 'dear Miss S.'[36] They were not, however, to meet again for many years during which Soane had married, and Anna's life had been beset with troubles.

Having hired a carriage, Soane now set off for Bologna, a two-day journey which involved stopping overnight at Pietramala on the way. If the stay in Bologna was itself short, he had time for 'my favourite walk to San Michele in Bosco', which apparently revived his sentimental mood for he then added 'Wrote to Miss S. at Florence.' After another night on the road, he reached Padua on 2 May and found accommodation at the Stella d'Oro. The next morning was spent in refreshing his memory and making notes or sketches of buildings first glimpsed on his visit with Rowland Burdon in the previous summer. He found little to like in the city with its 'streets narrow, dark and nasty in general', but conceded that 'there are some handsome palaces'. Later in the day he took a carriage to Vicenza for the night and next morning went on to Verona where he stayed for five days in which, although occupied with a prodigious number of notes and sketches, he was at least spared the wearisome jolting of a carriage over indifferent roads.

It seems that a plan had been made by letter for Charles Collyer and Edward Pratt, whom he had met in Venice, to have a brief reunion with Soane in Verona, or perhaps somewhere along the road leading from the city to Mantua since he noted only that he 'Went with Messrs Collyer and Pratt to Mantua 24 miles.' Although the rendezvous lasted only a few hours, it must have been a cheerful occasion, particularly for Soane. After dinner, though, he began the next stage of his journey and, by travelling until two in the morning, reached Parma. The reason for this detour to the south-west was probably twofold. Firstly, although he had decided not to compete for the premium offered in 1780 by the Royal Academy of Arts at Parma, he still wished to deposit there a drawing which might gain that body's diploma. Secondly, having set his heart on a visit to Genoa, he determined not to forgo this part of his original plan, even if the rest of his journey home had to be made through Germany and not France. The first mission was accomplished on 9 May when he left his design for a Triumphal Bridge (Plate 16) based on 'a series of studies made in Italy in 1778'.[37] This led to the desired

16. Design for a TRIUMPHAL BRIDGE, prepared for the Academy at Parma.

result, and in June he was informed that he had been accorded honorary membership of the Academy, subject to the submission of a plan and section corresponding to the elevation already received.[38]

Leaving Parma by coach at two a.m. on 10 May, Soane was travelling northward again and after a short stop at Piacenza, reached Milan by evening and took a room at the Tre Rei. Sightseeing on the following day and the making of many notes came to a close with a visit to the 'Great Theatre'—no doubt La Scala—for a performance of a comedy. Returning to the theatre next morning to look more carefully at its architecture, he then went in search of a carriage to take him to Genoa, eventually settling with a driver who agreed to undertake the two and a half day journey for three and a half sequins plus a tip. They set off in the afternoon (11 May), spending the first night at Pavia and the second at Novi where Soane noted 'Novi est la premiere ville des Etats de Gênes sur cette route', a route which ran for some thirty miles between 'pine woods and highly cultivated vallies' to Campo Marone 'where the Mountains finish and one continu'd plain of great richness and fertility . . . takes you to the most charmg. city of Italy'.[39] On arrival he took a room at the Croix de Malta for five nights and collected the *poste restante* mail which awaited him. It included letters from Rowland Burdon, Edward Pratt, and John Patteson, the latter by now back in Norwich. The last of these was short and only to advise Soane that Patteson had dispatched £25 to him on 11 March. Pratt, not knowing of the change in Soane's plans, gave an introduction to the Abbé of Tours, while Burdon, also thinking that Soane was travelling through France, wrote from Newcastle on Tyne reproaching him for writing only 'a *little* letter' and going on to give him various commissions including the purchase from Bonnivert, a tailor in Lyons, of ermine 'to line a suit with. You will choose it as white as possible and pay something from 9 to 12 louis d'or for it, but avoid anything which may have a yellow hue.'⁴⁰ Soane noted that he had answered this letter on 14 May, but it is doubtful if the others had an early reply since the following days were spent in a whirl of making notes and sketches as he sped from one to the other of the churches and palazzi listed in Louis Dutens's *Itineraire . . . d'un voyage aux villes principales de l'Europe*. When it was too dark to see, and the buildings had been closed, he allowed himself to relax in the city's agreeable social life. An introduction from Thomas Pitt allowed him to call on Madame Cileria, 'a most elegant accomplish'd woman with 2 charmᵍ daughters [who] treat'd me with uncommon politeness and attention'. He was received by Mrs Batt, wife of William Batt, the English doctor who had settled here some years before, and made the acquaintance of 'Sigʳ Gibbs—a most worthy young fellow', who was a cousin of his friend in Rome, Antony Gibbs; then followed breakfast with a Signor Carafino. Finally he gave a supper party at 'the English house' for his new-found friends. 'I shall ever feel pangs of regret in being obliged to quit [Madame Cileria] and other delightful society here', he confided to his notebook, and on Friday 19 May added 'Left Genoa at 6 o'clock in the Mornᵍ with heartfelt sorrow in firm hope of seeing it again.' The carriage hurried on to Campo Marone where there was an hour's rest before he 'began to cross the beautiful Alps of which all description must fall very short'.⁴¹ By 21 May he was back in Milan, but not for long. After a night at the Albergo Pozzo, and a morning making further sketches, he took a carriage bound for Como in the afternoon of 22 May and there transferred to a boat for a night journey northward along the Lake. Disembarking at Riva, horses were hired to take him and his baggage to Chiavenna where he had to wait for a day before joining other travellers for the first stage of ascending the Alps. After a night at Isola, they crossed by the Splugen Pass and then rode on to Tusano, now called Thusis, 'about 27 miles . . . by frightful precipices'. It was an experience in which his appreciation of the awe-inspiring scenery was not without some trepidation:

> Below this little road, 4, 5, or even 600 feet perp[endicular] [is a] Torrent, rumbling over immence pieces of the Mountains tumbled down from the tops on one hand. On the other lofty mount[ains] sometimes almost upright, other times hanging over you, immence quantities of fine lofty firs from the top to abᵗ the middle, pleasing[ly] diversified by nature in their dimensions & situations.

After supper the travellers pressed on to Coire (now Chur) for the night, proceeding next morning by coach to Walenstadt. From here Soane took a boat along the lake to

Vesey, reached in the evening. In spite of the fact that he wished to continue at once, the boatmen refused and he had to wait for daylight before making the last stage to Zurich where he landed and put up at the Épée inn.

Although he continued to make sketches, the entries in Soane's notebooks come more or less to an end at this point and the course of the remaining journey homeward can only be pieced together from random jottings in the margins of his copy of Dutens's *Itineraire*, or from a loose sheet of comments preserved with his drawings of bridges. These show that Zurich was left on the morning of 30 May, and that after a pause at Wettingen, where he made a measured sketch of the bridge,[42] he continued to Schaffhausen for the night and spent the next day making sketches of another celebrated Rhône bridge. On the morning of 1 June he and a fellow traveller, 'Mr Parker', took a coach to Basel where surviving correspondence from Anna Miller shows that he had sent off a letter to her.[43] From the same source comes evidence that it was on the way from Schaffhausen to Basel that Soane discovered the damage to his trunk, placed behind the carriage, whereby the bottom had broken open allowing most of the contents to fall out and be lost. It was a crushing blow for, by his own account in a copy of the letter subsequently sent to some unspecified local official, the missing items included his gold and silver medals from the Royal Academy, his silver drawing instruments, a number of architectural books, several of his drawings and a quantity of clothing which probably included the silk and black velvet breeches, waistcoats, shoes, spotted cravat and ruffles on which he had spent several pounds in Genoa.[44]

The most serious loss, however, was that of the letters received from the Bishop of Derry, now Earl of Bristol, promising him future employment. As Soane explained to the unnamed recipient of his letter:

C'est une grand honte pour un etrange a vous donner cette incommode, mais quand je vous dis l'absolu necessite d'avois les papiers, lesquelles me toucheront par toute ma vie, je crois et espere d'avoir vos bonnes concills et assistance . . .[45]

Neither the letter not his own enquiries while at Basel brought any result, and his anguish is evident from the fact that although he extended his stay here to six days in the hope of news, he had not the heart to make a single drawing or note. Abandoning local enquiries, he finally moved on to Freiburg im Breisgau, where on 7 June a stop was made for lunch. From there he probably followed the course of the Rhine, eventually reaching Cologne by, or possibly just before, 15 June. The next day he crossed into Belgium where a night was spent at Liège and then at Louvain on 18 June from where he set off for Brussels. Whether he then made for the port at Flushing or Ostend is not known, nor whether he landed at Harwich or Dover, but the end of June certainly found him once again on English ground and heading for London.

During his absence, Henry Holland's house in Hertford Street had been Soane's *poste restante* address, and here he found several letters awaiting him, including one from Anna (now Lady) Miller, thanking him for the present which he promised her of a sketch of the Temple of Clitumnus. She also gave him a pressing invitation to visit Bath and attend one of her celebrated literary gatherings, held every Thursday at her Batheaston villa. This he had to decline owing to his commitment to work for the earl bishop. As it transpired, there would be no future opportunity, for the cough of which she complained in her letter proved to be the onset of a fatal illness from which she died a few months later.

In his *Memoirs* Soane stated that, within a few days of his return, he obeyed the earl bishop's instruction to proceed to the Hervey seat at Ickworth and there survey the site on which it was proposed that a new house should be built to his design. Travelling to Suffolk by chaise early in July, he spent eight days in plotting and collecting the necessary data. Returning to town for a week, he then set out for Ireland in about the third week of July, arriving at Downhill late on the evening of the 27th when he began to make entries in a small paper-backed notebook.[46]

Soane's meeting with the earl bishop next morning augured well, and during the next few days it was agreed that the proposed additions to the existing house should occupy part of a large stable-yard. On one side of this a new room was to be built, while across the centre of the yard a colonnade would lead from an imposing gateway in the outer wall to the main entrance of the house itself. Extensive general repairs were also required, for the roofs leaked, every chimney smoked, the doors, windows and shutters were falling apart, and there was no proper water supply. Soane had reservations about the proposed colonnade which, he pointed out, would be draughty in bad weather while doing nothing to hide the cleaning of carriages and removal of dung in what was left of the courtyard. However, he noted on 7 August that the earl bishop was 'anxious to build the room and form the cortile', urging that the work should be started without delay. The architect was instructed to write to Richard Holland in London for help in procuring two good joiners, while estimates were to be obtained from James Brown of Ballycastle for best quality stone. Mr Louch of Armagh had apparently already agreed to find timber.[47] On 23 August the earl bishop 'expressed himself perfectly satisfied in warm terms with what I [Soane] had done', and two days later work began on making drawings.

There are a few small sketches in the Downhill notebook, as well as brief outlines of what was intended, from which it seems that the whole of the south front of the house, with parts of the east and west fronts, were to be faced with stone while the roofs were to be raised, and the stable block roughcast. On the principal bedroom storey the floors were to be taken up and sound-proofing inserted, ceilings were to be replastered and general improvements carried out. By this time, though, the earl bishop was beginning to show signs of the vacillation in building matters which was to be the despair not only of Soane but of those architects who were to follow him both here and at Ickworth. On 28 August he changed the idea of a courtyard entrance to one in the east front, there using a space previously intended for the butler's pantry. The new reception room was also changed from a rectangle of thirty-six feet by twenty-four feet into a gallery of forty feet in length and twenty feet wide, whereby, as Soane confided to his notebook, 'the whole house is an assemblage of Galleries and Passages. Surely if any thing were to be built it should be a good room which would doubly answer the intention of Room and Gallery. Added to this 20 feet will be too narrow to see the Aurora proposed for the Ceil[ing] to advantage.' He added other criticisms in which it is clear that he was experiencing some frustration. However, he seems to have kept this in check for the moment, and at least a few of his suggestions, such as that 'As the Building is much too low [I] propose for the south front and returns over the bows, a balustrade of wood, painted and sanded', were accepted.

Precisely what precipitated the earl bishop's volte-face remains a mystery. The entry in Soane's notebook under 'Monday' reads 'Every thing entirely changed'. His own account of the episode as given years later in his *Memoirs* recalls that 'after staying with his Lordship about six weeks without any prospect of professional employment, I asked permission to return to England, which was granted.' He left Downhill at two o'clock on the following Saturday, 2 September, having asked for an advance of £20 towards his travelling expenses. This, and the £30 sent to him at the outset were, in Soane's own words, 'all the remuneration I ever received from the right reverend Prelate for all my expenses and professional services, amounting to upwards of 400l'. Underlying this disappointment was no doubt some self-reproach—although he would not have admitted it—for not having curbed his exasperation when dealing with a notoriously difficult client. Early in December, 1780, he made an attempt to obtain what he considered his due by writing to Lady Hervey, then at Ickworth. This met with no success, and in her reply she had to tell him: 'I am sorry to inform you that I cou'd obtain nothing for you: and his only answer was that you had dismissed yourself from his service and protection. All I can say on ye occasion is, that I heartily wish it had been otherwise.'[48]

Notes

1. An engraving of one of the walls in the Caffè degli Inglesi, decorated in the Egyptian style is illustrated in Piranesi's *Diverse Maniere* of 1769, plate 45. See also J. Wilton Ely, *Piranesi*, 1978, plate 200.
2. The relevant note and sketch books in the Museum are in the Soane Bookcase, Shelf D (left), as follows:
   Notes, Italy and Italian Language etc., MS, 8vo (usually referred to as 'Notes, Italy')
   Italian Sketches, 1779, 8vo
   Italian Sketches and Memoranda, 1779, 8vo
   Miscellaneous Sketches, 1780–2, 8vo.
   On the same shelf there are also:
   Notes on Italian Language, MS, 8vo
   Notes on the French Language, MS, 8vo
   Notebook, French Language, MS, 12mo
   Notebook, French Language, MS, 8vo.
3. Lady (Anna) Miller, *Letters from Italy, describing the Manners, Customs, Antiquities, Paintings, etc. of that Country* . . . , 1777, 2 vols., 8vo. From her correspondence it would appear that Soane had made her acquaintance before leaving England, perhaps through George Dance.
4. SMC Div. XIV, B (1).
5. W. S. Childe-Pemberton, *The Earl Bishop . . . The Life of Frederick Hervey, Bishop of Derry, Earl of Bristol*, 2 vols., 1925. In a letter to his daugther, Mrs Foster, the bishop mentions that 'Our company of English multiplies very much, and some pleasant people among them, especially Mr Thomas Pitt, nephew to my hero.' Pitt was en route for Naples where Soane was to meet him again.
6. SMC Div. I, B (13).
7. Soane, Italian Sketches.

8. Soane, *Memoirs*. The Bishop's intentions were already apparent in a letter to Mrs Foster, to whom he wrote 'I am purchasing treasures for the Downhill which I flatter myself will be a Tusculanum.'
9. Ibid.
10. SMC Div. 1, B/13.
11. Travel note. SMC Div. XIV, B (1)
12. G. L. Lee, *The Story of the Bosanquets*, 1966. By 1807 Richard had returned to live at a house in Falmouth for which Soane designed slight additions.
13. A. T. Bolton, ed., *Lectures on Architecture by Sir John Soane*, 1929.
14. The Revd Thomas Bowdler whose expurgated edition of Shakespeare's works gave rise to the verb to bowdlerise.
15. British Museum, Add. MS 35,378, f. 302–5.
16. Unnumbered Journal 1781–97, folio 11, 'Drawing of the Corsini Chapel sent from Rome' etc.
17. Louisa, the bishop's youngest daughter, married in 1795 Robert Banks Jenkinson, 2nd Earl of Liverpool, and in spite of her father's ill-treatment of the architect, her friendship with Soane was to be lifelong. Her husband was to become one of his clients, and Soane was much grieved by her death in 1821. He was asked to attend her funeral in Hawkesbury Church, Glos., on 22 June, and accompanied Lord Liverpool and his son into the vault. SNB 1821.
18. Probably the Jacobite Andrew Lumisden, sometime private secretary to Prince Charles Edward, and author of *Remarks on the antiquities of Rome*, 1797. A copy is in Soane's library.
19. Henry Greswold Lewis's sister Anne Marie had married in 1773 the Hon. Wilbraham Tollemache. It may thus have been Soane's meeting with Lewis in Rome which led not only to his employment at Malvern Hall, but to an introduction to Tollemache, one of his earliest clients.
20. Norfolk and Norwich Record Office, Patteson Box 3/12, letter of 12 April 1779.
21. Ibid, letter of 19 April 1779.
22. Soane, *Description of the House and Museum*, 1830.
23. Norfolk and Norwich Record Office, Patteson Box 3/12, letter of 23 May 1779.
24. A. T. Bolton, ed., *Lectures . . .*, op. cit., p. 83.
25. Soane, *Memoirs*.
26. Norfolk and Norwich Record Office, Patteson Box 3/12, letter of 11 June 1779.
27. Ibid, letter of 5 July 1779.
28. Paul Oppé 'Memoirs of Thomas Jones', Walpole Society, Vol. XXXII, p. 90.
29. Soane, Notes, Italy.
30. British Museum, Eg. MSS 2002, f. 28.
31. SMC Div. IV P/I.
32. Soane, *Memoirs*.
33. Soane, Notes, Italy.
34. Ibid.
35. Sir George Grove, *Dictionary of Music and Musicians*, 1954. Storace was the first singer to take the role of Susanna in Mozart's *Nozze di Figaro*, 1786.
36. Soane, Notes, Italy.
37. Soane, *Memoirs*.
38. Diploma in SMC Div. XIV A.
39. Soane, Notes, Italy.
40. SMC Div. III B (2).
41. Soane, Notes, Italy.
42. On 25 January 1788 Soane supplied the Revd Mr Coxe with a 'drawing of Bridge at Wettingden to a small scale', no doubt from his measured sketch made when in that town.
43. SMC Div. XIII A.
44. Items listed in Soane, Notes, Italy.
45. Letter quoted in A. T. Bolton, ed., *The Portrait of Sir John Soane*, 1927.
46. Downhill Notebook, Soane Bookcase, Shelf D (left).
47. Ibid.
48. SMC Div. XIII A, dated 24 December 1780.

[3]

Setting up a Practice

A sad flaw in Soane's character was his inability to weigh his misfortunes against his blessings. It is understandable that the shock and disappointment of his abrupt departure from Downhill affected him deeply. 'I was keenly wounded,' he wrote in his *Memoirs* many years later, 'depressed in spirits, and my best energies paralysed', yet there is no hint of gratitude for those good friends and patrons who rallied round at this crucial period in his career. Even while he was still at Downhill, two of these men whom he had met in Rome, John Stuart and Rowland Burdon, had invited him to their respective estates to discuss projects which, although small by comparison with that of the earl bishop, showed their faith in Soane's talents. Further support was soon forthcoming from John Patteson and Thomas Pitt.

John Stuart, who was later to suceed his father as 4th baronet, had been contemplating the improvement of Allanbank, in Berwickshire, when still in Italy but on returning to Scotland was too much occupied with other interests to envisage building work until the beginning of September 1780. On 5 September, unaware of the contretemps with the earl bishop, he addressed a letter to Soane at Downhill, enclosing a rough plan of the principal floor of his house and requesting ideas for changing the entrance. 'I wish much to see you here', he wrote, 'I cannot fix a time as I don't know how soon some people may be here whom I know you would not like, but I desire to know when you may be over—and tell me what you can make of the plan and how you could bring into the front of it a green house. I want a plan of a *green house* too and of gates with porter's lodge neat genteel and plain.'[1] The letter could not have arrived at Downhill before Soane's departure on 2 September and must have been redirected. In fact it would seem that Soane had already written to Stuart proposing a visit to Allanbank where he must have arrived unexpectedly some time before 22 September, the date which is given on his measured plan of the house.[2] After a fairly short stay he then travelled south to Rowland Burdon's house, Castle Eden, south-east of Durham. As the house—gothic in style— had only been built some twenty years before by William Newton of Newcastle, Burdon would not have taken seriously the three small sketches which Soane drew out for a neoclassical villa on 7 October, unless they were proposed for a different site. On the previous day, however, he had sketched a new entrance porch and niches for the staircase of the existing house, and there also survives an undated and very rough sketch in sepia wash for a semicircular gothic stable block to accommodate thirty-six horses.[3]

While still at Castle Eden an urgent letter arrived for Soane from Stuart: 'If you are still at Mr Burdon's I insist on your returning if you have not business of consequence to oblige you to go South, in that case write me the soonest you could return here because more than a fortnight I can't promise to be in this country myself.'[4] Presumably Soane did return, for although there are no details as to his movements at this point, he would have been anxious to comply with the request. Eagerness would have been tinged with some trepidation, for Stuart was a somewhat outspoken and tactless character who, in spite of his good intentions, must have jarred the younger man's nerves as when he told him in a letter, 'I saw Mr Burdon who is inclined much to continue your friend but complains of Your *Fancies*, and I told him my mind on that score, that I had reason for the same complaint, but imagine it to be constitutional, therefore not to be helped.'[5] By *Fancies* he meant the often excessive reaction to any form of criticism which was to plague Soane throughout his life and led to many misunderstandings, and sometimes to the alienation of his friends. But while Stuart's diagnosis was correct, it was scarcely calculated to soothe Soane's highly strung feelings at this time, or make him feel entirely at ease at Allanbank. Rowland Burdon, in contrast, was a gentle and sympathetic character whose observation on Soane, made to Stuart in misplaced confidence, only served to show how well he understood the young architect's nervous temperament. For his part Soane was to return Burdon's trust and friendship by a lifelong regard.

Soane's second visit to Allanbank would have provided time for a discussion of details on the basis of which he was able, after his return to London, to set out his 'several designs for the alterations', together with working drawings 'for the whole building', drawings for a model, and an estimate. Subsequently there were to be 'sundry designs for the Village'.[6] During 1782, however, Stuart's eagerness for the work to begin started to flag, and although suitable stone and timber had already been selected, a shortage of ready money resulted first in postponement of the project, and finally in its being abandoned. Probably as a gesture of consolation, Stuart now entrusted Soane with the business of finding him a leasehold London house. After the producing of several possibilities which, for one reason or another, did not meet with his satisfaction, Soane found that No. 42 Wimpole Street was available. This met with approval, and he was to be responsible for its repair and partial redecoration.[7]

Meanwhile Soane, on returning to London at the end of October 1780, had problems of his own to resolve. The first essential was to find suitable lodgings, and by early December he had installed himself at No. 10 Cavendish Street, a few doors from the home of his old friend and fellow student at the Royal Academy, Edward Foxhall, now established as a decorator and purveyor of fine furniture and fittings. Documentation for the remainder of the year is scanty, nor is there any indication as to Soane's means apart from his few architectural earnings at the time, but the total can only have been meagre. Early in 1781 he seems to have faced up to the realities of his situation, and the necessity of adopting a business-like method of recording and accounting for such commissions as might now come his way. A narrow folio 'Accompt Book' was the first attempt, and although he continued to make random entries in it for some years, it was soon superseded by a folio 'Journal' which initiated a series to be continued throughout his years in practice. In devising this system it is more than likely that he had the advice of Richard Holland who was steeped in the business side of his family's building firm. In Soane's early Journals the entries are under the clients' names, the first being a retrospective account covering the designs made for John Stuart, including £21 for those relating to the house at Allanbank, plus £5.15.5 for travelling expenses. Additional entries to the same account in 1781 covered the designs for the village, and subsequently the work which he supervised in redecorating No. 42 Wimpole Street.

Equally important as records were the chronological pocket memoranda books (now called Soane Notebooks) which he began slightly later in the same year, and which continued until his death although there are a number of gaps, probably due to the occasional moods for destroying papers which overtook Soane in his later years, and which also resulted in the loss of a good deal of his correspondence. The entries in these notebooks were extremely terse and served merely as an *aide-mémoire*. Only rarely, and in moments of exasperation or stress, was any comment of a personal nature allowed to appear. From 1784, when Soane's practice warranted the employment of assistants, and taking of pupils, the accounting system was expanded by Bill Books, Ledgers and Day Books in which the young men's daily tasks were meticulously recorded.

It is the Soane notebooks which provide useful clues as to his work in the first difficult years, and show that in addition to Foxhall and Richard Holland, such old friends as George Dance and James Peacock rallied round. Dance in particular was able to provide some temporary employment for Soane in assessing, with Peacock, the rebuilding work necessary at Newgate Gaol following its partial destruction in the Gordon Riots of June 1780. For Dance, too, Soane undertook the provision and installation of a new chimneypiece at Cranbury, in Hampshire, for the former's prospective sister-in-law, Mrs Dummer. He also helped in the preparation of drawings for Dance's new St Luke's Hospital, built as a replacement of an earlier institution.

The same notebooks also reveal how much Soane was to be indebted not only to Stuart and Burdon, but to several others of the Grand Tourists whom he had met in Italy. Thomas Pitt—still travelling through Europe—now wrote asking him to undertake repairs at his Petersham villa, and before 1781 was out, Philip Yorke gave him the designing of lodges for Hamels in Hertfordshire, the first of several other and more important commissions (Plate 17, 18). John Patteson, Charles Collyer, Edward Roger Pratt and Henry Greswold Lewis followed with work of varying extent and—equally important—recommendations to other clients. It was to the latter that Soane owed, during the 1780s, many of the East Anglian commissions which provided a mainstay of his early practice. Meanwhile in London his reputation was gaining ground in mercantile circles, probably due to recommendations from George Dance. In July 1781 he was consulted by Francis Adams on the development of a property adjoining the Falcon Inn in Borough High Street (Plates 19, 20). His design for this, consisting of a pedimented three-bay façade to the street, with glazed shop fronts flanking a passage-way to tenements at the rear, was his first entirely new building to be carried out. The bricklaying was given to Richard

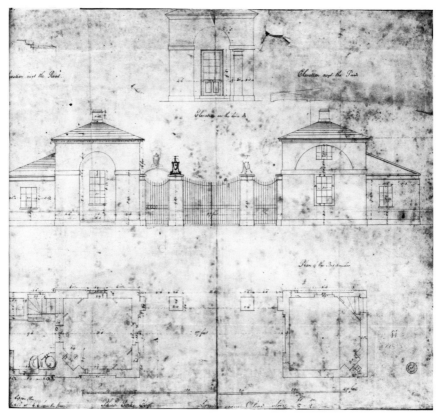

17. Design for lodges at HAMELS, 1781.

18. The Dairy at HAMELS, designed in 1783.

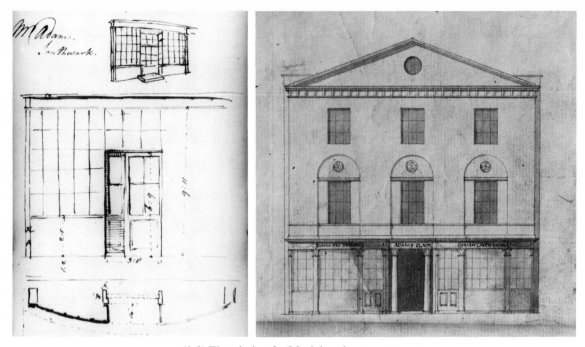

19. (*left*) First design for Mr Adams' SHOP FRONT.

20. (*right*) Mr Adams' SHOP FRONT.

Holland's firm, and John Hobcraft, with whom he had become acquainted while working with Henry Holland, carried out the joinery. In the same month Soane was surveying the Walthamstow house of a City merchant, James Neave and his son Richard, then deputy governor of the Bank of England. Here alterations estimated at £797 were carried out in 1783–4. Another early but unexecuted project was the classical bath house designed for Sir Joseph Mawbey of Botleys in Surrey (Plate 23).

Soane's preoccupation with building up his practice did not prevent him from preparing entries for the Royal Academy exhibitions, and in 1781 he had no less than five designs hung, three of which were for a mausoleum and were no doubt based on that designed to the memory of the Earl of Chatham when he was in Rome. The fourth drawing was for a 'Hunting Casine', while the fifth was a version of the 'Canine Residence' made for the Bishop of Derry after the visit to Terracina. During the summer news also reached Soane's ears of a competition to be launched in connection with the building of a penitentiary on Battersea Rise, which was the outcome of an Act of Parliament passed in 1779. He therefore set to work on preparing 'Designs in Competition for two Penitentiary Houses, the one to contain 600 males, the other for 300 females'. These were duly submitted under the motto 'Leve fit quod bene fertur onus'.[8] Ill-founded gossip that his was likely to be the successful entry raised his hopes, and added to his disappointment when the winner was announced as William Blackburn, who had been a fellow student at the Royal Academy in 1772 and was a subsequent gold medallist.[9] In plan, his alternatives show basically the same triangular arrangement of three blocks joined to each other at their inner angles and set within a circular wall in which the main entrance is flanked by accommodation for the governor and matron. Making the best of misfortune, Soane used one of the designs as his contribution to the Royal Academy exhibition of 1782, when it was catalogued as 'Elevation of a Design for a Prison'.

During the summer of 1781 Soane decided to move to more substantial accommodation at 53 Margaret Street where he leased from Miss Susannah Cecil rooms on the first and second floors 'for one year certain' from 24 June for £40 'to include dinner and service'.[10] Margaret Street at that time extended eastwards from Cavendish Square, and was not yet cut in two by John Nash's Regent Street. No. 53 was on the south side, near the crossing of John (now Great Portland) Street. Taking the sensible view that it was important for an architect—and particularly for one whose commissions then included a good deal of internal decoration—to present himself against a background of taste, he laid out a substantial sum on the furniture, carpets and curtains for the principal, though not very large, rooms which he was to occupy for the next five years. At first he did little entertaining here, and indeed the only hint of relaxation at this time seems to have been an occasional meal with James Peacock or Richard Holland with whom on rare occasions he went to a theatre or an exhibition at Spring Gardens.[11] The impression given by the notebooks is of his constantly hurrying from one job to another, preparing estimates, engaging workmen, or ordering materials. Probably his drawings were mostly done early in the morning when the light was good. As yet he did not have his own horse but, being a prodigious walker, relied on his long legs to carry him around, sometimes as far afield as Camberwell or Hampstead. Coach-hire at this time was reserved for really long distances or for when he was accompanied by less active companions. Two years later, however, Soane had the chance of purchasing a mare from his client William Cooke of Walthamstow for fifteen guineas after which there are many references in the notebooks to journeys on 'the grey mare', which from July 1783 was usually kept at one of the livery stables near Cavendish Square. It was apparently towards the end of this year that Soane adopted this spelling for his surname, previously spelt without an *e*. Presumably he thought that this gave it an added dignity, and he must have intimated the decision to various friends and clients such as Thomas Pitt who observed the instruction, while those books which Soane had collected before this date show that he had gone through them and added the *e* to any earlier inscription of his name.

The longer journeys undertaken in 1783–4 took Soane to Bath and Warwickshire, to his various works in Norfolk and Suffolk, and on one hectic excursion to County Durham whither he was carried by his client George Smith for whom he had already designed a semicircular cow-house at Marlesford in Suffolk, and alterations to his house in London. Smith now had the idea of building a large mansion at Burn Hall near Durham, and early on 21 July 1783 he and Soane and Mrs Smith set out on the long journey, reaching their destination on the afternoon of 23 July when the architect at once began to take measurements and survey the intended site. Next morning he continued his notes, and then in the afternoon accompanied the Smiths to Brancepath Castle where he sketched in his notebook the medieval gateway, a subject which he was later to work up as one of his drawings for the Royal Academy exhibition of 1784. Leaving Burn Hall that night, he travelled through Ferrybridge, Stilton and Cambridge, reaching London

21. (*left*) ANNA STORACE, the singer, friend of John and Elizabeth Soane.
A miniature by an unknown artist. See page 42.
22. (*right*) GEORGE WYATT, uncle of Elizabeth Soane; a pencil drawing by George Dance.

on the Saturday afternoon. Working under such pressure, it is not surprising that his health was beginning to suffer. A reference to feeling unwell in a letter to Thomas Pitt brought a solicitous reply (undated but at the end of 1783 or beginning of 1784),[12] and the practical suggestion that Soane should take a few days rest at the Petersham villa:

> I am griev'd my dear Soane that you continue so ill and do not doubt that the vexations of your mind greatly increase your distemper. We shall be extremely glad you should try the air of Petersham which we very much hope may be of service to you. There is a little green bed in a room adjoining to the steward's room which as being the best air'd and the most comfortable we always use when we come down. This apartment we recommend to you by all means not as the chearfulest but a great deal the most comfortable.

Reluctant to spare the time, Soane dismissed the idea and carried on at work, but providentially something now occurred to take his mind off his worries and steer it on a happier course.

The measuring work which Soane had undertaken for Dance at Newgate Gaol had led to an acquaintance with the City's Surveyor of Paving, George Wyatt (Plate 22), a substantial figure in the building world who was also a Common Councillor and the owner of a considerable amount of property. Although no relationship to James and Samuel Wyatt has been established, he was certainly a co-proprietor with the latter of the Albion Mills in Southwark, and occupied houses in the adjoining Albion Place, where he lived with a favourite niece, Elizabeth Smith, then aged twenty-three, who presided over the household.[13] George Wyatt's name first appears in Soane's notebooks in September 1783 in connection with supplying stucco and composition for houses in the Borough, no doubt those which Soane was building for Francis Adams. By the turn of the year, however, it is evident that Soane's interest was no longer confined to Wyatt's ability to supply stucco, but that the charms of his niece had now claimed his attention. By 10 January 1784 he was taking her to the theatre, noting 'expenses 10/6', and on 2 March she was dining with him in Margaret Street in company with Mr and Mrs Cooke, when he paid six shillings for wine, eight shillings and sixpence for sundries, and an extra five shillings to the serving maid, Betty. Two days later he was taking tea with the Cookes where he found Wyatt and his niece, although for some unspecified reason he was 'damnably vex'd'.[14] On 6 March he noted that he had again escorted Miss Smith to the theatre, and during the next four months the normally brief entries about work in the notebooks are interspersed with references to dining or supping with 'Eliza' at their respective homes, or visits to Vauxhall or the theatre, the latter being of particular interest to both. Another note records that on 6 May they went to sit for 'sketches by George Dance', and although Soane does not mention at what point their engagement officially began, it must have been recognised, at least by their friends, at this time.

As it transpired, Soane could not have made a better choice of wife for Eliza was not only endowed with agreeable looks, but with intelligence and a degree of patience which was to stand up to fairly rigorous testing until the onset of her last illness. Not only did she encourage Soane to make more frequent visits to see his elderly mother at Chertsey, but often went there by herself, and endeavoured to soften the hard feelings which Soane harboured towards his brother William. She ran the household efficiently, welcomed the guests and came to be regarded with affection by Soane's friends in all walks of life from the Duchess of Leeds and Lady Bridport to Turner and the ever-impecunious Gandy family.

During the early summer of 1784 Soane was frequently away, inspecting work or making surveys, mainly in East Anglia. Early in July he waited on Lord Bellamont with designs for a tomb in memory of Miss Elizabeth Johnstone, who had lived with her parents in Brompton. It took the form of a classical sarcophagus which, sadly neglected, still stands in St Mary Abbot's churchyard, Kensington (Plate 24). The last two days of July and first two of August were spent in Warwickshire, settling the alterations for Henry Greswold Lewis at Malvern Hall. Arriving back in London at six on the Tuesday evening, he had barely twelve hours at home before setting out for more visits to Norfolk and Suffolk lasting until 18 August during which time he called at Earsham, Letton, Taverham, Saxlingham, Langley Park and Costessey, discussing plans, making sketches and giving instructions to workmen. In Norwich he stayed with John Patteson, saw vari-

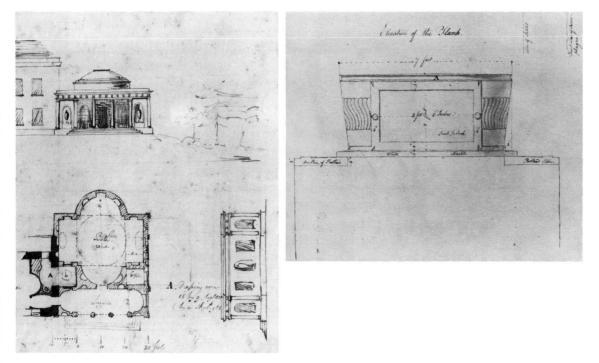

23. (*left*) Design for a bath house at BOTLEYS. *Page 53*.

24. (*right*) Tomb designed for MISS JOHNSTONE, St Mary Abbot's churchyard.

ous friends, and visited the cathedral where, to his annoyance, he 'gave by mistake 1.1.0' to the verger. After spending a night at Thetford, he arrived in London on Wednesday in time to settle Richard Holland's account for £200 in respect of various works, and then allowed himself two days of comparative calm, and a gap of four days without an entry in his notebook. It was during this weekend that his marriage to Elizabeth Smith took place.

The register of Christ Church Lambeth[15] records that on 21 August 1784, 'John Soane of the Parish of St Marylebone [was] married to Elizabeth Smith of this Parish by special licence' in the presence of George Wyatt and an aunt, Elizabeth Levick, the service being conducted by the Revd William Walker. The couple returned to the apartment in Margaret Street with which she was already well acquainted, but the honeymoon—if, indeed, it justified that name—could scarcely have been more brief for on the Monday Soane set off for Oxford *en route* for another four-day visit to inspect the work at Malvern Hall, leaving Eliza alone to take stock of the new life which lay before her, and the realisation that, however sincere her husband's protestations of love might be, she came second to his self-confessed passion for architecture. From this time until her death in 1815 references to her in those notebooks which survive are scanty, and then usually associated with some domestic detail. As there is a gap between Christmas 1784 and May 1788, it cannot be ascertained whether Soane noted the births of his children, but considering that he failed to comment on his marriage, it seems unlikely. Fortunately his wife, who had good reason to be more mindful of these events, entered the arrivals on the flyleaf of her copy of *The Whole Duty of Man*.[16] There were four children, all boys. John, the eldest, was born on 29 April, 1786, at 53 Margaret Street and Richard Holland agreed to stand as godfather.

In the autumn of 1784 Soane decided to take his first pupil, John Sanders, who was apparently introduced by Timothy Tyrrell. Up to this time Soane had only once employed outside help when, desperate to finish drawings for a house at Taverham, he employed Christopher Ebdon for four days.[17] Sanders was taken on for five years from 1 September at a premium of £50, and he was the only one of Soane's many pupils to be resident. It is a tribute to his good nature that he stayed the course in the cramped quarters at Margaret Street. From 1785, however, he was able to escape for a few evenings each week to pursue his studies at the Royal Academy School. No doubt it was because of this congestion that, in the same autumn, Soane began looking for other accommodation and finally settled on No. 77 Welbeck Street, the lease of which he took over from a Mr Little for £720,[18] and which he insured for £500 with the Westminster Office. As shown on Horwood's map of 1792, the house was wider than most at this southern end of the street, and had a garden at the rear. His neighbour at No. 76 was the Hon. Horatio Walpole, who had not yet succeeded as Lord Orford, and at No. 78 was James Boyd. Here the Soanes' second son, George, was born in the early hours of 21 December 1787, but he lived for only six months, the same christian name being given to the next child, born on 28 September 1789. The last son arrived on 10 October 1790, and was named Henry, but died of whooping cough in the following year.

In spite of the missing notebooks, the course of Soane's practice in the period following his marriage can be charted from his Bill and Account Books. The year 1785 found him travelling to Staffordshire about additions to Chillington, and to Norfolk about a new house at Shotesham. In the same year his somewhat erratic client, George Smith, having decided to build at Burn Hall nothing more than a new cow-house, which was a copy of the one which Soane had designed for him at Marlesford, switched his interest to remodelling Piercefield, on the equally distant estate in Monmouthshire which he had recently purchased. In fact, the design ultimately adopted for this house from the alternatives which Soane produced, after a visit in 1785, was almost identical with that chosen by Robert Fellowes at Shotesham, although Piercefield was faced with ashlar. Whether his clients were aware of this duplication is not recorded.

Of about this time is an undated sheet of paper preserved in Soane's correspondence with Thomas Pitt, who had been created 1st Baron Camelford in 1784. It sets out the latter's intention to offer to the Dilettanti Society the two empty houses adjoining his own in Hereford Street, Mayfair. It also shows that he had asked Soane to prepare a design for adapting these to suit the needs of the Society. The particulars state that they had cost 'above three thousand pounds, no expense having been spared' in their construction, and go on to say that 'they may be thrown together according to a plan of the invention of Mr Soane proper for a public museum in a gallery on the principal floor of upward of 120 feet, and on the ground floor one of 52 feet and two rooms that might serve as libraries of 30 feet each.'[19] Lord Camelford was willing to present them to the Society on condition that the Society would 'exonerate him of the ground rent', and would 'allow the ground not built upon [at the rear of the houses] to be thrown into his garden, as it will be of no use to them, and they will by that means save the expence of keeping it'. He also wished to have a door from his own house into the gallery. With this document is the draft of a letter, unsigned, to Sir Joseph Banks and dated 7 February 1785. It requested that Banks would take the matter up with the Society, but there is no indication as to Banks's reply. Certainly the Society did not follow up the offer, and the houses were subsequently let or sold to private individuals.

It was to Camelford that Soane was indebted for an introduction to the former's cousin, William Pitt who had, in December 1783, at the early age of twenty-four become prime minister. Pitt's country residence was Holwood, near Keston, in Kent, and he was to take a keen interest in the alterations which Soane was commissioned to make from 1786 onwards. These involved many visits in the course of which the architect would be invited, if his distinguished client were at home, to join him for breakfast or dinner. The importance of this work, however, lay less in its size or financial return than in the support which Pitt was to give Soane in his future applications for various posts, notably the surveyorship to the Bank of England in 1788.

Wiltshire was not a county with which Soane had any connection before he was asked, probably to his surprise, to make designs for a new picture gallery at Fonthill Splendens, the Palladian mansion built some thirty years before for Alderman Beckford. In 1769 the estate had passed to his son William who had subsequently fallen from grace on account of his indiscretions with young 'Kitty' Courtenay in 1784, after which he had been forced to live abroad with his wife, Lady Margaret. In January 1787, a few months after her death, Beckford returned to England for a brief and surreptitious visit during which he stayed at Fonthill and decided on various alterations which his mother was to put in hand after he left in March for a long period spent in Spain and Portugal. Mrs Beckford's selection of Soane as architect may perhaps have come on the advice of her cousin, the Hon. John James Hamilton, later Marquis of Abercorn, who was certainly acquainted with him by 1785.

On 25 April 1787, Soane visited Fonthill and took plans of that part of the house in which the 'intended gallery' was to be formed. Three days later he called on Mrs Beckford in London to show her his designs which were approved. They included chimneypieces for the tapestry-room and parlour, and later on he designed a 'great bed', the drawing being sent to his friend Foxhall to be executed. Foxhall was apparently also in charge of the redecorating. The work went ahead swiftly and on 2 December 1788 Soane's account for £284.14.10 was settled by 'Mr Wildman', one of the three brothers who acted as Beckford's solicitors over many years and were believed to have feathered their nest very comfortably in the process.

Soane would not have met Beckford himself at this stage for the work was finished by the time the latter returned in October 1789. What Soane did see, however, was Beckford's fine collection of paintings which made a lasting impression, and from which, when the contents of old Fonthill were dispersed, he acquired the eight *Rake's Progress* paintings by Hogarth.[20] Five years later he purchased from Beckford the large Canaletto *Venetian Scene* for 150 guineas.[21] Later on he and Beckford were on calling terms, both in London and in Bath, when Soane was taking a cure there in 1829. 'Left card for Mr Beckford', Soane wrote in his notebook after a walk to Lansdowne Crescent on 19 September. Two days later he noted 'Mr B[eckford] called early. Saw Mr Beckford home.'

In 1788 the death of two distinguished architects left vacant the official appointments which they had held for several years. James Stuart, who died suddenly on 2 February, had acted as surveyor to Greenwich Hospital since 1758. Soane at once applied to succeed him, but unsuccessfully, as the post was given to Sir Robert Taylor who was already surveyor to the Bank of England. As it transpired, Taylor was himself to be carried off by a fatal chill on the following 27 September when both posts became available again. Although he had professed disappointment over not getting the Greenwich appointment, Soane now decided to apply for the Bank post, realising that the work which he had carried out at Holwood might secure him the prime minister's support. This proved to be the case, and in a letter of 16 October the Bank secretary, Francis Martin, informed him that 'You are by the Court of Directors appointed Architect and Surveyor to the Bank of England in the room of Sir Robert Taylor deceased.'[22] Martin's letter instructed him to attend on the following Tuesday at one o'clock. No salary was mentioned, but subsequent accounts show that Soane received a commission of five per cent on the half-yearly total expenditure on building work, except on rare occasions involving considerable extra work such as illuminations or banquets.

Although Soane had sent the good news to Lord Camelford, his letter miscarried as the latter pointed out when writing from Carnoles in the South of France on 6 February 1789:

> I certainly received none of Your letters, Soane, and will own I was not a little surprised at it. I had heard from others of your disappointment at Greenwich, and of your success at the Bank from those who had contributed to it, and I could not help wondering at your silence. I am sorry you lost Greenwich, but at your time of life the Bank is such a step gained that it ought to reconcile you to your disappointment.[23]

For the first twelve months little work was involved at the Bank beyond routine maintenance, and Soane was able to complete his project for publishing in 1788 a new, and this time folio, volume of his designs under the title of *Plans Elevations and Sections of Houses, Lodges, Bridges, etc. in the Counties of Norfolk, Suffolk, Yorkshire, Staffordshire, Warwickshire, Hertfordshire et caetera*. Most of the designs had been carried out, the exceptions being a villa at Mottram in Cheshire for Philip Yorke, the mansion house at Burn Hall, and the proposed premises for the Dilettanti Society. The volume was prefaced by an imposing list of subscribers in which figured the various noblemen by whom he had already been patronised as well as friends and clients such as William

Pitt, Rowland Burdon, John Patteson, George Dance, Henry and Richard Holland, Edward Foxhall, and William Beckford. The names of Robert Adam, William Chambers and James Wyatt also appeared. Their support must have gone a long way towards the satisfactory launching of the edition by the publishers Isaac and Josiah Taylor, Soane agreeing to take a hundred copies at trade price for his own use. In his fulsome dedication he expressed his gratitude to George III:

> Enabled by Your Majesty's Munificence to finish my Studies in Italy and flattered by Your Permission for this Dedication, I am induced to hope that the small tribute of a Grateful Heart will not be unfavourably received and that Your Protection will be extended to a Work which owes its Origin to your Patronage.

While they testified to a creditable performance for an industrious architect of thirty-five, the designs themselves showed that he was still following the simple neo-Palladian formula made popular by Holland and Wyatt, and gave no hint of the highly idiosyncratic 'Soane style' which was to emerge two years later.

Notes

1. SMC Div. IV (3).
2. Soane, Drawer V, Set 3 (4).
3. Soane Bookcase, Original Sketches, Shelf C (left).
4. SMC Div. IV (3).
5. Ibid.
6. Soane Journal, 1781–97.
7. Ibid.
8. Soane, Drawer XIII, Set 1. Soane gives this as the motto in his *Memoirs*. It may be translated as 'Light is a burden gladly borne'.
9. Soane, *Memoirs*.
10. Soane, Notebook.
11. Ibid.
12. SMC Div. IV (I). The letter is signed 'T. Pitt' and was therefore written before he was created 1st Baron Camelford.
13. *European Magazine*, Vol. 63, 1813, p. 5.
14. Soane, Notebook.
15. Now in the Greater London Council's Record Office. Mrs Elizabeth Levick was a sister of George Wyatt and mother of Ann Levick, a lifelong friend of Soane and his wife.
16. W. Bent, *The Whole Duty of Man*, new edition 1785.
17. Journal, 10 February 1784, 'Mr Branthwaite 3 sections 1 elevation 1 plan . . . Ebdon, 4 days, self 3.'
18. Soane, Journal, 1781–97.
19. SMC Div. IV P.
20. As Soane had been ill, Mrs Soane attended the sale at Christie's on 27 February 1802, and made the successful bid of 570 guineas for the eight paintings.
21. The painting was No. 605 in the six-day sale held at Fonthill by H. Phillips from 17 August 1807. A 'Mr White' apparently bid on Soane's behalf, subsequently being paid £9.2.6 for 'half the expenses to Fonthill', Journal 1807.
22. SMC Div. XIV J.
23. SMC Div. IV P.

[4]

'Form, if you can, a style of your own'

advice from Sir William Chambers

For Soane the year 1790 could justifiably have been regarded as an *anno mirabilis*. Not only were a number of substantial commissions forthcoming, including Buckingham House, Pall Mall and Wimpole Hall, but the Building Committee of the Bank of England at last agreed to the total replacement of the by now decrepit Bank Stock Office. Nor was this all, for on 23 February Mrs Soane's uncle, George Wyatt, died leaving some valuable London property to Eliza and her husband.[1] Relieved from the drudgery of petty jobs, the architect was now able to develop that highly idiosyncratic approach to design which was to become recognised as the 'Soane style'. It relied on certain basic themes which, although employed on vastly differing scales, and emerging sometimes in stark simplicity and sometimes richly embellished, appeared in his work for nearly forty years, but with particularly striking effect in the Bank Stock Office and ultimately in the Law Courts at Westminster.

The most characteristic of these themes was the domed ceiling over segmental arches resting on four piers usually, although not always, lit by a glazed lantern. While the conception owed much to George Dance's Council Chamber at Guildhall, built in 1777, Soane's adaptation of the idea for the Bank Stock Office showed an entirely original interpretation of classical forms. His second favourite theme was a derivative from the first, but with the dome and lantern replaced by a shallow cross vault springing from the piers, an idea which again was indebted to Dance who had used this form for the City Chamberlain's Court and for the ballroom ceiling at Cranbury. Dance, in turn, is likely to have based his design on a plate in Pietro Santi Bartoli's *Gli Antichi Sepolchri* of 1768 (Plate 25), and probably introduced Soane to this source for he later acquired his own copy and found in it the inspiration for many of his decorative details.

A third theme to appear in Soane's designs over the years is that of the 'tribune', or open well, which rises through two floors and is lit by a lantern in the roof. A so-called 'tribune' of this form had been used by Lancelot Brown and Henry Holland at Benham in 1773, and Holland later employed it on a much larger scale for the octagonal hall at Carlton House. Soane's first domestic application of the idea was at Tyringham in 1793, and it later appeared in his own house at Pitzhanger, Ealing, but it was to play a major role in his National Debt Redemption Office of 1817, and in attenuated form, in the Court of Chancery.

The last, and certainly not the least, distinctive element in the 'Soane style' was the

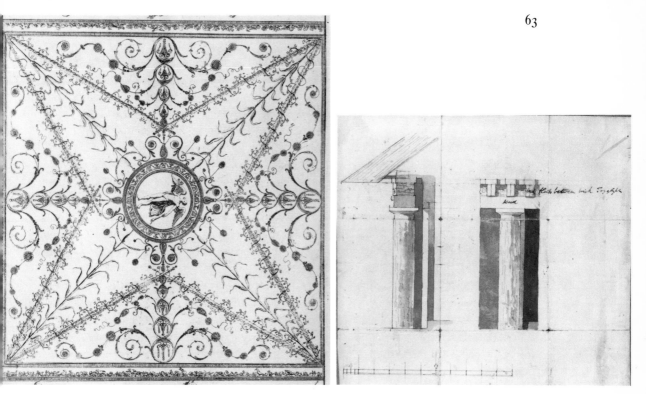

25. (*left*) A ceiling design from P. S. Bartoli's *Gli Antichi Sepolchri*.
26. (*right*) HAMELS, the dairy, an early instance of Soane's 'primitive' style.

'primitivism' which made use of 'prototypal' equivalents for the conventional orders. This is distilled largely from the theories expounded by the Abbé Laugier in his *Essai Sur L'Architecture*.[2] Soane's design of 1782 for the dairy at Hamels Park reveals a fleeting interest in rustic details (Plate 26), but after 1790 bark-covered tree trunks gave way to 'primitive' columns or pilasters of flint or brick, with a narrow band cut away below the abacus to form a retracted necking, while for the normal entablature he introduced his own version in which two bricks set upright took the place of triglyphs. While these innovations made their first appearance in designs for lodges, dairies or gateways, notably at Bagshot, Wimpole, and Cumberland Gate, Hyde Park, they were extended to the stable range at Betchworth Park and ultimately were to be reflected in the Dulwich Picture Gallery and Mausoleum.

Although the Bank Stock Office was to be the first major product of Soane's experimentalism, an embryonic version appeared a few months earlier in his design for a new drawing-room at Wimpole Hall to which his early client Philip Yorke had now succeeded as 3rd Earl of Hardwicke. Faced with a difficult T-shaped site wedged behind and between existing rooms on the north side of the house, he adopted the expedient of a domed, top-lit inner space flanked by semicircular apses. From the domed area a barrel-vaulted 'limb' extended to the line of the north front where two windows admitted more light.

The result could never have made a really enjoyable sitting-room, but it served its purpose as additional accommodation for entertaining, and as a link between the older Saloon and Red Room, which was what Lord Hardwicke wanted, and it was only one of the many alterations and additions which Soane was to carry out for him during this decade.

The fact that Soane's Bank appointment carried no salary may have been one reason why he decided to apply for the post of Clerk of the Works to St James's Palace, the Houses of Parliament, and other public buildings in Westminster which had become vacant on the death of Kenton Couse. This had a fixed salary of £300 a year. Once again he sought William Pitt's support and towards the end of October 1790, heard that he had been successful. Writing to the prime minister to express his thanks, he added his assurance that 'I shall always endeavour to deserve the honour you have done me in sanctioning my wishes by your approbation.'[3] The only worthwhile product of this post was the building of a new guard-room at St James Palace, begun in 1792. It was later rebuilt.

The spring of 1791 brought more work for Lord Abercorn who, with the first phase of alterations to Bentley Priory under way, decided to remodel the Irish house, Barons-court, Co. Tyrone, which he had inherited two years before. This involved Soane in a journey to Ireland for which he set out on 7 May by way of Chester and on to Holyhead where he embarked for Dublin, reaching Baronscourt by the end of the week and spending three days in making notes and surveys. On his return journey he travelled north to Donaghade, took a boat to Portpatrick, and then went by coach through Carlisle to Durham and on to Skelton Castle, near Middlesborough to stay with John Hall for whom he had carried out work here in 1787. By 24 May he was back in London and setting his draughtsmen on to drawing out the proposals for altering Baronscourt which he took to Lord Abercorn at Bentley on 28 May. These proving acceptable, it was decided that one of his most trusted clerks, Robert Woodgate, who had been with him since 1788, should go to Ireland and take charge of the work.[4]

The office staff had by this time grown to some size. With his first pupil, John Sanders, due to leave in 1790 on completion of his agreed five years, Soane had taken on John McDowell and Thomas Chawner as pupils, but these were joined in the course of 1790 and 1791 by David Laing, Frederick Meyer and Thomas Williams.[5] There were also Robert Morrison who came as an assistant, William Blogg who was an improver, and three new clerks of works, Walter Payne, Henry Provis and Robert Louch, while Soane's friend Christopher Ebdon also gave temporary help as an assistant.[6] The clerks were mostly engaged on outside work, but the rest were squeezed into No. 77 Welbeck Street together with Mrs Soane, the babies and domestic staff. However, it was not to last much longer for Soane's recently acquired wealth now allowed him to contemplate building a new house.

The site on which he eventually settled was No. 12 Lincoln's Inn Fields, then a residential area conveniently situated between his work at the Bank and his many commissions in Westminster. On 30 June 1792, he noted that he had 'Paid Mrs Barnard for the house in Lincoln's Inn Fields £2100',[7] and on 12 July his clerk Louch 'met Mr Jacques in

Lincoln's Inn Fields [and] measured the party wall next Lady Heathcote's', that is, No. 13. At first he contemplated alteration but then decided on total demolition and replacement with a building of white brick with Portland stone dressings. Richard Holland's firm undertook the bricklaying while most of the other work was carried out by artisans whom he had already employed at the Bank. The internal decoration of the house was subtle and restrained with the exception of the Breakfast Room where Soane introduced one of his shallow groined vaults over which spread painted decoration in the form of trelliswork entwined with flowers, doubtless the work of John Crace who was later to execute a similar ceiling at Pitzhanger Manor. Soane's interest in this trellis effect is likely to have been aroused by the 'landscape' room at Norbury Park, where, in a house built for William Locke by Thomas Sandby, George Barrett and Benedetto Pastorini had painted a room with rural scenes below a border of flower-entwined trellis.[8] The communicating north and south drawing-rooms on the first floor of No. 12, and the bedrooms above, were reached by a cantilevered stone staircase with a balustrade of the same scrolled ironwork as was used for the continuous balcony which extended at first-floor level across the façade of the house.

No. 12 was completed in eighteen months, and on 18 January 1794 Soane and his wife, with their two surviving sons, moved in. A water-colour drawing made by Joseph Gandy in 1798 shows the family in the Breakfast Room (Plate 27). Soane is seated at a table, examining a plan which has been sent to him, while Mrs Soane presides behind the tea-kettle and the boys disport themselves nearby. On the walls can be seen the engravings presented to him by Piranesi, and above the bookcases are two plaster lions and two Wedgwood 'Etruscan' vases which were probably those purchased from Flaxman shortly before. Through the window shown in the water-colour is a glimpse across a small courtyard of the low building which housed his new office. Although somewhat overshadowed by the house, it had a large window and purpose-made drawing tables which would have been a considerable improvement on the improvised working accommodation at Welbeck Street. Here the pupils and assistants, unless sent out on a job, were to work from seven to seven in the summer, and eight to eight in the winter from Monday to Saturday inclusive.[9] The more determined and serious-minded persevered with this strict regime, but a few fell by the wayside, including Thomas Williams who absconded with a large sum of money intended for the bank, and made off to sea. There was little opportunity for relaxation or high spirits while the master was within ear-shot, and no doubt there was a feeling of relief once his dark-suited figure had departed for a meeting or a journey. A letter from young Bob Smirke written to his father, during his brief stay in the office confirms the impression that being a pupil here was no easy task.

He [Soane] was on Monday morning in one of his *amiable* Tempers. Everything was slovenly that I was doing. My drawing was slovenly because it was too great a scale, my scale, also, being too long, and he finished saying the whole of it was excessively *slovenly*, and that I should draw it out again on the back [so as] not to waste another sheet about it.[10]

Taking this discouragement to heart, young Smirke left after a year, but those who did stay the course—among them John Sanders, C. J. Richardson, George Basevi, David Laing and David Mocatta—held their master in great esteem and found in him a helpful and generous friend. Nobody, however, was more indebted to Soane than Joseph Michael Gandy who, although described as 'odd and impracticable in disposition', struck a sympathetic chord in Soane's usually down-to-earth attitude in the running of his office. Born in 1771, Gandy attended the Royal Academy School where he won silver and gold medals and was then enabled, through the generosity of a patron, to travel to Italy for further study. From 1789 he exhibited at the Academy where Soane probably first saw his work and was struck by its originality and the skill of his draughtsmanship. Within a few months of Gandy's return from the Continent in 1797 Soane took him into his office, and furthermore lent him £20 to tide him over the first of the financial crises which became more frequent after his marriage and the arrival of nine children. There appears to have been no formal agreement, but Soane noted in his Journal that he intended to pay Gandy amounts totalling £80 'to Xmas 1798, and from thence £100 per annum'.[11] Of the £80, £20 was a 'present', presumably to offset Gandy's debt. Although the latter's name appears fairly regularly in the Day Books for this period, he does not seem to have been tied to set hours, and much of his work must have been done at home, or what passed for 'home' in a series of rather lowly lodgings. It was largely concerned with drawings for Soane's major commissions in hand such as the Bank Stock Offices and Rotunda, the Bagshot and Cumberland Gate lodges, the hall at Bentley Priory, the house, bridge and lodges at Tyringham, and new versions of Soane's mausoleum and triumphal bridge designs for exhibition at the Royal Academy in the summer of 1799. They leave no doubt that Gandy, more than any other of Soane's draughtsmen, entered into the spirit of the master's designs, and produced the most successful interpretations of it.

Gandy's own contribution to the Academy exhibition of 1799 is listed under the address 'Bold Street, Liverpool' to which he had moved earlier in the year. Here he formed an ill-fated partnership with the sculptor George Bullock, but subsequently returned to London and worked intermittently for Soane during the ensuing years. At Soane's death he was left an annuity of £100 a year.[12]

Soon after his purchase of No. 12 Lincoln's Inn Fields, Soane also paid attention to one of the London houses left to him by George Wyatt, No. 7 Orchard Street, Marylebone. This he never intended for his own use, but regarded as a source of income, and after it had been thoroughly renovated, it was let on a fourteen-year lease to a Miss Wynyard, and subsequently to a Mr Fanshawe. When added to the houses in Albion Place, Cow Cross Street, and Liquor Pond Street which he had also inherited, Soane's holding of rent-producing London properties was now considerable, and he could well have afforded to take life at a more leisurely pace. That, however, was not in his nature, and there was no lessening in the volume of work at this time although, from July 1789, when he made the first of several recorded purchases of fishing tackle, he allowed himself

27. No. 12 LINCOLN'S INN FIELDS, the Breakfast Room, a water-colour by J. M. Gandy. *Page 65*.

28. No. 12 LINCOLN'S INN FIELDS, the Breakfast Room, chimneypiece detail. *Page 65*.

29. HOUSE OF LORDS, unexecuted design.

an occasional Sunday's fishing, either in the streams near Chertsey, or in the Thames at Pangbourne with which he had been familiar as a child.

A misunderstanding as to the duties involved was the excuse put forward by Soane for resigning from his Westminster clerkship in 1793, soon after the completion of the new Guard Room at St James's Palace.[13] It is evident, though, that he really wished to be free for another project of which he had heard when a committee was appointed to consider the state of the House of Lords. In June 1794 he was instructed to suggest 'what alterations could be made to render the House of Lords, and the rooms and offices appertaining thereto, more commodious, consistent with the general plan of the adjacent buildings'. This was followed by a further direction to make plans for an entirely new House.[14] He responded with designs for an extensive classical building which fully exploited its riverside site while retaining within the complex such historic portions of the old building as St Stephen's Chapel and the Painted Chamber (Plates 29–31). The drawings were duly delivered to the lord chancellor and subsequently, on his direction, to various other members of the committee, all of whom made various suggestions which the architect had to incorporate. Finally they were shown to the royal princes and then to the king himself, by whom Soane 'had the honour to be most graciously received' at Windsor. 'His Majesty having examined the designs in all their details, with most accurate and scrupulous attention, expressed his entire approbation, particularly with the entrance into the House of Lords, in the centre of the new building, through the

30. HOUSE OF LORDS, unexecuted design.

31. HOUSE OF LORDS, unexecuted design.

Scala Regia, decorated with statues of our ancient monarchs.' Royal interest and approval was, however, the only satisfaction which Soane was to receive for his trouble. After being sent from one high official to another, he was informed that 'in the present state of the country it would be inexpedient to commence the work'. Hope was rekindled in December 1798, when a message came directing him to take the drawings to Lord Grenville, where they were again admired and left for others to see. These apparently included James Wyatt who at once claimed his right to design any new buildings for the House of Lords by virtue of having succeeded as surveyor general on the death of Sir William Chambers in 1796—two years after the unfortunate Soane had received and carried out his initial commission.[15]

It was probably when he first began to encounter the delays which bedevilled this project that Soane decided to apply for another official post. This followed a Treasury decision in 1795 that 'an experienced Architect should be appointed as Deputy Surveyor of His Majesty's Woods and Forests', with responsibility for such plans, estimates and repairs as were necessary for the numerous small buildings which came within these extensive areas of royal land, including the New Forest, Salcey Forest, and Windsor

Great Park.[16] The salary was £200 per annum with one shilling a mile for travelling over twenty miles, and one guinea a day for time and trouble. Much of the repair work was trivial such as brick arches built under the water-tables and ridings, fences and kennels in Bushey, Richmond, Hampton Court and Greenwich Parks, or maintenance of the lodges, and it is hardly surprising that Soane's enthusiasm for this aspect of the post began to evaporate. It did, however, produce two new buildings which, although small in size, emerged as important examples of Soane's growing interest in 'primitivism'. They were the Cumberland Lodge and gateway in Hyde Park, designed in 1797, and the entrance to Bagshot Park, carried out with alterations to the mansion itself, for the Duke of Clarence in 1798. They proved insufficient compensation for the monotony of the routine work, and on the completion of the work at Bagshot in 1799, Soane submitted his resignation to the Commissioners of the Treasury.

A venture which had attracted Soane's interest in the early years of this decade had been the foundation and subsequent meetings of the Architects' Club.[17] This had come into existence on 20 October 1791, through the deliberations of James Wyatt, George Dance, Henry Holland and Samuel Pepys Cockerell who had felt that there was a growing need for architects to have a meeting place of their own, and completely independent of the Royal Academy, where such matters as professional conduct and fees could be discussed, and matters of policy formulated. The subscription was proposed as five guineas, and it was agreed that the discussion of business should be combined with dinner on the first Thursday in each month at five p.m. Membership was to be restricted to Royal Academicians, Associates, or members of the Academies of Rome, Parma, Florence or Paris, while one black ball at the election would exclude a candidate. Soane was one of the original members who, in addition to the four founders, included Sir William Chambers, Thomas Sandby, Robert Adam, Robert Brettingham, Robert Mylne and ten others not all of whom were regarded by Soane with friendly feelings. Nevertheless, he seems to have attended the meetings fairly regularly, these taking place for the first year or two at the Thatched House tavern in St James's Street. Later on, they were held at other eating establishments such as the Globe in Fleet Street or the Freemasons' tavern in Great Queen Street. During 1795 storm clouds began to loom from two directions, one caused by Soane's attempt to compete for the design of a new East India House, and the other by furious reaction to some ill-judged criticism of his recently completed section of the external wall at the Bank of England.

Richard Jupp, who was some twenty-five years older than Soane, had served as surveyor to the East India Company from 1768, and had designed several of the Company's City warehouses. When the question of building a new House arose in 1796, it was felt that for so important a work designs should be sought from such eminent professionals as Wyatt, Holland and Soane. Jupp, particularly fearful that Soane's ambitious nature and position at the Bank might gain him the commission, sought to have his name removed from the list of competitors. When Soane learnt of this interference he was not unnaturally displeased and demanded an explanation which did little to mend matters, for Jupp, while endeavouring to excuse his conduct, showed Soane copies of two malicious skits which had been printed and were currently in circulation. In one of these, entitled *The Modern Goth*,[18] the anonymous author hurled abuse at the Lothbury façade of the Bank, but what made matters worse was the fact that James Wyatt had read it aloud at a private dinner party which he had recently given for fellow architects at the Globe tavern. While Soane's annoyance is understandable, the poem is not without wit:

> Glory to thee Great Artist Soul of taste,
> For mending Pigsties when a plank's misplaced,*
> Whose towering Genius plans from deep research,
> Houses and Temples fit for Master B——†
> To Grace his Shop on that Important day
> When large Twelve Cakes are rang'd in bright array,
> Each Pastry Pillar shews thy Vast design,
> Hail then to thee and all Great Works of thine.
> Come let me place thee in the foremost rank
> With him whose dulness discomposed the Bank,‡
> With him whose dulness darkened every Plan
> Thy style shall finish what his Style began.
> Thrice happy Wren, he did not live to see
> The Dome that's built and beautified by thee,
> O had he lived to see thy blessed work,
> To see pilasters scor'd like loins of pork,
> To see the Order in confusion move,
> Scroles fixed below and Pedestals above,
> To see defiance hurled at Rome and Greece,
> Old Wren had never left the World in Peace.
> Look where I will above around is shewn
> A fine disordered Order of thine own,
> Where lines and circles Curiously unite
> A base compounded Compound Composite,
> A thing from which it must with truth be said
> Each labouring Mason turns abashed his head,
> Which Sxwxt reprobates, which Dxxxe derides,
> While tasteful Wxxxt holds his aching sides.§
> Here crawl ye spiders, here exempt from cares
> Spin Your fine webs above the Bulls and Bears,
> Secure from harm enjoy the Chisel'd niche,
> No Maids molest ye for no brooms can reach,
> In silence build from models of Your own
> And never imitate the Works of Sxxne.

*Alluding to Soane's country practice.
†The Cornhill shop of Birch the pastrycook.
‡The work carried out at the Bank by Soane's predecessor, Sir Robert Taylor.

§As James Stuart was already dead, this may refer to George Steuart. The other references are to James Wyatt and George Dance.

It appears that Soane now considered retaliating against Jupp by preparing a design for the East India House, and tried to extract the necessary measurements, which had been withheld from him, from George Dance. The latter, however, suspecting that in matters of professional skirmishing Soane might not be over punctilious, refused to give them, and urged him to drop the idea:

I know of but one rule that comprehends all moral duties, do as you would be done unto. Under the influence of this principle I cannot do what you desire, I feel that I *ought not*; in everything that I can serve or oblige you, wch does not interfere with the rule of right, I shall always from real regard and friendship be eager to stand forward. In this case I wish from my soul you wou'd not add to the mortification of the individual [Jupp]. You do not want such means to forward your reputation and I am sure it will be consider'd as invidious, if you force yourself into this business. I am sure you will not conceive that any motives, that relate in the smallest degree to myself, actuate me in offering you this advice. At any rate let me not have any thing to do with it.[19]

To this wise counsel Soane replied:

You mistake me entirely, God forbid that I should wound the peace of any man. I certainly meant literally what I said, "to amuse myself". I request you not to think otherwise, for unless I hear of the subject, which by the way has not been attended to by me, from some of the directors I shall not go further.'

Soane certainly did prepare a design,[20] if only 'to amuse' himself, and although it was not submitted, he subsequently made a strong complaint to the directors of the East India Company about Jupp's behaviour, but without gaining any satisfaction. Jupp was responsible for the design adopted for the new building, and work was carried out under his supervision. At his death on 17 April 1799, Soane applied for the vacant surveyorship but without success, and the appointment went to Henry Holland.

After his first reaction to the printing of *The Modern Goth* in 1796, Soane should certainly have let the matter subside, but the irritation dragged on and in 1799 he unwisely obtained counsel's opinion that he had reason for prosecution against Philip Norris, a brother of the architect Richard Norris, on the grounds that he had caused the libel to be published. The case came to the King's Bench in the Easter term of 1799 and was promptly dismissed after wasting a great deal of the plaintiff's time and money.

Notes

1. George Wyatt's will, Prerogative Court of Canterbury. Wyatt also left £500 to each of Soane's two sons.
2. Ten copies of Laugier's *Essai*, in French and in English translations, are in the Soane library.
3. SMC. Quoted in A. T. Bolton, *The Portrait of Sir John Soane*, 1927.

4. Woodgate was so much attracted to Ireland in the course of this visit that he decided to settle there. Soane accepted his notice with regret but wished him well, and the young man set up his own practice in Dublin.

5. The articles for these pupils are in SMC Div. XV C.

6. After 1802 Payne became clerk of works at the Bank of England and remained there until Soane's resignation. He and his wife were left an annuity in Soane's will. Robert Louch was probably a relative of 'Mr Louch' of Armagh on whom Soane had called in connection with the Downhill proposals in 1780. Robert was killed by a fall from scaffolding during work at Buckingham House, Pall Mall, in 1792.

7. Soane, Journal.

8. Soane, Journal. A water-colour by G. Barrett, *View in Mr Lock's Park* is in the Soane Museum.

9. These hours were kept until 1807 after which the young men were expected to arrive at 9 a.m. and stay until 8 p.m.

10. SMC Div. II S 14.

11. Soane, Journal, 5 December 1796.

12. Soane paid tribute to Gandy's talent in his Royal Academy Lecture V when he stressed that 'a superior manner of Drawing is absolutely necessary. Indeed, it is impossible not to admire the beauties and almost magical effects, in the architectural drawings of a Clérisseau, a Gandy, or a Turner.'

13. SMC Div. XIV J, appointments and resignations.

14. Soane, *Memoirs*.

15. J. M. Crook, *The History of the King's Works*, ed. H. Colvin, Vol. VI, 1782–1851 (1973).

16. SMC Div. XIV J, appointments and resignations.

17. A concise account is given in *The Portrait of Sir John Soane*, op. cit.

18. SMC Div. XIV E. Copies of both *The Modern Goth* and the second skit entitled *Inscription for a Monument to the Memory of Sir William Chambers* are with other papers relating to the case against Norris.

19. SMC Div. III 5. Letter not dated, but in reply to one from Soane of 17 June 1796.

20. SMC Div. XIV E.

⎡5⎤

The Pitzhanger Dream

Soane's disappointment over the East India Company's surveyorship was no doubt mitigated by a new and enjoyable interest. He had been living at No. 12 Lincoln's Inn Fields for nearly six years when he began to think of building himself a villa outside, but not too far from, London. No. 12 was an attractive house, elegantly furnished, and displaying a growing collection of works of art: but it was not large, was incapable of expansion, and had no garden. Although he later maintained that his prime object in building and furnishing a second house was to attract his children to architecture, it is also evident that he intended to create a showpiece with which to impress his friends and clients.

His choice of the Acton–Ealing area is not surprising since he had long been familiar with it and had several acquaintances nearby, among them John Winter, solicitor to the Bank of England, whom he had first met in Italy and for whom he had more recently designed Heathfield Lodge in Gunnersbury Lane. It was probably through Winter that Soane heard of a piece of land available in Acton. After a visit to the owner, a Mr Selby, on 25 May 1800, he agreed to purchase this plot for £500 and at once put two of his draughtsmen to work on drawing out his alternative designs. These were followed by two wooden models, each labelled as for 'A house at Acton'.[1] He was on the point of deciding which to build when he heard that Pitzhanger Manor at Ealing was about to be sold by the family of Thomas Gurnell who had died a few years before. George Dance, as Gurnell's son-in-law and one of the trustees, would have been Soane's informant, knowing his association with the enlarging of the house in 1768, and the latter at once determined to acquire it for himself. The body of the house was a fairly nondescript building of the second quarter of the eighteenth century, to which the south wing containing the dining and drawing rooms had been added. To this, as Soane wrote in his later *Description* of the house, 'I was naturally attached . . . it being the first whose progress and construction I had attended at the commencement of my architectural studies in Mr Dance's office.'[2]

On 8 August Soane took his wife and her cousin Ann Levick to look over the property and three days later was there again with the lawyer, Mr Whetton. He had by now persuaded his obliging friend John Winter to take the Acton plot off his hands and was thus free to make an offer of £4,500 which was accepted, and paid to the trustees on 5 September. He had already been working on alternative designs, most of them related to those made for the Acton villa, although there were a few proposing a new house in flint and brick. In the design adopted, the main body of the older house was replaced

32. PITZHANGER MANOR, Ealing, Soane's remodelling of 1800.

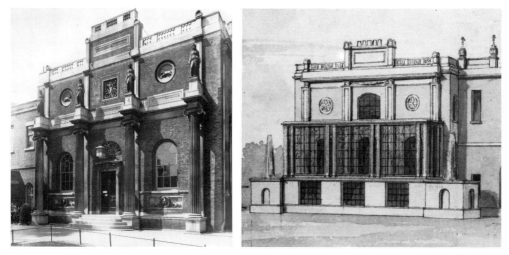

33. PITZHANGER MANOR, entrance front.   34. PITZHANGER MANOR, rear elevation.

by a rectangular brick building of two storeys over a basement. Its most striking feature was to be the frontispiece of Portland stone with free-standing fluted Ionic columns carrying an entablature on which were set four Coade-stone figures modelled from those of the Erechtheum at Athens. In fact, this composition echoed the dramatic archway which Soane had recently completed for the Lothbury Court at the Bank of England, and its conspicuous appearance on the west side of Ealing Green was a deliberate proclamation that Pitzhanger was now the country home of the Bank's architect (Plates 32–4).

35. PITZHANGER MANOR, front parlour.

At the beginning of October Walter Payne, the trusted clerk of works who had already been in charge at Ryston, Betchworth and elsewhere, arrived on the site and made himself a temporary lodging in the Dance wing, Soane noting on the sixth that 'Payne began pulling down at Ealing.'[3] Advice had already been sought from the garden designer, John Haverfield of Kew[4] who had submitted on 17 September a design for the miniature landscape with its surrounding plantations, cedar trees on the lawns, and serpentine stream, a good deal of which is still recognisable. This drawing was embellished with thumb-nail sketches in the margins of various houses in the area belonging to Soane's friends, including Samuel Wegg of Acton, John Raymond Way, also of Acton, and Lord Kinnaird of Elm Grove which was immediately to the south of Pitzhanger.

The house was ready for occupation in 1804 (Plates 35–7). In addition to the retained wing containing a large dining-room, and a drawing-room hung with Chinese wallpaper on the floor above, the rebuilt block had a breakfast room or front parlour, and a library or back parlour (see also pages 181–2). Adjoining the latter was another drawing-room of marked simplicity, the plain walls of which were obviously intended for the display

36. Wall-painting from
Campanella's engravings
of the Villa Negroni,
Rome, a source for
Soane's decoration in the
Front Parlour,
Pitzhanger Manor. See
Plate 35.

37. PITZHANGER MANOR, back parlour.

of pictures. It probably also held the pianoforte which Soane purchased from Anna Storace for £31.10 on 30 November 1804. For the next few years much of Soane's entertaining took place at Ealing, usually at the weekends when he felt free to escape from work for a day or two, and could preside over the 'Gothic scenes and intellectual banquets' to which as many as two two hundred friends would be invited to a *'dejeune a la fourchette'*.[5] Many of the dinner guests were fellow Academicians,[6] some with their wives such as the Flaxmans, de Loutherbourgs, and Hardwicks. The Maltons and Wheatleys are mentioned as are James Peacock and his wife, Augustus Callcott and Henry Howard. There were also clients including the Praeds from Tyringham, Mr and Mrs Peters from Betchworth, and the Thorntons from Albury. Anna Storace came with John Braham, as did the Duchess of Leeds, Lord and Lady Bridport, and the Duc d'Orleans—later King Louis Philippe of France—who was then living in exile at Orleans House, Twickenham, and who for a time taught at a celebrated school at Ealing.

While the visitors were doubtless impressed by the house itself, there were certain features which they must have found puzzling. One was the appropriation of a room in the basement, overlooking the garden, for what Soane called 'the Monk's Dining Room'. While he was never really at ease when called on to design in the gothic style, he had a profound respect for medieval buildings which he regarded as eloquent of those sublime and picturesque qualities essential to the 'Poetry of Architecture'.[7] It is therefore all the more surprising to reconcile this noble vision with his creation of a mock-gothic apartment at Pitzhanger, and his invention of a hypothetical monk as its custodian. A taste for 'gothic gloom' was, of course, current in such romantic literature as Mrs Radcliffe's *Sicilian Romance* and Matthew Gregory Lewis's *The Monk*, but Soane's recluse was neither of the roistering nor the sinister kind, and had more in common with Charles Hamilton's gentle hermit at Pain's Hill, or Sir Rowland Hill's mechanical anchorite at Hawkstone. It is conceivable that the idea may have owed something to Strawberry Hill, some five miles away in Twickenham. Soane would certainly have known the latter to which Horace Walpole (who had been his next door neighbour at 76 Welbeck Street), had added 'a small gloomy hall', a cloister, an oratory and a cabinet lit from above by a star-shaped pane of yellow glass. Moreover, in gothic matters Walpole had relied largely on the advice of his close friend Thomas Pitt, the earliest of Soane's patrons and one who would have encouraged his appreciation of gothic as well as classical architecture. Whatever its source, the Pitzhanger monk's apartment became a repository for various gothic acquisitions, and was, at least in its owner's eyes, of sufficient importance to be transferred, after the sale of this property, to his London house where not only the monk's parlour but his cloister and 'tomb' survive.

A hint of an even more bizarre project taking shape in Soane's mind during 1801 appears on a plan of that year where a window in an extension to the north of the house is marked as overlooking 'the Ruins of a Temple'. In his notebook Soane entered under 7 December that he had been to Ealing 'about [the] Ruins', and by the end of that month they were in course of construction. What emerged were the seemingly half-buried remains of a small classical temple round which he proceeded to invent an elaborate fantasy

38. MRS SOANE AND THE BOYS, water-colour by Antonio B. Van Assen, *circa* 1800.

whereby visitors were led to believe that the ruins had actually been found and partly excavated among the plantations in the grounds. No doubt some of the more simple minded of his friends swallowed the story, to his amusement; others may have seen through the charade but accepted it as a harmless form of eccentricity which could be enjoyed since their host's hospitality was generous, the company usually interesting, and the villa easily accessible for a day's expedition from London.

In spite of its five principal and two lesser reception rooms, the bedroom accommodation at Pitzhanger was limited, and it was only particular cronies such as J. M. W. Turner—whose friendship with Soane and his wife seems to have begun in about 1802—who were encouraged to stay for a few days. In fact, for Mrs Soane Pitzhanger proved to be a burden. As her husband later admitted, she 'never liked the country',[8] and the initial equipping of the house meant many visits from London and much shopping before they could sleep there or begin to entertain. Subsequently she had to cater for uncertain numbers of guests, make sure that sufficient staff were available, and appear to all who came as a delighted hostess. Soane may have been aware of this and certainly produced several handsome presents during the earlier part of the decade, such as £100 for a diamond necklace in May 1803, and a similar sum for a musical box. For a few years from January 1804 Mrs Soane began to write in notebooks of her own on the lines of those kept by her husband but neater, more comprehensible, and dealing with social activities or domestic matters. From these it appears that she still went frequently to the theatre or an opera. She enjoyed reading, did a good deal of needlework, bottled fruit when at Ealing, and often gave, or attended her friends' card-parties and dances. That Soane disliked both the latter is evident, particularly dances—'Mr Soane left town. Mr Peacock of Chertsey dined here—had a dance in the evening', and again, 'Mr S. out of town, had a little dance.'[9] In time, however, there are increasing references to her health when 'bad colds', 'ill with a headache', 'ill all day', or 'poorly' suggest that physical strain coupled with worry over the boys was sapping her vitality. For her husband, however, the first years at Pitzhanger were stimulating and enjoyable. In between the social activity he was able to find the odd hour or two in which to go fishing, or to take an interest in his garden, the peacocks, and the three pet dogs, Toby, Caesar and Little Lion.[10] It was probably the happiest period of his life.

In 1806 George Dance resigned from the post of professor of architecture to the Royal Academy, following growing criticism of his failure to produce the obligatory lectures to students. Soane was approached as a possible successor, and on 9 March replied to John Richards, the Academy's secretary, that he was willing to stand for election, adding:

> I have always considered lectures as particularly useful to the students, and have felt deep mortification and regret in their having been so long deprived of lectures in Architecture:- upon these considerations, provided no other Academician comes forward to fill the situation, I wish *then*, to be considered as a candidate for the vacant Professorship.[11]

As soon as his appointment had been confirmed, he began to assemble material not only from his own well-stocked library, but from fellow architects and various experts. It proved to be a far more laborious task than he had anticipated, and only after he had filled eighteen volumes with manuscript notes was the first series of lectures distilled. Probably as a gesture to show that he had the matter in hand, he gave the first lecture on 27 March 1809, at the end of the winter session, but the series proper began in the following autumn. He was, however, to continue expanding and improving the series over the years, and equally gradually built up the splendid collection of 'Lecture Diagrams', prepared by his draughtsmen, and intended for display during his talks.

It was during the course of his fourth lecture, given on 29 January 1810, that Soane ran into trouble with his fellow Academicians by referring obliquely to Smirke's recently erected Covent Garden Theatre as an example of a composition in which the entrance front was unsatisfactorily related to the side elevation. He was promptly reminded by a circular from the Academy's secretary that 'no comments or criticisms on the opinions or productions of living artists in this Country should be introduced into any lectures given at the Royal Academy'. Soane, infuriated by this communication which arrived on Sunday 4 February, declined to give his fifth lecture to the students on the following day and instead invited a few friends to hear it read at his own house. The ensuing rumpus led to a suspension of the lectures for nearly two years during which a good deal of heat was generated and he worked off his own feelings by writing a ponderous

'Appeal to the Public' which was privately printed but, fortunately, not published and went only to a few friends. After some talk of his resignation, and many meetings of the Council, Soane successfully defended his right to make reasonable criticism:

> The main point I required, namely that I should not be fettered by any new law in the faithful discharge of my duty as Professor of Architecture, being tacitly assented to, I resumed the Lectures on the 9th of January 1812.[12]

A few days later the breach with Smirke was—at least temporarily—healed, and Soane was able to record in his notebook under 18 January:

> Dined at the Academy. Queen's birthday dinner. Mr Smirke asked me to shake hands, which I did, and at dinner I sent to him by the waiter to say I wished to take wine with him, which we did.

Even the task of preparing his lectures had not entirely satisfied Soane's appetite for work, and in 1807, having heard of the sudden death of Samuel Wyatt on 8 February, he applied to be his successor in the post of clerk of the works at the Royal Hospital, Chelsea. The appointment carried a salary of £200 a year, with a small house within the Hospital grounds, and on 12 February he received 'Lord Temple's offer of Chelsea in answer to my letter'.[13]

It is understandable that Soane's preoccupation with the lectures on top of his other work kept him from paying much attention to his wife's frequent complaints of 'head-aches', but from about 1807 her life was far from easy. Running two homes was further complicated by a third at Chelsea, even though Soane, contrary to the regulations, did not use it regularly until he had made extensive improvements.[14] More wearing than physical effort, however, were her worries about the behaviour of the two boys whom, in her efforts to prevent friction between them and her husband, she tended to spoil with gifts of money, or by keeping silent about their misdemeanours now that they were tasting the freedom of college life. The attitude of John junior and his brother George was, in fact, the major reason for bringing the Pitzhanger dream to an end. Aged fourteen and eleven respectively when it began in 1800, they at first regarded the house and its grounds as a more enjoyable venue for the holidays than the constrained atmosphere of No. 12 Lincoln's Inn Fields. Their father's hope that it would ultimately induce them to pursue architectural careers had, however, little success and they were soon bored with this didactic experiment. Evidence of their wayward dispositions also began to appear, and produced problems a good deal more serious than an indifference to Pitzhanger.

For the younger son there is little to be said in his favour. A comment in one of Soane's notebooks that, after helping to catalogue some books, 'George hurled the inkwell on the floor' illustrates his increasingly ungovernable temper. From his college days onwards, his constant demands for money and dissolute conduct were to be a source of worry to his parents. The elder son, John, emerges as a weak but not entirely unsympathetic character whose apparent laziness was no doubt partly due to ill-health.

Both boys began their schooling as boarders with a Mr Wicks in 1797, but the results were poor. As Soane noted drily in July of the following year, 'Paid Mr Wicks for keeping the children in ignorance ½ year, 39.13.0.' However, they remained with him for another five months after which they were moved to the Revd Mr Appleby's establishment in Moorfields for two years. Probably on account of John's delicate health, it was decided that he should be sent to a school kept by Dr William Chapman at Margate, a resort which Mrs Soane, who believed in the benefits of sea air, had been visiting since 1796. In the summer of 1804 John gained admission to Trinity College, Cambridge where he was joined in the autumn by George. During their first winter vacation Soane commissioned a painting by William Owen which shows the two boys in their gowns, this being exhibited at the summer exhibition of the Royal Academy in 1805. John for some reason took a dislike to Trinity and obtained permission to move to Pembroke, but left in 1807 without taking a degree, leaving George to continue in Cambridge for the next two years during which, in spite of a generous allowance, he began the long trail of debts which continued throughout his life.

Early in 1807 John's health dictated a return to Margate with his mother. Renewing his friendship with Dr Chapman's family, and now aged twenty-one, he became involved in a brief romance with his former schoolmaster's daughter, Laura. A small packet of her letters, undated but with '1807' added later, were preserved by Mrs Soane among her private papers, and show Laura to have been an intelligent and high-minded girl who might well have made John an ideal wife,[15] but after a few months his feelings seem to have cooled, while Mrs Soane, fearful of her husband's disapproval, kept the affair to herself and encouraged him to comply with his father's wish that he should return to London and take the first steps towards an architectural career. Setting him to work in the Lincoln's Inn Fields office was not a success, and apart from his lack of enthusiasm, it is doubtful whether young Master Soane, sauntering in late, or seeking the consolation of his mother when things went wrong, was made welcome among the hard-working pupils and assistants.

Soane now suggested that Joseph Michael Gandy, who had moved to Liverpool, should take young John as a pupil, an arrangement which was adopted. On 6 June 1808, Soane recorded that 'John went to Mr Gandy for one year, 100 guineas.' By August the boy was ailing again and dispatched—this time to Ramsgate—for another dose of sea air. He recovered sufficiently to resume his studies on 11 October and remained in Liverpool until 10 March 1809, when a further bout of sickness interrupted them and he returned to the old haunts in Margate. By now, however, Soane had suspicions that he was idle rather than ill, and sent a letter urging him not to become 'one of the drones of society'.[16] John reluctantly returned to Liverpool and was still there in the late summer of 1810 when his parents made a short visit to the city, staying at the Liverpool Arms from 8 to 11 August. On the second day Gandy and his wife joined them for dinner, after which Soane recorded that they were 'At the theatre—*Othello*'. Next day he and Mrs Soane dined with the Liverpool architect John Foster, with whose second son young Soane had become friendly. During this visit Soane must have gathered that all was not well with Gandy's practice, and would therefore not have been surprised to receive a letter from the latter on 1 September, informing him that it had been dissolved, and that he would be returning to London. In it he offered to

> make some compensation for the loss of time to your Son, and promise to let him study under me a few months longer than the term we originally fixed on . . .

but he added significantly

> Mr Soane's constitution does not seem calculated to bear with the rough storms of life, nor can it go through the incessant fatigue with which you have overcome difficulties on the road to fame more successfully than many others.[17]

Soane had already faced up to the fact that John's interest in architecture was of the most ephemeral kind, and that neither he nor George—still disporting himself in Cambridge—showed the slightest concern as to the future of Pitzhanger. Pressed by Mrs Soane, he decided to sell and arranged with James Christie that an advertisement for 'an elegant villa at Ealing' should be placed in the morning papers in November 1809. Mrs Soane, writing from Margate, advised her husband not to let the house go for less than £10,000 which was the figure at which it was sold to General Cameron in the following year.

In July 1810, Soane spent his last three days at Pitzhanger, fishing nearby and entertaining a few friends, after which the contents were gradually packed up and dispatched to the already crowded house in Lincoln's Inn Fields.

When planning their short visit to Liverpool in August 1810, Soane and his wife decided to return through Herefordshire. He therefore wrote to Richard Holland, who had retired some years earlier to Madeley, and suggested calling on him. The letter, however, brought no immediate reply, having been redirected as Holland had recently moved to Combe Royal, near Kingsbridge, in Devonshire, from where he wrote on 15 August:

> I received at this place, only the last evening, your very friendly letter of the second ins‍ᵗ. I have not regretted leaving Hereford before. I do assure you, it would have given me very sincere pleasure to have had the opportunity of seeing you, and I am sorry for the disappointment to us both. May I hope any chance will bring you to so distant a county as this? If it should, I trust you would pass sometime with me here. South Devon is a renovating climate, and occasional relaxation *good*. Surely at some time of the year you might bring Mrs Soane with you, and come and see *our Lions*. You will meet an old *friend* with an *old face*, and a heart not less warm than your own.
>
> I left the neighbourhood of Hereford, about four months ago, after six years residence. Some family occurrences impelled me to the change, and I have found a situation in some respects much better suited to me. Rather a pretty place, about a mile from the town of Kingsbridge, where when you come I will shew you oranges and lemons trained against the garden walls like peach trees and almost as large abounding with fruit—the lemons *good*, but the fragrance and appearance of them *delightful*;

I have a tolerable garden and grape house, and many comforts which I would have you come and partake of, and I have a niece who will be much gratified in making them agreeable to Mrs Soane.

Your Sons must now be grown up and having some pursuits. May I ask what? I have the interest of an old friend for You and Yours.[18]

This warm letter obviously touched Soane deeply and produced a reply in similar vein:

You paint your scenes of retirement in such natural and glowing colours as make me sigh for tranquil shades, but, alas, my unfortunate attachment to Architecture is as difficult to be extinguished, as a passion for play in the mind of a professed gambler! Some two or three years past I was endeavouring to follow your truly philosophical example and leave the bustle of the world altogether, but was again roused to Architectural pursuits, by the Academy choosing me unanimously to fill the Professor's Chair. This circumstance destroyed all my plans of retirement, called forth all my zeal, and aroused the only half extinguished embers! . . .

You ask me, most kindly, respecting my two Sons, the one 25, the other 21. The eldest (your godson) will I trust follow the profession: he will have none of those difficulties to contend with that you and I have had—but will he therefore be equally active? To be happy he must be employed, idleness is the root of all evil, and fortune, without some pursuit beyond a town life, is at best but a negative blessing. The youngest is unluckily smitten with a passion for dramatic writing: pray heaven he may succeed! Mrs Soane, with every good wish towards you and yours, partakes of the satisfaction your letter gave me, and if we live until the spring you may certainly expect to see us, that we may have once more the pleasure of passing an hour with an old friend.[19]

It was to be the following summer, however, before the visit could materialise, for young John was now pursuing another line than architecture.

During his last visit to Margate the young man had made the acquaintance of Maria Preston who was staying there with a married sister. According to a later account by John's father, the sister, having ingratiated herself with Mrs Soane, then introduced Maria to John and 'very soon brought about a marriage with her . . . and my unfortunate son'.[20] Mrs Soane must have realised what was happening but, as on an earlier occasion, at first kept silent. By the beginning of 1811, however, Soane had discovered the situation and reluctantly agreed to a marriage on the understanding that Maria's father settled £2,000 on her, an arrangement which the latter did not fulfil. The wedding having been fixed for early June, Mrs Soane took herself off to Brighton in April where she persuaded young John to join her in the hope of setting him up with another dose of sea air. On receiving news of her intended return, Soane wrote a welcoming letter on 22 May:

With a small change in my dressing room you will find the house as you left it, that, and the repairing of the table, makes the sum total of my labours. I do not like the account of John's health, but I trust the apothecary is correct. If I understand you exactly it will be tea time before you return on Saturday, but at all events I will have some cold meat in the house, which at this season is, I think, preferable to hot. I never felt the weather warmer than yesterday, and this morning I walked to Clapham and back, not a coach to be had, all going the wrong way.[21]

John and Maria were married from the Prestons' house at Sewardstone on 6 June. His parents attended but left early, Soane complaining that he had not been introduced to anyone. As he wrote of Preston *père* afterwards, 'the old fox had given nothing—he had sent his daughter out a begger except [for] a pianoforte and gold watch and gold chain.'[22] The couple set off for a honeymoon in Tunbridge Wells, and that evening Soane, overcoming his misgivings, and anxious to provide a happy beginning to their married life, wrote to Maria and enclosed a draft for £500.[23] He subsequently invested money in India and Government stock in John's name, ensuring him of an income of at least £1,000 a year.

Three days after the wedding Soane set off for Devonshire by himself, Mrs Soane having declined to accompany him. Travelling by night on the Exeter Mail, he stopped at Honiton and took the opportunity of making a slight detour to visit Reymondo Putt at nearby Combe Raleigh, tentative plans for the rebuilding of his house having been made in 1808. Back in Honiton on 15 June, Soane took a coach on to Exeter and arrived at Combe Royal at four in the afternoon for what must have been a heart-warming welcome from Richard Holland and his niece. Apart from going to church next day, he rested but on the Monday went with Holland to neighbours at Moat House for a large picnic dinner party on the beach. There can be no doubt as to the happiness and relaxation which Soane enjoyed during this short visit which came to an end on 21 June when Holland's niece, Mary, and other friends escorted him as far as Exeter on the first stage of his homeward journey.[24] The next stage took him for two nights to more good friends, Lord and Lady Bridport at Cricket Lodge, from where he began a long and appreciative letter to Holland ending:

I shall send you a sketch, without a fee, for the Library. I think yours is a very good idea, but you must let me tickle it up a little. This you will say is vanity. Be it so:- it is my way, and you, my dear Sir, are too sincere a friend of him whose greatest pleasure is to assure you of his sincere regard for yourself, and for those under your roof . . .[25]

Soane was back in town by 25 June and it was ironic that, having returned in such good spirits, he should soon have to suffer another blow, this time delivered by his younger son.

According to an account written by Soane years later[26] George, on leaving Cambridge, had decided to study law and was therefore 'put into the care of Mr Kinderley, an eminent solicitor, and subsequently under another professional gentleman'. After a while he found the law 'too dry a profession for him', so his father arranged for him to be 'taken into the house of Mr Pennington, one of the most able practitioners of the present age'.[27] It was through Pennington that he first became acquainted with the family of James

Boaden, a play-writer and journalist who had been editor of the *Oracle* newspaper, and was now writing biographical accounts of various actors and actresses. Taken by Boaden behind the scenes at various theatres, George found a new interest as a result of which 'he became tired of physic, and so far neglected his studies that Mr Pennington was ultimately obliged to dismiss him. The Navy, Army and Church were then proposed; neither of which were accepted.' An additional misfortune was that George had formed a particular friendship with one of the Boaden daughters, Agnes, although on being questioned about his intentions, he assured his parents that he had no thought of marrying her. Mrs Soane was therefore dismayed to receive on 5 July—less than a month after her elder son's wedding—a note from George announcing that 'I have married Agnes to spite you and father.'[28] From now on his almost pathological hostility to his parents, and unscrupulous behaviour, became all too apparent in spite of receiving an allowance of £200 a year from his father and another £200 from his mother as well as having his debts settled by one or the other on innumerable occasions.[29]

While Soane had his work to provide a distraction from his disappointments, Mrs Soane had no such escape, and George's heartless conduct caused her much mental anguish. In September she went to Ramsgate for a short stay, and although the change brought some improvement in her general health, it was not sustained. 'For the last four days', she wrote to her husband, 'I found myself getting much better—indeed I may say *better* and *more quiet in my mind*, but unluckily for me, there always starts some demon to make me wretched—and which I am now sure will bring me to my end.'[30]

Notes

1. Soane Museum, models in store.
2. John Soane, *Plans, Elevations and Perspective Views of Pitzhanger Manor-House*, English edition 1802, re-printed in French 1833.
3. Journal, 6 October 1800.
4. Presumably a son of John Haverfield of Kew who worked in the Princess of Wales's garden there in the second half of the eighteenth century.
5. Soane, *Memoirs*.
6. Soane was elected an Associate of the Royal Academy in 1795, and a Royal Academician in 1802.
7. Soane, *Description of the House*, 1830, p. 54.
8. Soane, MS notes 'pour servie à l'histoire de ma vie', SPC Box 6.
9. Mrs Soane's Notebook, 15 January 1806 and 1 April 1811.
10. Soane, Notebooks, 2 August 1804: 'Caught 15 tench, 3 carp.' and 21 September 1806, 'Poor Lion died last week and is buried in the plantation.'
11. Soane, *Memoirs*.
12. Ibid.
13. Soane, Journal, 12 February 1807.
14. Soane Bookcase, Chelsea Sketches, Shelf B (left).
15. SPC Box 4.
16. Ibid.
17. SMC Div. III (7).
18. SMC Div. III (10).
19. Ibid.

20. Soane, *Memoirs.*

21. SMC Div. XIV C.

22. SPC Box 4.

23. Ibid.

24. SMC Div. III (10).

25. Ibid.

26. *Details respecting the Conduct and Connexions of George Soane* . . . , privately printed, no date, but *circa* 1835.

27. R. R. Pennington, physician, of Montague Place, Bloomsbury, was a personal friend of Soane and his wife over many years, as well as being their medical adviser.

28. SPC Box 4.

29. *Details respecting the Conduct* . . . , op. cit.

30. SPC Box 4.

[6]

Family Troubles

Long before the sale of Pitzhanger was envisaged, Soane had set covetous eyes on a stable building behind his neighbour's house at No. 13 Lincoln's Inn Fields. On raising the subject with the owner, George Booth Tyndale, it transpired that the latter would be willing to sell not only the stable, but the whole property provided that he could remain as a tenant of the house itself for a few more years. Soane therefore purchased the freehold of No. 13 in June 1808, for £4,200, leaving Tyndale in residence at a rent of £202 10s per annum while he could now rebuild the rear premises to form an eastward extension to his own offices behind No. 12.[1]

No. 13 was a good deal wider and slightly deeper than No. 12, and when, following the sale of Pitzhanger, crate after crate of paintings, sculpture, books and furniture began to arrive in Lincoln's Inn Fields in the autumn of 1810, Soane reopened negotiations with Tyndale which resulted in the latter agreeing to exchange houses, taking a sixteen-year lease of the front part of No. 12 at £130 per annum while Soane not only obtained possession of the whole of No. 13 but retained the rear portion of No. 12 as well. On 2 July 1812 he noted that he had been 'at home all day about plans of next house', and a fortnight later, on 17 July, the demolition of No. 13 began. Where Tyndale went to in the interim is not explained for although the new house went up at speed, the Soanes could not move in from No. 12 until October 1813.

While the architect faced the rebuilding of No. 13 in a mood of exhilaration, for his wife it augered only discomfort, noise and dirt. Young John's recent marriage had ended her frequent visits with him to the seaside, and her worries about her health were now exacerbated by George's endless and usually abusive letters demanding money, many of which she answered herself and did not show to her husband. It is evident that her previous composure was suffering under the strain, and although to the outsider, the Soanes presented an appearance of marital happiness, this masked an increasing feeling of tension as she picked on trivial incidents for criticism in her conversation or letters. Even Soane's preoccupation with his work could no longer blind him to this change in his wife's manner, and by the end of 1811 hints appear in the notebooks of his dismay caused by unaccustomed recriminations and chilly silences. At last, suspecting that she might have been using her private money to keep George quiet, he left a note for her on 13 February 1812, in which he expressed his concern:

It is, my dear friend,[2] with the most painful sensations and deep anguish that I have

for some time past observed Your mind less tranquil than formerly—to what cause
this change arises I have not been able to trace:- I think from occasional obscure
hints it is money—altho I do not see how it can be so:- with this impression I give
you the power of drawing at such times as you please whatever money may be of
mine in Mr Praed's Banking House, which at this moment exceeds two thousand
pounds:- this sum I shall not touch and, as I find it lessened, more will be added,
for the only object of my life is to see you truly happy.

    Yours with real regard, and unaltered affection . . .[3]

In the next few months there was comparatively little entertaining at No. 12, and on
the day that the demolition of No. 13 began, Mrs Soane retreated to Chertsey, returning
for only a few short visits to London until the end of September when she went to Brighton for a week. It was at about this time that she arranged to take as a paid companion
one of her Chertsey acquaintances, a Miss Sarah Smith.[4] Soane raised no objection,
hoping that it might restore her cheerfulness, but he probably had some misgivings.
Certainly from later correspondence Sarah appears as an unattractive character, and one
who returned Mrs Soane's kindness with intrigue and gossip.

With his wife's departure for Chertsey on 2 July, Soane sought to forget his domestic
troubles in the building operations next door but these were shortly to produce worries
of a different kind. While in height and fenestration the new house conformed with its
neighbours, it was distinguished by a Portland stone projection, to which Soane referred
as a 'loggia', consisting of two tiers of round-headed arches at ground and first-floor
level (Plates 39–40). The central bay extended to the second floor where it was flanked
by two small balconies at the extremities of which were placed Coade-stone caryatids,
modelled from those of the Erechtheum at Athens. Twelve years later, in 1825, four
fourteenth-century gothic 'corbels' which had originally adorned the north front of Westminster Hall, were set against the piers between the ground and first-floor windows.
No sooner had the lower stage of the 'loggia' appeared than the district surveyor, William
Kinnard, who had assumed this office at the age of nineteen, and was still only twenty-
four, took exception to it. On 12 August Soane noted that 'Kinnard called and behaved
impudently'. No doubt he gave the young man a forthright exposition of his own views
whereupon the surveyor retaliated by bringing a court action on the grounds that Soane
had contravened the Building Act. Accepting the challenge, Soane obtained support from
his old friend John Crunden, then district surveyor for St Pancras, and when the case
was heard at Bow Street on 12 October, the magistrates declared in Soane's favour.[5]
A subsequent application by Kinnard for a mandamus was refused by Lord Ellenborough
in the Court of King's Bench on 18 November, and there the matter rested. News of
the tussle had, however, reached Rowland Burdon who wrote to congratulate his friend
on 17 December:

I have more than once had a strong desire to have a peep at Your *Castle* in Linc's
Inn Fields, both for the sake of saying how d'ye do to its inhabitants, and also to

39. No. 13 LINCOLN'S INN FIELDS.

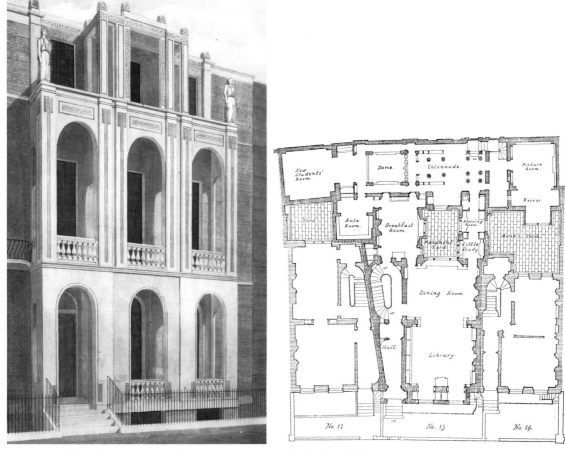

40. (*left*) No. 13 LINCOLN'S INN FIELDS, Soane's design of 1812.

41. (*right*) Nos. 12, 13 and 14 LINCOLN'S INN FIELDS, a later plan showing the ground floors of the three houses.

see by what extraordinary outworks you have fortified yourself, so as to provoke the attacks of an angry Surveyor.

I was glad to see however that you have defended Yourself and castle strenuously and successfully. You have, in martial language, 'Covered yourself with Glory'.[6]

It was not only the exterior of No. 13 which was in contrast to the simplicity of No. 12 (Plate 41). In the two 'parlours' at Pitzhanger Manor Soane had already achieved highly original decorative effects which clearly derived from some hand-coloured engravings by Angelo Campanella of painted walls from the Villa Negroni in Rome.[7] For the combined dining-room and library at No. 13 he took inspiration from the same source, using a deep 'Pompeian' red for the walls, and slender 'bronze' rods to give an illusion of supporting the flying arches which imply a spatial division between the two rooms

42. No. 13 LINCOLN'S INN FIELDS, dining-room.

(Plate 42). Elsewhere on the ground floor the honey-coloured graining of the breakfast-room (Plate 43) and dressing-room, the dark 'porphyry' of the entrance hall and richly marbled staircase well, the use of innumerable strips of mirror, coloured glass in the windows and lanterns, and contrived contrasts of light and shade, are eloquent of Soane's striving at this time to achieve the 'fanciful effects' which he considered to be the 'Poetry of Architecture'.[8]

It would seem that Mrs Soane, who had been happy with the simple arrangement of No. 12, was less appreciative of the complicated lay-out and somewhat gloomy richness of the ground floor of No. 13, and while the first-floor drawing-rooms (Plate 45) were in themselves cheerful enough in their pale yellow colouring, they, and the south-facing bedrooms above were partly shaded by the stone loggia. Even before moving into the new house, the prospect seems to have depressed her, but for this not only No. 13 was

43. (*left*) No. 13 LINCOLN'S INN FIELDS, breakfast-room.

44. (*right*) No. 13 LINCOLN'S INN FIELDS, section through dome.

45. No. 13 LINCOLN'S INN FIELDS, drawing-room, a water-colour of 1825.

46. No. 13 LINCOLN'S INN FIELDS, painting showing views of the house.

to blame, as Soane discovered when, on her return from a short stay in Bath early in
June 1813, he had to face more grumbles.

    The additional cause was the recent arrival in London of Miss Eleanora Brickenden,
a harmless but intense spinster of the 'blue stocking' variety, whom Soane had first met
when staying in Devon with Richard Holland. Described in a letter from the latter as
'a lady of strict virtue and honor', her portrait in water-colours drawn by Mrs Pope[9]
shows her to have been no great beauty such as might have caused Mrs Soane any pangs
of jealousy but, having sought permission to call at No. 12, she must have been unwise
enough to cast admiring glances in the direction of the elderly architect. After thirty
years of marriage in which her husband's loyalty and devotion were never in question,
Mrs Soane should not have given a second thought to the unfortunate Miss Brickenden's
ingenuous behaviour, but her reaction was probably one more instance of the general
irritability caused by poor health. On 21 June Soane, having been invited to a party
given by Mrs Desenfans, found Miss Brickenden among the other guests and offered
her a ticket for an exhibition of paintings in Lord Stafford's gallery. Whether on account
of this or some other chance meeting, Mrs Soane expressed her feelings strongly and
her husband had to appeal to Richard Holland for confirmation that, in making this
gesture, he had been complying with the latter's remark about being greatly obliged for
'any attention shown to [his] friend'.[10] Still suspicious, Mrs Soane went off to Chertsey
in July from where Soane noted that he had 'Recd. a strange letter . . . in consequence

47. No. 13 LINCOLN'S
INN FIELDS, the Dome
with a bust of Soane by Sir
Francis Chantrey, 1830.

48. No. 13 LINCOLN'S INN FIELDS, Soane's bedroom.

of something W. Daniell has said'. The letter has survived and although Miss Brickenden is not mentioned by name, there is no doubt that she was the cause of Mrs Soane's anger when she wrote:

> In my opinion any woman turned thirty that affects to be romantic and professes platonic love—t'is only a cloak for *intrigue*. She should recollect in *London*, as well as the *country*, there are allways gossips that are ready to propagate what they *see*—and what they *guess*. And I must say, t'is rather surprising your friend Mr Holland, who certainly *knows the World*, should have considered a romantic lady as fit companion for his *niece*. I can recollect, when my uncle would not have suffered me to have had any acquaintance with such a woman—much less recommended her to his friends— and believe me, the opinion I have formed of her is fixed; fixed too firmly to be explained away. I boast of being a plain *matter of fact woman*, that knows *right* from *wrong*.[11]

She must have continued the attack verbally when, on 8 August, Soane drove down to Chertsey to bring her home, entering in his notebook afterwards that it had been 'a gloomy day'. Although Eleanora Brickenden was to remain in London for at least three years, she soon realized that she was not welcome at Lincoln's Inn Fields and kept away until after Mrs Soane's death when she resumed her friendship with Soane. She eventually married a Herefordshire parson, the Revd Mr Davis of Brecon, from where she continued to write to the architect for nearly twenty years.

By October 1813 No. 13 was ready for occupation, and on the eleventh Soane recorded that Mr and Mrs Pope and Mr Monins—for whom he was designing a new house at Ringwould, near Dover—had 'dined here, last time in old house', after which they went into No. 13 and 'drank tea, first time in new study' (now the Breakfast Room). Next day he and Mrs Soane, with Sarah Smith, 'dined first time in new study'. On 26 October Mrs Soane left for a visit to young John and his wife at Brighton, and in mid-December she was off again to Chertsey.

It may have been partly as an escape from his domestic troubles that Soane was now attracted to the companionship offered by Freemasonry. He had long been familiar with the Freemasons' Tavern in Great Queen Street, and the lofty hall behind it which had been designed by Thomas Sandby in 1775–6. Here the students of the British Institution had held their Anniversary Dinner on 13 November 1812 when Soane had been honoured with a specially composed three-verse song of which the refrain ran:

> For Friendship, Soane, and joy are here,
> And Wit and Mirth the goblet share,
> And spread the Attic fire.[12]

On 14 August 1813 he noted a call on the Duke of Sussex—the Fraternity's Grand Master—and on 11 December he was bidden to attend at Freemasons' Hall where he was installed by the duke as Grand Superintendent of Works, an office which he held until his death. A 'purple apron handsomely trimmed with gold fringe' was purchased from Thomas Harper for £1.16.0.[13] His participation in the meetings over the years was an undoubted solace in return for which he not only assumed responsibility for the maintenance of the premises but designed a fine new Council Chamber, and contributed handsomely to the charitable funds of the fraternity.

The year 1814 began badly for Soane who was taken ill on the previous 27 December and 'continued a prisoner until Monday 28 March . . . except[g] that I went out three times for an hour or two before 1st March on which day the operation was performed and I did not go out until the 28 March'. The nature of the illness is not specified but is likely to have been gallstones. The surgeon was the celebrated Sir Astley Cooper, lecturer on comparative anatomy at the Royal College of Surgeons, who, in acknowledging a cheque for £100 sent by Soane, wrote: 'You bore Your operation so well that, next to Buonaparte, I consider You as the greatest hero of modern times.'[14] This ordeal over, Soane recovered fairly quickly which was fortunate since June was to bring considerable activity in the City in preparation for a visit by the Emperor of Russia during which he went round the Bank on the thirteenth. Reporting on this event the *Courier* informed its readers that:

> The Emperor desired to see the able Architect, when Mr Soane was introduced to him by Mr Manning [a director]. He complimented Mr Soane in a very particular manner on the grandeur of the work and shook him most cordially by the hand.[15]

Soane's own account in his first *Description* of the house (1830) records that:

> When the Emperor Alexander was in England, I had the honour to be presented to His Imperial Majesty in the Bank, who, after expressing great approbation of that building, was pleased to command me to attend at the Pultney Hotel with drawings of that great national structure. I took this opportunity of presenting other designs, which his Imperial Majesty accepted.

This took place on Sunday 19 June and shortly afterwards the emperor sent Soane a diamond ring.[16]

On the evening of 17 June there were more festivities when the Merchant Bankers of London gave a banquet at Merchant Taylors' Hall in honour of the Duke of Wellington, and presented him with the Freedom of the City. Soane was responsible for the accommodation and decorations for this occasion, and had his own invitation to the dinner.

Early in August Mrs Soane went again to stay in Brighton with her elder son and his wife. Soane, who had been working on the revision of his lecturers, felt that he, too, had earned a holiday, and, taking advantage of the restored peace with France, made arrangements to leave the office in the hands of his trusted assistant, George Bailey. Having obtained some French currency and spent £1.18.6 on a 'portmanteau', he set off for Paris on 15 August.[17] No entries were made in the current notebook for the three weeks during which he was away, but he resumed with the observation that he had returned to England on the evening of 5 September. This was in fact the day on which Mrs Soane had sailed from Brighton to Dieppe, not, as might have been expected, to join her husband on his homeward journey, but to spend eight days in the French port with 'a party of friends'.[18] It is evident, however, that he knew nothing of this expedition until he received Mrs Soane's rather casual account of it in a letter sent to him after her return to Brighton, and which must have caused him some surprise.

Any benefit which either might have reaped from their holidays was soon to be overshadowed by more trouble with George who, by the beginning of October, was again pestering his mother for money. This time it was for £800 to extricate him from some predicament to which she refers in her reply as 'defrauding people out of their property'. It is likely that part of the debt in this instance had been borrowed from Edward Foxhall, who is known to have lent him a large sum. Ignoring his mother's advice to come into the open with a true statement of his affairs, he was at last cornered by the solicitor acting for a Mr Richard Priestley of the New Road, St Pancras. In January 1814, George had apparently persuaded Priestley to purchase a number of books which he wished to sell, and having secured a cash payment of £46, promised to deliver them that evening as he did not like the neighbours to see things being taken out of the house in daylight. When no books turned up, Priestley made enquiries and found that the books in question had in fact been sold elsewhere. After some months had passed in which he failed to get his money back, Priestley took legal proceedings as a result of which George was found guilty of obtaining the sum under a fraudulent pretence, and was committed to the King's Bench Prison early in November 1814. Soane now refused to do anything further for the miscreant, other than giving him his usual allowance. As Mrs Soane wrote to the family friend John Perry, 'it is not more than 16 months since his father paid his debts and gave him a sum of money to go on with; since which he has had more than £700—and now his debts are near £1400, besides some he has not brought forward.' The parents felt that in view of what they had done for George, the Boaden family should at least take care of his wife whose extravagance had in part contributed to his debts. The couple's house, No. 11 Euston Place, was sold on 30 December together with the contents, and the proceeds distributed to the creditors, but the debt of £46 to Richard Priestley remained until 16 January 1815 when it was paid by Mrs Soane, and George was liberated.

The sudden death of James Wyatt as the result of a carriage accident on 4 September 1813, left vacant the office of surveyor general which he had held since 1796. During this time his negligence and mismanagement had led to an unprecedented state of confusion in the Office of Works which required a Commission of Military Inquiry, not only to sort out the problems but to recommend steps for the prevention of similar occurrences. The outcome was a general reorganisation of the Office whereby it would be in the charge of a non-professional surveyor general to whom three 'Attached Architects' would be responsible for delegated areas, these being John Nash, John Soane and Robert Smirke. In addition to a retaining fee of £500 per annum, they were also paid a percentage on the executed works. They were also allowed to continue in private practice.

The new surveyor general was Colonel (later Sir) Benjamin Stephenson who wrote to Soane on 4 July 1815 enclosing a 'List of the several Palaces, and Public Buildings allotted to your district'. This included Hampton Court Palace, the Queen's Palace (Buckingham House), and 'all the Public Buildings under the care and superintendence of H. M. Office of Works, viz. in Whitehall and Westminster, the New Forest, Bushey Park, Richmond Park and Kew Gardens'.[19] For the first few years the appointment entailed little work other than routine maintenance which was fortunate as Soane was soon to be overwhelmed by personal trouble.

On 3 January he noted that he had been 'At home alone all the even^g: with weak eyes, unable to read', and on 12 February made another note about 'bad eyes', but they had recovered sufficiently for him to read his fifth lecture at Somerset House on 16 March, and the last of the series on 23 March. Mrs Soane seems to have visited Chertsey several times and was certainly there for most of July when Soane joined her for the day on the seventh, and again on the sixteenth. On the twenty-second he was there for two days, when he 'Took Mrs S. a present', and noted that 'William offered £10 as part of the £20' owed him, but '[I] desired him to keep it, and suppose the debt settled'. Over the following weekend he was there again, and presumably hoped to go fishing as he took with him a bagful of worms, and subsequently noted that he had given the fish to his friend Douglas, together with a bottle of port wine. There was to be one more summer visit to Chertsey on Sunday, 10 August, when he was accompanied by his one-time pupil John Sanders—now established as a successful architect—and with three bottles of old sherry, two of madeira and one of champagne stowed away in the carriage. By this time the primary cause of Mrs Soane's illness had been diagnosed as gallstones for which a 'cure' at Cheltenham was recommended. On 21 August Soane sent his carriage to fetch her and Miss Smith from Chertsey, and three days later they set out from Lincoln's Inn Fields for Gloucestershire, with her little dog Fanny and the man servant Joseph in attendance. Although she wrote to let Soane know of their safe arrival on 26 August, and appeared to find the lodgings at 82 High Street satisfactory, she wrote again four days later to say that she had moved further along the High Street to No. 123:

My Dear Friend,

Perhaps you may think me very whimsical, but we have changed our Lodgings and I think much for the better for tho we were in a gay part, yet on better acquaintance there were many objections—both for little Fan[20] and ourselves. This morng. Joseph went to enquire about the coaches of which I send the account—4 inside from the Angel Inn, St Clements, every day except Sundays—Golden Cross every day except Sunday at half-past 5 o'clock morng.—but let us know when to expect you. I write in haste as the post is going out. Adieu.[21]

At first she thought that her health was improving, but when her husband arrived on the evening of 2 September, he found her 'very ill in bed'. Five days later he noted that she was 'much better, able to walk into the drawingroom', and thus reassured he returned to London on the eighth. A week later he was there again for three days, and on 28 September Mrs Soane wrote an encouraging letter to say that:

> I am on the whole much better and feel more myself than I have done for months. This morning I have seen Dr Boisragon and he . . . assures me the complaint is not dangerous but says if I do not get rid of it now, it may return in a few months with double force, and if I do get quite rid of it, I shall have better health than I have had for many years—so now I feel more satisfied to stay with the hope of returning quite well—pray let me hear from you.[22]

When writing, she was unaware that Soane had been shocked to discover that in the *Champion* for 10 and 24 September there had been published a two-part article by an anonymous writer under the title of *The Present Low State of the Arts in England and more particularly of Architecture*, in which his own work was singled out for vicious attack. Suspecting that they had been written by his younger son, he travelled to Cheltenham on 13 October and showed them to Mrs Soane who at once said 'Those are George's doing. He has given me my death blow. I shall never be able to hold up my head again.[23] Soane stayed with her for a week and then, when it seemed safe to leave her, drove into Somerset to see the progress of the alterations which he had designed for Thomas Horner at Mells Park. On his return to London he tackled Scott, the publisher of the *Champion*, who admitted that George had written the offending article.

Mrs Soane returned to London on 28 October, but although she was able to take short walks, and was able to call on her old friend Mrs Foxhall who had recently been widowed, it is evident that her improvement had been only temporary. Early on the morning of 21 November she had a severe spasm, appeared to recover, but then had a relapse and took to her bed, asking that Mrs Shee would act as hostess for her at the small dinner party which had been arranged for that day. No immediate danger was anticipated but on the following day her condition deteriorated rapidly. Both Mr Pennington and Dr Pemberton were sent for but agreed that there was no hope of her recovery, and shortly after one a.m. on the 23rd she died. Soane's notebook has blank pages for the next few days, the entries resuming on 1 December with 'Friday—melancholy day indeed! The burial of all that is dear to me in this world, and all I wished to live for.'

Her funeral procession to Old St Giles's Burial Ground (now St Pancras Gardens) included John junior and his wife Maria, James Spiller, John Taylor, Martin Archer Shee, John Perry, Dr Pemberton, and the pupils Basevi, Parke and Foxhall whose father, one of Soane's oldest friends, had died three weeks before. Her son George made neither an appearance nor any sign of contrition. On 2 December Soane went to Chertsey, staying three days at the house of Mrs Smith, the mother of Sarah Smith, and giving £5.0.0 each to his brother William and various friends, presumably for mourning rings.[24] During the next three weeks, he attended only to essential business, staying for most of the time at Chelsea. Part of Christmas Eve was spent quietly with Turner, but he apparently refused an invitation from John Britton and his wife for Christmas Day, instead remaining alone at Chelsea and recording in his notebook that it had been 'A gloomy day'.

49. MRS SOANE, a pencil drawing by John Flaxman, given to Soane by J. M. W. Turner.

Although it was to be nearly a year before Soane felt that he could resume his Royal Academy lectures, he gradually picked up the threads of his practice, making alterations to No. 13 Grosvenor Square for Lord Berwick, and designing a stable block for Carrington House, Whitehall. He also made designs for a national monument to commemorate the victories of Trafalgar and Waterloo, and for further alterations at Petworth, although neither of the latter were executed. Also much in his mind was the monument to be erected over the vault containing Mrs Soane's coffin in St Giles's Burial Ground which eventually emerged as a version of his favourite shallow dome, here forming a canopy over an upright marble sarcophogus, the pedimented 'lid' of which rested on four detached Ionic columns (Plate 50). In drawing out his various designs he had much help from George Basevi, who, having completed his term of five years as a pupil, was due to leave in February but stayed on for another three months before leaving for his tour of Italy and Greece. In appreciation of this, Soane subsequently sent him a draft for £25 but Basevi returned it, assuring him that as part of the time had

> been devoted to a subject in which my feelings were concerned, I could receive no greater remuneration than the gratification it afforded me. . . . Under this impression, I trust you will not be offended at my returning your draft, as I assure you I nevertheless retain a due sense of gratitude for your kindness to me.[25]

During the summer Soane was to find himself the object of a somewhat disconcerting amount of female attention in which Mrs Barbara Hofland, a literary lady of some talent but effusive nature, was the principal participant.[26] She and her husband, a painter in water-colours, had for some years been on friendly terms with the architect and his wife, and she rashly claimed to have 'seen further into [Soane's] heart' than any other of his friends. Eleanora Brickenden also reappeared after her banishment from Lincoln's Inn Fields, while Sarah Smith who had stayed on as housekeeper clearly hoped to remain and perhaps obtain a more elevated position. Fortunately for Soane there was another couple whose friendship he and his wife had enjoyed for some years. Sarah and Edward Conduitt were the tenants of one of Soane's houses, No. 3 Albion Place, probably in their late twenties, and intelligent without assuming any literary pretensions.[27] Being happily married, and young enough to have been his children, they were able to offer Soane genuine regard and companionship without any tiresome display of emotion or giving grounds for gossip.

Towards the end of June 1816 Soane arranged to visit Harrogate, and leaving George Bailey in charge of the office, he set out on 4 July in his own carriage accompanied by Mrs Hofland and Mrs Conduitt. After a night at Stamford and another at Doncaster, they reached Harrogate on the sixth and took rooms at the Dragon. Pouring rain on the Sunday brought on a mood of melancholy, and the entry in his notebook 'Oh Eliza! Eliza! how great is thy loss! here we should have rambled together and held converse sweet.' Recovering his spirits the next three weeks were spent in drinking the waters or sightseeing, which included Castle Howard, Studley Park and Fountains Abbey, Knaresborough and Beverley. By 13 August the travellers were back in London.

50. Design for the
SOANE TOMB as
executed.

The holiday had obviously been of benefit, and soon after his return Soane felt able to tackle the problem of settling the domestic arrangements at No. 13. Ignoring a deluge of well-intentioned but irritating letters from Mrs Hofland, with their hints that he should marry again, and having dismissed Sarah Smith on account of some unsatisfactory behaviour, he took the eminently sensible step of asking Mrs Conduitt to take charge of his household, a non-resident duty which she was to perform for the rest of his life, and for which she received an honorarium of £50 a year. This entailed visiting the house several times a week when she would usually stay for dinner with Soane, and often be joined by her husband. The servants seem to have settled down happily under this arrangement, while Mrs Conduitt also managed the more difficult feat of maintaining a friendly relationship with Mrs Hofland and Eleanora Brickenden.

In the summer of 1819 Soane decided to make another visit to Paris and suggested that the Conduitts should join him there. He also took his pupil Henry Parke who was to act as draughtsman. This time he kept a separate notebook,[28] and although the entries are sketchy, they record that after leaving London on 21 August with a letter of credit for £1,000 in his pocket, he crossed from Dover to Dunkirk, spent a night at Beauvais, and reached Paris on the twenty-fifth. Lodgings were taken in the house of Mme. Sophie Gaile at No. 18 rue Vivienne. On the first day he felt unwell, but quickly recovered and next morning 'Walked with Mrs C. on the Boulevards'. After dinner, when he was joined by Parke, he hired a carriage, drove through the boulevards and returned by the Louvre. From then on the days were spent in sightseeing, with visits to Neuilly, Sèvres, St Cloud, the aqueduct at Arcueil, Malmaison and Versailles, these being interspersed with hours spent in the Louvre and innumerable bookshops. The Conduitts apparently left Paris on 10 September, and Parke departed soon after, but Soane stayed on for another ten days. The day before leaving he noted that he had cashed a final cheque for £40, bought more books and prints, and taken a last look at the Jardin des Plantes, the Halle au Vins, Poste Royale and l'Eglise St Germain-des-Près—'Norman, large, simple and handsome'. Breaking the homeward journey at Clermont, Amiens and Abbeville, he reached Boulogne on 22 September, crossed to Dover for a night at the Ship Inn, and was back in London on the evening of the twenty-third.

Notes

1. Soane Museum, leases. George Booth Tyndale and his wife remained close friends of Soane's over the years. The former, a Cottonian Family Trustee of the British Museum, was instrumental in obtaining for Soane a reversion enabling him to purchase the sarcophagus of Seti I when the government decided against its acquisition for the British Museum in 1824.
2. SPC Box 4.
3. SMC Div. XIV C.
4. SMC Div. XIV C. Sarah Smith was a sister of Richard Smith of Chertsey.
5. The *Morning Chronicle* for 13 October 1812 gives an account of the case. Kinnard subsequently travelled abroad. John Sanders encountered him in Rome in 1818 and reported in a letter to Soane 'Your old friend Kinnaird [*sic*] is here . . . he looks not only fat but fierce, in consequence of being adorned with a magnificent pair of mustachios.' Div. XV A (I).
6. SMC Div. III B (2).
7. Soane acquired two sets of Angelo Campanella's coloured prints of murals from remains in the grounds of the Villa Negroni in Rome.
8. Soane, *Description of the House and Museum*, 1836, p. 54.
9. This hangs in the Dressing Room, Soane Museum, and is entitled 'Nora Brickenden'.
10. SMC Div. III H.
11. SPC Box 4.
12. SMC Div. XIV B (7). The British Institution was founded on 4 June 1805 'to promote the Fine Arts in the United Kingdom'. It occupied the gallery in Pall Mall originally designed by George Dance as the Shakespeare Gallery for John Boydell.
13. Soane, *Journal*.
14. SMC Div. I C (22).
15. Quoted in John Patteson's letter of 17 June 1814 to Soane, SMC Div. 2 P (1).
16. In his will Soane directed that 'my diamond ring which was [a] present from the Emperor of Russia and my gold ring with the hair of Napoleon Buonaparte therein . . . shall be considered and kept as heirlooms in my family.' They passed to his grandson John who married Marie Borrer but had no children and the subsequent whereabouts of the rings is not recorded.
17. He also took with him a letter from a Mons. Bondoni, the owner of a shop in London, to a friend in Paris, requesting the latter to give Soane, who wished to see Versailles, an introduction to 'our friend Blondele'. This was probably Merry Joseph Blondel (1781–1853), the historical painter, several of whose works are at Versailles.
18. SPC Box 4.
19. SMC Div. XIV J.
20. Mrs Soane's pet dog Fanny. She outlived her mistress by five years, dying on Christmas Day 1820 aged '16 or 17' and was buried in the Monument Courtyard behind No. 14. Soane wrote in his notebook: 'Alas poor Fanny! Faithful, affectionate, disinterested friend. Farewell.' Soane had portraits of her painted by James Ward and Antonio Van Assen. She is also shown sitting on her mistress's lap in the posthumous painting of Mrs Soane by George Jackson (Picture Room, Soane Museum).
21. SPC Box 4.

22. Ibid.

23. Soane mounted copies of these cuttings on a board to which was attached a separate piece bearing the inscription: 'Blows given by George Soane 10th & 24th Sept. 1815.' For many years they were hung in Soane's dressing-room, but are now on the second floor of the house.

24. Soane, *Journal*. Mrs Soane left no will. Edward Toller's receipt for £39.8.0, 'being the amount of Expenses in obtaining Administration of Elizabeth Soane deceased' is in SPC Box 16.

25. SMC Div. XV 2 (A) 15.

26. Barbara, wife of the artist Thomas Christopher Hofland. She was the author of several novels. In *The Merchant's Widow* Soane's name occurs in various passages, one being uttered by a precocious small boy who, after visiting the architect's house in Lincoln's Inn Fields, says 'Dear Mamma, make me a Mr Soane.' On reading the book the latter was much displeased, and admonished the author in a letter of 1 November 1814 (SMC Div. III H (9)), but she was subsequently forgiven.

27. A paper on Sir Charles Barry by Sir M. D. Wyatt in *Transactions of the Royal Institute of British Architects*, 1859–60, p. 118, refers to Edward Conduitt as accompanying Barry on the first stage of his Continental tour in 1817.

28. Soane Bookcase, Shelf D (left). Henry Parke had originally intended to follow a legal career but a speech impediment prevented this and he became one of Soane's pupils, being responsible for many fine Lecture Diagrams. When he left for travel abroad, Soane made him an allowance of £100 a year for three years. His long letters from Italy and Sicily (SMC Div. XV 2 (B) 17) would have been of considerable interest to Soane.

[7]

The Last Decades

From 1820 until his retirement, Soane was to be occupied almost entirely with official work. Only two noteworthy private commissions—Wotton and Pellwall—were squeezed into a demanding programme which suddenly sprang to life with the accession of George IV. Up to this time his duties as one of the three Attached Architects had been principally concerned with reports for the surveyor general, the only one of significance coming in 1818 when Parliament voted £1,000,000 for new churches to be built in the rapidly expanding cities of London and the provinces. The intended buildings were to be for maximum congregations at minimum cost and Soane, on being asked to suggest a figure for the latter, quoted £30,000. After lengthy discussion this was cut by the commissioners appointed under the Act who adopted £20,000 as the standard, a meagre sum which resulted in the erection of a number of gaunt structures few of which could claim any architectural merit. Soane was eventually assigned three of these churches, St Peter Walworth, Holy Trinity Marylebone, and St John Bethnal Green, the first begun in 1823, and the other two in 1826.

Meanwhile other and more urgent matters required attention in Westminster following the death of George III on 29 January 1820, and the prince regent's accession as George IV. Although now aged fifty-eight, corpulent, asthmatic and gouty, the new king had definite ideas as to the dignity of the Crown, and the architectural background against which occasions of state should be seen. His favourite architect, however, was John Nash who had already remodelled for him the Royal Lodge in Windsor Park, and the Pavilion at Brighton. When the Bill 'for the better Regulation of the conduct of the Business of the Office of Works' had been drafted in 1814, Nash, on the insistence of the prince regent, had been given charge of such royal palaces as were used by the prince for his own occupation, whether in Westminster or elsewhere. This removed specific buildings from what was geographically Soane's rightful area, and later deprived him of the commission to transform Buckingham House into Buckingham Palace. However, neither Nash nor his patron could dispute Soane's responsibility for any work done within the Palace of Westminster. As it happened, this was to begin with the uninspiring task of providing extra seating in the House of Lords for the trial of Queen Caroline whose recent and embarrassing arrival from abroad on 5 June was to cause a postponement of the coronation. By building out galleries on either side of the Chamber, supported on cast-iron columns and draped with crimson cloth, Soane achieved the desired accommodation and was duly complimented by the surveyor general on the result which the peers were anxious to retain 'not only as a useful but as a highly ornamental addition to their house'.[1]

In his first opening of parliament the new king had been shocked to see the mean approach—a contrivance of James Wyatt—by which he had to reach the House of Lords. Soane's next commission was therefore to produce designs for a more appropriate entrance. This took the form of a curving arcade enclosing Old Palace Yard, and leading to a vestibule from which a staircase rose in three stages. For the latter his inspiration clearly derived from Bernini's *Scala Regia* in the Vatican. The drawings, submitted early in 1822, met with royal approval although the king asked that there should be more enrichment at the entrance which he considered too plain. Building began at once and was sufficiently advanced for the Duke of York to inspect it on 3 December. Meanwhile Soane had received instructions to continue the work with a new Ante Room at the head of the staircase, and a Royal Gallery beyond to link it with the Painted Chamber. There was some delay before the designs received approval, but work began in August and involved the destruction of the old Prince's Chamber, a step which Soane regretted although he pointed out that it had already been greatly altered and was in a delapidated condition. The Painted Chamber—which he was later wrongly accused of destroying— was preserved intact, a new doorcase being the only addition.[2]

With characteristic impatience the king wanted his new gallery to be completed for the opening of parliament in February 1824. This entailed a tremendous effort on the part of the men employed who worked in continuous day and night shifts. Soane, wishing to acknowledge their achievement, arranged to hold a feast at his own expense, but when news of this reached the surveyor general the latter was much perturbed. Writing an admonitory letter to Soane on 22 January he pointed out that as

> these works were undertaken by orders of Government, and placed under the imme-
> diate direction and superintendence of this Office, I much fear so extensive public
> an entertainment given upon such an occasion, and under such circumstances, may
> draw down some unpleasant animadversions from those under whose authority this
> Department is placed.[3]

Soane, determined not to disappoint the men, went ahead with the feast but tactfully absented himself on the excuse of a summons to Windsor, and persuaded John Britton to take his place as host. Thus no official significance could be attached to the occasion and a hundred and fifty workmen sat down to a sumptuous dinner at the Freemasons' Tavern in Great Queen Street.

There were valid grounds for making attendance at Windsor an excuse, since a few months earlier the king had been advised to consider a complete rehabilitation of the inadequate accommodation and delapidated general condition of the Castle. In his official capacity Soane had to be consulted, together with Nash and Smirke, but although he produced a survey of the buildings, he showed little enthusiasm for the project and in the end the commission went not to an Attached Architect, but to Jeffry Wyatt, whose handling of this mammoth task later earned him the title of Sir Jeffry Wyatville.

While work in the House of Lords was proceeding, Soane was also engaged in other parts of the Palace of Westminster, the most important task being the provision of a new Court of King's Bench and other courts in the awkward spaces which lay between the buttresses of Westminster Hall and the Palladian 'Stone building' which stood a few yards to the west, and for which John Vardy had been largely responsible in the middle years of the eighteenth century. Soane felt strongly that the new building should be 'composed in a style totally different' to the gothic hall, and therefore produced a classical design with a rusticated ground floor and large venetian windows to the upper floor in keeping with the classical character of Vardy's work. This design was approved and work on the foundations began in October 1822, the shell of the building being virtually complete by March 1824 when a fierce attack on its design was launched in the House of Commons by Henry Bankes, MP for Corfe Castle. He had inspected the work on several occasions without adverse comment, yet on 1 March delivered a critical speech, supported by William Williams, MP for Weymouth. Describing it as 'so ugly that it ought to be immediately razed to the ground', they deplored that a gothic style had not been adopted. As a result of this attack all work was stopped and a Select Committee appointed to review the situation. After much discussion Soane was instructed to produce designs for a gothic façade, this to be set back from the original frontage by several feet. Work was resumed, and the building completed in 1827. Suppressing his inclination to resign, he worked off his feelings about the episode by preparing a *Brief Statement . . . Respecting the New Law Courts*, published in 1827, which left no doubt as to his contempt for the self-styled arbiters of taste who had interfered.[4] He was in fact to have another encounter with an officious member of parliament over his design for the State Paper Office a few years later, but in general Soane's work in the Whitehall area during the 1820s proceeded without incident. It included extensive alterations to the Privy Council and Board of Trade Offices, new rooms at Nos. 10 and 11 Downing Street, and the replacing of the crumbling façades of Inigo Jones's Banqueting House.

In 1823 Soane reached his seventieth birthday and it was inevitable that the years would now bring increasing gaps in the circle of his friends. They also brought concern about his family. On 21 October his elder son John died at Brighton aged thirty-eight. For two years from 1819 the latter and his wife, with their children and nurse, had travelled in Italy from where he wrote lengthy but carping letters[5] to his father whose affection and anxiety deepened as the serious state of John junior's health became apparent. He was buried in the vault below the monument designed seven years earlier for his mother in St Giles's Burial Ground. Within a few months the widowed Maria showed the unattractive side of her character by taking possession of Soane's official residence at Chelsea in defiance of the regulations, and subsequently by spreading unfounded rumours that Soane had made no provision for her and her family, this in spite of the fact that he had undertaken to pay for the education and all expenses of his grandson John. Soane therefore set up a Trust for the benefit of Maria's children, the capital sum being £10,000, and the trustees being Sir Thomas Lawrence and Sir Francis Chantrey.[6]

Soane was already paying for the education of his other grandson, Frederick, George's child, having found that this had been neglected during the boy's early years. The rift with George himself was, however, to be widened when Soane discovered that the latter had set up a ménage à trois, his wife's sister having lived with them for several years and become the mother of his second son, known as George Manfred, born in or around 1824. George, it seems had first tried unsuccessfully to have the baby admitted to the Foundling Hospital, but it was then secretly 'farmed out' with Sarah Smith at Chertsey. Soane's offer of further financial help was conditional on George ceasing to associate with his sister-in-law but the latter would not comply. Meanwhile Soane entertained the hope that the legitimate son, Fred, might become an architect, and on leaving school the boy was placed with John Tarring until unsatisfactory behaviour led to his dismissal. It was then found that he had formed an undesirable friendship with a Captain Westwood, at one time a fellow officer of a Captain Beauclerk and a Captain Nicholls, the latter subsequently being executed for an 'unnatural offence', while the former cut his throat while facing a similar charge. Although Fred apparently chose to have no further contact with his grandfather, he continued to receive an allowance from him of £100 a year paid through Praed's Bank.[7]

In 1825 Soane's elder brother William died aged eighty-five and was buried on 1 December in the churchyard of St Peter's, Chertsey.[8] It is doubtful, however, whether this loss affected him as deeply as had the death of his old friend and revered master, George Dance, who had died on the preceding 14 January, and whose burial in the crypt of St Paul's Cathedral Soane is likely to have attended. There is, however, a gap in the notebooks for the first three weeks of that month due to the operation for the removal of a cataract from one of his eyes which had been performed on the previous 24 December. Trouble with his eyes was to be a severe trial throughout his later years, and it was probably for this reason that in the summer of 1826 he decided to employ George Wightwick for several months as an amanuensis. Wightwick, who was desperately looking for work following his return from a year's study in Italy, had offered his services and Soane made it clear that he would be employed in a secretarial capacity. It was agreed that he should begin by accompanying the architect to Bath in September when the latter was to take a 'cure', and fill his spare time in writing his account of the New Law Courts episode.

Wightwick found that taking down Soane's dictation on this vexed subject for several hours each day was not the happiest employment, while being expected to return in the evening and take a glass of wine with the architect left him little free time. However, he remained with Soane after their return to London and was on happy terms with the pupils until one day when, having taken umbrage at an unintentionally slighting remark by Soane, he walked out. Soane apparently forgave him and when, a year later, Wightwick called to give him a copy of his newly published *Select Views of the Roman Antiquities*, he was received 'with much kindness'. Wightwick subsequently settled in Plymouth and built up a successful architectural practice in the west country. His brief appearance in the Soane story would scarcely warrant a mention were it not that after his retirement in 1851, he contributed an autobiography to *Bentley's Miscellany* which included a lively account of the months spent with Soane. Too long to be quoted in full,[9] the passage in which he recollected his arrival and impression of the architect is as valuable a record of the latter is as Lawrence's portrait of him (Frontispiece), painted three years later:

> Between the table and the window was a large folding screen, to dim the glare of the light. On the inner side of the table, with his back to the fire, stood the fully developed full-length of John Soane.
>
> He was certainly distinguished-looking: taller than common; and so thin as to appear taller; his age at this time about seventy-three. He was dressed entirely in black; his waistcoat being of velvet, and he wore knee-breeches with silk stockings. Of course the exceptions to his black were his cravat, shirt-collar, and shirt-frill of the period. Let a man's "shanks" be ever so "shrunken",—if they be but straight, the costume described never fails upon a gentleman. The idea of John Soane in a pair of loose trowsers and a short broad-tailed jacket, after the fashion of these latter times, occurs to me as more ludicrous than Liston's *Romeo*! The Professor unquestionably *looked* the Professor, and the gentleman. His face was long in the extreme; for his chin—no less than his forehead—contributed to make it so; and it still more so appeared from its narrowness. . . . It is true, he was ill when I saw him, and sorely worn with perplexity and vexation; and therefore I ought to say, that at *that* time, it can be scarcely said that he had any front face. In profile his countenance was extensive; but, looking at it "edgeways", it would have been "to any thick sight" something of the invisible. A brown wig carried the elevation of his head to the utmost attainable height; so that, altogether, his physiognomy was suggestive of the picture which is presented on the back of a spoon held vertically. His eyes, now sadly failing in their sight, looked red and small beneath their full lids; but through their weakened orbs, the fire of his spirit would often show itself, in proof of its unimpaired vigour.

Wightwick's second publication, *A Selection from the Museum of the Vatican*, was published shortly after Soane's death in 1837, and was dedicated to him, permission for this having been obtained some time before.

The 'unimpaired vigour' to which Wightwick referred was to be put to the test in Soane's last important work which was about to materialise in 1828. It stemmed from the problem of providing an adequate repository for the national archives which had been under discussion for several years before 1828 when it was decided to ask Soane to prepare surveys both of the existing premises in Great George Street, and a possible site in Duke Street, St James's Park. Early in February he noted that he had sent the surveyor general 'six drawings of proposals for the housing of the records' but of these there are no copies in the Museum. The earliest surviving drawing is for the entrance front, dated May 1829 and followed by one of 20 June for the east façade as carried out. They show that his New State Paper Office, as it was to be called, was to be a complete break from anything that Soane had produced before, and that his inspiration derived from Vignola's Villa Farnese at Caprarola. The fact that Charles Barry and C. R. Cockerell were soon to exploit the Italian villa theme in several of their works, many of which have survived, has somewhat overshadowed the originality of Soane's building which was doomed to a short life by lack of departmental forethought, and was soon forgotten. In the London of his time, however, it was a striking innovation.

Soane's admiration for Vignola's work went back to his student days in Italy, where he had studied it at first hand, and formed the opinion later expressed in his Royal Academy lectures, that the Villa Farnese was 'a building which can never be sufficiently admired or too much studied'. In addition to engravings of it by Le Bas and Debret, his library also contained eight editions of Vignola's book on the Orders, from a plate in one of which he noted that the principal entrance for the State Paper Office was to be copied.

Such scholarship was wasted on the egregious Henry Bankes who once again voiced his opposition to Soane's design and sought support from the chancellor of the exchequer, Henry Goulburn who, in the course of an interview with the surveyor general, scribbled on Soane's drawings his own idea for rows of small pilasters set between the windows on the two principal storeys. With predictable anger Soane protested to the surveyor general:

> Let me conjure you my Dear Sir to exert all your power to prevent the erection of such a monument of folly . . . from disgracing the Metropolis of the Empire. I trust you will listen to my prayer which is for the cause of Architecture and to prevent the reproach of Foreigners on our National taste.[10]

His plea was successful and his design was approved in unaltered form by the Lords of the Treasury. Its completion in 1831 made a fitting conclusion to his seventeen years as an Attached Architect, and an appropriate occasion for the conferring of a knighthood which he received from William IV on 21 September. By now Soane's private practice had come virtually to an end. George Bailey and C. J. Richardson were still with him, but the past pupils, David Mocatta and Stephen Burchell had left in 1827 and 1828 respectively, while the assistant David Paton departed in 1830 shortly before emigrating to America. Soane's surveyorship at Chelsea Hospital now involved very little work and was retained until his death, but two major decisions had to be faced as he approached his eightieth birthday. The first was to submit his resignation as architect to the Bank of England, and the second was to secure the future of his house and collection. Steps towards the latter were taken by a Bill, introduced in the House of Commons by Joseph Hume, MP. In spite of opposition by William Cobbett, and evidence given by George Soane, the *Act for settling and preserving Sir John Soane's Museum, Library and Works of Art, in Lincoln's Inn Fields in the County of Middlesex, for the Benefit of the Public, and for establishing a sufficient Endowment for the due Maintenance of the same* received royal assent on 20 April 1833.

Resignation from the Bank was a more painful step but eventually, on 16 October,

Soane steeled himself to inform the governor, deputy governor and members of the Building Committee that:

> Feeling myself unable, from impaired sight, to perform my professional duties as I have hitherto done, I must now, with heartfelt regret, retire from a situation which has so long been the pride and boast of my life.
>
> If at any time I can be useful to my successor, I shall be always ready to render every assistance in my power.
>
> With the most ardent and sincere wishes for the increasing prosperity of this great national establishment, and with grateful recollection which can only cease with my existence,
>
> I have the honour to subscribe myself, Gentlemen, Your faithful and most obedient servant.[11]

On the following day the Court of Directors passed a resolution

> That the resignation of the office of Architect and Surveyor to the Bank by Sir John Soane be accepted; and that the warmest thanks of this Court be given to him for the honourable and assiduous manner in which he has for forty-five years fulfilled, with unremitted zeal, the service that has been assigned to him. Further, that the Members of the Court express an earnest wish that every earthly enjoyment may be afforded him by Divine Providence during his retirement from the labours of his profession.[12]

By then Soane had already left London for Hastings where he stayed for a month while George Bailey and Mrs Conduitt took charge of No. 13.

Retirement for Soane did not mean idleness, and an entry in his notebook at the end of 1833 recorded that since his return to town he had been 'chiefly occupied in completing the *Professional Life* [the *Memoirs*] and other miscellaneous business to this day the 31st Dec. I hope a new year will be less fertile in painful incidents than the year past.'

In fact the remaining years of his life proved tranquil and rewarding, and although he gave up making entries in his notebooks he was pursuing various interests, of which the most important was a proposal for an Institute 'to be formed for the promotion of Architecture' as outlined in a circular over the names of P. F. Robinson, T. L. Donaldson, C. Fowler, J. Goldicutt and others.[13] Accompanying the copy sent to Soane was a note by Robinson expressing the hope that he might allow his name to be proposed as president. To this Soane was regretfully unable to accede as the rules of the Royal Academy prohibited members from belonging to any similar society. The presidency was therefore undertaken by Earl Grey to whom, on 13 June in 1835 Soane sent a cheque for £750 to be used 'for such purposes connected with your Society as shall appear to you most conducive to its advantage'.

By 1834 Soane had become generally regarded as the 'Father of the Profession', and in the spring of that year a meeting was convened at the Athenaeum Club to consider the presentation of a gold medal in recognition of his services to architecture. It was decided to form a committee including Charles Barry, Thomas Donaldson and George Bailey, and to invite subscribers at a guinea each.[14] The date chosen for the ceremony was Tuesday 24 March 1835, when the company was to assemble at No. 13 Lincoln's Inn Fields at noon. When the day arrived, the Duke of Sussex, who had hoped to attend, was prevented by illness and the presentation was made by Sir Jeffry Wyatville in the presence of Sir Francis Chantrey, Sir William Beechey and other close friends. Joseph Kay read the duke's letter with its expressions of regard and regret that 'the want of sight with which it has pleased the Almighty to visit me for a time' had prevented him from 'witnessing the warm reception with which you will be greeted on this day'.[15] It was followed by the reading of the formal Address by Thomas Donaldson. Soane, who feared that he might be overcome with emotion, asked his friend and solicitor John Bicknell to read his reply which concluded with his gratitude for the occasion and the gift, 'gilding the close of a long professional life with a reward so bright, so welcome and so honourable'. For his part Soane proposed to endow a charity whereby an annual sum should be distributed to distressed architects, their widows and children.[16]

That evening a great gathering of subscribers, organised by John Goldicutt, took place at the Freemasons' Hall when silver and bronze versions of the gold medal were distributed in a setting decked with flowers and a display of drawings of Soane's principal works. On a pedestal in the main hall, Chantrey's bust of Soane dominated an assembly of other busts representing Vitruvius, Palladio, Michelangelo, Jones and Wren which Goldicutt had somehow managed to borrow. The festivities ended with a ball, and there was general agreement that they were worthy of the occasion.

Having completed his *Memoirs*, which were privately printed by J. Levy in 1835, Soane worked on a new *Description of the House* to replace the inadequate editions of 1830 and 1832. In the spring of 1836 he was troubled by ill-health and on the advice of his doctor spent a few weeks in a house on Richmond Hill from where he wrote on 10 June to R. J. Jones who had sent him an invitation to attend the official opening of the newly formed King William Street in the City. Regretting his inability to accept, he still hoped 'at some future time to have the satisfaction of seeing what at present I can only imagine'. He appears to have been back in London towards the end of July when copies of the new *Description* were dispatched to various eminent people. Two copies went to Kensington Palace for the Duchess of Kent and her daughter, Princess Victoria, whose accession as queen Soane was to miss by five months. Sir John Conroy, acknowledging the books on their behalf, assured Soane that both had received their copies with 'great interest'. Other recipients included Isaac d'Israeli, Charles Barry and Rowland Burdon, who acknowledged his copy on 13 August:

It has raised in my mind a cloud of recollections, which overshadow some of the pleasantest days of my life. Few expeditions have been begun, continued and ended, with more uniform and satisfactory results than our visit to Naples and its environs, our circuit of Sicily, our Maltese expedition, Syracuse, Messina, Stromboli and various

51. The SOANE TOMB, in
St Giles's Burial Ground, now
St Pancras Gardens.

52. The SOANE TOMB, detail of
panel inscribed to Soane.

Speranaro adventures, and the close of our travels in the classic cities of Lombardi. For how much of enjoyment in the earlier and better period of our lives have we to be grateful to divine Providence! and can we doubt that the same Providence, though visiting us with that mixture of evils, which a state of trial makes essential to our future prospects of happiness, is not at hand to crown our honest efforts.[17]

It was the last letter from Burdon, on the threshold of eighty, to Soane who was to be eighty-four in the following month. On 20 January 1837 Soane died at his house in Lincoln's Inn Fields. His funeral service was held privately, and he was buried in St Giles's Burial Ground beneath the monument which he had designed for his wife twenty-one years before (Plates 51–2).

The future of the house and collection had already been secured by the Act of 1833. In that year Soane had also made a will, a lengthy document in which many friends and servants were remembered.[18] It also set out his wish that George Bailey should become the first curator of the Soane Museum, and that Mrs Sarah Conduitt should act as inspectress, duties which both were to fulfil until their deaths within a fortnight of each other in December 1860.

53. Caricature of SOANE in old age,
probably by Daniel Maclise

Notes

1. SMC Div. XI D (2).
2. A description of the Royal Suite is given in John Britton and Augustus Pugin, *Public Buildings of London*, Vol. II, 1825–8.
3. SMC Div. II S (22).
4. The *Brief Statement* was superseded by Soane's *Designs for Public and Private Buildings* published in the following year (1828).
5. In these and several of his earlier letters John Soane junior frequently adopted a disagreeable sarcasm or derogation, referring to his father's good friend and neighbour, George Booth Tyndale, as a 'half bred attorney', J. M. W. Turner as 'pig Turner', and the British Consul in Rome as a 'broken down banker'.
6. Soane, *Memoirs*, p. 60 footnote.
7. SPC Box 4 Envelope 5.
8. For many years William Soane had lived in a small house at Goose Poole, adjoining 'the Chamblins Field' at Chertsey (SMC Div. XIV C (I)). Although John had provided his elder brother with an annuity, relations between them were never close. William's wife, Mary, died in 1813 when Soane made the only reference to her in his notebooks: 'Mary died this day – I believe' (13 December).
9. The full account is given in Bolton, *Portrait*, pp. 395–410.
10. SMC Div. XI K (2).
11. SMC Div. XIV J (2).
12. Ibid.
13. SMC Div. V A (6).
14. SMC Div. XIV G (2).
15. Dated 24 March 1835. Quoted in full, Soane *Memoirs*.
16. Soane, *Memoirs*. The capital sum of £5,000 was invested in Bank of England annuities. The annual distribution of the interest took place in March each year and continued until 1978 when, with the consent of the Charity Commissioners, the fund was transferred to the Architects' Benevolent Society.
17. Soane Bookcase, Shelf A (left). Bound letters of thanks from various friends for presentation copies of Soane's *Description of the House and Museum*, 1835–6.
18. The will also made provision for his surviving but unrepentant son George, his wife Agnes, and their legitimate children, Frederick, Clara and Rose. George died in August 1860.

[Part Two]

THE
ARCHITECTURAL WORKS
OF SIR JOHN SOANE

54. Bridge over the River Wensum, NORWICH, designed by Soane in 1783.

Major Commissions

Early Works 1781–1792

Hamels Park, Hertfordshire (Plates 17, 18, 26)

Philip Yorke, later 3rd Earl of Hardwicke, was one of the earliest of Soane's patrons. From 1780, when he commissioned a drawing of the Corsini Chapel (Plate 14), based on one made by Soane while in Rome, Mr Yorke and his family continued to consult the architect on a variety of undertakings during the course of some forty years.

At Hamels, Mr Yorke's early home, Soane carried out alterations in the house between 1781 and 1789. The lodges were built in 1782, and are still in use, and in 1783 he produced a design for the rustic dairy which he described as 'roughcasted, and the roof . . . covered with reeds; the pillars are the trunks of trees, with the bark on, decorated with woodbines and creepers'. This was the first example of the 'primitivism' which was later to become an important element in the style which Soane evolved. The dairy disappeared many years ago, and the house itself has been largely remodelled but the gardener's cottage survives.

Adams Place, Southwark (Plates 19, 20)

In 1781 Soane was engaged with Jupp and Allen to survey a small estate in the Borough for Francis Adams and subsequently supplied a design 'for improving the said estate'. It comprised a three-storey three-window façade to Borough High Street containing two small shops between which an entrance gave access to two rows of tenements at right angles to the main street. Soane was later to supervise the letting of the tenements and collection of the rents. In 1783 he advised Mr Adams on a house in Powis Place, Bath, but there are no details.

Norwich, Blackfriars Bridge, Norfolk (Plate 54)

Soane attended a meeting of the City Corporation in March 1783 with his design for a bridge over the river Wensum which was approved in the following month and subsequently built by the mason John de Carle. Soane noted that for '12 journies, time and expenses, model, fair drawing and c. the Court voted me their thanks and also £63'. The bridge survives although it was later widened and has lost its original ironwork. Soane's design for a bridge at Hellesdon, on the outskirts of the city, was drawn out in 1785 but was not executed on the grounds of expense.

Letton Hall, Norfolk (Plates 55–60)

The building of Letton was commissioned by Brampton Gurdon Dillingham in 1783. Of the alternative designs prepared, that finally selected was built in white brick with Portland stone dressings. The original entrance had a segmental Doric porch carrying a balcony with an iron balustrade, but this was replaced by a two-storey projection built in the nineteenth century. The compact plan of the house centres round an oval staircase which is top-lit and has a wrought-iron balustrade of unusual design. Much of the interior remains as completed by Soane, as do the domestic offices adjoining.

55. LETTON HALL, engraved design.

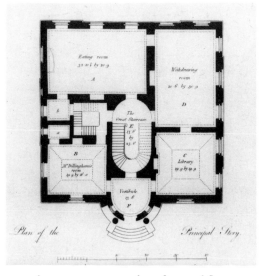

56. LETTON HALL, plan of ground floor.

57. LETTON HALL, garden front.

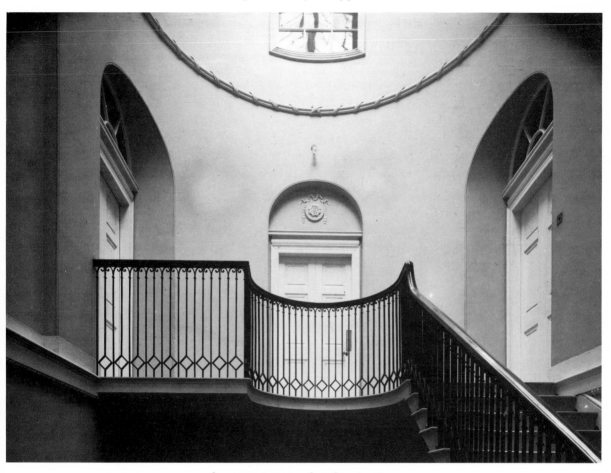

58. LETTON HALL, first-floor landing.

59, 60. LETTON HALL, details of drawing-room chimneypiece.

Malvern Hall, Warwickshire

Henry Greswold Lewis was one of the party of grand tourists with whom Soane visited Sicily in 1779. He was also the brother-in-law of the Hon. Wilbraham Tollemache for whom Soane was refurbishing 148 Piccadilly in 1781–2, for either or both of which reasons he was to consult the architect in the summer of 1783 on alterations to Malvern Hall, a late seventeenth-century house which he had inherited some ten years before. Soane's first visit was on 20 August 1783, when he inspected the old house and made the first plans. Apart from one large elevation, and an engraved plate in his *Plans* of 1788, the only drawings to survive in the Museum are those in the 'Precedents' which show plans with proposed alterations for the ground floor and basement, and some details for chimneypieces and a doorway. There are, however, accounts for the work in Soane's Journal and it is evident that he replaced the old balustrade with a stone cornice and blocking course while the entrance front was given an Ionic portico of Meriden stone. Two wings were added to the main block, that on the north containing an eating-room, bedchamber and dressing-room, while that on the south had a drawing-room, bedchamber and dressing-room. There were staircases in both wings, while the main staircase of the old house was altered and given a 'new moulded handrail with enriched ironwork'.

During 1784–5 Soane made many journeys to Malvern Hall to inspect the work in hand, the principal craftsmen being William Swan, bricklayer, George Wyatt and John Holmes, joiners, and John Mackell, smith. Edward and Martin Foxhall were responsible for carving and painting.

Decoration continued in a desultory way over the rest of the decade, and there is a note in the accounts that as late as 1794 Soane was sending patterns of borders for wallpapers. A further note, added to the account in Soane's Journal, records that on 2 May 1798 he sent Mr Lewis a 'Design for a Barn à la Paestum'. Now designated 'Doric Barn, 936 Warwick Road, Solihull', this remarkable small building, which originally served as a store and cart shed, was built in red brick which was also used for the four

61. SOLIHULL, Soane's 'Barn à la Paestum.'

pairs of Doric columns which adorn its façade, and the pilasters of the return walls. They support a timber entablature. A central archway leads to a cart-yard at the rear (Plate 61). The building is now converted to a dwelling, and the ground on which it stands is no longer part of the Malvern Hall estate.

Langley Park, Norfolk (Plates 62–3)

In August 1784 Soane made his first design for an entrance to Langley Park, the seat of Sir Thomas Proctor-Beauchamp. Further designs were sent for the brick lodges which stand a short distance along the road from the main gateway. The latter are referred to in the accounts as in course of construction during 1786, but the completion of the gateway appears to have been delayed as the pateras and chimneypots for it were not ordered from Coade and Sealy until 1791. There is a reference in a Bill Book to £26 5s 0d paid for '2 grey hound dogs as per agreement'. These support the shields flanking the central archway which were supplied by the mason, James Nelson.

62. LANGLEY, the main gateway.

63. LANGLEY, entrance and lodges.

Earsham, Norfolk (Plates 64–5)

Soane was asked by William Windham of Earsham to design a greenhouse in 1784, but half way through its construction it was decided that it should be used as a music-room instead. It is rectangular in plan with an apse at either end, and the five-bay façade has an Ionic order. The central entrance is surmounted by a fanlight, and the four Ionic columns support a pediment in which is a plaque and swags. The ceiling of the interior is coffered, and the walls were originally painted in chiaroscuro decoration by de Bruyn but this has now disappeared.

From 1786 Soane carried out some alterations in the mansion itself but this was principally concerned with the domestic quarters.

Saxlingham Rectory, Norfolk (Plates 66–7)

At least four alternative designs were prepared by Soane for the Revd John Gooch who wished to build a parsonage house at Saxlingham in 1784. The simplest version was chosen and built in white brick. The main block is of two storeys only, but the elliptical bays in the centre of the north and south fronts continue through both floors to form an attic room above the parapet. The original library and dining-room have lost their Soane chimneypieces, but that in the drawing-room survives, as does the scroll-pattern plaster frieze in this room. There has been some internal rearrangement in recent years.

Tendring Hall, Suffolk (Plates 68–9)

Soane's designs for Tendring Hall were prepared in 1784, when Admiral (later Sir) Joshua Rowley wished to replace an earlier house which he and his eldest son had inherited. Legal difficulties caused delay in beginning the new house which was to be on a different site, but it was completed by 1786. Rectangular in plan, it had an Ionic entrance porch on the north, and a three-window semicircular bay running through the ground and first floors of the south front. The materials used for the exterior were white brick with Portland stone for the portico and dressings.

A vestibule with a shallow barrel-vaulted ceiling led to the main hall in the centre of the house, extending through both floors and lit by a glazed lantern. A cantilevered stone staircase followed the curve of the southern wall. Opposite the stair, two marble columns and two antae, with gilt capitals and bases, supported a gallery at first-floor level from which in turn rose further columns with capitals of a Corinthian type. Between the latter the simple ironwork of the staircase was continued as a balustrade. A drawing-room with segmental ends occupied the centre of the south side of the house. The decoration of this and the other principal rooms was simple, but they had fine mahogany doors and marble chimneypieces.

The house was considerably damaged during military occupation in the Second World War and was subsequently demolished.

64. EARSHAM, the music-room designed in 1784.

65. EARSHAM, the music-room. From Soane's engraved *Designs*.

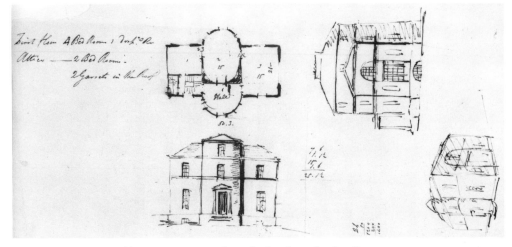

66. SAXLINGHAM, Soane's sketches of 1784. *Page 124.*

67. SAXLINGHAM, garden façade. *Page 124.*

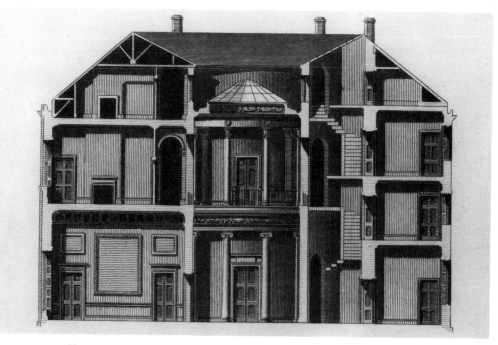

68. TENDRING HALL, section from Soane's engraved *Designs. Page 124.*

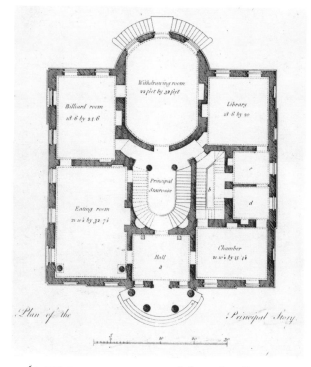

69. TENDRING HALL, ground-floor plan. *Page 124.*

Entrance front.

70. SHOTESHAM, engraved design.

71. SHOTESHAM, original entrance front.

72. SHOTESHAM, vestibule.

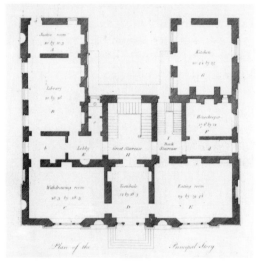

73. SHOTESHAM, plan from
Soane's engraved *Designs*.

Shotesham Hall, Norfolk (Plates 70–3)

The first designs for Shotesham (spelt Shottisham in Soane's time) are dated 1785, but the work which was carried out for Robert Fellowes extended over several years and there are details for some of the internal finishings as late as 1789. The house is built in brick with Portland stone dressings. Against its principal front are set six irregularly spaced pilasters of brick with Ionic capitals in Coade stone carrying an entablature over which rises an attic storey. At ground level three venetian windows with solid tympana occupy the wider spaces between the pilasters, while the two narrow bays contain round-headed brick niches.

From the central doorway a small vestibule leads to a hall with a geometrical staircase occupying three sides. The drawing-room and dining-room on either side of the vestibule are simply decorated but these rooms and the library contain fine chimneypieces of earlier date. As Soane noted in his Journal for 1787 that he had received £178 15s 0d from Mr Fellows for purchases at the sale of Sir Gregory Page's house at Blackheath, it is possible that these chimneypieces may have come from that source.

Chillington, Staffordshire

Prior to the alterations carried out by Soane for Thomas Giffard between 1785 and 1789, Chillington consisted of a modest block with an irregular range of domestic offices projecting at the rear. His first proposal was to incorporate a chapel in the centre of the house, but this idea was dropped and the space which this would have occupied was used for a saloon. The remodelling of the house consisted of lengthening the principal two-storey front from nine to eleven bays, the additions at either end being of three storeys. An Ionic portico of stone was set against this façade which remained in brick although Soane noted that it was intended to be stuccoed—a fact which probably accounts for the outline of the relieving arches being visible above the ground-floor windows. The principal masons employed were Bird and Brown, and the slater was Philip Kirkbride.

The saloon in the centre of the house has a shallow dome supporting a glazed lantern. Originally it was decorated with fluted plasterwork, but this has been changed. Soane's chimneypiece has also been replaced. The entrance vestibule, however, with its Ionic columns and antae, remains intact.

Designs were made for a separate chapel to be built in the grounds, but neither this, nor the bridge for which Soane also made drawings, were executed.

Lees Court, Kent (Plate 74)

All traces of the extensive alterations made to the interior of Lees by Soane for the Hon. Lewis Thomas Watson in 1786 were destroyed by fire early in the present century. They included the remodelling of the library and the reroofing of the house and chapel. Soane's stable block and the adjoining range of offices survive, both being built in brick with stone dressings. The entrance to the stable court is through an archway over which rises a clock turret in two stages. At the angles of the first stage stand giant 'oil jars', similar to those which Soane perched on the chimneystacks of his official residence at Chelsea Hospital.

74. LEES COURT, stables

75. RYSTON HALL, as remodelled by Soane.

Ryston Hall, Norfolk (Plate 75)

Among the English travellers with whom Soane became acquainted during his stay in Italy was Edward Roger Pratt of Ryston. Mr Pratt inherited the house in 1784 and two years later consulted Soane as to its remodelling. As originally built by his kinsman Sir Roger Pratt *circa* 1668, the house consisted of a rectangular block with a high basement. The centre portion was surmounted by a lantern, and the slightly lower ranges on either side had steeply pitched roofs and dormers. Soane visited Ryston on 9 October 1786, and drawings of his proposals were sent on 13 November. A rough sketch for roof-timbers is the only drawing to have survived in the Museum, but two plans and an elevation were included in Soane's published *Designs*, and there are accounts for the work carried out. The lower roofs of the house were raised to the same height as the centre block, and the whole reroofed with Westmorland slates. Small pavilions containing domestic quarters were added on either side of the main block, and linked to it by single-storey corridors. Fifty thousand bricks were made in a nearby field for the work at Ryston, which began on 15 January 1787.

Changes have been made to the exterior since Soane's time, but a good deal of his work remains. The principal staircase has a wrought-iron balustrade with decorative panels, and there are good chimneypieces in the main rooms.

Holwood House, Kent

One of the many kindnesses shown to Soane by his early patron, Thomas Pitt, was an introduction to the latter's cousin William, then prime minister. In 1786 William Pitt commissioned the architect to carry out a number of alterations at his country house, Holwood, beginning with the staircase hall and dining-room. A new drawing-room with bedroom above was built, a porch was added, and new rooms for servants were made over the nearby brew-house. Bricklaying and carpentry were carried out by Richard Holland's firm, and two of the new chimneypieces were obtained from the mason James Nelson.

Further work was carried out in 1795, including repairs to the roof and roughcasting the front of the house. In the following year Soane went to Holwood on 31 May to breakfast with Mr Pitt, when they 'settled about [the] new room'. This was a library, with rooms above. Subsequently it was agreed that another porch, or conservatory, should be added on the south-east, and that the whole of the exterior of the house should be whitewashed.

Although the prime minister toyed at one time with the idea of building a new house, he decided instead to make the existing building more symmetrical. In 1797 Soane was therefore asked to prepare further plans, based on a rough pencil sketch made by William Pitt himself. A number of alternatives were drawn out, and included a staircase hall which would have occupied the full height of the house. These schemes were not carried out for reasons explained by Soane in his *Public and Private Buildings* of 1832: 'Mr Pitt, having approved of this Design, added "the work must be carried on slowly, commensurate with my limited means", hence it followed that the Building was never completed.' The prime minister died in 1806, and the house was later burnt down, being rebuilt by Decimus Burton in 1823.

Blundeston House, Suffolk (Plate 76)

In Soane's *Plans* of 1788 this house is described as designed for Nathaniel Rix at Oulton. In fact it is in the village of Blundeston, within a short distance of the church, and is sometimes claimed to be the 'Rookery' described by Charles Dickens in *David Copperfield*.

It is a modest house consisting of a central block, three storeys high, which originally had lower projections to north and south. That on the south was, however, subsequently raised to provide an extra bedroom. Although Soane states that the brick walls were to be roughcast, this was not done, and the bricks were painted white. The slate roof has steeply projecting eaves on wooden brackets and the entrance front has a Doric porch with fluted columns of timber, probably contemporary with the building of the house although not shown in the surviving designs.

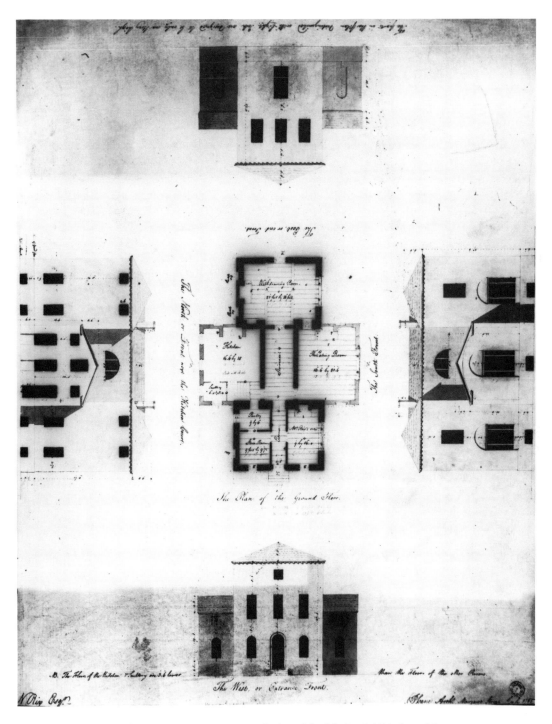

76. BLUNDESTON HOUSE, designed for Nathaniel Rix in 1786.

Fonthill, Wiltshire (Plates 77–8)

In 1787 Soane received a request from William Beckford to prepare a design for a picture gallery at Fonthill Splendens. That selected and put into execution replaced what had previously been bedrooms, and was lit by two shallow domes with glazed lanterns, set in the long barrel-vaulted ceiling of coffered plasterwork.

Some work was carried out in other rooms at old Fonthill, and there are references in the ledger to niche heads and chimneypieces for the Tapestry Room, designs for 'state beds', and a chimneypiece in the south-east parlour. Soane's designs for the beds were sent to his friend Edward Foxhall to be carried out. The house was demolished after James Wyatt had built Fonthill Abbey for Beckford.

Castle Hill, Devonshire

Although Soane first visited Castle Hill in April 1786, when plans were taken of the existing house, and proposals for alteration were supplied later in the year, it was apparently 1788 before anything was settled, and the architect made his second journey at the end of January, following which drawings were made for the library, 'White Room', and rooms in the south wing. There were also drawings for the domestic offices, working details being sent to a local foreman, Sharland, to be carried out. Soane also sent in May that year a 'fair drawing of the library table', while 'Several drawings for the alterations and improvements of the mansion house and offices' were supplied to Lord Fortescue in July 1790, but a single elevation and four plans are all that remain in the Museum. Lord Fortescue apparently paid for the building work himself, but Soane received his commission and expenses amounting to £238.6.3½ from which it is evident that the alterations were fairly extensive. There were additions by Edward Blore in 1843, and the central block of the house was burnt and rebuilt in 1934.

Wardour Castle, Wiltshire, the Chapel

As originally designed by James Paine in 1776, the Chapel in the west wing of Wardour Castle was quite small. In 1788 Lord Arundell wished to enlarge it, and for this purpose obtained alternative schemes from Soane since Paine had by now retired to France. Soane visited Wardour in the spring of that year, submitting drawings in April, and setting out the foundations in September. The addition comprised a new domed chancel flanked by apsidal transepts, in each of which was a small gallery supported on scagliola columns. Paine's Corinthian order and enriched frieze were continued in the new work, and the wall behind the altar, as well as the dome and soffits of the arches, was decorated with plasterwork. The building is in a good state of preservation.

77. FONTHILL, Soane's section through the new gallery.

78. FONTHILL,
chimneypiece design.

Bentley Priory, Middlesex (Plates 79–83)

Extensive Victorian rebuilding and two post-war fires have eliminated much of the work which Soane carried out at Bentley Priory for the Hon. John James Hamilton, later 1st Marquis of Abercorn, between 1788 and 1801. In plan, however, the extensions made by Soane to a small mid-eighteenth-century house are still easily definable, particularly on the east side, where he first built a library, breakfast-room and circular 'tribune' for the display of pictures and sculpture. To these were added, a few years later, a new

79. BENTLEY PRIORY,
rear elevation as enlarged.

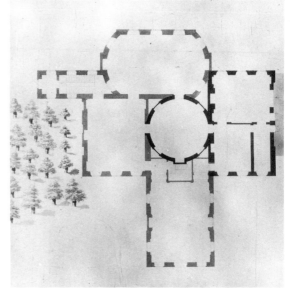

80. BENTLEY PRIORY,
plan showing the
first extensions.

81. BENTLEY PRIORY, the new entrance.

82. BENTLEY PRIORY,
interior of the hall.

83. BENTLEY PRIORY,
the music-room,
now demolished.

drawing-room, dining-room and music-room. The latter, with its frieze of aegicranes and an organ placed between Ionic columns at the southern end of the room, has long since disappeared, although under the lawn where it stood there is still a cellar of corresponding dimensions.

The most interesting survival at Bentley is the Greek Doric entrance vestibule which Soane built as a projection from the north front in 1798. Originally decorated with marbling to resemble Sienna, and lit by windows filled with bands of coloured glass, it was heated by a stove in the form of the upper part of a suit of armour complete with helmet. The hinged breast-plate opened to reveal a fire, and smoke was carried off by a concealed flue at the back. Although it does not survive, it is recorded in various views of the vestibule and there is an account for its construction.

A thatched lodge, which had a flattened, rusticated, stone arch set in each of its four flint walls, was built in the grounds, also a hexagonal dairy and a greenhouse, but these were probably removed when the property was bought by Sir John Kelk, B! in the middle of the nineteenth century. Bentley Priory has for many years been in occupation by the Royal Air Force.

Piercefield, Gwent (Plate 84)

The Piercefield estate was bought by George Smith in 1784. In the following year he asked Soane to prepare designs for a new house which would incorporate part of an earlier building at the rear, but only the rejected drawings survive in the Museum. There was some delay before work began on the chosen design the façade of which was almost identical with that employed at Shotesham, and illustrated in Soane's *Plans* of 1788, but whereas the latter was built in brick with stone dressings, Piercefield was faced entirely with stone. The clerk of the works was John Pullinger who wrote to Soane on 14 January 1793 that the roof was ready for the slater. By then, however, George Smith had become involved in financial difficulties and the property was put up for sale at Christie's in London in December of that year when the catalogue described the house as 'a capital new-built mansion . . . designed by Mr Soane'. It was bought by Colonel (later Sir Mark) Wood who later employed Joseph Bonomi to add a saloon and 'elegant winding staircase'. The house was sold in 1923 to the Chepstow Race Club, and has been derelict for many years.

Pembroke Lodge, Richmond

The Countess of Pembroke who employed Soane on alterations to this house, and later to her house in Grosvenor Square, was Elizabeth wife of the 10th earl. As a military man spending much of his time with his regiment, he seems to have left her in control of the work at the 'cottage', as it is described, in Richmond Park to which Soane was summoned in 1788, and for which he made designs for additions. The plan and exterior of the building still correspond fairly closely to the drawings in the Museum, but the interior is now of little interest since the trellis decoration of what later became the dining-room has entirely disappeared, as has his decoration of the other principal rooms.

84. PIERCEFIELD, the façade in ruins, 1958.

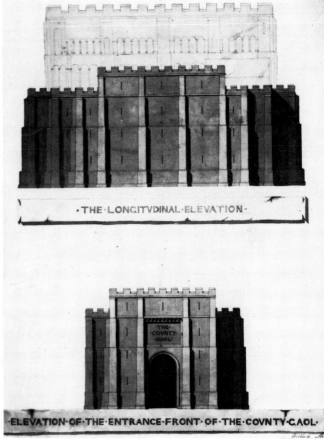

85. NORWICH GAOL, Soane's design for additions.

Norwich Castle Gaol, Norfolk (Plate 85)

In 1789, largely through the influence of Robert Fellowes of Shotesham, Soane was asked by the Norfolk Magistrates to alter the Castle Gaol. A copy of John Howard's book, *The State of the Prisons* (1780), is in Soane's library, and the architect's particular attention to the planning, ventilation and sanitation in his designs may be taken to reflect Howard's recommendations. Within the castle walls Soane formed new felons' cells over an arcaded basement, with a central airing court. Accommodation for male and female debtors, with a chapel and offices, was provided in an embattled addition to the east of the keep.

The appearance of the new building was severely criticised by the elder William Wilkins in a paper read to the Society of Antiquaries in 1795. Soane comments on this criticism in his *Memoirs*, defending his designs, and referring to Wilkins as 'an able stuccatore of Norwich', from which it would seem that the latter was related to James Wilkins, a plasterer employed by Soane for some of his early houses in the area. Thirty years later the younger William Wilkins removed all traces of Soane's work at the castle.

86. GUNTHORPE HALL, before late Victorian refacing.

Gunthorpe Hall, Norfolk (Plate 86)

Soane's designs were made for Charles Collyer, whom he had met in Italy. The first was dated 16 February 1789 but it was followed in June of that year by two more, one in the style adopted for Shotesham, with a pilastered façade, and the other with the windows of both floors set in arched recesses running the whole height of the entrance façade. All three were set aside in favour of a very simple design for a two-storey three-window block, the ground-floor windows having round heads in arched recesses, and the central entrance having a tetrastyle Doric porch. Work was in hand before the end of July 1790 when an earlier building was demolished. Foundations were dug in August, and although the workmen had to break off for four days in September to give a hand with the harvest, the framing of the roof was nearing completion in early October. It was duly covered with what are described in the accounts as 'glazed tiles'.

Mid-nineteenth-century photographs of the house correspond in almost every detail with Soane's drawings in the Museum and provide a valuable record as the whole was encased in Victorian brickwork with stone dressings *circa* 1880, when bow windows were built out on the entrance front, and the portico removed.

Sydney Lodge, Hamble, Hampshire (Plate 87)

Sydney Lodge was built between 1789 and 1798 for the Hon. Mrs Yorke, stepmother of Soane's client Philip Yorke, 3rd Earl of Hardwicke. Its north and west walls are of Beaulieu stock bricks, but on the south and east it is faced with matching mathematical tiles which were considered a better protection against driving rain. The entrance front, on the west, has a segmental Doric porch of stone from which a small vestibule leads

87. SYDNEY LODGE, entrance façade.

to an oval hall, top-lit, and with a cantilevered staircase balustraded with wrought iron. The walls of the hall are decorated with plaster swags, and the principal doorway, on the axis of the entrance, has fluted pilasters. It leads to the drawing-room, with windows occupying the semicircular bay on the east. The adjoining library has bookcases set in segmental-headed recesses, and a ceiling in the form of a depressed cross-vault. There are Soane chimneypieces in the principal rooms of the house which is well maintained by the Hawker Aircraft Company.

Tawstock Court, Devonshire

Lysons' *Magna Britannia* (Vol. VI, 1822) says of Tawstock that it was 'nearly burnt down in 1787' and 'soon afterwards rebuilt from a design of Sir Bourchier Wrey's'. A number of details for the house were, however, provided by Soane whose first visit there was made in February 1789. On a second visit in the following April he measured carpentry already carried out by a local man—no doubt the 'Rough Carpenter's Work' for which a copy of an agreement between Sir Bourchier and Edward Boyce is preserved in the Museum. On this occasion Soane made all the necessary drawings for 'finishing the several works . . . viz. the Chamber Floor, the Principal Floor, the Great Staircase, the Galleries, the Frontispiece, etc.' He subsequently supervised the execution of these designs, on which his commission amounted to £100 plus expenses for travelling, and his clerk of the works, Piper, presumably a local man.

Drawings for two gothic porches and some details for the staircase hall and internal doorcases survive, one of the former corresponding to an existing entrance at Tawstock which was moved from the east side of the house to the south in the nineteenth century.

88. SIMONDS BREWERY, as designed by Soane.

89. SIMONDS BREWERY, shortly before destruction.

90. CHILTON LODGE, as designed by Soane.

Simonds Brewery, Reading, Berkshire (Plates 88–9)

Soane's designs for a new brewery and residence in Bridge Street were prepared for William Blackall Simonds in December 1789. The house was built of brick, four giant Ionic pilasters with stone capitals adorning the main façade. Over the principal entrance was a stone tablet with hops and leaves supplied by Soane's friend Edward Foxhall. Hop leaves also featured in the wallpapers for the principal rooms, patterns being sent to Mr Simonds in 1792. The house was completed in 1794, and the brew-house was built in 1796. In 1803 Soane supplied further designs for offices which were carried out, but of these and his other buildings nothing now remains.

Chilton Lodge, Berkshire (Plate 90)

Plans and elevations of this house were included in Soane's *Cottages and Villas* of 1793. In the caption he describes it as 'now building for William Morland Esq.', and he goes on to explain that 'as most of the materials were furnished from the buildings pulled down, the adoption of certain forms did not always depend on the wish of the architect, particularly in the portico', a tetrastyle Doric composition which stood uncomfortably against the semicircular bay which was the central feature of Soane's original design. The house had a short life, being pulled down in 1800 to make way for a house designed by William Pilkington for a new owner of the property.

91. BUCKINGHAM HOUSE, Pall Mall.

Buckingham House, Pall Mall, London (Plates 91–3)

George Nugent-Temple-Grenville, 1st Marquis of Buckingham, employed Soane on the remodelling of two early eighteenth-century houses to form Buckingham House in 1790. This involved taking out the party wall so that the wells of the two previous staircases provided space for a spectacular approach from ground to first floor. Externally, the new house was given a seven-window three-storey façade of Portland stone, rusticated on the ground floor and carrying a stone balustrade at roof level with the Buckingham coat of arms in Coade stone placed as a central feature.

Between 1790 and 1793 numerous plans were prepared for the principal reception rooms, and the oval vestibule which led from the entrance to the staircase hall. In 1813 a library was made out of the dining-room, the latter being moved to what had hitherto been a ground-floor drawing-room. The new staircase in its oval well rose by a short single flight before dividing and turning to reach the first floor where, at either end, eight Ionic columns supported an entablature which continued round the opening. At second-floor level an iron balustrade guarded open corridors on the two long walls while the solid apsidal ends were each set with Coade stone caryatids, corresponding in position

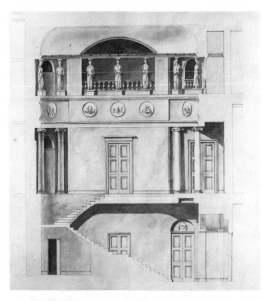

92. BUCKINGHAM HOUSE,
section of staircase hall.

93. BUCKINGHAM HOUSE,
upper stages of hall.

to the columns on the floor below. Above these rose the deep cove of the ceiling which carried an oval lantern. The walls of this staircase well were painted blue, and the columns were painted to resemble Sienna marble. Abstract Book No. 2 shows that the cost of carrying out Soane's alterations to Buckingham House came to a little over £10,944.0.0.

Early in the present century Buckingham House formed part of the old War Office building, but it was later demolished to make way for the Royal Automobile Club's building.

Norwich, Surrey Street, Mr Patteson's house, now Norwich Union Fire Office
(Plates 94–5)

John Patteson was another of the good friends whom Soane had made in Rome and for whom he was subsequently to make considerable additions to the family house in Norwich. These included new kitchens with a bedroom, dressing-room and nursery above, which were to form a wing behind a screen wall to the south-west. He also refurbished the first-floor drawing-rooms, adding marble chimneypieces for one of which his original design survives in the Museum. Other drawings include details for the friezes in the bedroom, nursery and dressing-room, the latter consisting of a row of classical heads. None of this plasterwork survives, however, and these rooms have been adapted for offices.

94, 95. NORWICH, John Patteson's house in Surrey Street, chimneypieces designed by Soane.

96. WIMPOLE HALL, drawing-room.

Wimpole Hall, Cambridgeshire (Plates 96–100)

When the Hon. Philip Yorke succeeded his uncle as 3rd Earl of Hardwicke in 1790, and inherited the family seat at Wimpole, he at once commissioned Soane to make plans for alterations to the interior of the existing house. The principal requirements were an additional drawing-room, book-room and staircase, all of which were in hand during the following year. The drawing-room was contrived behind and between existing rooms

97. (*left*) WIMPOLE HALL, design for drawing-room. *Page 147*.
98. (*right*) WIMPOLE HALL, the *castello d'aqua*.

99. WIMPOLE HALL, the ante-library, designed by Soane.

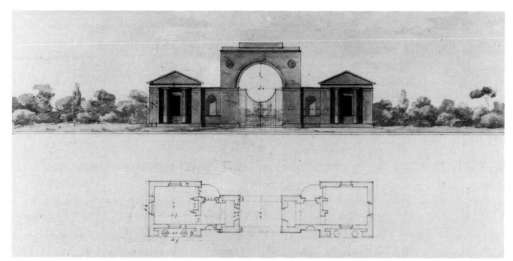

100. WIMPOLE HALL, lodges and entrance.

on the north side of the house. To solve the problem of lighting the T-shaped room which emerged, Soane set a toplit dome over the inner central space, this latter being flanked by semicircular apses under semi-domes. To the north extended a barrel-vaulted 'limb' lit by a pair of windows in its external wall.

The 'book room', which serves as an ante-room to a gallery leading to the original library which once housed the Harleian collection, differs slightly in execution from the rough drawings preserved in the Museum. Soane's first suggestion shows only one arch spanning the room whereas the executed scheme incorporated three segmental arches which spring from narrow, projecting piers faced with bookcases on either side of the room.

Between 1791 and 1794 Soane supplied Lord Hardwicke with designs for cottages, entrance lodges and a gateway, a *castello d'aqua*, an ice-house and farm buildings. Of the three estate cottages only one can be identified with certainty. This is now called French House on the Arrington Road, but in the accounts it appears as 'Mud Cottage' from its construction in *pisé*. Whether it acquired its subsequent name from this Gallic association, or whether it came from the local builder, Samuel French, who worked on it, is not explained. The two other cottages which were built were apparently later remodelled and cannot be identified among the number of 'picturesque' brick cottages added in the 1860s. The entrance gateway and lodges were almost identical with those built for Tyringham in the same decade, but they were demolished in the nineteenth century and replaced with the present gates of ornamental ironwork. The *castello d'aqua* also disappeared, but not before it had been described by the authoress Mary Berry in her *Journal* for 1810 where she noted that work had begun on 'cutting down the trees, and clearing away about the reservoir, the only building in real good taste about this place. It is like a Roman Sepulchre, and will look well when no longer choked up with trees—two beautiful yews behind and a fine cedar in front excepted.'

Baronscourt, Co. Tyrone, Ireland (Plates 101–2)

In 1789 Soane's client, the Hon. John James Hamilton of Bentley Priory, succeeded his uncle as 9th Earl of Abercorn, and inherited Baronscourt for which, two years later, he was to ask Soane to make designs for alterations. The existing house, built by George Steuart a decade earlier, consisted of a rectangular block with a Doric portico on its south side and projecting service wings.

Soane's first proposals were submitted in 1791 but later revised. As carried out from the following November onwards, the additions included a new portico on the north from which ran curved screen walls reaching to the extremities of the existing service wings, and thus masking their uninteresting elevations. The screens also accommodated a number of small rooms for the housekeeper and steward, a 'doctor's shop', and three schoolrooms. Within the main body of the house, the walls between the drawing-room, dining-room and saloon on the south were knocked down to form one long gallery. The staircase was moved to another position and its site used for a billiard room, and a new dining-room was formed in the west wing. Soane, who had spent some twenty-three days in visiting Baronscourt in the late spring of 1791, arranged that the work should be supervised by his assistant Robert Woodgate, who was to receive £100 a year plus his travelling expenses. The latter found Ireland so congenial that he decided to stay

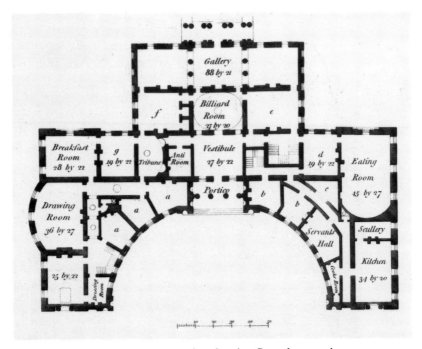

101. BARONSCOURT, plan showing Soane's extensions.

102. BARONSCOURT, the new entrance.

on after the work was completed and wrote to tell Soane of his decision. Soane accepted the loss of a useful assistant with good grace, advising him to 'weigh well before you determine, and having once made up your mind, act steadily and be assured success will attend you'. In fact Woodgate's presence of mind helped to save the wings of the house when fire broke out and gutted much of the main block in December 1796. Following his employment on repairs here he set up his own architectural practice and, meeting with success, later moved to Dublin.

Baronscourt was considerably altered in the early 1830s by William Vitruvius Morrison and there are now only traces of Soane's work remaining, notably in the entrance hall and the portico which was altered to form a *porte-cochère*.

The Bank of England, London, work from 1791 onwards (Plates 103–28)

The magnitude and complexity of Soane's work at the Bank can be gauged from the two chests of accounts, fourteen bill books, a great deal of correspondence and over six hundred drawings which are preserved in the Museum. This great task occupied forty-five years of his life, and while the resultant building did not entirely escape contemporary criticism, it was generally acclaimed, both by his own and later generations, as a master-

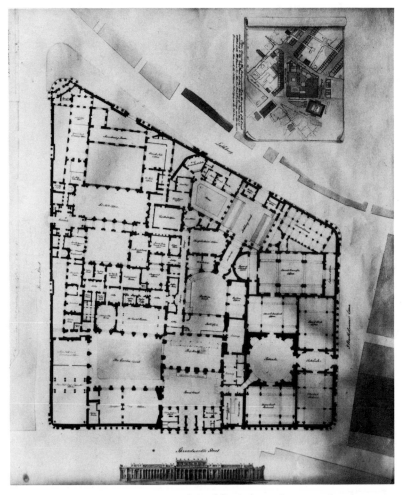

103. BANK OF ENGLAND, plan of Soane's work as completed.

piece. Few English architects at that time were offered so wide a scope for expressing their ingenuity, yet Soane never lost sight of the purposes which the halls and offices were to serve. With meticulous attention to construction and detail he achieved for this national institution a setting which was unique, dignified and practical.

Soane's appointment as architect and surveyor to the Bank in succession to Sir Robert Taylor was made on 16 October 1788. The nucleus of the building for which he then assumed responsibility consisted of the house in Threadneedle Street originally built for George Sampson *circa* 1732, and described by Soane as in 'a grand style of Palladian simplicity'. To this Taylor had added single-storey wings on either side of the forecourt, a Rotunda and Stock Offices, a Court Room suite and a library. These buildings occupied about two-thirds of an island site of irregular shape, bounded by Threadneedle Street on the south, Lothbury on the north, Bartholomew Lane on the east and Princes Street

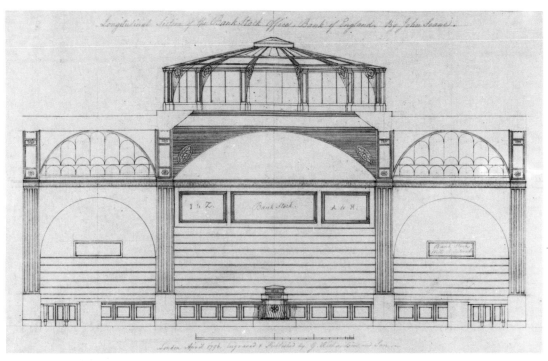

104. BANK OF ENGLAND, section through the Bank Stock Office, 1792.

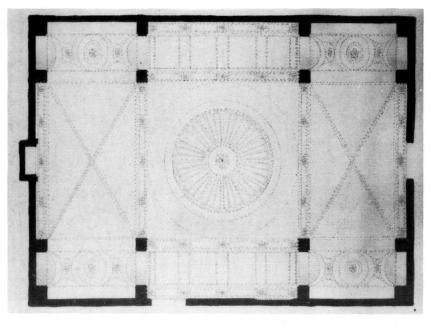

105. BANK OF ENGLAND, Bank Stock Office plan showing dome and vaults.

106. BANK OF ENGLAND,
Bank Stock Office. *Page 156.*

107. BANK OF ENGLAND,
Bank Stock Office,
detail of pendentive. *Page 156.*

108. BANK OF ENGLAND, Rotunda, as rebuilt by Soane, 1794. *Page 152.*

109. BANK OF ENGLAND,
Soane's design
for the Rotunda. *Page 152.*

110. BANK OF ENGLAND, Consols Office, first design, 1797.

on the west. During the next ten years, the remaining third, comprising the Haines Estate on the north-west, and some small houses along Lothbury and Bartholomew Lane, was acquired by the Bank, so that the whole area was ultimately available for its extensions.

The first major work after Soane's appointment was the rebuilding of the Bank Stock Office, initial drawings for which were made at the end of 1791. As carried out in 1792, it was to be one of the most important expressions of the 'Soane style', and became the prototype not only for four other banking halls but, on reduced scales, for many rooms elsewhere in his works. Although the idea of a vaulted hall of three compartments with 'aisles' was present from the outset, the arrangement underwent a number of changes as Soane proceeded with his drawings, the final version of 1792 having a large central space top-lit by a twelve-sided lantern, while the smaller end bays were lit by glazed lunettes over their side arches. To render the building as fireproof as possible, the Stock Office was built of brick, and vaulted with hollow earthenware cones to lighten the weight of the superstructure. A similar design was used for the Four and Five Per Cent, or Old Shutting, Office begun in 1794; also for the Consols Office of 1797, and the much later Colonial and Dividend Offices of 1818.

The first section of the screen wall, which was eventually to encircle the Bank, was

111. BANK OF ENGLAND, Consols Office, in course of construction.

begun in 1795. For this Soane used an order deriving from the Temple of Vesta at Tivoli—a monument which he much admired, and of which he had made measured drawings when in Italy (Plate 9). The acquisition of the Haines Estate made it possible for the wall to be continued round the north-west corner of the site, where the acute angle at the junction of Princes Street and Lothbury provided an opportunity for an imposing feature. A large folder of drawings devoted entirely to designs for this shows the variety of ideas which passed through Soane's mind in 1804 and 1805. His final solution was to round off the corner with what is virtually a segment of the peristyle of a circular temple—in other words, a composition based on the Temple of Vesta at Tivoli.

The Tivoli order also appears in Soane's treatment of the Lothbury Court where it is used for an open colonnade on the west. The approach from here to the inner Bullion Court is, however, treated as a Roman arch, its Corinthian order breaking forward and supporting, over the entablature, four figures representing the continents, modelled by Coade and Sealy and supplied in August 1801 at a cost of £88.10. each.

Routine repairs at the Bank were continuous, and Soane was also responsible for supervising the furnishing of the rooms and offices, as well as the maintenance of Garden

112. BANK OF ENGLAND, Lothbury façade, east end. *Page 157*.

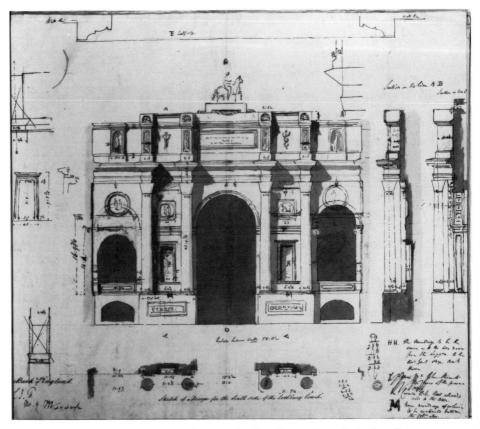

113. BANK OF ENGLAND, archway to Bullion Court, Soane's design. *Page 157*.

114. BANK OF ENGLAND, archway as built. *Page 157*.

115. BANK OF ENGLAND,
Lothbury Court. *Page 157.*

116. BANK OF ENGLAND,
loggia to
Waiting Room Court.

117. BANK OF ENGLAND,
Princes Street entrance,
vestibule. *Page 157*.

118. BANK OF ENGLAND,
Princes Street entrance,
vestibule. *Page 157*.

119. BANK OF ENGLAND, £5 Note Office. *Page 168*.

120. BANK OF ENGLAND, Soane's final design for the Tivoli Corner. *Page 157*.

121. BANK OF ENGLAND, the Tivoli Corner as built. *Page 157*.

122. BANK OF ENGLAND,
passage to Rotunda. *Page 152.*

123. BANK OF ENGLAND,
Old Dividend Office.
Page 156.

124. BANK OF ENGLAND,
Colonial Office. *Page 156.*

125. BANK OF ENGLAND,
Colonial Office. *Page 156.*

126. BANK OF ENGLAND, Views in various parts, elaborated water-colour drawing.

127. BANK OF ENGLAND, Threadneedle Street front. *Page 152.*

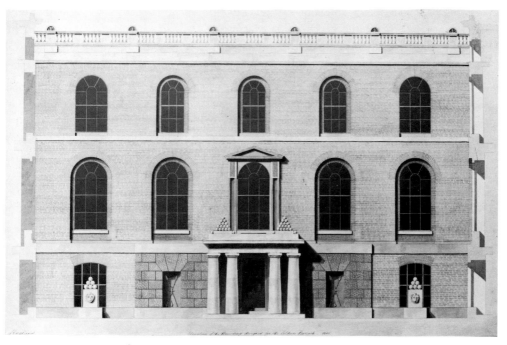

128. BANK OF ENGLAND, Barrack Building. *Page 168.*

Court which at the appropriate times of year was filled with an assortment of plants and shrubs including azaleas, china roses, hydrangeas and lilac. Gas lighting was introduced in 1816 when, in July, the Gas Light and Coke Company were paid for fitting up sixteen lamps with cocks and burners.

Soane's work at the Bank can briefly be summarised as follows:

1791–1800   Bank Stock Office, first design November 1791, built 1792. Accounts Office and Lobby, 1793–4. Four and Five Per Cent (later Old Shutting) Office, 1794. Rotunda, 1794–5. Screen wall, first section to Lothbury, 1795. Bullion Court, north wall remodelled, 1796. Lothbury Court, with Residence Court adjoining on west, 1797. Consols Office, 1797. Library, 1798.

1800–18   Development of north-west angle, with Printing House Court, 1801–5. Extension of screen wall, 1803. Waiting Room Courtyard and Loggia, 1804–5. 'Tivoli Corner', 1805. Barrack Building, 1805–6. Accountants' Room (later £5 Note Office and finally Public Drawing Office) with four small Note Offices and waiting rooms, 1805. New suite for governor and deputy governor, 1805. Discount Office, 1805. Bullion Court, east and west walls remodelled, 1806–7, south wall, 1810. Vestibule leading to Rotunda from Front Court, 1815. Enlargement of Treasury, 1815.

1818–33   Rebuilding of old offices in south-east angle, i.e. Four Per Cent Office (later Three and a Half Per Cent Consols Transfer Office and finally Old Dividend Office) 1818. Five Per Cent Office (later Warrant Office and finally Colonial Office) 1818. Rebuilding of older ranges of external wall (Threadneedle Street façade, and southern ends of Princes Street and Bartholomew Lane) 1823–6. Dome of Rotunda re-covered in lead, and lantern increased in height, 1830. Five Pound Note Office rearranged as Drawing Hall, 1830.

In January 1826, The Court of Directors appointed a committee to consider 'how far it may be practicable to establish Branch Banks'. As a result of this committee's deliberations, and following consultation with the prime minister and chancellor of the exchequer, the directors ordered that a plan should be drawn up for the establishment of branches. The list of places considered suitable included Leeds, Birmingham, Gloucester, Liverpool and Manchester. In May 1826, the 'respectable gentry' of Swansea put in a successful plea for a branch to be opened there, and later on it was decided to add to the list Newcastle, Hull, Bristol, Exeter and Norwich. For the surveying of suitable buildings, and their alteration to provide not only business accommodation but a residence for the agent or sub-agent, Soane assumed responsibility. He was, however, now in his seventies, and was largely assisted in the negotiations and plans by George Bailey.

The Middle Period 1792–1820

Tyringham House, Buckinghamshire (Plates 129–37)

Writing about Tyringham in his *Memoirs*, Soane says 'this villa, with its numerous offices, greenhouses, hothouses, and extensive stabling, the great bridge, and the lodge, were completed and occupied in the year 1797, after having engaged a large portion of six of the most happy years of my life.' His client was William Mackworth Praed, a banker of Fleet Street, who inherited the Tyringham property through his wife. The first mention of the old house in Soane's notebooks comes in August 1792, when he visited it in company with the Marquis of Buckingham. Suggestions were made for remodelling, but Mr Praed eventually decided to build a new house. This was to be rectangular in plan, with shallow segmental bows on the south-east and north-west fronts. That on the south-east has an Ionic order supporting an entablature which continues round the house. Both bays rise to an attic storey. The external masonry is rusticated to first-floor level, and between the ground and first-floor windows are long panels of incised Greek fret.

129. TYRINGHAM, design for the entrance front.

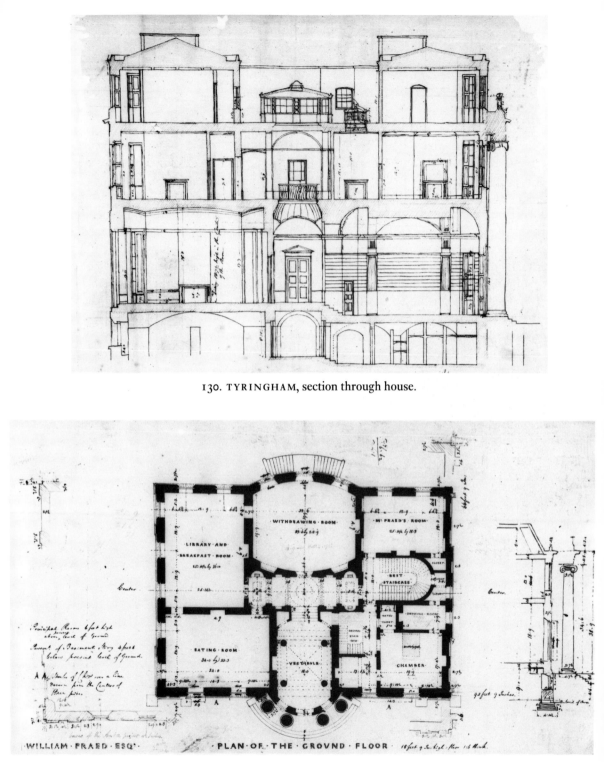

130. TYRINGHAM, section through house.

131. TYRINGHAM, Soane's plan.

132. TYRINGHAM. The dome
was a later addition.

133. TYRINGHAM, hall,
as built by Soane; now
destroyed.

134. TYRINGHAM, gateway and lodges.

135. TYRINGHAM, the bridge.

136. TYRINGHAM, proposal for church, unexecuted.

137. TYRINGHAM,
interior for
the proposed church.

The entrance originally led to a vestibule and an inner hall on the final details of which Soane spent much time and thought. The former had walls plastered to simulate rusticated masonry. At the angles were set Greek Doric columns, with stopped flutes, carrying an entablature from which sprang a groined vault. Five steps led up to the inner hall or 'tribune', consisting of a rectangular central space the ribbed dome of which had a wide circular opening to the floor above. At first-floor level this was protected by an iron railing, and light was admitted to both floors by a glazed lantern in the roof. This tribune was to be the prototype of other Soane works, notably the National Debt Redemption Office, and the hall at Wotton.

The principal ground-floor rooms were entirely redecorated in the early years of the present century, but some marble chimneypieces of Soane's design were removed to the first-floor rooms, where his hand can also be detected in such details as doorcases, a small vaulted lobby, and a glazed lantern which retains a few panes of coloured glass.

The stables designed by Soane have survived, as has the bridge carrying the drive to the house, and the entrance gateway with its flanking lodges.

No. 12 Lincoln's Inn Fields, London (Plates 27–8)

Up to 1792 Soane had not owned a house of his own, but in that year, with his practice flourishing, and having recently benefited under the will of his wife's uncle, he felt justified in acquiring a property. Lincoln's Inn Fields offered a convenient locality, being midway between Soane's various works in the City and in Westminster. No. 12 became available at this time, and on 27 May he went to Richmond to negotiate with the owner, when the price of two thousand guineas was agreed. His first intention was to alter the existing house but he then decided to rebuild.

As first designed the new house was of three bays and three storeys, but an extra floor was added in the 1820s. It was built of white brick with Portland stone dressings, the bricklaying being carried out by Richard Holland's firm. The rest of the principal craftsmen—James Nelson, mason, Thomas Martyr, carpenter, and the leadworker Ramelly—were already working for Soane at the Bank of England. The curious angle of the party wall between Nos. 12 and 13—due to an ancient boundary between two fields—accounts for the irregular plan of both houses, the rear of No. 12 being considerably narrower than its front. It has an entrance hall plastered in imitation of rusticated masonry. This leads to the cantilevered staircase with its simple iron balustrade of the same serpentine pattern as that to the external balcony overlooking the Fields on the first floor. There are handsome marble chimneypieces in the principal rooms but the decoration is extremely restrained with the exception of the ceiling in the Old Breakfast Room which is painted with trelliswork entwined with flowers for which the painter John Crace was responsible. In recent years it has been recovered from beneath sixteen coats of white paint, applied after the house had been let for office purposes.

The house took eighteen months to complete, and on 18 January 1794 Soane and his wife and sons slept in it for the first time. From the turn of the century Soane's collection of books, paintings and sculpture was growing rapidly, as was his office, and space became a problem. In the summer of 1808 the possibility of an extension being built on ground behind No. 13 was discussed with Soane's neighbour George Booth Tyndale, and there are three sheets of sketches dated 11 June of that year which show proposals for a top-lit 'plaister room' and adjoining galleries over 'catacombs' in the basement. Later in this month the architect and his wife dined at No. 13 when Tyndale consented to the scheme. Thus Soane was able to build on the site of what is now the 'Dome' of the Museum.

In 1812 Soane and Tyndale, under a previous agreement, exchanged houses, and the architect at once set about rebuilding No. 13 (see page 203).

Winchester, Hampshire, The Revd Mr Richards's Academy in Hyde Close
(Plates 138–9)

The small brick building, which subsequently became a Salvation Army headquarters and then a drill hall for the Hampshire Carabineers, was originally designed by Soane in 1795 for Mr Richards, a schoolmaster of some distinction who at one time had numbered Lord Liverpool and George Canning among his pupils. A new road later deprived the building of its original entrance lobby containing a staircase to a small gallery overlooking the schoolroom, and an entrance was then made through one of the window openings on the east side. Apart from this, the structure remains much as Soane designed it.

138. WINCHESTER, Mr Richards' Academy in Hyde Close.   139. WINCHESTER, Mr Richards' Academy.

140. CUMBERLAND GATE, Hyde Park.

Cumberland Gate, Hyde Park, London (Plate 140)

This north-east entrance to Hyde Park stood on the site now occupied by Marble Arch. The gate, with its adjoining lodge, was designed by Soane in 1797 while he was deputy surveyor of Woods and Forests. It consisted of a central archway of brick with stone imposts and a brick cornice, flanked by lower arches and joined to them by halberd-headed iron railings of similar pattern to those forming the gates. Recumbent consoles supporting lamp-holders topped the side arches, while the central arch carried the royal arms. The adjacent keeper's lodge was of brick with flint pilasters and a three-bay loggia linked it to the gateway. Its central chimneystack was surmounted by two smoke-pots disguised as oil jars.

Bagshot Park, Surrey (Plate 141)

Similar in composition and materials to the Cumberland Gate, Hyde Park, was Soane's design for an entrance to Bagshot, also carried out in his capacity as deputy surveyor of Woods and Forests, in 1798. Bagshot was a hunting box occupied at this time by the Duke of Clarence, later William IV. In the same year he was consulted as to alterations

141. BAGSHOT LODGE, the entrance gateway and lodges.

in the domestic quarters of the house, and on 5 March 1799 noted that he had met the prince who 'agreed that the front [of the house] should be made regular, and that he would pay £300 towards the expence, in addition to £330 he had before agreed'. In April they also 'settled [the] arcade from offices to house'. There are no drawings in the Museum for the work on the house, but there are several for the entrance and its two flanking lodges which were demolished when the property was acquired by the 1st Duke of Connaught.

Betchworth Castle, Surrey (Plates 142–4)

Only a few stones remain of the mansion at Betchworth which Soane altered extensively for Henry Peters in 1799. From the drawings the alterations apparently included the remodelling of the drawing-room, and the building out of a new breakfast-room and 'Mrs Peters Room'. The dairy in Soane's 'primitive' style was also demolished, but there are drawings for it in the Museum while a water-colour, painted a few years after it was built, is in a private collection. Soane designed the stable block about half a mile to the north of the site of the mansion. Ranged round three sides of a courtyard, the building has a two-storey central feature, and two wings terminating in pavilions with

142. BETCHWORTH CASTLE,
a chimneypiece design.

143. BETCHWORTH CASTLE, the stables, 1798–9.

144. BETCHWORTH CASTLE, the dairy.

widely projecting eaves. Flint with brick banding is used both for the walls and for the pilasters which divide the bays. The stables have now been converted into small residences.

Aynho Park, Northamptonshire (Plates 145–8)

The house to which Soane was asked to make additions in 1798 consisted of a Jacobean core, largely remodelled by Edward Marshall after the Restoration, with further work carried out in the early eighteenth century, when Thomas Archer is likely to have been the architect employed.

Soane's client, Richard Cartwright, wanted a new library, dining-room and drawing-room, with bedrooms above. The architect therefore extended the house on the west by a wing corresponding to the existing orangery on the east, which was raised to two storeys by an additional floor. The balustrading which had hitherto surmounted the central block of the north and south fronts was removed and replaced by pediments. Soane was also responsible for the pair of 'triumphal arches' which were built as a link between the house and two previously unattached service and stable blocks on either side of the entrance forecourt. For these arches his sketches survive, and on one of them the orders are marked 'old column, base and capital' although there is no indication as to their previous use or situation.

145. AYNHO, south front, with Soane's extensions.

146. (*left*) AYNHO, north front, with Soane's archway on the east.

147. (*right*) AYNHO, façade to the Soane library.

148. AYNHO, the library.

The reception rooms added by Soane remain largely as he designed them, as does the top-lit west staircase of stone with a simple iron balustrade. The elaborate decoration proposed for another staircase, and for a small vestibule, was, however, considerably modified in execution.

Pitzhanger Manor, Ealing, Middlesex (Plates 32–7)

In purchasing and rebuilding Pitzhanger Manor, Soane's particular wish was that it might stimulate an interest in architecture in his two sons, and ultimately provide a home for the elder when he came of age. It was a house which he had known since his early days in George Dance's office when the latter was adding a wing to it. In 1800 Soane purchased the house with twenty-eight acres of land. He retained the rooms designed by Dance, which he considered to be in 'exquisite taste', pulled down the older building, and in its place erected a villa of unique design. As built, it reflected many of the elements which he was then using at the Bank of England: the Roman triumphal arch, for instance, which was to be adopted for the frontispiece of the villa, had already appeared on the south side of the Lothbury Court, although the order at Ealing was Ionic instead of Corinthian, and caryatids in Coade stone took the place of the four statues of the Continents surmounting the Bank arch. The north façade of the house is a solid version of the open loggia which formed one side of the Waiting Room Court; while inside the house, the hall, with its rusticated walls and coffered archways, echoes the Court Room corridor, and the plaster medallions of Thomas Banks's 'Morning' and 'Evening' (modelled on reliefs from the Arch of Constantine) were copies of those in the Lothbury Court. The curving drive to the house is not, however, entered through a strictly classical archway, but through one conceived in Soane's 'primitivist' style, pairs of flint pilasters being set against a brickwork arch, and carrying, over a retracted frieze, cappings in the form of stone sarcophagus lids. Another rustic feature is the small bridge which crosses a stream in the grounds.

The principal new rooms in the villa were the front and back parlours, the former having a shallow domed ceiling resting on four piers against which were set Egyptian-type caryatids, supplied by Coade and Sealy, and painted in copper-bronze. The walls had panels of painted decoration deriving from a set of hand-coloured engravings based on wall paintings found in the Villa Negroni in Rome. These engravings by Angelo Campanella, were published in the late 1770s and Soane acquired two sets. Double doors in the west wall led to the back parlour or library where the ceiling was a shallow groined vault painted with trelliswork and flowers, almost identical with the breakfast-room at No. 12 Lincoln's Inn Fields. The painter was almost certainly John Crace, who was responsible for decorative painting elsewhere in the house. Both these parlours were provided with niches and shelves intended for the books, antique urns and other treasures which Soane was then collecting. While there is now no trace of their painted decoration, it is known from the accounts that in the front room there was a good deal of simulated porphyry, the doors being of rosewood and satinwood with ebony fillets. The dome was in two shades of light blue with figures in silver bronze. The windows of the back parlour opened into a long glazed gallery with a fountain at either end. This, usually referred to in the accounts as the 'greenhouse', was described by Soane as 'enriched with antique cinerary urns, sepulchral vases, statues and other sculptures, vines and odoriferous plants, the whole producing a succession of beautiful effects, particularly when seen by moonlight, or when illuminated, and the lawn enriched with company enjoying the delights of cheerful society'.

On the floor below—a semi-basement with windows at garden level at the rear—were a room for architectural models and a 'Monk's Dining-room', the monk being a symbolic figure invented by Soane as representative of the gothic interest prevalent at that time, and a suitable 'custodian' for his collection of casts from medieval fragments which were here displayed. The Monk's Dining-room was in fact to be the forerunner of the Monk's Parlour which Soane was to create, and which still survives, behind his house in Lincoln's Inn Fields after Pitzhanger Manor had been sold. Beyond the domestic quarters adjoining the north of the villa he added a gallery for the display of his collection of plaster casts, and still further to the north he was to construct, towards the end of 1801 another fantasy which can best be described as a miniature 'forum', in which stood a cluster of seemingly half-buried classical remains—two pairs of fluted Corinthian columns, three incomplete pairs of the same order with matching responds, a pair of fluted Doric columns, and several detached capitals and broken shafts.

Pitzhanger, now generally known as Walpole Park, survives although shorn of much of its internal decoration, and without Soane's 'ruins' which later owners failed to appreciate. It is maintained by the London Borough of Ealing.

Praed's Bank, Fleet Street, London (Plate 149)

A new banking house at 90 Fleet Street was built for William Praed of Tyringham in 1801. The façade, of three bays, with incised pilaster strips and panels of Greek fret, has a good deal in common with the second house which Soane was to build for himself in Lincoln's Inn Fields some eleven years later. On the ground floor there were offices and strong rooms as well as the banking hall, while on the floors above were a drawing-room, dining-room and bedrooms. The building progressed rapidly, and by the end of the year Mr Praed was writing to Soane: 'We have much to talk over before the first of Jany. when I expect to find myself in the character of a London Banker seated in full form in the most elegant convenient House in the City of London.' Further work was carried out in 1812 when Soane added a waiting-room, clerk's sitting-room, lobby and staircase at the rear. The building was demolished in 1923.

149. PRAED'S BANK, Fleet Street, Soane's design for the façade.

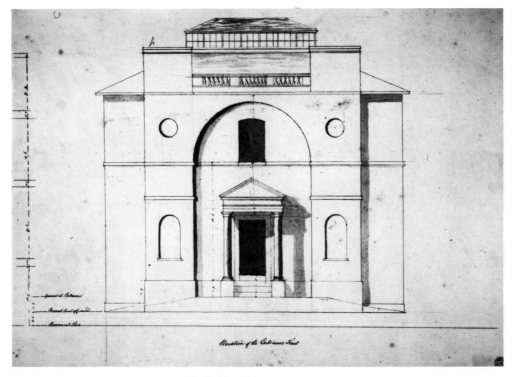

150. Mr Robins' house at NORWOOD.

Norwood Green, Middlesex, a house for John Robins (Plate 150)

From 1796 the name of John Robins of Warwick Street, Golden Square, London, occurs frequently in Soane's notebooks. Little is known about him except that in addition to his furniture business he acted as an estate agent, and through him a number of small commissions for alterations and redecorations came to the architect who reciprocated by ordering furniture from Robins for the Bank of England and elsewhere.

In 1801 Soane supplied him with designs for a house at Norwood, the foundations of which were laid in August of that year. A number of plans and elevations survive, from which it is evident that the house was of two storeys with basement and attics, and that the central hall was top-lit. The façade was an unusual composition reflecting a 'triumphal arch' theme, with a central Doric porch. There are accounts from the principal tradesmen engaged on the work, but the house itself was apparently destroyed many years ago.

Cricket Lodge, Cricket St Thomas, Somerset (Plate 151)

This house has been extensively altered, and only a few traces survive of the work which Soane carried out for Lord and Lady Bridport, who were close friends of the architect and his wife.

151. Soane's design for Lord Bridport's library at CRICKET LODGE.

The first plans for alterations were sent in 1786 but from the accounts these were not of importance and it was not until 1801 that designs for additions and further alterations were submitted. Of the drawings in the museum, the elevations bear little relation to what was finally carried out, but two fragmentary pen sketches among the Bridport correspondence show part of the existing south front, and the incised decoration of its stonework. The plans, however, indicate that the entrance was then on the west side of the house, leading to a columned hall which is now a drawing-room. To the south is a smaller drawing-room, and both this and the bedroom over it have chimneypieces of Soane's time. His most interesting feature in the house was the library, to the north of the original entrance hall. For this the drawings in the Museum show a rectangular central space flanked by apses, the former having a shallow domed ceiling with incised decoration. The walls were lined with bookcases to three-quarters of their height. Only the outline of the room survives, all traces of its original decoration having disappeared.

152. Mr Knight's hall, No. 48 GROSVENOR SQUARE.

Grosvenor Square, London, No. 48 (later No. 49) (Plate 152)

Soane's first work here was carried out for Lady Pembroke in 1797–8 when alterations were made to the first-floor drawing and ante-rooms and the insertion of a new staircase. Designs of this time for the library, and for various chimneypieces, are in the Museum.

By October 1801, the house had passed into the hands of Robert Knight for whom Soane proposed further alterations to the ground and first floors. One of the more striking changes was the entrance hall which was extended by a semicircular bay with windows flanking the front door. Between these were placed fluted Ionic columns. Opposite the front door a short flight of steps led up to a small lobby from which was approached a new library, its chimneypiece placed in a curved wall, and the bookshelves set in arched recesses. Crace, the painter, refers in his account to 'graining the greater part of the Library satinwood'. On the first floor a new south drawing-room was formed over the library, and the old north drawing-room overlooking the Square was given a curved east wall and tripartite window. In 1805 the library was altered to make a dining-room.

The house was destroyed when the present flats were built on the corner of Grosvenor Square and Carlos Place (formerly called Charles Street).

Port Eliot, Cornwall (Plates 153–6)

In 1804 John Eliot, for whom Soane had already designed alterations or supervised repairs to Down Ampney in Gloucestershire and houses in London, succeeded as 2nd Baron Eliot. Within a short time he sought Soane's advice on the family seat, Port Eliot at St Germans in Cornwall, which Soane first visited on 28 October, staying for three days. He subsequently submitted designs both for alterations to the nearby Church, and for the house which was then partly medieval and partly mid-eighteenth century in date. The work carried out on the house included a new south and east front containing a dining-room, library, saloon, hall and circular drawing-room, the latter forming a 'tower' at the north-east angle. An extensive stable range was built a short way to the west of the house. Building began towards the end of the year and continued through 1806 with Matthews acting as clerk of the works. Much of Soane's alterations remains except at the west end of the house which was remodelled by Henry Harrison *circa* 1829, when a new entrance was made.

153. PORT ELIOT, Soane's refacing of the south front.

154. PORT ELIOT, the stables.

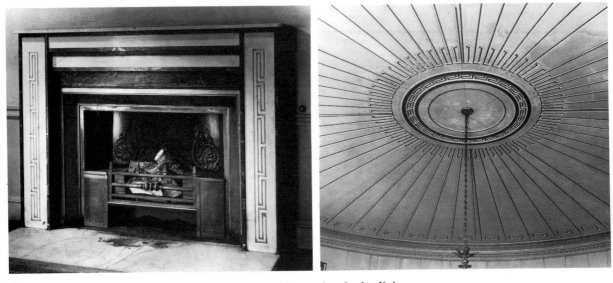

155. PORT ELIOT, chimneypiece in the dining-room.
156. PORT ELIOT, the drawing-room ceiling.

Ramsey Abbey, Cambridgeshire (Plate 157)

Ramsey Abbey House was built over the remains of the Lady Chapel of the Abbey of SS Mary and Benedict, granted at the Dissolution to Sir Richard Cromwell. His son Henry erected a small Tudor house, which early in the nineteenth century came into the possession of William Henry Fellowes, nephew of Soane's client at Shotesham, who asked for designs in 1804.

Soane set an oval porch, or vestibule, in the centre of the north front, this being approached by a flight of five curved steps. The porch opened into a long arched corridor extending across the main front and giving access to the tower blocks at either end. On the west he built a three-storey addition which accommodated a new staircase, eating-room and 'Mr Fellowes Room'. Most of this work survives, although new grates, panelling and doors were inserted, probably when Edward Blore was at work here, adding an angular bay on the south, and pierced balustrading to the roofs. Soane's work at Ramsey, including a lodge which has now disappeared, came to over £10,000.

157. RAMSEY ABBEY, with Soane's additions.

158. CEDAR COURT, as enlarged by Soane.

Cedar Court, Roehampton (Plate 158)

This house stood to the south-west of the junction of Roehampton Lane and Clarence Lane. The owner was John Thomson for whom Soane prepared alternative designs early in 1804. That selected was for a two-storey block with wings at either end, canted towards the garden, and surmounted by a balustraded parapet in Coade stone. Soane noted that the foundations were set out on 23 July and during the next two years he supervised the work and supplied drawings for details in the hall and saloon. By 1807 the total cost had risen to over £13,600. The outline of the house was still shown on a London map of 1920 although in fact it had been demolished some years earlier.

New Bank Buildings, London (Plate 159)

Built at the direction of the Bank of England on land which it owned at the north-west end of Princes Street, New Bank Buildings consisted of five mercantile residences described by Soane as 'presenting more of the appearance of one grand hotel than of several distinct mansions'. They were begun in the autumn of 1807, and when completed were leased to prominent city firms including the London Dock Company (No. 1) and Thellus-

159. NEW BANK BUILDINGS.

sons (No. 2), both of whom had large counting-houses at the rear with trade entrances in the adjoining Meeting House Lane.

The Princes Street façade consisted of three storeys with an attic storey over the five central bays. The windows throughout were set in round-headed arches, and below those on the ground floor were decorative panels. The end bays projected slightly and at first floor level carried a pair of fluted columns of an Ionic order which supported, above their entablature, a section of pierced balustrading. In spite of threats to mutilate the northern end of the block in connection with road-widening proposals in 1825 and 1831 (both strongly opposed by Soane), New Bank Buildings survived until 1891 when new offices were built on the site.

Stowe, Buckinghamshire, Gothic Library and Vestibule (Plates 160–1)

The Library at Stowe is the only instance of Soane's use of gothic for a domestic interior, a style in which he was never entirely happy. Lord Buckingham, however, had expressly asked that the new repository for his 'Saxon manuscripts' should take this form, and it seems that Soane, apprehensive as to the correctness of his gothic detail, prevailed on John Carter, the antiquarian, to act as draughtsman in the early stages of the work,

160. STOWE, Lord Buckingham's library.

though he later dispensed with his help. Formed out of some nondescript rooms on the south side of the basement the new library was to have its own vestibule and staircase to the floor above. The first designs were dated January 1805, and work began a few months later although details for the bookcases were still being discussed in February 1806 when Lord Buckingham wrote: 'I think you have departed a little too much from Hy 7ths Screen which I wish to take as the bookcase round the room. I would therefore beg you to be so good as to send one of your draughtsmen simply to sketch one of the upper squares of that composition, unless you have Dart's *Westmr. Abbey* in your collection.' Soane had, in fact, purchased this book some months before for £3.13.6.

Detailed accounts are preserved for the work in Soane's Cost Book for 1805–7. The

161. STOWE, vestibule to library.

four 'carved canopies very richly ornament[d.] with crockets, pinnacles, drops, tracery in pannels, battlements and rosettes' were supplied by the metalworkers, Underwood and Doyle, and the 'enriched face of [the] Cieling . . . in 509 Pannels large imbost and executed as per Design' was executed by William Rothwell. Almost the last feature to be installed in the library was the 'large brass Gothic chimneypiece made to drawing' and a 'handsome Gothic brass stove', both of which were supplied by Thomas Catherwood.

162. MOGGERHANGER, the entrance façade.

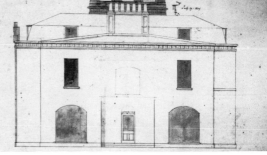

163. MOGGERHANGER, 'flank elevation' as designed

Moggerhanger, Bedfordshire (Plates 162–3)

Soane's earliest plans for this house are dated 1791, and suggest the alteration of an unpretentious existing building which belonged to Godfrey Thornton, a director of the Bank of England. The scheme was, however, delayed, and during the next few years his client's ideas became more ambitious, a number of proposals being drawn out and culminating in the final design of 1809 which was put into execution.

The entrance front consists of a three-storey three-window central block flanked by projecting two-storey wings, these being linked by a single-storey range which passes in front of the main block and contains the entrance hall. It is entered by a semicircular Doric porch, the columns being partly fluted. All the windows of this façade have semi-circular heads, and the central block carries a pierced balustrade. The accounts show that the house was faced with Parker's Metallic Stucco, originally coloured to imitate stone, but now painted white.

Internally almost all the original decoration has gone, although the staircase retains its simple ironwork balustrade, and two marble chimneypieces remain in what were the dining and drawing-rooms.

Charlotte Street (now Hallam Street), London, No. 38 (Plates 164–5)

This house at the north end of the east side of the street, was occupied by Sir Francis Bourgeois during the later years of his life. In 1807, he was to inherit a considerable part of the collection of paintings which had been formed by the art dealer, Noel Desenfans. The first intention of Bourgeois on receiving this gift was to build a gallery for it in Charlotte Street, but negotiations for a site were unsuccessful which ultimately led him to make a will by which these pictures and others of his own collection, should go to Dulwich College with sufficient money to build a gallery for them there (see page 200). In the meantime, he decided to erect a mausoleum adjacent to his house to receive the coffin of his benefactor who had an aversion to being buried below ground. A space was also to be available for the coffins of Mrs Desenfans (who did not die until 1813) and himself.

Soane was asked to supply designs for this small sepulchral building and the first set was submitted on 15 August 1807. One design was for a short 'aisle' set between columns with an apse at the far end. The alternative, which was adopted, was for a lobby opening into an oval top-lit space beyond which was a vaulted sanctuary flanked by apses. It was here that the coffins, in their fluted sarcophagi, were to be placed. Work went ahead without delay, the bricklayer, John Labern, obtaining a licence and erecting a hoarding on 27 August. Two days later he was joined by Richard Martyr, carpenter, when demolition began of the old stables which had occupied this site. The new building was sufficiently advanced for the mason, Thomas Grundy, to lay the paving early in the following November. He also supplied the sarcophagi for the coffins. Sir Francis died on Monday 7 January 1811, following which a new mausoleum was constructed adjoining the picture gallery at Dulwich. When completed his remains and those of Desenfans were moved there, to be joined by the coffin of Mrs Desenfans after her death.

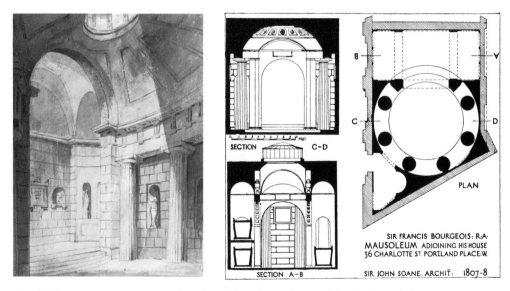

164. (*left*) CHARLOTTE STREET, London, Mausoleum designed for Sir Francis Bourgeois.

165. (*right*) CHARLOTTE STREET, sections and plan of Mausoleum.

166. ROYAL HOSPITAL, CHELSEA, a composite drawing showing Soane's various works.

The Royal Hospital, Chelsea, London (Plates 166–71)

Soane succeeded Samuel Wyatt as clerk of the works to the Royal Hospital on 20 January 1807—a post which he was to hold for exactly thirty years until his death in 1837. It provided him with a salary of £200 per annum and a small residence which he was to improve, and to which he later became much attached.

Neither Wyatt nor Robert Adam before him had made any great changes in the Hospital buildings, but Soane was to carry out extensive repairs and alterations to the existing fabric, and to design several new buildings.

The first of these was the Infirmary, begun in 1810 on the site of Yarborough House, once the residence of Sir Robert Walpole. Soane's building consisted of a long east-west range from which a wing at either end extended south towards the river. Along the south front of the main block was set a single-storey loggia, linking the two wings, this having round-headed arches and providing a sheltered place in which the convalescents could sit. The materials of the new building were stock brick with stone dressings, and the royal arms in Coade stone were placed above the cornice on the north front. The chimneys of the Infirmary, like those of all Soane's buildings at Chelsea, were treated in an original and decorative manner, pairs of panelled shafts being linked by brick arcading. The entire block was destroyed by a war-time bomb in 1941.

167. ROYAL HOSPITAL, CHELSEA, the Infirmary.

The next building of consequence was the stable block of 1814, formed round a court-yard, and approached by an archway in the centre of its eastern range which is a remark-able composition carried out almost entirely in stock brick, stone appearing only in the narrow footing, as a strip above the cornice, and for the top courses and acroteria on the chimneyshafts. The central stable archway is flanked by two larger arched recesses in the brickwork, in each of which smaller recesses frame a doorway to a set of apartments. A typical 'Soane cornice' of two bricks set edgeways continues round the block, to the north and south of which are single-storey pavilions. The north and west external walls of the stables are also remarkable for their arrangement of blind arches in the brickwork.

To the west of the stables, and fronting Royal Hospital Road, stood Soane's official residence, originally small and of irregular shape. In 1814 he enlarged it with a new study, staircase and bedroom, by building out bays at either end, and an attic over the central portion. In this new work the chimneys were even more unusual, pairs of diagonal brick shafts being set over panelled rectangular bases, each shaft being topped with a smoke-pot in the form of an oil jar, similar to those which Soane had placed on the Cumberland Lodge in Hyde Park some twenty years earlier.

A new Bakehouse was built in the West Road of the Hospital precincts in 1815, and a Gardener's House in the following year. In 1818 a new Guard-house was erected in the East Road, and work began on the Secretary's Office facing Light Horse Court, the

168. ROYAL HOSPITAL, CHELSEA, the stables, east front.

169. ROYAL HOSPITAL, CHELSEA, the stables, external wall to Royal Hospital Road.

170. ROYAL HOSPITAL, CHELSEA, East Road and Secretary's offices.

171. ROYAL HOSPITAL, CHELSEA, the Secretary's Offices, hall.

secretarial staff having by this time increased from five to fifty. As it was flanked by the Old Guard-house and the original Gardener's House, both by Wren, Soane was asked to make his front elevation accord with them by using red brick with stone quoins and a timber cornice. The principal office still contains furniture and fittings supplied under his direction in 1819.

The last buildings erected in the Royal Hospital grounds to Soane's designs were the Smoking Room at the north end of the West Road, built in 1829, and a garden shelter set up in 1834. The Smoking Room was similar in construction to Soane's Guard-house of 1818 and was in fact adapted to this purpose in 1857. The shelter stands in Ranelagh Gardens, to the south-east of the Hospital. It is a simple but unusual construction of brick piers supporting a pitched roof which was originally thatched but is now slated. In the centre of its longer side facing south is a pedimented porch projected on a pair of reeded timber columns with retracted necking and bases. Pairs of similar columns are set at either end of the shelter between the piers. There are no drawings for it in the Museum, but Soane is known from the Hospital records to have prepared four designs from which this 'doric barn' was selected.

Mells Park, Somerset

Soane was consulted by Colonel Thomas Horner after difficulties had arisen with James Spiller, the architect previously employed for alterations at Mells Park. He visited the house in July 1810, and subsequently submitted designs for the decoration of the drawing-room and library, and for forming a new domestic range and stables. Five years later he made detailed drawings for a new porch and for a library, and himself travelled to Mells, where he stayed from 21–24 October to see the work in progress.

The house was gutted by fire in 1917 when the site was cleared to make way for a house designed by Sir Edwin Lutyens.

Dulwich Picture Gallery, Greater London (Plates 172–7)

Sir Peter Francis Bourgeois, RA, died on 7 January 1811, bequeathing the paintings which he had inherited from the art dealer Noel Desenfans, as well as his own important collection, to the Master, Warden and Fellows of Dulwich College. In addition he left them a sum of money to build a gallery for the pictures, and a mausoleum to contain the remains of Mr and Mrs Desenfans and himself. The mausoleum was to be similar to that which Soane had designed for him in Charlotte Street (page 195), where the body of Mr Desenfans had reposed since 1807.

It had been agreed some time before the death of Sir Francis that Soane should under-take the work, and within twenty-four hours of this event the architect was at Dulwich inspecting the site. Several sets of designs were, however, to be prepared before the Master and his colleagues settled on a scheme for a gallery with a mausoleum projecting from the centre of the east front, and flanked to north and south by six small apartments for the almswomen whose previous accommodation had occupied the site. The new build-ing was to be of stock brick, with Portland stone dressings, and the same stone was used

172. DULWICH ART GALLERY.

173. (*left*) DULWICH ART GALLERY, in course of construction.

174. (*right*) DULWICH ART GALLERY, before recent rearrangement.

175. DULWICH ART GALLERY, the Mausoleum. From one of Soane's Lecture Diagrams.

176. (*left*) DULWICH ART GALLERY, exterior of the Mausoleum.

177. (*right*) DULWICH ART GALLERY, the Mausoleum, roof lantern.

for the lantern, vases and sarcophagi over the mausoleum. At the north and south extremities shelters were recessed behind arches in the return walls to provide seating for the old ladies in warm weather.

The foundations of the building were set on 11 October, but a month later the Master and Warden changed their minds as to the orientation of the mausoleum, as a result of which Soane had to turn his plans around so that the main entrance would face College Road, while the 'Sisters' Apartments' and mausoleum would lie on the west, approached by a curving drive from what is now called Gallery Road.

Internally, the gallery comprised five main areas in which the paintings were to hang, each lit by a lantern with a flat, solid top which deflected downwards the light admitted from its glazed side lights. Semicircular headed archways led from one area to another giving an uninterrupted view from north to south through the building.

Several of the craftsmen who had been employed on work at the Bank of England were responsible for the building of the gallery including Thomas Grundy, mason, Martyr & Son, carpenters, and William Watson, painter and glazier. Their bills amounted to £9,644 3s 2d, with £119 17s for the clerk of the works, and £24 14s 9d for a dinner given to them on completion of the building. Soane did not charge a commission for his designs or supervision.

In 1944 the Gallery was seriously damaged in an air raid, the contents fortunately having been removed. It was restored and reopened in 1953, and has recently benefited from further redecoration and rearrangement of the paintings.

No. 13 Lincoln's Inn Fields, London (Plates 39–48)

Being on good terms with his neighbour, George Booth Tyndale, whom he often visited, Soane was well aware that No. 13 Lincoln's Inn Fields was appreciably larger than the house in which he was then living, No. 12. As his collection grew and No. 12 proved increasingly inadequate to contain it, Soane began to cast envious eyes on a stable building at the rear of No. 13 for which Tyndale seemed to have no particular use. In the course of conversation he learnt that the latter was willing not only to sell the stable but the residential part of No. 13 as well on condition that he and his wife might continue as tenants for a few more years. The outcome of their negotiations was that Soane acquired the freehold of the property for £4,200 in June 1808, Tyndale agreeing to pay a rent of £202.10s. while in occupation of the house, and Soane obtaining immediate possession of the stable. In 1808–9 he converted his old office into a library and, eastwards of this, on the site of the stable of No. 13, built what he called a 'Plaister Room' (now the Dome) and, eastward again, an office building with 'upper' and 'lower' offices.

Further negotiations took place in 1812 when the Tyndales agreed to take a sixteen-year lease of the residential part of No. 12 so that Soane could have possession of No. 13. He was to retain the rear portion of No. 12, which contained what was now his library. On 2 July 1812 Soane noted that he was at work on the plans of the 'next house', the demolition of which began on 17 July. In spite of trouble with the district surveyor over the architect's design for the façade, and in particular the Portland stone projection to which he referred as a 'loggia', the building proceeded without undue delay, and was ready for occupation in October 1813.

Most of Soane's favourite themes and motifs are to be found in the internal treatment of No. 13, but assembled with infinite care so as to create those dramatic effects of light and shade, of vistas and surprises, which he regarded as the 'Poetry of Architecture'. For the first two years few changes were made, and Mrs Soane's death in 1815 left her husband in too great a state of misery to pay much attention to the house or its contents. Towards the end of 1816, however, his interest began to revive, and for the next twenty years there was hardly a year when alterations of a greater or lesser degree were not being made in some part of the house or galleries. In 1821 he reconstructed the upper and lower offices, raising the floor-level of the lower office and building, the present 'colonnade', as well as re-creating the upper office as the present Students' Room.

In 1823, Soane purchased the house adjoining his on the east, No. 14. He immediately demolished the stables and started to build the Picture Room and Monk's Parlour. In March 1825 he started to rebuild the main house with a façade corresponding with that of No. 12. He never used this house and eventually sold the freehold.

Four fourteenth-century stone corbels which Soane brought from the north front of Westminster Hall were set into the façade of No. 13 in 1825, and in 1834 the glazing of the ground and first-floor windows was moved to the outer side of the 'loggia', thus giving additional space to the library and south drawing-room. By then William Kinnard had long since relinquished the district surveyorship, and his successor lodged no complaint against this subtle move which virtually extended three floors of No. 13 by three and a half feet beyond the accepted building line on this side of Lincoln's Inn Fields.

Ringwould House, Kent (Plate 178)

Soane designed this small country house, built high up on the cliffs to the west of Dover, for the Revd John Monins in 1813. It is of two storeys in stock brick with sharply projecting eaves and a slate roof. Two drawings of the exterior, unsigned but obviously by Soane, came to light in the house some years ago and correspond to the designs in the Museum. The internal treatment is simple, decoration in the entrance hall being restricted to a run of ball-beading oulining the ceiling. The cantilevered staircase, top-lit by an oval lantern, is in wood with plain balusters and a mahogany rail. The library has later panelling and there is nothing of note in the other principal rooms. The porch by which the house is entered has lost its original pediment shown in the Soane drawings, and the wing to the north has been raised to two storeys.

Soane's accounts show that he made four journeys to Ringwould in connection with the work which was begun in December 1813, and carried out under the supervision of Henry Harrison.

Cricket St Thomas, Somerset, Monument to Lord Bridport in St Thomas's Church (Plate 179)

Soane's friend and client, Alexander Hood, 1st Viscount Bridport, died on 3 May 1814, and his widow subsequently asked the architect to design a monument to him. Ten alter-

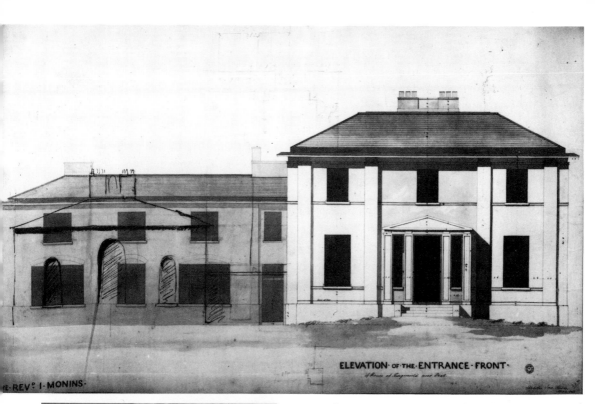

178. RINGWOULD HOUSE, Soane's design of 1813.

179. Lord Bridport's tomb
in the Church at
CRICKET ST THOMAS,
erected 1816.

natives were drawn out during the next two years, that finally chosen having an inscription on it composed by Lady Bridport. It was executed by Thomas Grundy at a cost of £251.

Butterton Farm House, Staffordshire (Plate 180)

Although the designs which Soane prepared for a large country house at Butterton did not materialise, a smaller farm house was commissioned by the same client, Thomas Swinnerton, in 1815, and was begun in the summer of the following year. The exterior has survived intact, and is remarkable for the splayed angles of its brick walls, each being flanked by a brick pilaster with retracted necking. The entrance in the centre of the south front is recessed, and is set, as are the ground-floor windows, within a semicircular headed brick arch. To the north, a dairy is built out from the main block. The roof, with sharply projecting eaves, has a central chimneystack of stone pierced by a small arched opening, and capped by a miniature 'sarcophagus'.

The absence of any characteristic features within the house was partly due to Mr Swinnerton's decision to call a temporary halt for reasons of economy soon after the carcase was completed; and partly to the interference of the tenant farmer, Harding, for whom the house was intended. During his landlord's absence abroad, and without consulting

180. BUTTERTON FARM HOUSE.

the architect, he gave orders for work to be resumed. Writing to Mr Swinnerton's agent, he reported with self-satisfaction 'I have nearly finished my new house but do not inform Mr Soan of it, but I will assure you it is nearly finished and well, and at half the expense.' This conduct resulted in considerable embarrassment, and several apologetic letters to Soane in which Harding's drinking habits and tendency to madness are given as excuses. Although it was suggested that the interior should be stripped and rearranged, this was not done, and Harding's nondescript finishings were allowed to remain.

The Soane Family Tomb, St Pancras Gardens, London (Plates 50–2)

Three months passed from Mrs Soane's death on 22 November 1815, before her husband felt equal to the task of designing 'Eliza's monument', and a number of alternatives were prepared. One of the early designs, dated 14 February 1816, was eventually chosen, and the mason Thomas Grundy was employed to carry out the work. By 18 April the canopy had been completed, and the angle blocks of the surrounding balustrade were in position. Further inscriptions were added to the tomb after the burial here of Soane's elder son, John, in 1823, and of Soane himself in 1837.

National Debt Redemption Office, London (Plate 181)

Soane's first connection with this Office was in 1808 when it occupied a house in Bank Street, previously known as Will's Coffee House. This he altered and repaired over several years until larger premises became imperative. In 1817 he was asked to submit plans to the directors of the Bank of England for a new building on a site in Old Jewry.

Several alternatives were prepared, that chosen being for a three-storey building of five bays with a loggia of round-headed arches at ground-floor level. In addition to offices, it was to contain a memorial to William Pitt, at whose instigation a Commission 'For the Reduction of the National Debt' had been set up in 1786. The statue was to be a life-size figure of Pitt by Richard Westmacott, and as its setting Soane designed a lofty hall reminiscent of the inner hall or 'tribune' which he had built at Tyringham in the mid-1790s. It occupied a rectangular space defined by four round-headed arches between which pendentives were linked to form the rim of a circular opening to an upper storey. Here a peristyle of eight Corinthian columns supported an entablature and a dome with a glazed lantern. The dome was decorated with incised Greek fret.

On either side of this hall were the offices, for the equipping of which John Robins was mainly responsible. The items included mahogany chairs, desks and library tables, worsted hearth-rugs, foot-mats with coloured borders, yellow gauze curtains, and fifty-six yards of floor-cloth painted with 'a large oak pattern'. A 'sarcophagus stove' was supplied for the dining-room, and a brass-topped wire fireguard for the nursery, since the manager and his family resided on an upper floor.

The building was demolished in 1900, when the statue of Pitt was removed to the garden of the Royal Humane Society in Hyde Park where it remained for many years. It has now been acquired by Pembroke College, Cambridge, where Pitt had obtained his MA degree in 1776.

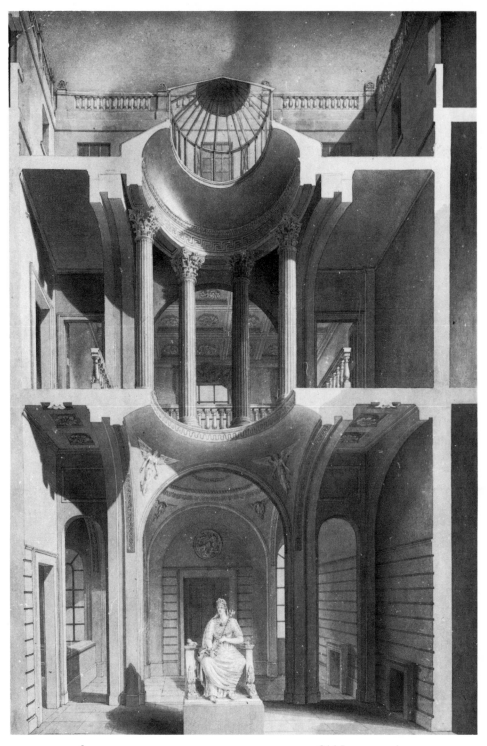

181. NATIONAL DEBT REDEMPTION OFFICE, Old Jewry, section through the central 'tribune'. *Page 207*.

Marden Hill, Hertfordshire (Plates 182–3)

Marden Hill was acquired by Claude George Thornton in 1818, when he asked Soane to design a new vestibule and staircase hall. The projecting, two-storey porch which was added does not appear on the first plans and was apparently an after-thought since a reference in Soane's Journal shows that its Ionic columns had originally been intended for New Bank Buildings in Princes Street. For some reason they were not used there, and came instead to Marden Hill where they support a stone balustrade in front of the projecting bay.

The vestibule to which the porch leads has a pedimented doorcase on either side leading to the dining-room and a sitting-room. Beyond is the staircase hall where the stair rises in a single first stage and then divides. It is constructed of wood (unusual in Soane's works, as he preferred stone for reasons of safety in case of fire), and has iron balustrading similar to the staircase balustrading in No. 13 Lincoln's Inn Fields.

182. (*left*) MARDEN HILL, the Ionic entrance porch.
183. (*right*) MARDEN HILL, entrance to vestibule and hall.

Late Works 1820–1833

Wotton House, Buckinghamshire (Plates 184–6)

The early eighteenth-century house at Wotton was seriously damaged by fire in 1820 when Lord Buckingham sent an urgent note—undated but probably on 29 October— telling Soane that 'Poor Wotton is burned down', and urging him to 'get one of your foremen ready to set off immediately'. James Cook was dispatched at once and arrived to find that fire was still breaking out in parts of the basement. Nevertheless he set to work on what must have been the uncomfortable job of obtaining measurements of such walls as were still standing.

Soane's designs for rebuilding were ready by December. In accordance with Lord Buckingham's wishes, he kept closely to the original external appearance of the house although reducing its height by omitting the attic storey.

Within he introduced a lofty central hall which had much in common with that in the National Debt Redemption Office, which in turn derived from the tribune at Tyringham. It rose through two storeys with a gallery at first-floor level, and terminated in a dome carrying a glazed lantern. The spandrels of the arches were filled with '4 casts of angels'. Of the alternative treatments suggested for the balustrading, that selected appears to have been of solid stonework composed of panels bearing shields below which hung '20 pendant ornaments'. Extensive remodelling of the interior of the house early in the present century destroyed these details, but elsewhere traces of Soane's work have come to light in the course of structural work and restoration.

Regent Street, London, houses for John Robins, on the east side (Plates 187–8)

The creation of Regent Street by John Nash in the second decade of the nineteenth century was largely dependent on the speculative procedure of letting sites to men who would be prepared to erect buildings either designed by him, or conforming to his specifications. One such site, lying on the east side between Chapel Court and Beak Street, was acquired by Soane's friend John Robins in conjunction with David Jonathan. Nash had apparently intended to supply the design himself, but was probably too busy to proceed with it, and in 1820 Soane was asked to prepare a scheme for six shops with residences above. A note on the back of one of his drawings records that David Jonathan 'called on Mr Nash at his house in Dover Street by desire of Mr Robins with his Elevation of the Intended Houses . . . which he approved of and left intirely to Mr Soane'.

The façade was of stuccoed brick, and the premises were entered by three pairs of projecting porches carrying balconies with iron balustrading. The upper part was divided by pairs of pilaster strips with incised decoration, and above the blocking course were three attic blocks, that in the centre having a 'pediment' in the form of a double console. The work was carried out between 1 July 1820 and 17 February 1821.

184. WOTTON HOUSE, as rebuilt by Soane after a fire.

185. WOTTON HOUSE, drawing showing the reduced height of the new building.

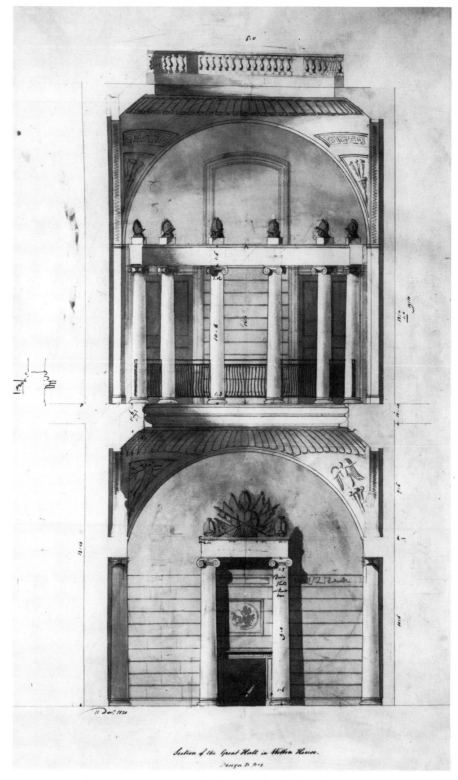

Section of the Great Hall in Wotton House.

Design D No. 9

186. WOTTON HOUSE, the inner hall or 'tribune'. *Page 210*.

187. REGENT STREET, a block of shops with houses above, designed for John Robins. *Page 210.*

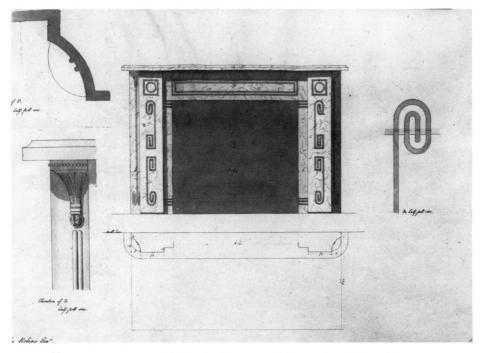

188. REGENT STREET, Mr Robins' houses, a chimneypiece design. *Page 210.*

189. PELLWALL, entrance façade. The porch was rebuilt later in the nineteenth century.

Pellwall House, Staffordshire (Plates 189–90)

This was to be the last of Soane's country houses and was designed for his friend Purney Sillitoe in 1822. The builder was John Carline of Shrewsbury. The house is of two storeys above a basement, and with attics behind a parapet. The principal façade carries four pilaster strips with incised lines representing a 'token' order akin to those appearing on the Regent Street houses recently completed. Although a new and higher porch has been added, it incorporates the four Ionic columns used in the original entrance.

The interior has been altered extensively and the present staircase occupies part of the position of the original large drawing-room. Here and there, however, traces of Soane's work survive, notably in a marble chimneypiece in the hall, and one in the small

190. PELLWALL, the triangular lodge.

drawing-room which also retains a shallow vaulted ceiling with a ribbon beading. The house is now in a precarious state.

At the end of the north drive stands the triangular lodge which is an expression of Soane's attempt to unite gothic and classical motifs. Pointed openings are used for the porch and the windows in the two corresponding projections, while the windows of the central room have mullions and leaded casements. All three projections carry parapets of angular stone balustrading and from the centre of the roof rises a hexagonal glazed lantern surmounted by a weathervane. A modern extension has been added on the north.

191. HOUSE OF LORDS, new Royal Entrance.

The Houses of Parliament, London (Plates 191–6)

As the Attached Architect responsible to the surveyor general for public buildings in Whitehall and Westminster, Soane's later work was almost entirely concerned with official buildings. The first major undertaking came in 1822 with instructions to plan a new entrance and staircase for the use of George IV when attending the House of Lords. This was to take the form of a curving arcade across Old Palace Yard, leading to a vestibule from which the stair—inspired by Bernini's *Scala Regia* in the Vatican—ascended in three stages. After some delay during which adjustments were made, the design was finally approved by the king and completed by January 1824, by which time Soane had received further instructions for an ante-room and Royal Gallery, as well as additional committee rooms. His designs and an estimate of £21,800 were approved in July and put into execution at once. The rectangular ante-room had three doorways and a window flanked by pairs of scagliola columns supporting massive 'pediments' in the form of pierced balustrades. From this apartment the processional way took a turn towards the House of Lords through a long, wide gallery over which were three domes supporting lanterns with stained glass.

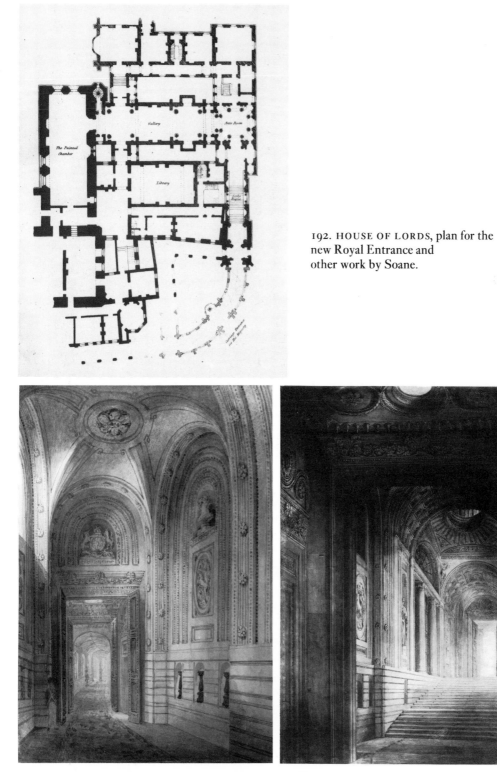

192. HOUSE OF LORDS, plan for the
new Royal Entrance and
other work by Soane.

193. (*left*) HOUSE OF LORDS, the new vestibule.

194. (*right*) HOUSE OF LORDS, the Scala Regia leading to the Ante Room.

195. HOUSE OF LORDS, Ante Room.

196. HOUSE OF LORDS,
the Royal Gallery.

Four new committee rooms, with smaller rooms and two staircases, were built to the east of the Royal Gallery and separated from it by a narrow open well. A library for the Lords was accommodated to the south of the Gallery.

For the House of Commons Soane's work during the next few years was to include alterations to the Speaker's House, and a new library as well as committee rooms, clerks' rooms and stores. His work on both Houses was, however, to disappear in the fire of 1834 and the subsequent clearance of the site.

The Insolvent Debtors' Court, Portugal Street, London (Plates 197–8)

This Court is now a forgotten building of Victorian London of which Charles Dickens's short and unflattering account in *The Pickwick Papers* is one of the few records. He made it the haunt of Solomon Pell, with whom Sam Weller had various transactions, and described how 'there sit nearly the whole year round one, two, three, or four gentlemen in wigs, as the case may be, with little writing desks before them, constructed after the fashion of those used by the judges of the land, barring the French polish: a box of barristers on their right hand: an inclosure of insolvent debtors on their left: and an inclined plane of most especially dirty faces in their front.'

Soane waited on the Commissioners of the Insolvent Debtors' Court in 1821 when the first plans were prepared, but the final set was not approved until January 1823. The exterior as built in that year had a two-storey façade with a central main door, flanked by windows and, beyond these, smaller doors. The windows of both storeys had semicircular heads, and over the roof of the building two groups of chimneystacks were linked by arcaded stonework to form a decorative feature which screened the top-light of the court room occupying the full height of the building.

197. INSOLVENT DEBTORS' COURT, Portugal Street.

198. INSOLVENT DEBTORS' COURT, the Court Room, demolished *circa* 1903.

Rectangular in plan, the court room had the effect of being divided into three compart-ments by the defining of its central space with four compound piers. From these sprang four semicircular arches without impost mouldings, and supporting over heavy cross beams a square opening covered by a glazed lantern. The end compartments of the room were lit by windows, and the walls of the whole court were panelled for half their height.

The Insolvent Debtors' Court was abolished in 1861 when the building was used by the Compensation Court. It was subsequently demolished and the site used for part of the Land Registry offices.

The New Law Courts, Palace of Westminster, London (Plates 199–205)

On 12 July 1820, Soane 'surveyed the buildings attached to Westminster Hall for the purpose of considering the site for a new Court of King's Bench'. This was the first step towards improving the cramped and awkward quarters in the 'New Stone Building', built by John Vardy and extended by haphazard additions, in which the Law had been administered since the middle of the eighteenth century.

Soane's instructions from the surveyor general were to retain the original building—a five-bay block with a wing on its south side—and to plan new accommodation for the Courts of Chancery and King's Bench between this and Westminster Hall. In addition to the six massive buttresses of the latter which projected on to this scanty site, there was also the ancient Court of Exchequer which Soane at first hoped to retain, although its defective condition ultimately made demolition necessary.

The building of a corner block with one façade to St Margaret Street and another to Palace Yard now posed a question as to the architectural style to be employed for the exterior. It was not easily resolved and led to fierce controversy. Soane had a deep veneration for Westminster Hall and wished that his new building should be isolated from it so as not to diminish its grandeur. As, however, lack of space precluded this, he maintained that the new façades should be 'composed in a style *totally* different' to the Hall. He therefore designed them in the same Palladian manner as the existing building in St Margaret Street, with a rusticated ground floor and Venetian windows at first-floor level.

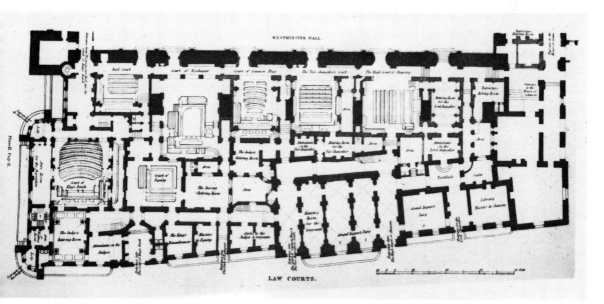

199. Soane's plan for the NEW LAW COURTS, abutting Westminster Hall.

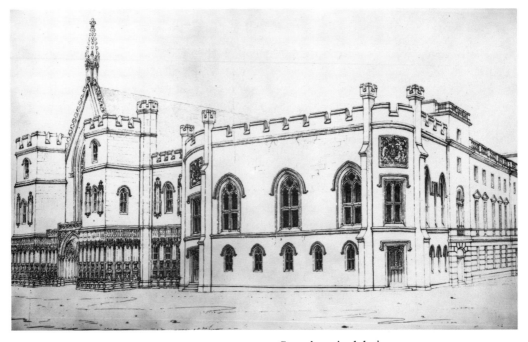

200. NEW LAW COURTS, Soane's revised design.

The new building was to accommodate the five Courts of Exchequer, Chancery, Equity, King's Bench and Common Pleas, as well as the Vice-Chancellor's Court and the Bail Court. In consultation with the Lord Chief Justice, Soane was urged to keep the Courts small, which was fortunate since he had to fit five of them into the spaces between the buttresses of Westminster Hall. His ground plan was submitted to the Treasury on 13 December 1821 and approved. At this meeting Lord Palmerston raised the question of gothicising the exterior, but no action was taken. Soane showed his design to the king in February 1822 and on the twenty-eighth of that month was informed that the latter 'highly approved of all the arrangements'. The foundations were laid in October, and the shell finished by February 1824.

In the following month an attack on the new building was launched by Henry Bankes, MP for Corfe Castle, who, without warning, delivered a virulent criticism of the design during a House of Commons debate. He was supported by William Williams, MP for Weymouth, who was even more abusive. The work was described as a 'frightful projection ... so ugly that it ought to be immediately razed to the ground', and views were expressed that it should have been designed in a gothic style. There was much publicity for the criticisms as a result of which Soane was ordered to suspend work while a Select Committee was appointed to inspect and revise the design.

After many meetings of this Committee, and the preparation of a number of alternative schemes, Soane was instructed to pull down the Palace Yard façade, to set back the building line by several feet, and to rebuild in a gothic style. This meant that he had

201. NEW LAW COURTS,
Court of King's Bench.

202. NEW LAW COURTS,
Court of King's Bench,
side gallery.

203. NEW LAW COURTS,
Court of Chancery.

to sacrifice the three separate entrances originally provided for judges, counsel and barristers, as well as a vestibule and staircase, offices and storage space. Although he prepared a Petition to the House of Commons, which was delivered by Edward John Lyttelton, it was without effect, and on 24 June 1824 the *Morning Herald* reported that work had begun on pulling down 'such portions . . . as were condemned by the Commons' *Committee of Taste*'.

Rebuilding followed immediately, and on 21 January 1825, the first case was tried in the Court of King's Bench. Although they varied considerably in detail, the Courts shared a common form of construction, all being rectangular in plan with windows set high in their walls, and with further light admitted from glazed lanterns above square or circular openings in ornately plastered ceilings. The Courts of Chancery and King's Bench had galleries, and the walls of the latter were plastered to simulate rusticated masonry. The rest were panelled for almost their full height and painted with light oak graining. Red carpets and red velvet curtains were used for the Courts and Judges' rooms. The passages were mostly lit by lanterns glazed with pale amber glass.

On the completion of George Edmund Street's Royal Courts of Justice in the Strand, the buildings in St Margaret Street became redundant. They were pulled down in 1883 and the site left open to give a view of this side of Westminster Hall.

225

204. NEW LAW COURTS,
Vice Chancellor's Court.

205. NEW LAW COURTS,
Lord Chancellor's
Robing-Room.

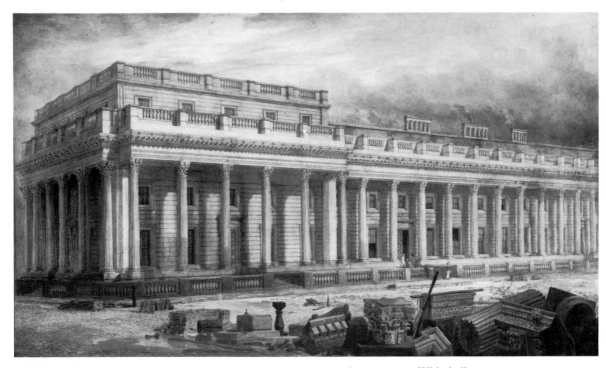

206. PRIVY COUNCIL OFFICES and TREASURY, Whitehall.

Privy Council and Board of Trade Offices, Whitehall (Plates 206–7)

Soane first drawings for new offices facing Whitehall, but with a return wall to Downing Street, are dated May 1823. In the following year, however, the Lords of the Treasury decided that the designs were too plain and asked for one 'composed in a more enriched character'. The architect complied with a design for a two-storey building in which a continuous Ionic order was set above a rusticated ground floor, but this again was rejected. A further design was submitted in June 1824, and this time proved successful, although he was subsequently instructed that the proposed 'Tivoli' order should be replaced by one based on that of the Temple of Jupiter Stator. In this design the free-standing giant order was set in front of rusticated stonework, and continued through two storeys to carry an entablature and pierced balustrade behind which rose an attic storey.

The portion of the building containing the Board of Trade extended northward from Downing Street to the Old Tennis Court, while the Privy Council Offices occupied the wing which extended westward and faced Downing Street. Although the internal decoration of the offices and the staircases in both blocks was restrained, in the Privy Council Chamber Soane, no doubt remembering the taste of the Lords of the Treasury for 'enrichment', provided a setting of considerable magnificence. The Chamber was in effect divided into one wide and two narrow compartments by his favourite device of four

207. PRIVY COUNCIL
CHAMBER.

piers. From these sprang arches carrying a shallow vaulted ceiling or 'canopy' over the central space, while the flanking aisles received light from lofty glazed lanterns as well as windows set high up in the walls. The principal doorways were flanked by Ionic columns of Sienna marble supporting an entablature topped by recumbent consoles. Soane's effort to please their Lordships was, however, misjudged for no sooner had the decoration become apparent than protests were voiced, resulting in a sharp exchange of words between the architect and the clerk to the Privy Council. On 6 September 1827 the former was ordered to remove the columns, 'their Lordships being of the opinion that these . . . interfere with . . . the transaction of Business in that apartment.' Soane sensibly suggested that as the room was almost finished, they should try the effect for one year, and at the same time appealed to the chancellor of the exchequer for support. In the end his decoration was allowed to remain, although for little more than a decade, as Charles Barry removed the columns and substituted a flat ceiling for Soane's groined vault and its decorative plasterwork in the course of his drastic alteration to the whole building.

Downing Street, Westminster, Nos. 10, 11, 12, and the Old Foreign Office
(Plates 208–10)

Between 1824 and the end of 1826 a good deal of Soane's time was taken up in supervising
work on houses in this street, Nos. 10 and 11 being on the north side, while the Old
Foreign Office occupied the south-west angle of what was then called Downing Square.
Of the latter all traces disappeared in the 1860s, but Soane's plans and accounts show
the considerable amount of alteration which he carried out there. Externally, the old
entrance was removed, and a corridor built across the front of the house at ground-floor
level, linking two projecting bays. In the centre of this he placed a tetrastyle portico.
Many of the rooms were remodelled to form a new Cabinet Room, Foreign Minister's
Room, libraries and clerks' rooms, while the large drawing-room was decorated with
wallpaper of 'blush colour with scroll borders, white paintwork picked out lightly in
gold, and pilasters of giallo antico'.

Soane's first summons to No. 10 Downing Street came in a letter of 3 July 1824, in
which the surveyor general explained that a new dining-room was required. The house
was then occupied by the chancellor of the exchequer, Frederick Robinson, the prime
minister having decided to remain in residence at his own house in Whitehall. After
much discussion during the rest of the year it was agreed that the new dining-room
and a small ante-room should be built over the kitchens which had been added to the
east side of the house in 1781. Soane made a number of sketches in 1825 although only
a few remain in the Museum. 'Shewn to the Chr. of the Exchequer' he wrote on one
surviving sheet, adding 'Appd. Plan 2 and Groined Cieling [sic] No. 3. To begin in August
and to complete in three months'. Both these rooms are panelled in oak, and have oak
floors with margins of mahogany. While the ante-room has a plain, flat ceiling, the dining-
room has a shallow groined vault enriched with plasterwork, forming the 'star-fish' pattern which was one of his favourite motifs. This was modelled by Thomas Palmer who
also supplied the plaster medallions which are set above the panelling of the walls at
either end of the room.

This work, and the minor alterations which Soane carried out elsewhere in the house,
was completed by the early spring of 1826. On 26 March the chancellor wrote to the
architect 'A small party will dine in my new room (for the *first* time) on Tuesday next
the 4th April. I wish you would be of the party that you may see how well it looks
when lighted up.'

During 1825 Soane was also to work on the two houses which adjoined No. 10 on
the west and which had previously been numbered 11 and 12. No. 12 was in the course
of this work to be merged with No. 11, the party wall being underpinned, and the 'back
front' being rebuilt. A new staircase was built as was a new room on the site of what
had been a small courtyard in an angle between No. 11 and a projecting wall of No. 10.
This room, which it was eventually decided to use as a dining-room, has a resemblance
to the breakfast-room at No. 13 Lincoln's Inn Fields which Soane had built for himself

208. No. 10 DOWNING STREET, dining-room.

209. No. 11 DOWNING STREET, breakfast-room.

210. No. 10 DOWNING STREET, dining-room ceiling detail.

in 1812. The rectangular central space has a shallow vaulted ceiling with fluted plaster-work radiating from an enriched panel. On either side of this 'canopy' are two long top-lights which originally contained coloured glass. A new chimneypiece has been installed, but the room is otherwise much as designed by Soane.

The Commissioners' Churches, London: St Peter, Walworth (Plates 211–12); Holy Trinity, Marylebone (Plates 213–14); St John's, Bethnal Green (Plate 215)

Soane was to design these three churches in the 1820s. The same plan was used for each, consisting of a rectangular nave with side galleries supported on columns, and approached by small staircases on either side of the entrance vestibule. The chancel extends beyond an elliptical arch, and is flanked by a robing room and a vestry.

Although Soane's assignments began with Holy Trinity for which his early designs are dated 1820, many difficulties ensued over the next three years, and it was St Peter's, designed in 1822, which was the first to be built in spite of his estimate having exceeded the stipulated amount. This he was ordered to reduce, resulting in fewer vaults below the church, and by a proposal to substitute Bath for Portland stone, and grey stock instead of white brick. In the end, through the generosity of the mason, William Chadwick, who bore the extra cost, Portland stone was used for the four Ionic columns which form the west entrance to the church. Building began in 1823 and St Peter's was consecrated

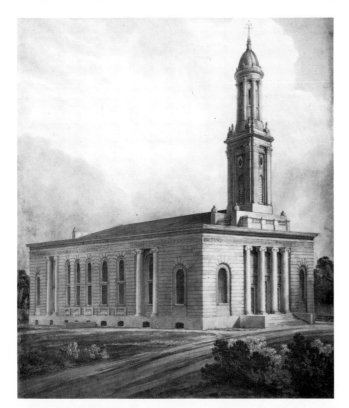

211. ST PETER'S CHURCH
WALWORTH,
as designed by Soane, 1822.

212. ST PETER'S CHURCH, WALWORTH, interior.

213. HOLY TRINITY CHURCH,
MARYLEBONE,
a cut-away perspective
showing the internal
arrangements.

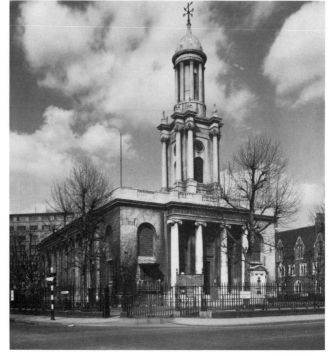

214. HOLY TRINITY CHURCH,
MARYLEBONE, from the
south-west.

on 28 February 1825. It is the best preserved of Soane's churches, and was carefully restored after damage in the last war.

The final versions of Soane's designs for Holy Trinity were approved in 1824 and the foundations laid in the following year after problems as to siting had been resolved by giving the building a north-south orientation. The tower, for which Soane clearly drew his inspiration from Robert Adam's twin towers for the church at Mistley, in Essex, came near to being omitted, again on grounds of cost. A public subscription, headed by the Duke of Portland, was however successful in raising sufficient money for the tower to be completed. In recent years the church had been adapted to provide office accommodation for the Society for the Promotion of Christian Knowledge while retaining the chancel and part of the nave for public worship.

St John's, the last of Soane's churches, was built in 1826 as a chapel of ease in the parish of St Mary, facing the junction of Cambridge Road and Green Street. The contract drawings were signed by the architect and Robert Streater as builder, the amount agreed by the commissioners for the work being £15,999. The exterior differs from its two predecessors in not having an Ionic order at the west end, this being replaced by six pilaster strips of Portland stone which divide the façade into three bays separated from each other by narrow recesses in the brickwork. The pilasters are given 'token' capitals in the form of small rectangles of groved masonry.

The windows of the church were altered at the end of the nineteenth century, when they were filled with tracery, and the interior has also been altered, but the vestibule and gallery staircases at the west end retain their original character, as does the rectangular stone tower supporting a small domed bell turret.

216. FREEMASONS' HALL, the Council Chamber.

Freemasons' Hall, Great Queen Street, London (Plate 216)

Soane's nomination as Grand Superintendent of Works followed immediately on his join-ing the Grand Master's Lodge in 1813 and he continued in this office until his death. Although during the first few years he supervised minor repairs and alterations for the Freemasons' Tavern and the adjoining hall, he made no important changes until 1821, when he increased the accommodation of the latter with a new gallery.

In 1826 he prepared four plans for a new hall to be built behind two houses which stood to the east of the Tavern, but the project was delayed. Further plans were drawn out in 1828 and approved by the Duke of Sussex as Grand Master. They provided for a large room which was to serve as a council chamber, with a smaller room placed at a right angle to its southern end, with access to a staircase which communicated with a kitchen and scullery in the basement.

As built and decorated, the Chamber was an interesting example of Soane's later style. At either end of the two longer walls were windows over fireplaces. Each of the windows on the east was linked to its counterpart on the west by a wide, coffered, elliptical arch spanning the room. In the east and west walls between the fireplaces, were pedimented doorcases, and arched recesses one of which contained an organ. From the central com-partment of the ceiling was suspended a square canopy in the form of a shallow vault with a wide circular opening above which was a glazed lantern. From the four extremities of the canopy were suspended bronze lamps. The walls and ceiling of the Chamber were grained and varnished, and there was a good deal of gilding and bronzing of details. The pilasters of the doorcases were painted in imitation of Sienna marble, and the windows were filled with coloured glass including strips with a diaper pattern on an orange ground, 'frette borders', rosettes and signs of the zodiac. There are also references in the accounts to yellow glass patterned with the 'Five Orders of Antiquity'.

The hall was completed in 1831. Although he claimed to have been as economical as possible in its execution, the cost had amounted to £8,820 4s 6½d, towards which the architect made a personal contribution of £500.

The New State Paper Office, St James's Park (Plates 217–20)

This was to be the last of Soane's major public buildings. He was now seventy-six yet he seems to have welcomed the project although fully aware of the obstructions and changes of mind which seemed to be inevitable where official undertakings were concerned.

When, after lengthy discussion, a decision was made in 1829 to move the national archives from an unsatisfactory repository in Great George Street, Soane was instructed to prepare a new building of brick and stone to be built on the site of Suffolk House, in what was then Duke Street on the east side of St James's Park. In addition to storage, the building was to include residential accommodation for the deputy keeper of State

217. NEW STATE PAPER OFFICE, St James's Park, Soane's design.

218. NEW STATE PAPER OFFICE, view from the lake in St James's Park.

Papers. The design, submitted to the surveyor general in May, was a complete departure from anything that Soane had previously produced. The source of his inspiration stemmed from Vignola's Villa Farnese at Caprarola by which he had been greatly impressed when he had visited it as a student some fifty years before, and of which a number of engravings were in his library.

The new Office was to be of four storeys and a basement. In Soane's design the most obvious debt to the Villa Farnese was the rusticated treatment of the end bays of the west elevation and the main entrance in Duke Street, which was his version of Vignola's famous doorway. From the villa, too, came the idea of the bracket cornice supporting wide eaves carrying a slope of pantiles which screen a flat roof behind in which were set a number of glazed lanterns providing light for the rooms below. No sooner had the design become available for inspection than Henry Bankes, whose interference had played havoc with the exterior of Soane's Law Courts, voiced his criticism, this time urging the chancellor of the exchequer to insist that two rows of pilasters be added to the façades of the building. Soane, knowing that this would be totally inappropriate to the essence of his design, protested strongly and pointed out that the suggestion would in any case increase the cost by nearly £3,000. Fortunately good sense prevailed, in no small measure due to the support of the keeper of State Papers, and Bankes's proposals were dropped. Writing to congratulate Soane on 26 June 1830, the keeper expressed

219. NEW STATE PAPER OFFICE,
entrance elevation with a section
through the building,
inset on the left.

220. NEW STATE PAPER OFFICE,
doorway details.

221. Composite painting of SOANE'S WORKS up to 1815, from a water-colour
by Joseph Michael Gandy.

the hope that 'our anchor is now heaved, and we are under way . . . I know the interest
you take in the work, and am sure that no exertion on your part will be wanting to
bring it to perfection.' The building was ready for occupation by the end of 1831 but
was to have a relatively short life. It was demolished to make way for the Foreign and
India Offices in 1868, when the archives were moved to the new Public Record Office
in Chancery Lane.

List of Works

The following list includes all executed works so far as they can be traced. It also includes designs commissioned but not executed. It does not include ideal designs or, on the other hand, minor repairs, decorations or surveys for valuation. 'London' denotes Inner London; outer suburbs such as Acton, Dulwich, Richmond, etc. are designated as in Greater London.

*Important surviving buildings or work by Soane
•Other buildings with some surviving Soane work

1780	**Downhill,** Co. Derry 4th Earl of Bristol and Bishop of Derry	Designs for alterations, unexecuted.
	Allanbank, Berwickshire John Stuart, later 4th Baronet	Designs and working drawings for alterations to house, followed by plans for new village, unexecuted.
	Castle Eden, Co. Durham Rowland Burdon, MP	Porch and other details, perhaps executed, but house later rebuilt.
	London, Battersea, proposed Penitentiary Commissioners for Prisons	Competition designs, unexecuted.
1781	**Petersham Lodge,** Greater London Thomas Pitt, later 1st Baron Camelford	Extensive repairs and decorations. Now demolished.
	London, No. 63 New Cavendish Street Hon. Philip Yorke, later 3rd Earl of Hardwicke	Extensive alterations and decorations.•
	Hamels Park, Hertfordshire (Plates 17, 18, 26) Hon. Philip Yorke, later 3rd Earl of Hardwicke	Gateway and lodges followed by dairy and work in the mansion. Also spelt Hammels or Hammells, the house was for a time known as Crofton Grange. See page 119.•
	Spencerswood, Berkshire William Sotheby	Design for a house, followed by design for a library. Probably unexecuted.
	Walthamstow, house in Grove Lane, Greater London James Neave	Survey and alterations followed by plans for a new room. Executed but later demolished.

	London, No. 148 Piccadilly Hon. Wilbraham Tollemache	Completetion and decoration of house carried out. Demolished 1972.
	London, Adams Place, Southwark (Plates 19–20) Francis Adams	Designs for shops and tenements carried out. See page 119.
	Garden buildings, unidentified Lady Rivers (sent through Lady Craven)	Four designs.
1782	**Belvedere,** Kent Sir Sampson Gideon	Designs for garden buildings. Unexecuted.
	London, Berkeley Square The Hon. Mrs Perry	Alterations carried out. 'Drawings of frontispiece for mason' are among those mentioned, but the house has not been identified.
	Coombe House, Surrey Hon. Wilbraham Tollemache	Repairs and alterations carried out. The house was later acquired by Lord Hawkesbury (subsequently 2nd Earl of Liverpool) for whom Soane carried out further work between 1801 and 1819. Demolished.
	Botleys, Surrey (Plate 23) Sir Joseph Mawbey, Bart.	Soane's sketch survives for a classical bath house to adjoin the mansion, but it was evidently not carried out.
1783	**Dunmow,** Essex Michael Pepper	Soane's accounts refer to supplying designs for a villa. Apparently unexecuted.
	London, No. 42 Wimpole Street John Stuart, later 4th Baronet	Alterations and decorations carried out.
	Walthamstow, Rectory Manor, Greater London William Cooke	A new reception room and kitchen added on the east. Soane may also have been responsible for the simple entrance gateway of brick with stone coping. The property was sold in 1897 and demolished to form Aubrey and Howard Roads.
	Burnham Westgate Hall, Norfolk Thomas Pitt, later 1st Baron Camelford	Alterations and redecorations as well as a large flint and brick barn and other farm buildings. The accounts also refer to a prospect tower but this does not appear to have been built. The house is now a home for the elderly.*

Letton Hall, Norfolk (Plates 55–60)
Brampton Gurdon Dillingham

A new house designed and built. See page 120.*

Norwich, Blackfriars Bridge, Norfolk
(Plate 54)
Norwich City Corporation

Designed and built. It survives but has been widened. See page 119.*

Malvern Hall, Warwickshire
Henry Greswold Lewis

Extensive alterations carried out to an earlier house. See 1798 for barn. See page 122.•

Marlesford, Suffolk
George Smith

Cow-house designed and built but burnt down in present century. It was similar to one built for the same client at Burn Hall, Co. Durham.

Burn Hall, Co. Durham
George Smith

Soane prepared designs for a large new house, and a model was made, but the project was abandoned after Mr Smith purchased the estate of Piercefield in Monmouthshire (see 1785). A cow-house similar to that at Marlesford was, however, built and survives.

Tyttenhanger, Hertfordshire
Hon. Mrs Yorke

Repairs carried out to an important 17th century house. See also 1789.

1784   **Cockley Cley,** Norfolk
J. R. Dashwood

Soane's ledger shows that many drawings for the house and offices were made but only two for the latter are in the Museum. The house was sold by the Dashwood family early in the nineteenth century, and in 1870–1 it was rebuilt in an Italianate style.

Herringfleet, Suffolk
John Leathes Esq.

Following a visit in October Soane sent designs for alterations and improvements but these do not appear to have been carried out.

Costessey, Norfolk
Sir William Jerningham

There are no drawings in the Museum but Soane's accounts show that he visited Costessey in 1784 and subsequently sent designs for stables and a dove-house for which a site had been agreed. A red-brick stable block with slightly curved extensions survived into the 1950s and was probably the local workmen's interpretation of Soane's design, but has since been demolished. There is no trace of the dove-house.

London, ? No. 18 Savile Row
Lady Banks

Alterations to the drawing-room. The house was later rebuilt.

Binfield, Berkshire
Dr Teighe

Soane supplied drawings and estimates for a farm house but none remain in the Museum, and it has not been possible to identify the building. As Soane 'gave directions to the workmen', the designs must have been executed but were probably demolished in the late nineteenth century.

Yorke Place, ? location
Hon. Philip Yorke

Design for a crescent of small houses. A site near Hamels has been suggested but seems unlikely as the houses have an urban or suburban character.

Saxlingham Rectory, Norfolk
(Plates 66–7) Revd John Gooch

Designed and built as a parsonage. It survives with slight alterations. See page 124.*

Tendring Hall, Suffolk (Plates 68–9)
Admiral Sir Joshua Rowley

Designed and built to replace an earlier house. It was left in poor condition after military occupation in the Second World War, and was subsequently demolished except for the porch. See page 124.

Taverham Hall, Norfolk
S. Branthwayte

Considerable alterations were designed including a new drawing-room and dining-room, and Soane made several visits to see the work in progress. The house was entirely rebuilt *circa* 1858 and no trace of Soane's work survives.

London, house in Park Street
Hon. Philip Yorke

Soane made surveys and estimates for repairs to an unidentified house here after Mr Yorke had moved to New Cavendish Street

London, Park Street, probably No. 48
Hon. John James Hamilton, later 9th Earl
   and 1st Marquis of Abercorn

Extensive repairs and decorations were carried out for this early and important client, but the house was entirely rebuilt at the turn of this century.

Earsham, Norfolk (Plates 64–5)
William Windham

Some work was carried out in the mansion itself, but Soane's most important contribution was the Music Room in the grounds, originally intended as a greenhouse but elaborated in the course of construction. It survives although without some of its painted internal decoration. See page 124.

Walthamstow, Greater London, St Mary's Church
William Cooke

Unspecified work was carried out in the church at the expense of Mr Cooke, but it cannot now be identified.

Langley Park, Norfolk (Plates 62–3)
Sir Thomas Proctor-Beauchamp

Two entrance gateways, one with lodges, were built to Soane's designs. They have recently been restored. See page 123.*

London, St Mary Abbot's Churchyard, Kensington (Plate 24)
The Earl of Bellamont

Soane was asked to design this tomb for Miss Elizabeth Johnstone. It took the form of a sarcophagus and still stands in the north-west part of the churchyard although in poor condition. The inscription is now illegible.*

1785 **Benacre Hall,** Suffolk
Sir Thomas Gooch

Designs for lodges, not executed.

Felbridge, Surrey, monument in the grounds to Mr Evelyn's parents
James Evelyn

After standing at Felbridge until 1927 the column was sold to Sir Stephen Aitchison of Lemmington Hall, Northumberland. It was then transported, probably by sea, to form a feature in his park where it still stands. In 1786 Soane supplied Mr Evelyn with designs for a chapel which may have been used for one built at Felbridge but there are no drawings for it in the Museum, and the building was replaced in 1865.*

Solihull, Warwickshire
W. Moland

Design for a bridge, unexecuted.

Shotesham Hall, Norfolk (Plates 70–3)
Robert Fellowes

New house designed and built. See page 129.*

Chillington, Staffordshire
Thomas Giffard

Additions to an existing house carried out. Designs for a chapel and a bridge unexecuted. See page 130.*

London, Hereford Street, proposed rooms for the Dilettanti Society
1st Baron Camelford

A scheme for adapting two of Lord Camelford's houses. Not adopted.

Nayland Church, Suffolk
Mr Alston

Designs and working drawings for internal alterations

Hingham Church, Norfolk
Revd P. Wodehouse

Designs sent for alterations in chancel and sketch of steeple. Working drawing sent for the former.

Piercefield, Gwent (Plate 84)
George Smith

Designs for additions and new façade to existing house. These were carried out, but the building has been derelict for many years. See page 138.•

1786 **Lees Court,** Kent (Plate 74)
Hon. Lewis Thomas Watson

Alterations to house and new stables built. The latter and a range of estate offices stand, but Soane's work in the house was destroyed in a fire. See page 130.•

London, 37 Pall Mall
Royal Exchange Assurance

A drawing in the Museum shows a stone or stucco façade with a fluted Doric porch. This has an enriched frieze and supports an iron balcony rail. There are references to bricklayers' work.

Cricket Lodge, Cricket St Thomas, Somerset
1st Viscount Bridport

Extensive alterations and additions were designed and carried out between this year and 1802 both for the house and out-buildings, but only fragments remain.•

London, St Stephen's Church, Coleman Street, Monument to Claude Bosanquet
Samuel Bosanquet

This was designed by Soane and carried out at a cost of £128.19.0, including lettering and a carved coat of arms. Slight alterations were made to it in the following year. It was destroyed with the greater part of the church by a bomb in the Second World War.

Worlingham Hall, Suffolk
Robert Sparrow

Designs for a house, unexecuted.

Tofts, Norfolk
Payne Galwey Esq.

Designs made for alterations to the house, and for a keeper's lodge. This village is now in the Army Battle School Area and it has not been possible to ascertain whether the buildings survive.

Ryston Hall, Norfolk (Plate 75)
Edward Roger Pratt

Extensive remodelling of the house carried out and surviving. See page 131.*

Boconnoc, Cornwall
1st Baron Camelford

Extensive repairs carried out in house, and a new top placed on the obelisk in the park after damage by lightning.•

Castle Hill, Devonshire
1st Earl Fortescue

Alterations carried out to house and offices. See page 134.

Mulgrave Castle, Yorkshire
2nd Baron Mulgrave

Additions and alterations carried out to house. Surviving in part.•

Hockerill, Hertfordshire
Ralph Winter

Small house built.

Beauport, Sussex
General Murray

Designs for a greenhouse and an obelisk which cannot now be traced.

Blundeston House, Suffolk (Plate 76)
Nathaniel Rix

House designed and built. It survives almost unchanged. See page 132.*

Nackington, Kent
Richard Milles

Soane made many journeys and carried out alterations to the house. This became derelict after use as a hospital in the First World War, and was demolished *circa* 1922.

A 'house in the country', unidentified
William Dinwody

There is a ledger entry for making 'two fair drawings of the plan and elevation of an addition' but no location is given.

Ossington Hall, Nottinghamshire
John Dennison

Although no drawings for Ossington remain in the Museum, a ledger entry refers to designs made by Soane for a proposed prospect tower, a temple, and lodges. These are presumably the drawings now in the Department of Manuscripts at Nottingham University. None of the designs appears to have been executed.

London, No. 16 Bedford Square
Thomas Wildman

Soane noted on 29 March that he had 'Called and settled Alterations' of this house, which included a 'design for a new kitchen'.

Holwood House, Kent
Rt. Hon. William Pitt

Additions and alterations carried out. Further work 1795. See page 132.

Forest House, Leytonstone, Greater London
Samuel Bosanquet

In this and the following year Soane supervised considerable alterations to the house, now part of Whipps Cross Hospital.

1787 **Skelton Castle,** Yorkshire
John Hall (later assumed the name of Wharton)

Alterations to house, new lodges and stables carried out.•

Lyndford Hall, Norfolk
George Nelthorpe

Following a journey to Lyndford, Soane supplied 'two fair drawings of a design for the alterations and additions' to the house. The house was rebuilt by William Burn 1856–61.

Fonthill, Wiltshire (Plates 77–8)
William Beckford

A picture gallery and other work carried out. The house was demolished after the building of Fonthill Abbey. See page 134.

1788 **Hetherset,** Norfolk
J. F. Iselin

On 24 August Soane took to Mr Iselin's London house three designs for Hetherset. Further designs were sent in November but there is no indication that any of them were carried out.

Kelshall Rectory, Hertfordshire
Revd Mr Waddington

Soane visited the house in early August to settle alterations and subsequently supplied four drawings, but no copies were kept, and it is not possible to identify what the work may have been.

Bentley Priory, Middlesex (Plates 79–83)
Hon. John James Hamilton, later 9th Earl and 1st Marquis of Abercorn

The first remodelling of this house was begun with a small extension on the east. The work continued until the end of the eighteenth century. See page 136.*

London, No. 21 St James's Square
Mrs Sturt

Soane made drawings for alterations to rooms on the principal floor including the 'Long Room'. There is also a reference to a design for an addition. The Long Room was probably the 'ball room' also mentioned. Soane received a commission on the tradesmen's bills, but the house was remodelled in the nineteenth century and nothing can now be identified as Soane's work.

? Melton Constable (or possibly Burrough Hall), Norfolk
Jacob Astley

After staying with Charles Collyer of Gunthorpe on 27–28 August 1788, Soane went on in the latter's carriage 'to Mr Astley' but does not give the name of the house which may have been either of these. He subsequently submitted a design for 'several alterations and additions'. Working drawings were sent in 1789 and later Richard Holland and James Nelson were paid small amounts, but it has not been possible to identify the work.

Wardour Castle, Wiltshire
8th Baron Arundell

Enlargement of the Chapel adjoining the house. See page 134.*

Shadwell Lodge, Norfolk
Robert Buxton

Soane supplied designs 'two fair drawings' for alterations but there are no details as to their execution and the house was rebuilt by S. S. Teulon *circa* 1856.

London, St James's Church, Piccadilly
Vestry of St James's Parish

Soane made three plans, two elevations and many other drawings for the 'reparations and improvements' together with descriptions and estimates. There is no indication that these were carried out, and a note in Soane's Journal that on 29 January 1789 'Hardwicke [*sic*] gave his drawings this day' probably means that the latter's designs were adopted.

Bemerton Rectory, Wiltshire
Dr William Coxe

Plans for improvements, probably executed.

Pembroke Lodge, Richmond Park, Greater London
Countess of Pembroke

Enlargement and alterations carried out. Further work 1796.•

Gawdy Hall, Suffolk
Revd Mr Holmes

Soane supplied drawings for alterations although only one—for a chimneypiece—is now in the Museum. There are ledger references to working drawings for the library bookcases, and Soane made seven journeys to see the work in progress. The house has been pulled down, and there is a housing estate on the site.

London, Queen Anne Street West
William Martin

Soane supervised alterations to Mr Martin's house and its subsequent decoration.

248 *List of Works 1788–1789*

Norwich Hospital, Norfolk
Through Robert Fellowes of Shotesham

Soane gave advice on minor alterations to the hospital which has been founded by Mr Fellowes' father, and built by Thomas Ivory *circa* 1770. The work was carried out, but Soane made no charge for his advice.

Bury St Edmunds, No. 81 Guildhall
Street, Suffolk
James Oakes

Alterations and additions carried out.●

Honing Hall, Norfolk
Thomas Cubitt

Although no drawings survive in the Museum, two plans for alterations, unsigned, but inscribed 'Welbeck Street, 6 Dec. 1788' remain at Honing and are undoubtedly by Soane, who made a new dining-room and a secondary staircase. Mid-nineteenth-century alterations have made the precise extent of his work difficult to determine.●

1789 **Wokefield,** Berkshire
Mrs Brocas

A 'drawing of additions' to this house is mentioned in Soane's Journal but no copy was kept. There are also references to a gateway. The house was much altered towards the end of the nineteenth century. Soane designed the Brocas chapel in Bramley Church (q.v.) for the same client in 1801.

Norwich Castle Gaol, Norfolk (Plate 85)
Norfolk Magistrates

Soane's commission was to alter and enlarge the gaol accommodation within the keep of the castle where he formed new cells for felons over an arcaded basement round a central airing court.

Male and female debtors were to be housed in an embattled addition to the east side of the keep, where there were also a chapel and offices.

The appearance of the new building was severely criticised by the elder William Wilkins in a paper read to the Society of Antiquaries in 1795. Soane defended his designs in his *Memoirs*, referring to Wilkins as 'an able stuccatore' which implies that he was related to James Wilkins, a plasterer employed by Soane for some of his Norfolk works. Thirty years later the younger Wilkins removed all traces of Soane's work at the castle.

Sydney Lodge, Hamble, Hampshire
(Plate 87)
Hon. Mrs Yorke

New house built for the stepmother of the 3rd Earl of Hardwicke. See page 140.*

Tyttenhanger, Hertfordshire
Hon. Mrs Yorke

Further repairs and improvements carried out.

Tawstock Court, Devonshire
Sir Bourchier Wrey

Alterations to house and new staircase built following a fire. See page 141.•

Wreatham Hall, Norfolk
William Colhoun

Designs for house illustrated in Soane's *Sketches* of 1793, where they are described as 'intended'. There is no indication as to whether they were carried out and a later house by Sir Reginald Blomfield was demolished some years ago.

Reading, Simonds' Brewery, Berkshire
(Plates 88–9)
William Blackall Simonds

Soane submitted designs for a new residence, with an office on the ground floor, and for a new brew-house and stables. Working drawings were sent in the following year. White bricks were obtained from Richard Holland, slates from R. Jones and artificial stone from Sealy, natural stonework being carried out by James Nelson. The house was completed in 1794, and an additional office building was erected in 1803, but none of these Soane buildings have survived. See page 145.

Fairford House, Gloucester
J. R. Barker

Soane made designs for altering the house, including a new staircase, and remodelling the dining-room and library. Only the drawings for three chimneypieces and one plan of the house are now in the Museum. The house was demolished in the 1950s when the ironwork staircase balustrade was acquired for a secondary staircase at Corsham Court in Wiltshire.

Westhill, Wandsworth, Greater London
D. H. Rucker

Plans for alterations, probably unexecuted.

Gunthorpe Hall, Norfolk (Plate 86)
Charles Collyer

New house built. See page 140.•

Halsnead, near Rainhall, Lancashire
Richard Willis

Designs supplied for a new façade and portico for an existing house, previously called Red Hall. The copies of the designs in the Museum have dimensions on them and it is evident that the work was carried out by local workmen. The house was pulled down *circa* 1930.

Chilton Lodge, Berkshire (Plate 90)
William Morland

Soane designed this house to replace an earlier building. See page 143.

Stanmore, The Old Church of St John the Evangelist, Middlesex
At Lord Abercorn's request

Soane designed a gallery for this church which became a ruin after the new church had been built in 1850.

1790   **Ireland**
Lady Granard

Two plans and an elevation of a villa were included in Soane's book of 1793, described as 'proposed to be built'. It has not been located.

London, No. 23 or 24 Bruton Street
Sir William Milner

A plan of 1790 shows Soane's proposals for enlarging rooms at the rear of an eighteenth-century house, but both Nos. 23 and 24 have been much altered, with shops on the ground floor, and nothing relating to the plan survives.

Wycombe Abbey, Buckinghamshire
? Earl of Shelburne

Three undated plans marked 'Wycombe House c. 1790' are in the Museum. One is marked 'Intended Alterations', the others show the old house and proposed new stables. The proposals appear to have been set aside.

Woodeaton Manor House, Oxfordshire
John Weyland

Additions and a new porch executed.•

Steephill, Isle of Wight
Hon. Wilbraham Tollemache

Designs for alterations, probably executed but the house was rebuilt in the 1830s.

London, Buckingham House, Pall Mall
(Plates 91–3)
1st Marquis of Buckingham

Considerable alterations carried out to exterior and interior of the house. See page 144.

London, No. 104 Pall Mall
Mr Crook

Soane gave a design for a shop front followed by working drawings. Crook and Eyston are given in Kent's *Directory* of 1807 as haberdashers and hosiers, but the premises were subsequently rebuilt.

Colne Park, Essex
Philip Hills

A copy of Soane's design for a memorial column to be erected in the park survives, as does the column itself, of the Ionic order surmounted by entwined snakes and a pineapple.*

Norwich, house in Surrey Street (Plates 94–5)
John Patteson

Designs followed by working drawings for additions to the house. See page 146.*

Wimpole Hall, Cambridgeshire (Plates 96–100)
3rd Earl of Hardwicke

Extensive alterations to the house and buildings in the grounds including a dairy, lodge, barn and *castello d'aqua*. See page 147.

1791   **Baronscourt**, Co. Tyrone (Plates 101–2)
1st Marquis of Abercorn

Extensive additions to house but centre gutted by fire in 1796. See page 150.•

Williamstrip, Gloucestershire
Hicks Beach

Library and other alterations carried out but no longer surviving.

London, Old Cavendish Street
Edward Foxhall

Soane designed a shop front for his old friend, Foxhall, but it was later demolished.

London, Leicester Square, proposed Opera House

A design survives for this project which did not materialise.

Whichcotes, Hendon, Greater London
John Cornwall

Repairs were carried out to this house, and a new marble chimneypiece was set in the drawingroom. The client was related by marriage to Charles and P. I. Thellusson for whom Soane worked in London. Whichcotes has now been demolished.

Wiston Hall, Suffolk
Samuel Beachcroft

Mr Beachcroft, a director and governor of the Bank of England, commissioned Soane to enlarge his small country house near Nayland. No elevational drawings survive but there is a plan in the Museum and accounts for the work carried out. The house was partly rebuilt and enlarged during the 1860s, but a tablet with the initials 'S.B.' and the date 1791 is on the east wall.•

London, No. 43 (?renumbered 23) Hill Street
1st Earl Fortescue

A considerable amount of alteration and decoration was carried out by Soane, but the house was destroyed by enemy action in the Second World War.

London, No. 56 Pall Mall
Ransom, Morland and Hammersley

Alterations and decorations were carried out, and a new office was built at the rear. No drawings survive in the Museum. Mr Morland was later a co-director with Soane of the British Fire Office.

Designs for a porch to a country house,
   ? location
Hon. Henry Fane

Probably unexecuted.

Moggerhanger, Bedfordshire
Godfrey Thornton

First designs for a house. Set aside until 1809. See page 194.

Netheravon House, Wiltshire
Hicks Beach

Soane designed a three-storey addition with kitchen quarters in the basement and a new drawing-room and bedrooms above. The work was carried out, as was the smaller of two designs for lodges. The latter, in flint with a thatched roof, survived until the present century. Soane's additions are now somewhat obscured by further additions.•

Cambridge, Senate House, proposed new
   Museum, etc.
Vice Chancellor, University of Cambridge

Drawings delivered, but not put into execution.

London, house in St James's Place
Robert Smith, later 1st Baron Carrington

Plans for improvements. Work carried out, but house not identified and probably one of those later demolished.

London, No. 147 Piccadilly
Charles-Alexandre de Calonné

Design for a chimneypiece supplied to M. Calonné, a French refugee who leased No. 147 for some years. The house has been demolished.

London, House of Commons
Office of Works

As clerk of the works responsible for buildings in Whitehall and Westminster at this time Soane supervised, in consultation with Henry Holland, new systems of plumbing, heating and ventilation.

London, Bank of England (Plates 103–28)
The Governor and Court

Although Soane was appointed architect to the Bank on 16 October 1788, this involved only minor work until 1791 when he was directed to prepare first schemes for rebuilding the Bank Stock Office. See pages 151–68.•

1792 **Wydiall,** Hertfordshire
'Mr Ellis'

Designs sent for cottages. No charge made, and the cottages have not been identified.

Wandsworth Common, Greater London
Benjamin Cole

Designs for alterations to a house which has not been identified.

London, No. 15 Philpot Lane
P. I. Thellusson

Extensive repairs and decorations carried out.

London, house in Hereford Street,
? No. 14
Joseph Smith

Extensive repairs and decorations carried out under Soane's supervision.

Buckland, Berkshire
Sir John Throckmorton

Design for a library and 'improvements' supplied after Soane had visited the house, but the present library does not appear to be his work, and much redecoration was carried out in about 1910.

Winchester, Hampshire, The King's
House
Commissioners of H.M. Treasury

Repairs and alterations carried out.

Taplow, Buckinghamshire
Lady Wynn

Lady Wynn was Lord Buckingham's sister Charlotte, and the design for adding a drawing-room with a bow window, and a bedroom above, was sent to Stowe. The work was carried out, but the house has not been identified.

Tyringham House, Buckinghamshire
(Plates 129–37)
William Mackworth Praed

Designs for a new house, gateway and bridge carried out. See page 169.*

Cambridge, Caius College
The Syndics

Plans for improvements and restoration of the old hall. Three elevations in the Museum show that the latter was given a barrel vault with coffered plasterwork, each coffer having a large flat rosette. At the north end a glazed lunette was placed above cornice level. The work was carried out with Henry Provis in charge. The new hall was divided up in 1853 and nothing of Soane's work is now visible.

Cambridge, St John's College
The Syndics

Soane was asked to superintend repairs in the First Court, and to give plans for 'the general improvement of the College buildings'. No copies remain in the Museum, and it seems that only the repairs were carried out.

Norwich, Norfolk
Alderman Crowe

Designs given for a house which has not been identified.

London, house in Fenchurch Street
Charles Thellusson

Decorations and repairs to a large city house which does not survive.

London, house in Mark Lane
Samuel Boddington

Alterations and repairs to the counting house of Mr Boddington, who was a director of the Bank of England.

London, house in Cloak Lane
J. F. Iselin

There are accounts for repairs and decorations, carried out for Mr Iselin for whom Soane had made designs for a house at Hetherset in 1788. Nothing remains of the Cloak Lane premises.

Sulby Lodge, Northamptonshire
René Payne

In October Soane visited Sulby taking with him six drawings for alterations, based on surveys made previously by his draughtsman Meyer. Soane went again in November, and also visited nearby Dunton where the same client wanted alterations to a farm house (q.v. 1793). Work proceeded during the next two years, and designs were also given for stables and a bridge in 1794 and 1798. In 1824 Mr Payne wished to make further alterations and alter the entrance façade, when Soane made two journeys. The house was drastically altered at a later date, and was demolished *circa* 1948.

London, St James's Palace, New Guard Room
Office of Works

Following the preparation of plans of the whole range of Palace buildings, Soane submitted designs for a new Guard Room in December 1792, but in the following May three alternatives were drawn out for the 'Entrances into the Officers' Apartments &c.' The simplest design was chosen and a working drawing is dated 4 October 1793. Accounts show that the brickwork was mainly in reduced stocks with gauged arches of best Malms set in putty. The present Guard Room and officers' rooms occupy the site of Soane's block but have been entirely rebuilt, and there is no trace of his work.

Arrington, Cambridgeshire, The
    Hardwicke Arms Inn
3rd Earl of Hardwicke

Improvements were carried out to the inn, chiefly by Richard Holland who was responsible for carpentry and for supplying '3 chimneypieces complete with pateras'.

London, 1 Upper Grosvenor Street
Mrs Brocas

Redecoration and repair work carried out.

? location
Sir Frederick Eden

In this year Soane gave his future neighbour at No. 22 Lincoln's Inn Fields two designs for a villa, but no clue is given as to the intended site.

London, No. 12 Lincoln's Inn Fields
    (Plates 27–8)
Soane for himself

No. 12 was Soane's first house in Lincoln's Inn Fields.*

1793 **Sheerness,** Kent
The Levant Merchants

Designs for a Lazaretto, unexecuted.

Wimborne, Dorset, St Giles' House
5th Earl of Shaftesbury

Soane visited the house and sent a clerk to take measurements for the designs subsequently sent to the earl for improvements to the house and offices. There are no further references, but the drawings may have formed the basis for work carried out by local builders as the staircase hall, with its groined vault and glazed lantern, has a Soanic quality although attributed to Thomas Cundy who made alterations here in 1813–20.

Barselton House, Hertfordshire
Hon. Mrs Yorke

This may be identified with Berkesden, on the outskirts of Buntingford, a manor which belonged to the Yorkes. The work included carpentry in the house, and the building of a mason's shop, a privy, and three sheds for the clerk of the works.

Dunton Bassett, Leicestershire
René Payne

In March 1793 Soane supplied plans for a farm house apparently to replace an old building which he had seen when visiting Sulby in the previous year. It has not been identified, but must have been built as Soane was paid for the working drawings and for measuring the works on completion.

London, No. 105 Pall Mall
Lady Louisa Manners

Alterations and repairs carried out to her house.

London, Grand Junction Canal,
    Paddington
? Bishop of London's Estate

Design for a decorative feature with four Ionic columns and a central niche in which stands a youthful figure in whose hands is an urn from which water flows. Perhaps intended for a scheme in which new streets were to be laid out on this estate, in which the canal terminated.

Palmer's Green, Middlesex
Thomas Lewis

More than £1,000 was spent on alterations and decorations to this house which has not been identified. They included a chimneypiece originally intended for Lord Hardwicke and purchased for £35 to be used in Mr Lewis's drawing-room.

? location
Richard Crichton

Designs for a castellated house. Not executed.

1794 ? location
Edward Darell

Design for a chimneypiece.

? location
R. Gervas Kerr

Design for a portico.

Sunderland, Co. Durham, bridge over the
    Wear
Rowland Burdon

Soane's advice was sought on the possibility of constructing a stone single-span bridge of 236 feet and, on surveying the situation, he expressed his doubts. It was eventually decided to drop the idea of a stone bridge and to build one of cast iron, a venture which Soane supported, and in which he took shares.

Cairness, Scotland
Charles Gordon

Portico designed by Soane and carried out, completing work on this house begun by James Playfair shortly before his death.●

Cuffnels, Hampshire
George Rose

South front refaced, new orangery built, and internal alterations including a library for which Soane supplied designs. The work was apparently carried out by a local builder, previously employed at Cadlands. The house has now been demolished.

Pitshill, Sussex
William Mitford

In March 1794 Soane provided this client with several designs for altering Pitshill and subsequently met Mr Mitford's builder on the matter. This led to misunderstanding, and Soane claimed to have destroyed the drawings following this meeting. There are, however, sketches for doorways on the reverse of an elevation in the Museum which correspond to details which survive in the house and suggest that the builder followed at least some of the ideas which had been put forward by Soane.

Reading, Berkshire, houses in London
    Place
W. B. Simonds

Designs for a terrace of houses, presumably not carried out.

Sunbury House, Middlesex
Roger Boehm

Soane supplied drawings for alterations to the house but it has since been drastically remodelled and no trace of his work survives.

London, Houses of Parliament
Office of Works

Designs for a new House of Lords, unexecuted. See pages 68–9.

London, No. 51 Lincoln's Inn Fields
John Pearse

Considerable alterations carried out under Soane's direction, including a new geometrical staircase. A room at the rear was given a shallow vaulted ceiling with fluted plasterwork, while the dining-room ceiling was embellished with a plaster flower which had previously belonged to Soane. House later demolished.

1795 **Beauport,** Sussex
James Bland Burgess

This house had previously belonged to General Murray for whom Soane had designed gardens in 1786. It was acquired by James Bland Burgess in 1794, and in the following year Soane noted that he had supplied him with designs. There are, however, no details as to these, and the architect apparently had difficulty in obtaining settlement of his account for many years.

Dunninald House, Scotland
David Scott

Soane called many times in the course of this year on David Scott, chairman of the East India Company, at his London houses in Harley Street or Streatham. This was to discuss plans for Dunninald, for which plans by Playfair had been cut short by the latter's death. Soane's designs were for gothic and classical alternatives. He later supplied a 'plan for the digger', and recommended a young man called Farquhar as clerk of the works (perhaps Colin Farquhar who exhibited at the Royal Academy, 1791–9). Soane also supplied detailed plans and elevations with estimates amounting to over £16,530, and in 1799 he was paid £203.19.6 for his part in the project. It seems unlikely that any part of it was carried out before Mr Scott's death in 1805, when the property passed into other hands.

London, No. 429 The Strand
Westminster Insurance on Lives

Plans for alterations, probably executed.

London, No. 12 Stratton Street
Colonel Thomas Graham, later
 Baron Lynedoch

House designed and built. It was on a narrow site so that the façade was only two bays across with a dining-room on the ground floor, and a drawing-room and library on the first floor. The curving staircase was top-lit. The work was completed in 1799, and the house stood until the present century when it was destroyed.

London, No. 56 South Audley Street
Miss Anguish

Repairs and decorations carried out. It was later rebuilt.

Winchester, Hampshire, Hyde Close
(Plates 138–9)
Revd Mr Richards

Soane gave Mr Richards a design for his celebrated 'Academy' which was built of brick with a slate roof. It survives although slightly altered. See page 175.*

London, Nos. 57 and 58 Lincoln's Inn
Fields
'Late Lord Mansfield's'

Soane drew up plans for the division of the house after Lord Mansfield's death in 1793.•

Palmer's Green, Middlesex
Samuel Boddington

Alterations carried out to Mr Boddington's house, including Soane's plan for a new 'eating room'.

Southgate, Middlesex
John Grey

A new gardener's house and rustic lodge built.

London, No. 70 (originally 25) Portland Place
Sir Alan Gardner

Extensive repairs and alterations carried out. Further repairs 1810. Now demolished.

Bagdon Lodge, Wiltshire
1st Earl of Ailesbury

Soane was asked to prepare alternative designs for converting the lodge into a residence for this client's son, Lord Bruce. The approved scheme was, however, modified in execution. It was renamed Savernake Lodge but was burnt down in the middle of the nineteenth century when its stables were converted into a small residence which now bears this name.

Hinton St George, Somerset
4th Earl Poulett

Designs were prepared for extensive alterations, but from a remark in Soane's *Memoirs* it seems that his proposals were set aside in favour of designs by James Wyatt.

Little Green, Sussex
T. P. Phipps

Although designs were prepared both for altering the existing house and for building a new one, neither was executed.

? location
Mr Henderson

Soane's Journal records that an elevation and two plans for a cottage for Mr Henderson were left at Lord Abercorn's house in Grosvenor Square, but there are no further details.

Richmond Park, Surrey
Office of Works

A sheet of elevations and plans for a lodge and gateway into the park at the top of Richmond Hill are marked 'approved by His Majesty' but Soane's name is not mentioned in the Declared Accounts for the building of the present lodge in that year by 'Messrs Kent, Claridge and Pearce'. Soane was, of course, deputy surveyor at this time.

London, No. 21 St James's Square
5th Duke of Leeds

Soane was called in to complete a house begun by Robert Brettingham after some fault in the construction had led to the latter's dismissal. Soane not only took over the direction of the work but supplied designs for alterations. The house was demolished in 1934.

1796	**London**, St Botolph, Aldgate Vestry Committee	Surveys of steeple and designs for alterations made in conjunction with James Spiller.
	Reading, Berkshire Lancelot Austwick	Following a visit to survey the site, Soane submitted designs for a small house of three bays, but a plan of 1796 indicates that the size was increased to five bays. It seems that in the course of building there were also other additions. The house was pulled down and rebuilt following a Ministry of Housing inquiry in 1959.
	London, Park Lane 2nd Earl of Mornington	Repairs and alterations to his house. Now destroyed.
	Tortworth Court, Gloucestershire 3rd Baron Ducie	Soane submitted alternative designs for lodges but they do not appear to have been built.
	London, No. 12 Downing Street Hon. John Eliot	A small amount of repair and decorative work was done here for Mr Eliot who, on succeeding as 1st Earl of St Germans, was to employ Soane on extensive work at Port Eliot.
1797	**London**, The Strand, an unspecified house	Soane's drawings include plans and an elevation for a house and shop on the south side and on the east corner of Strand Lane (later numbered 163A). There is no indication that they were put into execution and the present structure is modern.
	London, Cumberland Gate and lodge, Hyde Park (Plate 140) Office of Woods and Forests	Designed and built. Demolished for the resiting of Marble Arch. See page 176.
	Weston, nr. Southampton, Hampshire W. Moffat	Additions designed for a house at Weston but there are two references in Soane's accounts which suggest that the work may have been handed over to Willey Reveley.
	London, Constitution Hill Office of Woods and Forests	Lodge and gateway designed and built but later destroyed.
	North Mymms Park, Hertfordshire 5th Duke of Leeds	Considerable repairs, new greenhouse, dairy, etc.

? location
'Miss Backwell' (? Backall)

Designs for an almshouse. This lady was probably a sister-in-law of William Praed of Tyringham. A drawing shows a single-storey building containing six apartments.

London, No. 48? Grosvenor Square
Countess of Pembroke

Alterations carried out. See page 186.

1798   **Glasgow,** house in Buchanan Street
Robert Dennistoun

Alternative designs were sent to Robert Dennistoun for a house which was built on the west side of the street. It subsequently became the Buchanan Hotel but was later demolished, and the site used for the Monteith Rooms.

Wandsworth, Greater London, house
  on Clapham Common
Thomas Abbot Green

Plans for alterations to house supplied and carried out.

Malvern Hall, Warwickshire (Plate 61)
Henry Greswold Lewis

'Design for a Barn à la Paestum' sent to Malvern 2 May 1798. Now designated 'Doric Barn, 936 Warwick Road, Solihull'. See page 122.*

Bagshot Park, Surrey (Plate 141)
Prince William, Duke of Clarence (later
  King William IV)

Alterations to house carried out and new lodge built. Later demolished. See page 176.

Betchworth Castle, Surrey (Plates 142–4)
Henry Peters

Considerable alterations made to house, also new stables, garden buildings, etc. See page 177.•

Acton, Greater London, Heathfield Lodge
John Winter

Soane supplied two elevations of the front and one end, also a perspective view for two small tenements. The lodge, which survives, is eighteenth century in stock brick with an addition which may be from Soane's design but there are no drawings in the Museum. A two-storey cottage to the north may be one of those referred to in Soane's Bill Book where measuring the bricklayers' and slaters' work is mentioned.•

Richmond Park, Surrey, Thatched House
  Lodge
Office of Woods and Forests

Alteration to dining-room, etc. carried out. It survives in altered form.•

London, No. 34 Gower Street
Mrs Peters

Soane made plans for alterations and a thorough overhauling of this house and its stables for which the work began on 13 March. No. 34 was on the east side of the street and was later demolished.

High Wycombe, Buckinghamshire
Elisha Briscoe

Alterations designed for an unidentified house.

Stanmore, Middlesex, 'Thieves Hole'
Mrs Brewer

Alterations proposed for a house (unidentified) belonging to this lady who was introduced through Lord Abercorn.

? Perthshire, Scotland
Colonel Graham, later Baron Lynedoch

There are drawings for a two-storey farm house with adjacent stables, etc. Soane was paid £26.5.0 for the scheme but there is no reference to its execution.

London, Fountain Court
W. A. Jackson

Repairs to an old building in this year were followed by schemes between 1802–5 for a new building when a choice was made, Soane endorsing his final drawing 'No. 99,999th design for Fountain Court, supposed to be the last!!!' This was carried out but later replaced by a Victorian building.

1799   **Cosgrove Hall,** Buckinghamshire
Mr Mansel

Soane supplied Mr Mansel with six drawings for a new house and offices, but it does not appear to have been built.

Dublin, Ireland, Bank of Ireland
The Court of Directors

Soane was approached for plans of which copies survive in the Museum. Negotiations were conducted through Mr John Puget whose firm acted as London agents for the bank, and who in due course took the designs 'wound round a wood roll' to Dublin. After some three years, however, Soane was informed that it had been decided to adapt the existing building.

Clapham, Greater London
Mrs Adams

Alterations suggested for a house following Soane's visit with a Mr Marsham. Drawings were prepared but do not survive, and there was no charge or indication as to whether the work was carried out.

Aynho Park, Northamptonshire
   (Plates 145–8)
Richard Cartwright

Extensive alterations and additions carried out. See page 179.*

Down Ampney House, Gloucestershire
Hon. John Eliot

Soane designed alterations which were carried out by local artisans.•

London, No. 7 Austin Friars
Commercial Commissioners

Repairs carried out and rooms furnished under Soane's direction.

London, Lincoln's Inn Fields
Trustees of the Fields

Proposals designed by Soane for a new block to be built on the east side. Not executed.

London, No. 22 St James's Square
Samuel Thornton

Extensive alterations carried out. Further work, mainly repairs, in 1805 and 1811.

London, No. 1 Mansfield Street
Charles Mills

A Bill Book contains accounts for extensive work, including a bow window added to this house which stood at the south end of the west side. Now rebuilt.

London, Nos. 6 & 7 Kings Arms Yard
Thornton, Bayley & Amyand

Repairs and decorations carried out.

London, Frederick's Place
J. W. & I. Whitmore

Extensive repairs carried out.

London, No. 24 St George Street
Dr Pemberton

This was the house of Soane's friend and physician for whom he planned alterations for which there are drawings in the Museum. The house has been rebuilt in recent years.

London, No. 25 (formerly No. 26)
   Grosvenor Square
1st Marquis of Abercorn

Alterations and repairs carried out.

1800   **London**, ? 67 Grosvenor Street
Duchess of Leeds

There are no surviving drawings. A Bill Book gives details of fairly extensive decorations carried out by Soane but none appears to survive.

London, No. 54 Old Broad Street
Stephen Thornton

Alterations carried to first and second floors. Neither the building nor the drawings for Soane's work survive.

Bath, Somerset, Seymour Street
Christopher Barnard

Designs for eating-room, probably carried out. A large part of this street was destroyed in the last war.

Albury Park, Surrey
Samuel Thornton

Soane was consulted on alterations soon after Mr Thornton's purchase of the house and made his first designs in 1800, although those surviving in the Museum date from 1801–5 and concern the remodelling of the principal reception rooms and staircase. Most of these survive although the house was extensively altered by A. W. Pugin in the 1840s.•

Wall Hall, Hertfordshire
G. W. Thellusson

New entrance and rooms designed but apparently unexecuted.

Tyringham Church, Buckinghamshire
W. M. Praed

Designs for a classical church prepared but not carried out.

Ealing, Greater London, Pitzhanger
   Manor (Plates 32–7)
Soane for himself

Rebuilt by Soane, but retaining two rooms by George Dance. See page 181.

Rickmansworth, Hertfordshire, The
   Moat House
T. H. Earle

Alterations and additions noted and probably carried out but the house has not been identified.

Micklefield Hall, near Rickmansworth,
   Hertfordshire
Elisha Briscoe

Minor alterations carried out but house has not been identified.

1801   **London,** No. 22 Dunraven Street
   (formerly New Norfolk Street)
J. Hammet

Seven sheets of drawings for alterations were prepared for work to cost about £1,500 but after this had begun a misunderstanding arose when Hammet accused Soane of 'neglect and inattention'. Soane maintained that the client had interferred in the course of the work by instructing the men to alter floor levels, etc. Hammet called in James Spiller to take charge. The house has been much changed but the porch of the house has a Soanic character.

London, No. 54 Park Street
Kenelm Digby

Repairs and alterations to the extent of £279 were carried out under Soane's direction.

London, Bartholomew Lane
Down, Thornton and Free

Soane supervised alterations to this City counting house when the 'back front' was rebuilt and other alterations and redecorations were carried out. It was later rebuilt.

London, No. 90 Fleet Street (Plate 149)
W. M. Praed

This new banking house was designed by Soane for his client at Tyringham. The site was on the north side of the street, to the west of Clifford's Inn Passage. Demolished in 1923. See page 182.

South Hill Park, Bracknell, Berkshire
Rt. Hon. George Canning

Two surviving plans suggest that Soane's alterations were confined to the replacing of a doorway in the library, the building of a loggia between the two slightly projecting wings of the garden front, and work in the domestic quarters. Soane's charge for the designs was £9 but his client was so delighted with them that he sent the architect £42. No traces of the work survive as the house was almost entirely rebuilt in 1853.

Aldenham House, Hertfordshire
Lady Dalling

Soane visited this early eighteenth-century house and subsequently gave Lady Dalling an estimate for repairs and redecorations amounting to just under £1,000, which were carried out, John Crace being responsible for the painting. Extensive changes were made in the 1870s and Soane's work has disappeared.

Norwood Green, Middlesex (Plate 150)
John Robins

New house designed and built. See page 184.

Bramley, Hampshire, Church of St James
Mrs Brocas

Soane designed a chapel to be built on the south side of this church as a memorial to the husband of Mrs Brocas, a sister of Samuel Bosanquet. It has a ribbed vault and a five-light window supplied to Soane's design by Coade and Sealy. The chapel houses a monument to Bernard Brocas by Thomas Banks.*

London, Chelsea, General Wilford's House
General Wilford

Soane supplied several designs for the alteration of this house, originally called Prospect Place, which was some way to the east of the Ranelagh Rotunda. An early nineteenth-century drawing shows a long three-storey façade with an Ionic portico, but there is no clue as to whether Soane's designs were executed. The house was demolished for the setting out of Chelsea Bridge Road in 1854.

Cricket Lodge, Cricket St Thomas,
  Somerset (Plate 151)
1st Viscount Bridport

Further work carried out. See page 184.●

Coombe House, Kingston
  Surrey
1st Baron Hawkesbury, later 2nd Earl of
  Liverpool

Further work carried out (see 1782)

including addition of a library.

1802   **Uxbridge Treaty House,** Middlesex
Grand Junction Canal Co.

Soane held a number of shares in this Company. Plans of the early sixteenth-century building were required in this year when draughtsman Seward was sent to take measurements. Soane subsequently proposed minor alterations including a small additional block containing a staircase and rooms on the north. The work was probably carried out but some demolition has taken place on the north side of the building.

Macartney House, Greenwich, Greater
  London
Hon. G. F. Lyttelton

Soane made drastic changes to this early eighteenth-century house by projecting from its northern half a two-storey wing, and making alterations to the earlier rooms such as the dining-room which became a library. Much of this work survives.●

London, No. 48 Grosvenor Square
  (Plate 152)
Robert Knight

Further alterations carried out. See page 186.

1803   **Little Hill Court,** Hertfordshire
Mrs Saunders

Designs for internal alterations are preserved in one of Soane's folios, but the house has not been located and there is no reference in the account books.

London, Breadalbane House, Park Lane
4th Earl of Breadalbane

Soane's Account Book refers to 'altering some of the windows on the principal floor and directing the execution of the same'.

Taymouth Castle, Perthshire, Scotland
4th Earl of Breadalbane

Soane prepared a series of schemes for the redecoration of the castle including the dining and drawing-rooms, the breakfast and music-rooms. Copies are in the Museum. It was, however, 1818 before he received payment of £105 for his trouble. They were apparently not executed as A. & J. Elliot rebuilt the castle on a different site in 1806.

London, No. 14 Upper Grosvenor Street
Thomas Raikes

Considerable alterations carried out. The house has now been rebuilt.

London, No. 19 (now 27) Curzon Street
Sir John Sebright

Extensive alterations carried out, the cost of which amounted to £2,333. The house has, however, been entirely rebuilt.

1804 **Reading,** Berkshire, Simeon Monument in
Market Place
Edward Simeon

Although a director of the Bank of England, and resident in London, Mr Simeon's connection with Reading was no doubt through his brother, Sir John Simeon, the recorder and twice member of parliament for that town. A trust was made for the obelisk designed by Soane several of whose drawings remain in the Museum, as well as a mahogany model. In the chosen version the obelisk has fluted panels on each of its three faces, and a border of Greek fret along the three splayed angles. The mason responsible was James Marshall, the bricklayer J. Lovegrove, and the smith Thomas Russell. John Neville supplied three large lanterns and their iron supports. The obelisk, although still standing, has been mutilated by the local authorities in recent years.*

Port Eliot, Cornwall (Plates 153–6)
Hon. John Eliot, 2nd Baron Eliot, and later
Earl of St Germans

Alterations to house, new stables and family pew in church. See page 187.*

Ramsey Abbey, Cambridgeshire
(Plate 157)
W. H. Fellowes

Between 1804 and 1806 Soane prepared many designs for remodelling the house. See page 189.*

Reading, Berkshire, house in Castle Street
W. B. Simonds

Soane drew out designs for this house and attached offices described as 'intended to have been built'. A note in Ledger D, however, states that an account for preparing these should be transferred to

W. May Esq. of Burghfield and it seems that the latter had acquired the property. There is no indication as to whether the house was built but if it was, it does not now exist.

Roehampton, Greater London, Cedar Court (Plate 158)
John Thomson

Soane's designs incorporated part of an earlier late seventeenth-century house, and were carried out at a cost of nearly £14,000. The house was demolished between 1910 and 1913, and only a pair of gate piers survive. See page 190.

Beechwood, Hertfordshire
Sir John Sebright

Soane certainly supplied Sir John with designs for a library, and in May 1804 made 'drawings . . . for the workmen'. The library today, however, suggests that the bookcases were changed at a later date.•

1805   **Stowe,** Buckinghamshire (Plates 160–1)
1st Marquis of Buckingham

'Gothic Library' and vestibule built. They survive almost intact. See page 191.*

London, No. 31 St James's Square
2nd Baron Eliot

Extensive alterations carried out in this year and again in 1817, but the house has been greatly altered and only traces of Soane's work remain.•

London, St Giles's Church
Parish Council

Designs for a lobby and porch. Unexecuted.

Astrop Park, Oxfordshire
Revd Mr Willes

Additions to the house including a dining-room. Further additions in the nineteenth century obliterated most of Soane's work, although the columns in the dining-room survive.•

Banbury, Oxfordshire
James King

Alternative designs for a house survive, but appear not to have been executed.

Combe House, Devonshire
Reymundo Putt

Soane made designs for additions to an existing house but these were shelved until 1811 when there were proposals for a new classical house, several drawings surviving at Combe. Mr Putt's sudden death, however, put an end to the project.

1806   **Englefield House,** Berkshire
      Richard Benyon

A Cost Book for 1806–7 has entries for repairs carried out to this house under Soane's supervision. These followed minor repairs carried out in 1805 to Mr Benyon's London house No. 6 Audley Square.

      Leytonstone, Greater London, St Mary's
        Church
      Bosanquet family

Samuel Bosanquet of Forest House was a governor of the Bank of England for whom Soane had carried out repairs over the years to this house and to the same client's properties at 25 Watling Street and 75 Gracechurch Street. Following Mr Bosanquet's death Soane designed his tomb in which other members of the family were also later buried. It stood until about 1960 when, with other nearby tombs, it was demolished.

1807   **London,** Dean (now Deanery) Street
      Robert Knight

A good deal of alteration and redecoration was carried out by Soane for Mr Knight at a house which stood in the angle formed by a bend in this street. A later house on this site was demolished during the Second World War.

      London, New Bank Buildings, Princes
        Street (Plate 159)
      Bank of England

Built as mercantile residences. See page 190.

      Whitley Abbey, Warwickshire
      1st Viscount Hood

Soane was first consulted on the restoration of an Elizabethan house in this year although alternative schemes continued to be produced until the final selection in 1810. This proposed a new drawing-room, dining-room and hall within the old house, with additions at either end of the building. The house was demolished in the early 1950s.

      London, Royal Hospital, Chelsea
        (Plates 166–71)
      The Governor and Board

Soane was appointed clerk of the works to the Hospital in this year and held the office until his death. See page 196.

      Oxford, Brasenose College
      The Seniority of the College

Soane produced a plan for four suites of additional accommodation, each consisting of a sitting-room bedroom and closet, these being contrived on the east side of the seventeenth-century cloister range. The work was carried out and remains with only slight alterations. His grandiose classical design for a new building extending along the High Street did not materalise.

London, No. 34 (later 39) Grosvenor Square
Mrs Benyon

Extensive alterations were carried out and are detailed in Soane's accounts, but the house was entirely remodelled in the late nineteenth century when his work disappeared.

London, No. 38 Charlotte (now Hallam) Street (Plates 164–5)
Sir Francis Bourgeois

The mausoleum designed by Soane for the remains of Bourgeois's benefactor, Noel Desenfans, was built at the rear of this house. It was demolished after a new mausoleum had been erected as part of the gallery designed by Soane at Dulwich College, q.v. See page 195.

1808   **Hagley,** Worcestershire, Church of St John Baptist
2nd Baron Lyttelton

Soane designed a memorial urn to the 1st Baron Lyttelton and although no designs have survived, the urn appears in the large water-colour fantasy by Gandy showing all Soane's architectural works up to 1815. The urn was apparently destroyed in 1858.

Herne Hill Cottage, Greater London
Mme Anna Storace

Soane and his wife befriended Anna Storace after the break-up of her marriage to J. A. Fisher, and during her attachment to John Braham, when she resided at this cottage. Accounts show that Soane made additions to it, but there are no drawings, and it was subsequently demolished.

Belfast Academical Institution, N. Ireland
The Management Committee

Soane was approached for a plan and in fact by the end of this year had submitted seven alternative schemes for which he refused to accept a fee. Expense proved a problem, and the architect agreed to modify the designs. The foundation stone was laid on 3 July 1810. The remodelling of the interior on several occasions has left no trace of Soane's hand in the rooms.•

London, Southwark Cathedral, Monument
   to Abraham Newland
Governor of the Bank of England

A tablet on the south wall of the south
choir aisle was designed by Soane to
commemorate Abraham Newland who
had served the Bank as chief cashier for
thirty years, and in another capacity for
thirty years before that.*

1809   **Butterton Hall,** Staffordshire (Plate 180)
Thomas Swinnerton

Soane's designs proposed incorporating a
mid-eighteenth-century house. A model
was also prepared but the project hung fire
for several years and was eventually
abandoned although the same client
commissioned a farm house in 1815, q.v.

London, Fife House, Whitehall
2nd Earl of Liverpool

This house came up for sale in 1809 when
Soane negotiated its purchase on behalf of
Lord Liverpool for £12,000. He
subsequently supervised extensive repairs
and improvements for which the accounts
amount to over £3,724. Further work was
carried out in subsequent years partly to
stem damp caused by the nearby river.
Fife House was demolished *circa* 1868.

Moggerhanger, Bedfordshire
   (Plates 162–3)
Godfrey Thornton

New designs drawn up for this house and
carried out. See page 194.•

1810   **Mells Park,** Somerset
Colonel Thomas Horner

Soane was called in after James Spiller had
relinquished the commission for
alterations. See page 200.

Jersey, Channel Islands
Clement Hemery

At the request of this client Soane
supplied designs for enlarging the
principal reception rooms and adding a
tetrastyle Doric porch to this three-storey,
five-window house. Mr Hemery had sent
with his request a plan and elevation of the
existing house, one of which is inscribed
'Chateau belonging to Thomas Pipon Esq.
Lieut Bailiff' which suggests that Mr
Hemery had recently acquired the
property. It has not so far been identified.

? location
Sir John Coxe Hippisley

In September Soane sent Sir John eight
drawings 'for the cottage' which the latter
apparently intended to build in the
countryside for a retired friend and his
wife, but the precise location is not

mentioned nor is there any reference to the designs having been executed. Two years later Soane supplied Sir John with a plan and elevation for 'an octangular seat', and in 1813 he sent him six drawings for 'alterations of a house at the Isle of Wight'. Sir John had cousins, the Oglanders, at Nunwell on the island, and he himself later commissioned a 'marine villa' to be built by John Nash at West Cowes.

1811   **Lampton,** ? location

There are six drawings for a villa, and six for a 'bungalow' marked 'Lampton', and prepared in this year, but with no indication as to the precise location or client. The design is simple but typically Soanic, being mainly on the ground floor but with a bedroom in a central attic.

Dulwich Picture Gallery and Mausoleum, Greater London (Plates 172–7)
The Master and Wardens of Dulwich College

Designed and built. See page 200.*

Everton House, Bedfordshire
William Astell

William Thornton of Everton assumed the surname of Astell in 1807 after succeeding to his uncle's estate. Four years later he consulted Soane on additions to the house. A single plan and elevation only remain in the Museum, Mr Astell having asked to keep the many drawings prepared. The work was put in hand under Richard Matthews, and there are accounts in the Museum. Writing to Soane in December 1815 Mr Astell refers to his house as 'warm and comfortable, thanks to your skill and kind attention'. Minor work carried out for this client at a house in Old Broad Street and at No. 4 Portland Place is listed in Bill Books 1 and 2. Everton was destroyed early in this century.

1812   **Chiswick,** Churchyard of St Nicholas, Greater London
Mrs de Loutherbourg

In April of this year Soane was asked to design a tomb for Philippe Jacques de Loutherbourg. Three designs are on a single sheet, one of them endorsed by the widow, 'Here I fix my choice', although as executed the tomb departs slightly from the drawing. It stands close to the north walk of the churchyard.*

Walmer, St Mary's (Old) Church, Kent
At request of 2nd Earl of Liverpool

As warden of the Cinque Ports, Lord Liverpool took an interest in this church and asked Soane to prepare alternative schemes for enlargement. Neither appears to have met with approval by the parish council and the church was later enlarged by another architect.

Walmer, Kent, Walmer Cottage
At request of 2nd Earl of Liverpool

In the accounts for work done for Lord Liverpool Soane noted 'Sent Capt. Lee three plans and a perspective view for his proposed addition' in March of this year. On 11 May Captain Lee wrote: 'Your plan has been submitted to the bricklyrs. and carpenters which have begun the Room and are getting on with it.' The cottage has not been identified.

London, No. 22 (later 18) Park Lane
John Robins

The drawings show a three-storey house with basement and attics, the latter appearing above a Soanic brick cornice. The first-floor windows opened on to a balcony with serpentine ironwork. The estimate for the house was £5,000 and the work was carried out under the supervision of Soane's clerk, James Cook. The house was considerably altered and enlarged in the late nineteenth century and was damaged by enemy action in 1942 after which it was demolished.

London, No. 13 Lincoln's Inn Fields
Soane for himself

This was Soane's second house in Lincoln's Inn Fields. See pages 203–4.*

? location
Captain Mason

There are drawings for a two-storey three-window house, its façade divided by incised pilaster strips, and with tripartite windows to the ground floor, but no clues are given as to its situation or execution.

1813   **Ringwould House,** Kent (Plate 178)
The Revd John Monins

Until recently Mr Monins's descendants still lived in this two-storey house of pale stock brick with sharply projecting eaves and a 'secret' gutter in its slate roof. Soane made four journeys to inspect the course of the work which was carried out by Henry Harrison.*

Petworth House, Sussex
3rd Earl of Egremont

After a visit to Petworth Soane submitted three alternative designs for a portico for the east front of the house but the idea was dropped. Three years later he supplied four designs for a tower 'at Blackdown' (probably a prospect tower). As he later noted in his Journal 'no charge ever made' it would appear that this project was also dropped, and the existing 'tower' in the park was probably from another hand.

1814   **Cricket St Thomas**, Somerset,
       St Thomas's Church (Plate 179)
       Lady Bridport

At the request of the widow of his previous client, Viscount Bridport, Soane designed the monument to him which was set up in the church. The work was executed by Thomas Grundy at a cost of £251 plus expenses.

Putteridgebury, Hertfordshire
John Sowerby

Soane was asked to make surveys of 'the new buildings' and give 'directions for amendments' which suggests that recent work carried out for John Sowerby by another architect had proved unsatisfactory. Soane also supplied elevations for stables. His clerk James Cook was paid £21.10.6 for attending the work for thirty-nine days, but the rebuilding of the house in 1910 precludes establishing precisely what was done.

1815   **Camolin Park**, Co. Wexford, Ireland
       Viscount Valentia

Soane supplied designs for alterations. As a guide in preparing these he had been sent two sheets of drawings of the existing house, these signed 'George Papworth, Dublin, 1814'. There were apparently three alternative proposals by Soane although only plans survive. They show the addition of wings, and a portico of four, six or eight columns on the principal façade. The house is now a ruin, but it does not seem that his plans were put into execution.

Butterton Farm House, Staffordshire
(Plate 180)
Thomas Swinnerton

Designs for the exterior carried out. See page 206.*

	Sudeley Castle, Gloucestershire 2nd Marquis of Buckingham	Surveys made and alterations proposed but not carried out.
1816	**London**, Carrington House, Whitehall 1st Baron Carrington	Stable block built. Minor alterations to house made two years later. They were demolished in 1886.
	London, No. 13 (later 14) Grosvenor Square 2nd Baron Berwick	Alterations to house carried out but there is no evidence as to their nature and the house has been rebuilt.
	London, Westminster. Designs for a National Monument	Five drawings for a monument to commemorate Waterloo and Trafalgar and dated 1816–18 are among Soane's lecture diagrams, and are mentioned in his *Memoirs*. The project was, however, abandoned.
	London, St Giles's Burial Ground, now St Pancras Gardens (Plates 50–2) Soane for his family	Following his wife's death Soane designed a monument to her to be built over the vault in which she was buried. See page 207.*
1817	**London**, St Mary's Church, Lambeth Mrs Storace senior, mother of Anna Storace	Anna Storace died on 24 August 1817. Soane attended her funeral and subsequently designed her memorial tablet erected on the west wall of the church. The inscription reads

> To the Memory of
> ANN SELINA STORACE
> who died on the 24th day of
> August 1817 aged 51
> her affectionate mother
> Elizabeth Storace
> has erected this tablet

There follows a laudatory verse. The work
was carried out by the mason Thomas
Grundy.

	Snaresbrook, Greater London Jeremiah Harman	Soane supplied this client with two drawings for a 'gothic viranda' for his house at Snaresbrook, but there is no reference to their execution. A pencil note in Soane's journal reads 'No charge ever made. Mr H. dead many years.'

1818　**Canada,** Government House for Upper
　　　　Canada
　　　William Halton, Provincial Agent

In the autumn of this year Soane was
approached by Mr Halton for plans of 'a
Government House of Residence for the
Lt. Governor of Upper Canada'. The
requirements listed a 'substantial *plain*
house' in brick, as well as a separate
building for the Assembly, the Legislative
Council, Courts and accommodation for
officials. Four rough plans survive, but it
is evident that Mr Halton wished for the
drawings without delay. Soane refused to
be hurried, and on being pressed further
in December, he informed the Provincial
Agent that he had now 'discontinued the
subject intirely'.

Upper Clapton, Greater London
Thomas Bros.

Copies of accounts show that extensive
alterations and repairs were carried out
here between 1818 and 1820 but it has not
been possible to identify the house, which
appears to have been elegantly furnished.

London, No. 62 Threadneedle Street
Grote Prescott and Grote

Alterations amounting to over £9915.0.0
were carried out under Soane's direction
but there are no drawings in the Museum
and nothing survives of this banking
house, where Soane had a personal
account for many years.

Marden Hill, Hertfordshire (Plates 182–3)
C. G. Thornton

Alterations carried out to the house and a
new porch added. See page 209*

London, No. 3 St James's Square
3rd Earl of Hardwicke

Soane designed additional rooms at the
rear of this house and supervised the work,
but the house was demolished in 1933.

London, National Debt Redemption Office
　　　(Plate 181)
Commissioners for the Reduction of the
　　　National Debt

Although Soane was first instructed to
prepare plans and estimates for a building
to replace the old office which he had
repaired in 1808, it was March 1818 before
a design was selected. See page 207.

Stowe, Buckinghamshire
2nd Marquis of Buckingham

Soane supplied further designs for 'the
alteration and improvement of the family
apartments', but there is no reference to
their having been carried out.*

1819　**Sudeley Castle,** Gloucestershire
　　　2nd Marquis of Buckingham

On 7 August Soane visited Sudeley again
to make notes and in the following March

submitted plans of the existing building
and designs for proposed alterations, but
these did not materialise.

1820   **London,** No. 14 New Burlington Street
       Admiral Sir Joseph Yorke

From 1819 to 1831 the admiral occupied
this house on alterations to the dining-
room of which he consulted Soane. A plan
was submitted but apparently not
executed as Soane noted in his Journal
'No charge ever made, Sir J. S. Yorke
dead many years.'

Wotton House, Buckinghamshire
       (Plates 184–6)
2nd Marquis of Buckingham

House reconstructed to Soane's design
after a fire. See page 210.*

London, Holy Trinity Church,
       Marylebone (Plates 213–14)
Commissioners for Church Building

Soane's instruction to produce designs for
a new church in Marylebone came in 1820
when his first designs were produced,
although the final set was not approved
until 1824. See page 230.*

London, No. 16 Montague Place
Henry Hase

Henry Hase, chief cashier to the Bank of
England, lived in Montague Place. Soane
carried out extensive repairs and
decorations here in 1820 and 1821.

London, Nos. 156–70 Regent Street, east
       side (Plates 187–8)
John Robins and others

Soane designed a block of shops and
houses lying between Chapel Court and
Beak Street on John Nash's newly formed
Regent Street. Demolished and rebuilt.
See page 210.

London, Houses of Parliament,
       Westminster (Plates 191–6)
Office of Works

Works executed from 1820 onwards. See
page 216.

1821   **Wootton,** Somerset
       Sir Alexander Hood

Designs prepared for additions to the
house, but Soane relinquished the
commission on finding that Sir Alexander
had thoughtlessly superimposed some of
his own ideas on the architect's drawings.

London, Portugal Street, The Insolvent
       Debtors' Court (Plates 197–8)
Commissioners of the Insolvent Debtors'
       Court

A court and offices designed and built.
Demolished *circa* 1903 for building of the
Land Registry Office. See page 219.

Fan Grove, near Windsor, Berkshire
Vice Admiral Sir Henry Hotham

Soane visited Fan Grove and 'viewed the
situation', subsequently supplying the

admiral with 'several slight sketches', but there are no further references.

London, Freemasons' Hall, Great Queen
   Street (Plate 216)
Grand Master's Lodge

Although Soane supervised minor repairs from the time of his appointment as Grand Superintendent of Works in 1813, his first important work was the forming of a new gallery in 1821. His designs for a new Council Chamber were approved and built in 1828. See page 234.

1822 **Pellwall House,** Staffordshire
         (Plates 189–90)
       Purney Sillitoe

New house dsigned and built. See page 214. •

London, The Law Courts, Westminster
   (Plates 199–205)
Office of Works

On 7 February Soane submitted his drawings for the new Courts to the surveyor general. See page 221.

London, St Peter's Church, Walworth
   (Plates 211–12)
Commissioners for Church Building

Designed in this year, St Peter's was the first of Soane's three churches for the commissioners to be completed. See page 230.*

1823 **London,** Board of Trade and Privy Council
         Offices, Whitehall (Plates 206–7)
       Office of Works

Soane's first designs for new offices facing Whitehall are dated May 1823 but were subsequently revised and the work continued until 1827. See page 226. •

London, No. 14 Lincoln's Inn Fields
Soane for subsequent sale

Built with a façade corresponding to No. 12. The site of the stables at the rear retained by Soane for the building of his Picture Room. See page 204.*

1824 **London,** Downing Street, Nos. 10, 11, 12
         and the Old Foreign Office
         (Plates 208–10)
       Office of Works

Between this year and 1826 Soane carried out a good deal of work on these houses, including the addition of a new dining-room at No. 10 and a breakfast-room at No. 11, both of which survive. See page 228. •

1826 **London,** St John's Church, Bethnal Green
         (Plate 215)
       Commissioners for Church Buildings

This was the last of Soane's three churches to be built for the commissioners. See page 230.*

Branch Banks of England
Bank of England

Reports, repairs and alterations between 1826 and 1828. See page 168.

1827 **London,** Horse Guards Parade

Soane proposed a monument to the Duke of York, one of the framed designs for which is described as 'Monopteral Temple, to enshrine a colossal statue of His late Royal Highness'. It was not executed.

1828   **London,** The Banqueting House, Whitehall
Office of Works

Following instructions from the surveyor general, Soane carried out a careful examination of the external stonework and reported that a thorough restoration was necessary. This was begun early in 1829 and continued until 1832 by which time the repair and redecoration of the interior were in hand. See page 108.*

1829   **Hardenhuish,** Wiltshire
Thomas Clutterbuck

Alterations and additions to the house carried out but have been largely obliterated by later work.•

London, New State Paper Office, Westminster (Plates 217–20)
Office of Works

Designs made by Soane for this new repository for the national archives. It was demolished *circa* 1868. See page 235.

1830   **London,** No. 30 Belgrave Place
Sir Francis Chantrey

Soane designed and supervised the building of an ante-room for his friend and fellow Academician.

1831   **London,** 'Wellington Memorial'

A folder of eight sheets is labelled 'Designs for the Wellington Memorial' and although the date 1831 is given on a preceding sheet, three of the following drawings are in fact dated December 1836. One has the endorsement 'Mr R[ichardson] from my direction. This is what I wish for.' The drawings must therefore represent Soane's last project for he died in the following month.

Drawings Exhibited at the Royal Academy

by Sir John Soane

	No.	
1772	315	*"Omitted"*. John Soan, at Mr Holland's Half Moon Street. Front of a nobleman's town-house.
1773	281	J. Soan, at Mr Holland's, Half-moon-street, Piccadilly. Front, next The Thames, of The Royal Academy, from actual measurements in 1770.
	282	Garden front of a gentleman's villa.
1774	296	John Soan, at Mr Holland's, Hertford Street. A garden-building, consisting of a tea-room, alcove, bath, and dressing-room to ditto.
1775	298	John Soan, Orange Court, Leicester-fields. Elevation for a town house.
	299	Section through the hall.
1776	289	John Soan, at Mr Holland's May-fair. The Principal façade of a design for a royal academy.
1777	330	John Soan, at Mr Holland's, May-fair, or at No. 7 Hamilton-street, Piccadilly. Elevation of a mausoleum, to the memory of James King, Esq.
1779	308	John Soan, Rome. Plan, elevation, and section of a British senate house.
1781	471	J. Soan. Design for a doghouse.
	488	Elevation of a mausoleum.
	489	Design for a mausoleum.
	498	Plan of a mausoleum.
	524	Plan and elevation of a hunting casine. (J. Soan, Member of The Royal Academies of Parma and Florence, No. 10 Cavendish Square.)
1782	534	J. Soan. Elevation of a design for a Prison. (J. Soan, Margaret Street, Cavendish Square.)

	No.	
1783	362	J. Soan. Design for a Gateway.
	367	Design for a Dairy.
	388	Design for an Observatory.
		(J. Soan, 53 Margaret Street, Cavendish Square.)
1784	420	J. Soane. Gateway at Brancepath Castle.
	471	Blackfriars-bridge, Norwich.
	485	Design for a Mausoleum.
	489	Offices at Burnhall.
	500	Design for a museum.
	523	Malvershall [Malvern Hall].
		(J. Soane, Margaret Street, Cavendish Square.)
1785	496	J. Soane. Front of a Villa designed for a gentleman in Norfolk.
	563	Entrance front of Burnhall, the seat of Geo. Smith, Esq.
		(Margaret Street, Cavendish Square.)
1786	478	J. Soane. Elevation of a Bridge for a gentleman in Staffordshire.
		(Margaret Street.)
1787	452	J. Soane. The Great Room at Chillington, built in the year 1786.
	466	Entrance front of Chillington, erected in the year 1786.
		(Welbeck Street.)
1788	—	—
1789	—	—
1790	—	—
1791	—	—
1792		JOHN SOANE, R.A. Parma, Great Scotland-Yard.*
	550	Design for a Villa; ditto for a mausoleum; and a view of Chilton Lodge.
	558	Vestibule at the Bank of England; the great hall, Bentley Priory; and the withdrawing room at Wimpole.
1793		JOHN SOANE, R.A. Parma, Florence and Scotland-Yard.
	710	Geometrical elevation and perspective view of the entrance front of a seat of the Marquis of Abercorn's.
1794		JOHN SOANE (R.A. Parma and Florence) Lincoln's Inn Fields.
	592	The Bank Stock office constructed without timber.
	635	Interior parts of a design, intended to be built at Cambridge.
1795		(address as above)
	648	A design for the entrance front of a Public Building.
	649	Interior of Designs for a Public Building.

*In the original Royal Academy catalogues, Soane's name is in capital letters from this year. He was elected an Associate in 1795, and an Academician in 1802.

	No.	
1796		JOHN SOANE A. (R.A. Parma and Florence)
	731	Design for an entrance into Hyde and the Green [parks].
	735	Part of the elevation of a design to render the House of Lords more commodious.
1797	1070	[titles omitted]
	1071	
1798	927	The Entrance to Hyde Park, opposite Great Cumberland Street.
	960	The Hall at Tyringham, the seat of W. Praed, Esq.
	1006	The intended mansion of David Scot, Esq. in Scotland.
1799	935	The hall now building at Bentley Priory, a seat of The Marquis of Abercorn.
	942	Design for a National Mausoleum.
	953	Design for a triumphal bridge, for which the Diploma of the Academy of Parma was given.
	956	The bridge at Tyringham, belonging to W. Praed, Esq.
	1007	Design for a triumphal bridge.
	1013	The entrance into Bagshot Park, a seat of H.R.H. Prince William of Gloucester.
	1018	A Vestibule at the Bank.
1800	960	View of a staircase designed for the Right Hon. Wm. Pitt.
	1036	View of the New Consols Office in the Bank, built in the year 1799.
	1041	View from Old Palace Yard, of a design for a new House of Lords.
	1045	View of a design for the National Bank of Ireland.
	1047	View from the Thames of a design for a new House of Lords.
1801	865	Part of the design for the new House of Lords.
	890	Part of the design for the new House of Lords.
	956	A Sepulchral Church.
	957	A Villa now building at Ealing.
1802		JOHN SOANE, R.A. Lincoln's Inn Fields.*
	898	View of the new building in the Bank of England, erected in 1800.
	905	View of part of a design for the new House of Lords.
1803	435	A design for the royal entrance into the new House of Lords, as submitted to His Majesty.
	562	View of a library now finishing in a villa on Ealing-green.
	1021	View of one of the designs for the new House of Lords, as submitted to His Majesty.
1804	821	View of a Public Building.

*After this date, Soane's address is given in the index for each year as Lincoln's Inn Fields.

	No.	
1805	805	View of part of the design for the new House of Lords.
1806	797	Design for a Triumphal Bridge.
	901	A view of part of the Bank of England.
	907	A view of the new entrance into the Bank of England from Princes Street.
	912	A view of part of a design for the new House of Lords.
1807	1051	View of one of the interior quadrangles in the Bank of England.
	1056	Design for the new House of Lords, with the buildings connected.
	1060	View of one of the interior quadrangles in the Bank of England.
1808		JOHN SOANE, R.A. Professor in Architecture.
	849	View next the river, of a design made for the new House of Lords in 1795, by order of a Committee of the House of Lords.
	855	Entrance hall at Croome's-hill, a seat of the Hon. G. F. Lyttelton; and two views of a corridor in the Bank of England.
	889	Mausoleum to the memory of N. Desenfans, Esq.
	931	View of a vestibule in the Bank of England.
	984	View of the anti-room to the Discount-office in the Bank of England.
1809	778	View of the north front of the Bank of England.
	828	View of part of the proposed design for the New House of Lords, made in obedience to an order of the House of Lords.
1810	692	View of the houses in Princes-street, Lothbury, erected in the year 1808.
	710	Design for the Opera-house proposed to be built on the site of Leicester-house and garden.
	716	[as above]
	759	Design for a Sepulchral church.
	832	Design for the Opera-house, proposed to be built on the site of Leicester-house and garden.
	866	Part of the north front of the Bank as originally intended.
	877	Sketch of a design for one of the fronts for a new House of Lords, made in obedience to an order of a Committee of the House of Lords, in the year 1795.
1811	880	View of a mausoleum to the memory of the late Sir F. Bourgeois, Knt.
	881	View of the royal entrance into the proposed new House of Lords.
	892	View of the north front of the Bank of England, as originally designed.
1812	804	A view of a design for a Senate-House, from the original drawings made in Rome, in the year 1779.

	No.	
	810	View of a design for a mausoleum, to the memory of Sir F. Bourgeois, and a gallery for the reception of his collection of pictures bequeathed to Dulwich College.
	811	View of the new entrance hall to the Bank of England.
1813	812	Design for three houses, intended to form a centre, on the north side of Lincoln's Inn Fields, in part erected.
	836	Design for the mausoleum attached to the gallery now building at Dulwich College, for the reception of the pictures bequeathed to that establishment by the late Sir F. Bourgeois.
1814	701	View of part of one of the designs for a new House of Lords.
1815	769	Dulwich College.
1816	799	[A Design for a] Monument.
	810	[A Design for a] Monument.
1817	877	View of part of a design for a public building.
	889	Sketch of an elevation of a National Monument, forming part of a general design for the improvement of the two Houses of Parliament, the Courts of Judicature, . . .
1818	908	View of the new buildings forming the principal alterations and additions in the Establishment of the Royal Hospital at Chelsea.
	914	The elevation, plan, longitudinal perspective section, and other parts of a design for a National Monument, to perpetuate the glorious Achievements of British Valour by sea and land.
	915	A selection of parts of buildings, public and private, erected from the designs of J. Soane, Esq., R.A. in the metropolis, and in other places of the United Kingdom between the years 1780 and 1815.
	925	The perspective representation of the exterior of a design for a National Monument, forming one side of a quadrangle; the other sides intended for sites of a Royal Palace, the two Houses of Parliament, and the Courts of Judicature.
1819	1034	A Cenotaph now building, to the memory of the late Right Hon. William Pitt.
1820	894	Architectural visions of early Fancy, in the gay morning of youth; and dreams in the evening of life.
1821	949	Bird's eye view of a design for a royal residence.
	950	Sketch for a Church proposed to be built in the Regent's Park.
	964	Sketches for a Church proposed to be built in the Regent's Park.
	978	Sketch for a Church proposed to be built in the Regent's Park.

	No.	
1822	854	Design, showing part of the exterior and interior of the Bank of England.
	875	Design, showing part of the exterior and interior of a house in Lincoln's Inn Fields.
	906	Continuation of a design, shewing part of the exterior and interior of a house in Lincoln's Inn Fields.
1823	974	View of the Scala Regia of His Majesty's entrance to the House of Lords.
	979	An Architectural Study: subject, the national debt redemption office, and the cenotaph to the memory of the late Rt. Hon. W. Pitt.
	984	View of the Scala Regia, leading to the House of Lords.
	987	View of one of the Consol Offices in the Bank of England, in its progressive state of construction.
	1050	An architectural study: subject, a church.
	1056	An architectural study: subject, the picture gallery and mausoleum of the late Sir Francis Bourgeois, at Dulwich.
1824	838	View of the Bank of England, from the N.W. corner.
	873	View of the Bank of England, from the W. corner.
	884	View of the Bank of England, from the N.E. corner.
	965	View of a design for His Majesty's entrance into the House of Lords, erected between the 3rd October 1823, and the 29th January 1824.
1825	902	A group of churches, to illustrate different styles of architecture.
	903	Design for a sepulchral church, and mausoleum—a study.
	913	View of a design for a part of the exterior of a public building.
	923	View of part of a public building now erecting.
1826	869	Plans, elevations, sections and perspective view of a design for completing the south side of Downing Place and connecting the same with the new Council Office, the Board of Trade and the Treasury, by a Triumphal arch. [caption continues at length]
	870	Plan, elevation and perspective view of a design for the western barrier of the metropolis with entrances into the two Royal Parks.
	879	A design for a national entrance into the metropolis, intended to combine the classical simplicity of the Grecian architecture, the magnificence of the Roman [etc. etc.].
	889	Plans, elevations and perspective views of a design for entrances from Piccadilly into the two Royal Parks made under the direction of John Robinson, Esq. Surveyor General of H.M. Woods and Forests.
1827	905	View of the interior of new Council Chamber.
	910	General plan and different views of the new Law Courts at Westminster.

	No.	
	911	View in the Portico with the principal entrance; being part of a design for a Royal Residence.
	954	Exterior view of the Portico with the Principal entrance; being part of a design for a Royal Residence.
	967	View of the design for the Interior of the Court of King's Bench, with the additional space adjoining the Court of Equity.
	968	View of the interior of the High Court of Chancery.
	977	General view of a design for a Royal Residence.
1828	983	Design to render the entrances into the House of Lords and the rooms and offices appertaining thereto more commodious . . .
	984	Interior of a design for a Sepulchral Chapel. [To late Commander-in-Chief: long caption.]
	990	Design for completing the Board of Trade and new Council Offices.
	1033	View of one of the Courts of a Royal Palace.
	1127	Exterior of a design for a Sepulchral Chapel.
	1128	Bird's-eye view of a design for a Royal Palace, from studies made in 1779.
1829	989	Perspective elevation of a design to complete the north front of Westminster Hall, by making the exterior of the new Law Courts and a corresponding wing in the same style of architecture . . . This design is most humbly inscribed to His Majesty.
	998	Design for completing the buildings at the corner of Downing Street. Inscribed to the Rt. Hon. Viscount Goderich.
	1039	The interior of a room erected in the year 1828, for the Society of Freemasons, under the auspices of the Grand Master . . .
	1128	Designs to combine in the same uniform style of architecture, the entrances into Hyde Park, St James's Park, and the western entrance into the metropolis. These designs, altered from those exhibited in the Royal Academy in 1817, are inscribed to his Grace the Duke of Wellington.
1830	1031	An architectural pasticcio.
	1042	An evening view of the new Masons' Hall, in Freemasons' Tavern.
	1052	A bird's-eye view of the Bank of England.
1831	981	Design for the new State-paper Office.
	987	Architectural sketches.
	990	Design for a monopteral temple to enshrine a colossal statue of his late R.H. the Duke of York . . . .
	997	Design for the New State Paper Office, enlarged . . .
	1004	View of the entrance into the Sculpture gallery of Francis Chantry.

	No.		
1832	992		Architectural ruins—a vision.
	998		Interior of the edifice devoted exclusively to Freemasonry adjoining Freemasons' Hall, in Great Queen Street—an evening view made after the completion of the building.
	1106		An entrance to a park.
1833	996		A sketch of the first design for a new State Paper Office, to be erected in Duke Street . . .
1834	870		Model of the principal front of a design for completing the buildings in Whitehall, north and south of Downing Street . . .
	871		Model of part of the new State Paper Office, as originally designed.
1835	975		An architectural sketch.
1836	951		A design for the improvement of the buildings adjacent to Westminster Hall, for two new Houses of Parliament, the Courts of Judicature; from the original drawings made in the year 1796.
	952		A portfolio design for a British Senate House; from the original drawings made in Rome in 1779.
	953		A design for a new House of Lords, made in obedience to an order of a Committee of the House of Lords, 1794.

Drawings exhibited at the Royal Academy under the name of George Bailey or John Soane junior

	No.		
1811	882	G. Bailey.	View of various architectural subjects belonging to J. Soane Esq. R.A., as arranged in the year 1810.
	883	J. Soane, jn.	View of various architectural subjects belonging to J. Soane Esq. R.A., as arranged in the year 1809.
	889	J. Soane, jn.	Design for a public bath.

Select Bibliography

1. Books by Sir John Soane (excluding pamphlets):

   Designs in Architecture, Consisting of Plans . . . for Temples, Baths, Casines, Pavilions, Garden-Seats, Obelisks and other Buildings, 1778, 1797
   Plans . . . of Buildings erected in the Counties of Norfolk, Suffolk, etc., 1788
   Sketches in Architecture containing Plans . . . of Cottages, Villas and other Useful Buildings, 1793
   Plans, Elevations and Perspective Views of Pitzhanger Manor House, 1802
   Designs for Public and Private Buildings, 1828
   Description of the House and Museum . . . Lincoln's Inn Fields, 1830, 1832, 1835–6 (privately printed)
   Memoirs of the Professional Life of an Architect, 1835 (privately printed)

2. Books and Articles Relevant to the Life and Work of Sir John Soane:

   J. Britton, *The Union of Architecture, Sculpture and Painting*, 1827
   T. L. Donaldson, *A Review of the Professional Life of Sir John Soane*, 1837
   A. T. Bolton, *The Works of Sir John Soane, R.A.*, 1924
   H. J. Birnstingl, *Sir John Soane*, 1925
   A. T. Bolton, *The Portrait of Sir John Soane, R.A.*, 1927
   A. T. Bolton (ed.), *Lectures on Architecture by Sir John Soane, R.A.*, 1929
   H. R. Steele and F. R. Yerbury, *The Old Bank of England*, 1930
   J. Summerson, *Sir John Soane*, 1952
   D. Stroud, 'The Early Work of Soane', *Architectural Review*, February 1957
   D. Stroud, *The Architecture of Sir John Soane*, 1961
   D. Stroud, *George Dance*, 1971
   H. Colvin (ed.), *The History of the King's Works*, VI (by J. Mordaunt Crook and M. H. Port), 1973
   J. Summerson, 'Sir John Soane and the Furniture of Death', *Architectural Review*, March 1976
   P. de la R. du Prey, *John Soane. The Making of an Architect*, 1982
   J. Summerson, David Watkin, G.-Tilman Mellinghoff, essays by, *John Soane*, Academy Editions Monograph, 1983

Index

Page numbers in italics refer to illustrations

Abercorn, Marquis and Earl of, *see* Hamilton, Hon. John James
Acton, house in, 74
Adam, Robert, 61, 70, 233
Adams, Mrs, 262
Adams, Francis, 51, 56, 119, 240, *53*
Agrigento, 37–8
Ailesbury, 1st Earl of, 259
Albury Park, Surrey, 264
Aldenham House, Hertfordshire, 265
Alexander, Emperor of Russia, 97
Allanbank, Berwickshire, 49–51, 239
Allen, —, surveyor, 119
Alston, Mr, 244
Anguish, Miss, 258
Appleby, Revd Mr, 82
Archer, Thomas, 179
Architects' Benevolent Society, 7, 113, 116n.16
Architects' Club, 70
Arrington, Cambridgeshire, 255
Arundell, 8th Baron, 134, 247
Astell, William, 272
Astley, Jacob, 247
Astrop Park, Oxfordshire, 268
Austwick, Lancelot, 260
Aynho Park, Northamptonshire, 179, 181, 263, *179–80*

Backwell (?Backall), Miss, 261
Bagdon Lodge, Wiltshire, 259
Bagshot Park, Surrey, 63, 66, 70, 176–7, 261, *177*
Bailey, George, 97, 102, 111, 112, 113, 115, 168; drawings exhibited, 287
Baker, William, schoolmaster, 18
Banbury, Oxfordshire, 268
Bank of England, 151–2, 156–7, 168, 181, 252, 269, 271, *152–67*
    architect and surveyor, 60, *see also* Soane, Sir John
    Bank Stock Office, 62, 66, 156, 252, *153–4*

Branch Banks, 168, 278
Colonial Office, 156, *165*
Consols Office, 156, *156–7*
external wall, 70–1, 156–7, *158, 162–3, 167*
furniture, 184
Lothbury Court, 75, 157, 181, *160*
plan, *152*
Princes Street entrance, 160–2
Rotunda, 66, *155*
Tivoli Corner, 157, 162–3
Bankes, Henry, MP, 108, 111, 222, 236
Banks, Lady, 242
Banks, Sir Joseph, 59
Banks, Thomas, 181, 265
Barker, J. R., 249
Barnard, Mrs, 64
Barnard, Christopher, 264
Baronscourt, Co. Tyrone, 64, 150–1, 251, *150–1*
Barrett, George, 65
Barry, Charles, 111, 113, 227
Barselton House, Hertfordshire, 255
Bartoli, Pietro Santi, *Gli Antichi Sepolchri*, 62, *63*
Basel, 45
Basevi, George, 66, 100, 102
Basildon, Berkshire, 17
Bath, Somerset, 60, 94, 109
    Powis Place, 119
    Seymour Street, 264
Batt, Dr and Mrs William, 44
Beach, Hicks, 251, 252
Beachcroft, Samuel, 251
Beauport, Sussex, 245, 257
Beckford, Mrs, 59
Beckford, William, 59–60, 61, 134, 246
Beechey, Sir William, 113
Belfast Academical Institution, 270
Bellamont, Earl of, 56, 243
Bellew, Abbé, 39
Belvedere, Kent, 240
Bemerton Rectory, Wiltshire, 247
Benacre Hall, Suffolk, 243
Benevento, 36

Benham, Berkshire, 24, 62
Bentley Priory, Middlesex, 64, 66, 136, 138, 246,
    136–7
Benyon, Mrs, 270
Benyon, Richard, 269
Bernini, Gianlorenzo, 216
Berry, Mary, 149
Berwick, 2nd Baron, 102, 275
Betchworth Castle, Surrey, 63, 76, 177, 179, 261,
    178
Bicknell, John, 113
Binfield, Berkshire, 242
Bird, –, mason, 130
Blackburn, William, 53
Blogg, William, 64
Blondel, Merry Joseph, 104n.17
Blore, Edward, 134, 189
Blundeston House, Suffolk, 132, 245, *133*
Boaden, James, 85–6
Boconnoc, Cornwall, 25, 245
Boddington, Samuel, 254, 258
Boehm, Roger, 257
Bologna, 40, 42
Bonomi, Joseph, 138
Boodles Club, 24
Bosanquet, Claude, monument to, 244
Bosanquet, Richard, 34–5
Bosanquet, Samuel, 35, 244, 246, 265; tomb, 269
Botleys, Surrey, 53, 240, *57*
Bourgeois, Sir Francis, 195, 200, 270
Bowdler, Revd Dr Thomas, 36–7
Boyce, Edward, 141
Boyd, James, 58
Braham, John, 78, 270
Bramley, Hampshire, Church, 265
Brancepath Castle, Durham, 54
Branthwayte, S., 242
Brayley, Edward Wedlake, 18
Breadalbane, 4th Earl of, 266
Brescia, 40
Brettingham, Matthew, 24, 28n.17
Brettingham, Robert Furze, 24, 28n.17, 29, 32, 34,
    70, 259
Brewer, Mrs, 262
Brickenden, Eleanora, 94, 96, 102, 103
Bridgewater, Duke of, 28n.18
Bridport, Lady, 56, 78, 85, 184, 204, 206, 274
Bridport, Lord, *see* Hood, Alexander
Brighton, Sussex, 84, 89, 96, 97–8, 108
    Pavilion, 106
Briscoe, Elisha, 262, 264
Bristol, Earl of, *see* Hervey
Bristol Fire Office, 252
British Institution, 96, 104n.12

Britton, John, 107; and his wife, 100
Brocas, Mrs, 35, 248, 255, 265
Brocas, Bernard, monument to, 265
Broughton, Oxfordshire, 17
Brown, –, mason, 130
Brown, James, of Ballycastle, 46
Brown, Lancelot ('Capability'), 21, 24, 62
Buckingham, Marquis of, *see* Grenville
Buckland, Berkshire, 253
Bullock, George, 66
Burchell, Stephen, 111
Burdon, Rowland, MP, 44, 49–50, 51, 61, 89, 91,
    113, 115, 239, 256; in Italy, 37–40
Burgess, James Bland, 257
Burn Hall, Co. Durham, 54, 58, 60, 241
Burnham Westgate Hall, Norfolk, 240
Burrough Hall, Norfolk, 247
Bury St Edmunds, Suffolk, 248
Busbridge, Surrey, 24
Butterton Farm House, Staffordshire, 206–7, 274,
    206
Butterton Hall, Staffordshire, 271
Buxton, Robert, 247

Cadland, Hampshire, 24
Cairness, Scotland, 256
Callcott, Augustus, 78
Calonné, Charles-Alexandre de, 252
Cambridge
    Caius College, 253
    Pembroke College, 82, 207
    St John's College, 253
    Senate House, proposed museum etc., 252
    Trinity College, 82
Camelford, Lord, *see* Pitt, Thomas
Cameron, General, 83
Camolin Park, Co. Wexford, 274
Campanella, Angelo, engravings, 91, 181, *77*
Canada, Government House for Upper Canada, 276
Canaletto, *Venetian Scene*, 60
Canning, Rt. Hon. George, 265
Capaccio, 36
Caprarola, 41, 111, 236
Capua, 34, 36
Carafino, Signor, 44
Carle, John de, mason, 119
Carline, John, builder, 214
Caroline, Queen, 106
Carrington, 1st Baron, 275
Carter, John, 191
Cartwright, Richard, 179, 263
Caserta, 34, 36
Castle Eden, Co. Durham, 49–50, 239
Castle Hill, Devonshire, 134, 245

Catania, 38

Catherwood, Thomas, 193

Cecil, Susannah, 54

Chadwick, William, mason, 230

Chambers, Sir William, 21, 24, 26–7, 61, 70

Champion, 100

Chantrey, Sir Francis, 109, 113, 279; bust of Soane, 113, *95*

Chapman, Laura, 82

Chapman, Dr William, 82

Charlton House, Wiltshire, 28n.17

Chawner, Thomas, 64

Cheltenham, Gloucestershire, 99–100

Chertsey, Surrey, 18–19, 56, 68, 100, 109, 116n.8; Mrs Soane at, 89, 94, 96, 99

Chillington, Staffordshire, 58, 130, 243

Chilton Lodge, Berkshire, 143, 250, *143*

Chiswick, St Nicholas churchyard, 272–3

Christie, James, 83

Cileria, Madame, 44

City Lands Committee, 20

Clapham, Greater London, 262

Claremont, Surrey, 21, 24, 31, 34

Clarence, Duke of, *see* William IV

Clive, Robert, 1st Lord, 21

Clutterbuck, Thomas, 279

Coade and Sealy, 123, 181, 265, *see also* Sealy

Cobbett, William, 111

Cockerell, Charles Robert, 111

Cockerell, Samuel Pepys, 70

Cockley Cley, Norfolk, 241

Cole, Benjamin, 253

Collyer, Charles, 42, 51, 140, 247, 249

Colne Park, Essex, 251

Combe House, Devonshire, 85, 268

Combe Royal, Devonshire, 83–4, 85

Como, 44

Conduitt, Sarah and Edward, 102–4, 112, 115

Cook, James, 210, 273, 274

Cooke, William, 54, 240, 243; and his wife, 56

Coombe House, Surrey, 240, 266

Cooper, Sir Astley, 97

Cornwall, John, 251

Corsham Court, Wiltshire, 249

Cosgrove Hall, Buckinghamshire, 262

Costessy, Norfolk, 56, 241

Couse, Kenton, 64

Coxe, Revd Mr, 48n.42

Coxe, Dr William, 247

Crace, John, 65, 174, 181, 186, 265

Cranbury, Hampshire, 51, 62

Craven, Lady, 240

Crichton, Richard, 256

Cricket St Thomas, Somerset

church, monument, 204, 206, 274, *205*

Cricket Lodge, 85, 184–5, 244, 266, *185*

Crofton Grange, *see* Hamels

Crook, Mr, 25

Crook and Eyston, 250

Crowe, Alderman, 254

Crunden, John, 24, 89

Cubitt, Thomas, 248

Cuffnels, Hampshire, 256

Cuma, 35

Cundy, Thomas, 255

Dalling, Lady, 265

Dance, George, the elder, 20

Dance, George, the younger, 18–21, 25, 47n.3, 51, 61, 62, 70–2, 80; death, 109; drawings by, 56, *55*; letter from, 28n.18; work at Pitzhanger, 74, 181

Dance, Sir Nathaniel, RA, 21; drawing by, *19*

Dance, Captain Sir Nathaniel, 20

Daniell, Thomas, 18

Daniell, W., 96

Darell, Edward, 256

Dashwood, J. R., 241

Davis, Revd Mr, 96

de Bruyn, Theodore, 124

Dennison, John, 245

Dennistoun, Robert, 261

Derry, Bishop of, *see* Hervey

Desanfans, Mrs, 94, 195, 200

Desanfans, Noel, 195, 200, 270

Dieppe, 97–8

Dilettanti Society, 58–9, 60, 244

Dillingham, Brampton Gurdon, 120, 241

Dinwody, William, 245

d'Israeli, Isaac, 113

Donaldson, Thomas L., 112–13

Down, Thornton and Free, 265

Down Ampney House, Gloucestershire, 263

Downham, John, portrait by, *19*

Downhill, Co. Derry, 32, 34, 46–7, 49, 239; design for a dog-house, 34, *33*

Dublin, Bank of Ireland, 262

Ducie, 3rd Baron, 260

Dulwich Picture Gallery and Mausoleum, 63, 195, 200, 203, 272, *201–2*

Dummer, Harriet, 51

Dunmow, Essex, 240

Dunninald House, Scotland, 257–8

Dunton Bassett, Leicestershire, 254, 255

Earle, T. H., 264

Earsham, Norfolk, 56, 124, 243, *125*

East India Company, 70–2

Ebdon, Christopher, 58, 64
Eden, Sir Frederick, 255
Egremont, 3rd Earl of, 274
Eliot, John, 2nd Baron, later 1st Earl of St Germans, 187, 260, 263, 267, 268
Elliot, A. & J., 267
Ellis, Mr, 253
Englefield, Mr, 253
Englefield House, Berkshire, 269
Etna, Mount, 38
Evelyn, James, 243
Everton House, Bedfordshire, 272

Fairford House, Gloucester, 249
Fan Grove, Berkshire, 277
Fane, Lady, 17
Fane, Hon. Henry, 252
Fanshawe, Mr, 66
Farington, Joseph, diary of, 18, 20, 24
Farquhar, Colin, 258
Fatio, John, 35
Felbridge, Surrey, 243
Fellowes, Robert, 58, 129–30, 139, 243, 248
Fellowes, William Henry, 189, 267
Fisher, John A., 270
Flaxman, John, 65; drawing by, *101*; and his wife, 78
Florence, 40–2
Fonthill Abbey, Wiltshire, 134
Fonthill, Wiltshire, 59–60, 134, 246, *135*
Fortescue, 1st Earl, 134, 245, 251
Fossanova, Abbey of, 36
Foster, John, 82
Fowler, C., 112
Foxhall, Edward, 50, 61, 98, 100, 251; his son, 100; work by, 59, 122, 134, 143
Foxhall, Fanny, wife of Edward, 100
Foxhall, Martin, 122
Free Society of Artists, 21
French, Samuel, 149
Furze, Robert, *see* Brettingham, Robert Furze
Fuseli, Henry, 20

Gaeta, 36
Galwey, Payne, 244
Gandy, Joseph Michael, 66, 73n.12, 82–3; and family, 56, 82; water-colours by, 65, 270, *31*, *67*
Gardner, Sir Alan, 259
Gawdy Hall, Suffolk, 247
Genoa, 42–4, 45
George III, 21, 24, 61, 68, 106
George IV, 106–7, 222
Gibbs, Antony, 44
Gideon, Sir Sampson, 240

Giffard, Thomas, 130, 243
Glasgow, Buchanan Street, 261
Goldicutt, John, 112, 113
Gooch, Revd John, 124, 242
Gooch, Sir Thomas, 243
Gordon, Charles, 256
Goring-on-Thames, Oxfordshire, 17–18
Goulburn, Henry, 111
Graham, Colonel Thomas, later Baron Lynedoch, 258, 262
Granard, Lady, 250
Grand Junction Canal Co., 266
Gravina, Prince Ferdinando Grancesco, 37
Green, Thomas Abbot, 261
Greenwich Hospital, surveyorship, 60
Grenville, George Nugent-Temple-, 1st Marquis of Buckingham, 144, 169, 191–2, 250, 268
Grenville, Richard Nugent-Temple-, 2nd Marquis (later 1st Duke) of Buckingham, 210, 275, 276, 277
Grenville, William Wyndham, Baron, 69
Grey, Charles, 2nd Earl, 112
Grey, John, 258
Grote Prescott and Grote, 276
Grundy, Thomas, mason, 195, 203, 207, 274, 275
Gunthorpe, Norfolk, 140, 249, *140*
Gurnell, Thomas, 19, 74

Hagley, Worcestershire, 25, 270
Hall (later Wharton), John, 64, 246
Halsnead, Lancashire, 250
Halton, William, 276
Hamels Park, Hertfordshire, 51, 63, 119, 239, *52*, *63*
Hamilton, Gavin, 32
Hamilton, Hon. John James, later 1st Marquis and 9th Earl of Abercorn, 59, 242, 250, 259, 262, 263; at Baronscourt, 150, 251; at Bentley Priory, 64, 136, 246
Hamilton, Sir William, 35
Hammet, J., 264
Hardenhuish, Wiltshire, 279
Harding, Mr, 206, 207
Hardwick, Thomas, 29; and his wife, 78
Hardwicke, Earl of, *see* Yorke
Harman, Jeremiah, 275
Harper, Thomas, 97
Harrison, Henry, 187, 204, 274
Harrogate, Yorkshire, 102
Hase, Henry, 277
Hastings, Sussex, 112
Haverfield, John, 76; his father, 86n.4
Hawkesbury, Lord, *see* Jenkinson
Heathcote, Lady, 65
Heathfield Lodge, Acton, 74, 261

Hemery, Clement, 271
Henderson, Mr, 259
Hereford, 83
Herne Hill Cottage, 270
Herringfleet, Suffolk, 241
Hervey, Frederick, 4th Earl of Bristol and Bishop
    of Derry, 32, 34–6, 40–1, 45–7, 239; his wife, 32,
    34, 36, 47
Hervey, Louisa, later Countess of Liverpool, 32, 34,
    36, 48n.17
Hetherset, Norfolk, 246
High Wycombe, Buckinghamshire, 262
Hills, Philip, 251
Hingham Church, Norfolk, 244
Hinton St George, Somerset, 259
Hippisley, Sir John Coxe, 39, 271–2
Hobcraft, John, joiner, 53
Hockerill, Hertfordshire, 245
Hofland, Barbara, 102–3
Hofland, Thomas, 102
Hogarth, William, *Rake's Progress*, 60
Holgate, Mr, 41
Holland, Bridget (née Brown), 21
Holland, Henry, 21–2, 24, 31, 45, 61, 70; work by,
    21, 62, 72, 252
Holland, Mary, 84, 85
Holland, Richard, 21–2, 46, 51, 54, 58, 61, 83–5, 94,
    96; work by, 53, 65, 132, 174, 247, 249, 255
Holmes, Revd Mr, 247
Holwood House, Kent, 59, 132, 245
Honing Hall, Norfolk, 248
Hood, Alexander, 1st Viscount Bridport, 78, 85,
    184, 244, 266; monument to, 204, 206, 274, *205*
Hood, Sir Alexander, 277
Hood, Samuel, 1st Viscount, 269
Horner, Colonel Thomas, 100, 200, 271
Hotham, Vice Admiral Sir Henry, 277
Howard, Henry, 78
Hume, Joseph, MP, 111
Hunneman, Christopher, 28n.14

Ickworth, Suffolk, 40–1, 46–7
Incorporated Society of Artists, 21
Iselin, J. F., 246, 254

Jackson, George, 104n.20
Jackson, W. A., 262
Jacques, Mr, 64
Jagger, John, 24
Jenkinson, Robert Banks, Lord Hawkesbury, later
    2nd Earl of Liverpool, 48n.17, 240, 266, 271, 273
Jerningham, Sir William, 241
Jersey, 271
Johnstone, Elizabeth, tomb, 56, 243, *57*

Jonathan, David, 210
Jones, John, joiner, 122
Jones, R., 249
Jones, R. J., 113
Jones, Thomas, 39
Jupp, Richard, 70–2, 119

Kay, Joseph, 113
Kelshall Rectory, Hertfordshire, 246
Kenny, Nicholas, 24
Kent, Duchess of, 113
Kent, Claridge and Pearce, 259
Kerr, R. Gervas, 256
Kinderley, Mr, 85
King, James, 22; design for monument, 25–6, *25*
King, James, of Banbury, 268
Kinnaird, Lord, 76
Kinnard, William, 89, 104n.5
Kirkbride, Philip, slater, 130
Knight, Robert, 186, 266, 269

Labern, John, bricklayer, 195
Laing, David, 64, 66
Lampton, 272
Langley Park, Norfolk, 56, 123, 243, *123*
Laugier, Abbé, 63
Lawrence, Sir Thomas, 109, 110; portrait by,
    frontispiece
Leathes, John, 241
Lee, Captain, 273
Leeds, Duchess of, 56, 78, 263
Leeds, 5th Duke of, 259, 260
Lees Court, Kent, 130, 244, *131*
Lemmington Hall, Northumberland, 243
Letton Hall, Norfolk, 56, 120, 241, *120–1*
Levant Merchants, 255
Levick, Ann, 61n.15, 74
Levick, Elizabeth, 57
Lewis, Henry Greswold, 37–9, 48n.19, 51, 56, 122,
    241, 261
Lewis, Thomas, 256
Leytonstone
    Forest House, 246
    St Mary's Church, tomb, 269
Licata, 38
Lipari Islands, 38
Little Green, Sussex, 259
Little Hill Court, Hertfordshire, 266
Liverpool, 66, 82–3
Liverpool, Earl of, *see* Jenkinson
Locke, William, 65
London
    Adams Place, 51, 53, 56, 119, 240, *53*
    Albion Place, 66, 102

7 Austin Friars, 263
Banqueting Hall, Whitehall, 22, *23*
Banqueting House, Whitehall, 108, 279
Bartholomew Lane, 265
Battersea, proposed penitentiary, 53, 239
16 Bedford Square, 245
30 Belgrave Place, 279
Berkeley Square, 240
Board of Trade Offices, Whitehall, 108, 226, 278
23 or 24 Bruton Street, 250
Buckingham House, Pall Mall, 62, 73n.6, 144, 146, 250, *144–5*
Carlton House, 62
Carrington House, Whitehall, 102, 275
10 Cavendish Street, 50
38 Charlotte (Hallam) Street, 195, 270, *195*
Chelsea, General Wilford's House, 265
Chelsea Royal Hospital, 81, 196–7, 200, 269, *196–9*; Soane's official residence, 81, 100, 108, 130, 197
Cloak Lane, 254
Constitution Hill, 260
Covent Garden Theatre, 80
Cow Cross Street, 66
Cumberland Gate, Hyde Park, 63, 66, 70, 176, 260, *176*
19 Curzon Street, 267
Dean (Deanery) Street, 269
Downing Street, 108, 228, 231, 260, 278, *229–30*
22 Dunraven Street, 264
Fenchurch Street, 254
Fife House, Whitehall, 271
90 Fleet Street, 265
Fountain Court, 262
Frederick's Place, 263
Freemasons' Hall, 96–7, 113, 234–5, 278, *234*
Freemasons' Tavern, 96, 107, 234
34 Gower Street, 262
75 Gracechurch Street, 269
Grand Junction Canal, 256
13 (14) Grosvenor Square, 102, 275
25 Grosvenor Square, 263
34 (39) Grosvenor Square, 270
48 (49) Grosvenor Square, 186, 261, 266, *186*
67? Grosvenor Street, 263
31 Half Moon Street, 21–2
Hereford Street, 24–5, 58–9, 244, 253
Hertford Street, 22, 45
43 (?23) Hill Street, 251
Holy Trinity Church, Marylebone, 106, 230, 233, 277, *232*
Horse Guards Parade, 278–9
House of Commons, 219, 252, 277
House of Lords, 68–9, 106–7, 216, 219, 257, 277,

68–9, 216–18
Insolvent Debtors' Court, 219–20, 277, *219–20*
6 and 7 Kings Arms Yard, 263
Law Courts, Westminster, 62, 108, 109, 221–2, 224, 278, *221–5*
Leicester Square, proposed Opera House, 251
Lincoln's Inn Fields, east side, 263
12 Lincoln's Inn Fields, 64–5, 74, 88–9, 174–5, 255, *67*
13 Lincoln's Inn Fields, 65, 88–96, 175, 203–4, 228, 273, *90–5*
14 Lincoln's Inn Fields, 204, 278
22 Lincoln's Inn Fields, 255
51 Lincoln's Inn Fields, 257
57 and 58 Lincoln's Inn Fields, 258
Liquor Pond Street, 66
1 Mansfield Street, 263
53 Margaret Street, 54, 56, 57–8
Mark Lane, 254
Minories, 20
16 Montague Place, 277
National Debt Redemption Office, 62, 174, 207, 276, *208*
New Bank Buildings, 190–1, 269, *191*
14 New Burlington Street, 277
63 New Cavendish Street, 239
Newgate Gaol, 20, 51
Old Broad Street, 272
54 Old Broad Street, 263
Old Cavendish Street, 251
7 Orchard Street, 66
37 Pall Mall, 244
56 Pall Mall, 252
104 Pall Mall, 250
105 Pall Mall, 256
Park Lane, 260
Park Lane, Breadalbane House, 266
22 (18) Park Lane, 273
Park Street, 24, 242
54 Park Street, 264
15 Philpot Lane, 253
147 Piccadilly, 252
148 Piccadilly, 240
4 Portland Place, 272
70 Portland Place, 259
Privy Council Offices, Whitehall, 108, 226–7, 278, *226–7*
Queen Anne Street West, 247
156–70 Regent Street, 210, 277, *213*
St Botolph, Aldgate, 260
St George Street, 263
St Giles Burial Ground, 100, 102, 108, 115, 275, *114*
St Giles Church, 268

St James's Church, Piccadilly, 247
St James's Palace, guard room, 64, 254
St James's Place, 252
3 St James's Square, 276
21 St James's Square, 246, 259
22 St James's Square, 263
31 St James's Square, 268
St James's Street, 24
St John's Church, Bethnal Green, 106, 230, 233, 278, *233*
St Luke's Hospital, 51
St Mary Abbot's churchyard, 56, 243, *57*
St Mary's Church, Lambeth, memorial, 275
St Peter's Church, Walworth, 106, 230, 233, 278, *231*
St Stephen's Church, monument, 244
18 Saville Row, 242
Somerset House, 21, 22, *23*
56 South Audley Street, 258
Southwark Cathedral, monument, 271
State Paper Office, 108, 110–11, 235, 238–9, 279, *235–7*
Strand, The, 260
429 Strand, The, 258
12 Stratton Street, 258
62 Threadneedle Street, 276
1 Upper Grosvenor Street, 255
14 Upper Grosvenor Street, 267
25 Watling Street, 269
77 Welbeck Street, 58, 64
'Wellington Memorial', 279
Westminster, designs for national monument, 102, 275
    Westminster Hall, 89, 204
    42 Wimpole Street, 50–1, 240
    see also Bank of England
Louch, Mr, of Armagh, 46, 73n.6
Louch, Robert, 64, 73n.6
Loutherbourg, Mrs de, 78, 272
Loutherbourg, Philippe Jacques de, 78; tomb, 272–3
Lovegrove, J., bricklayer, 267
Lucullus, Villa of, 34
Lumisden, Andrew, 36, 48n.18
Lyndford Hall, Nofolk, 246
Lyons, 29, 44
Lyttelton, Edward John, 224
Lyttelton, Sir George, 28n.18
Lyttelton, Hon. George Fulke, later 2nd Baron, 266, 270
Lyttelton, William, 1st Baron, 270

Macartney House, Greenwich, 266
McDowell, John, 64

Mackell, John, joiner, 122
Maclise, Daniel, *115*
Malta, 38
Malton, Thomas, and his wife, 78
Malvern Hall, Warwickshire, 48n.19, 56, 57, 122–3, 241, 261
Mann, Horace, 41–2
Manners, Lady Louisa, 256
Mansel, Mr, 262
Mansfield, Lord, 258
Mantua, 42
Marcy, Mr and Mrs, 27n.3
Marcy, Revd, 17
Marden Hill, Hertfordshire, 209, 276, *209*
Margate, Kent, 82–4
Marlesford, Suffolk, 54, 241
Marsala, 37
Marshall, Edward, *179*
Marshall, James, mason, 267
Marsham, Mr, 262
Martin, Francis, 60
Martin, William, 247
Martyr, Thomas, carpenter, 174, 195; & Son, 203
Mason, Captain, 273
Matthews, Richard, 187, 272
Mawbey, Sir Joseph, 53, 240
May, W., 268
Mells Park, Somerset, 100, 200, 271
Melton Constable, Norfolk, 247
Meyer, Frederick, 64, 254
Micklefield Hall, Hertfordshire, 264
Milan, 40, 43, 44
Miller, Lady Anna, 29, 35, 45–6, 47n.3
Milles, Richard, 245
Mills, Charles, 263
Milner, Sir William, 250
Mitford, William, 257
Mocatta, David, 66, 111
Modern Goth, 71–2
Moffat, W., 260
Moggerhanger, Bedfordshire, 194, 252, 271, *194*
Moland, W., 243
Molesworth, Sir William, 35–6
Monins, Revd John, 96, 204, 273
Morland, Mr, 252
Morland, William, 143, 250
Morrison, Robert, 64
Moser, George Michael, 21
Mottram, 60
Mulgrave, 2nd Baron, 245
Mulgrave Castle, Yorkshire, 245
Murray, General, 245

Mylne, Robert, 70

Nackington, Kent, 245
Naples, 32, 34–7, 38–9
Nash, John, 98, 106, 210
Nayland Church, Suffolk, 244
Neave, James, 53, 239
Neave, Richard, 53
Nelson, James, mason, 123, 132, 174, 247, 249
Nelthorpe, George, 246
Netheravon House, Wiltshire, 252
Neville, John, 267
Newgate Gaol, 20, 51
Newland, Abraham, monument, 271
Newton, William, 49
Norbury Park, Surrey, 65
Norris, Philip, 72
North Mymms Park, Hertfordshire, 260
Norwich, 56–7, 254
    Blackfriars Bridge, 119, 241, *118*
    Castle Gaol, 139, 248, *139*
    Hospital, 248
    Surrey Street, 146, 251, *146*
Norwood Green, Middlesex, 184, 265, *184*
Novi, 43

Office of Woods and Forests, 69–70, 176, 260, 261
Office of Works, Westminster, 64, 68, 98, 106–7, 252, 254, 259, 277, 278, 279
Orleans, Duc d', 78
Ossington Hall, Nottinghamshire, 245
Owen, William, 82
Oxford, Brasenose College, 269–70

Padua, 40, 42
Padula, monastery of San Lorenzo, 36
Paestum, 35–6
    'Barn a la', 122–3, 261, *122*
    Temple of Ceres, 36, *33*
Page, Sir Gregory, 130
Paine, James, 134
Palagonia, Villa, 37
Palermo, 37
Palladio, Andrea, 27, 27n.1, 32, 40
Palmer, Thomas, 228
Palmer's Green, Middlesex, 256, 258
Palmerston, Henry, 3rd Viscount, 222
Pangbourne, Berkshire, 68
Papworth, George, 274
Paris, 29, 97, 103–4, 104n.17
Parke, Henry, 100, 103–4, 105n.28
Parker, Mr, 45
Parma, 40, 42–3; Academy, 42–3
Pastorini, Benedetto, 65

Paton, David, 111
Patteson, John, 44, 49, 51, 56, 61, 146, 251; in Italy, 34, 37–8
Pavia, 43
Payne, René, 254, 255
Payne, Walter, 64, 73n.6, 76
Peacock, James, surveyor, 18–19, 20, 27n.8, 51, 54, 80; and his wife, 78
Peacock, Thomas Love, 19, 27n.8
Pearse, John, 257
Pellwall, Staffordshire, 106, 214–15, 278, *214–15*
Pemberton, Dr Robert, 35–6, 100, 263
Pembroke, Elizabeth, Countess of, 138, 186, 247
Pembroke Lodge, Richmond Park, 138, 247
Pennington, R. R., 85–6, 87n.27, 100
Pepper, Mr, 41
Pepper, Michael, 240
Perry, Hon. Mrs, 240
Perry, John, 98, 100
Perthshire, 262
Peters, Mrs, 78, 262
Peters, Henry, 78, 177, 261
Petersham Lodge, 51, 55, 239
Petworth House, Sussex, 102, 274
Peyre, M. J., 22
Phipps, T. P., 259
Piacenza, 43
Piercefield, Gwent, 58, 138, 244, *139*
Piranesi, Giovanni Battista, 22, 26, 27, 29, 32, 47n.1, 65
Pitshill, Sussex, 257
Pitt, Thomas, 1st Baron Camelford, 24–5, 49, 51, 54, 55, 60, 78, 132, 239, 240, 244, 245; and the Dilettanti Society, 58–9; in Italy, 28n.18, 32, 35–6, 39, 40, 41, 44, 47n.5
Pitt, Rt. Hon. William, 59, 60–1, 64, 132, 245; memorial, 207
Pitt, William, Earl of Chatham, mausoleum, 31, 53, *31*
Pitzhanger Manor, Ealing, 19, 62, 65, 74–81, 91, 181–2, 264, *75–7*; Monk's Dining Room, 78, 182; sale of, 83
Playfair, James, 256, 258
Pompeii, 35, 40
    Temple of Isis, 35, *33*
Pontine Marshes, 34, 36
Pope, Alexander, 96
Pope, Clara Maria (formerly Mrs Francis Wheatley), 78, 94, 96
Port Eliot, Cornwall, 187, 267, *187–8*
Portland, Duke of, 233
Poulett, 4th Earl, 259
Pozzuoli, 35
Praed, William Mackworth, 169, 182, 253, 264, 265;

and his wife, 78
Praed's Bank, 89, 109, 182, 265, *183*
Pratt, Edward Roger, 42, 44, 51, 131, 245
Priestley, Richard, 98
Proctor-Beauchamp, Sir Thomas, 123, 243
Provis, Henry, 64, 253
Puget, John, 262
Pullinger, John, 138
Putt, Reymondo, 85, 268
Putteridgebury, Hertfordshire, 274

Raikes, Thomas, 267
Ramelly, —, leadworker, 174
Ramsey Abbey, Cambridgeshire, 189, 267, *189*
Ramsgate, Kent, 82, 86
Ransom, Morland and Hammersley, 252
Reading, Berkshire, 18, 260
    Castle Street, 267–8
    London Place, 257
    Simeon Monument, 267
    Simonds' Brewery, 143, 249, *142*
Reveley, Willey, 260
Reynolds, Sir Joshua, 22, 24
Rhône valley, 29, 45
Richards, Revd Mr, 175, 258
Richards, John, 80
Richardson, C. J., 66, 111
Richmond Park, Surrey, 259
    Pembroke Lodge, 138, 247
    Thatched House Lodge, 261
Rickmansworth, Hertfordshire, The Moat House, 264
Ringwould House, Kent, 96, 204, 273, *205*
Rivers, Lady, 240
Rix, Nathaniel, 132, 245
Robins, John, 184, 207, 210, 265, 273, 277
Robinson, Peter Frederick, 112, 228
Roehampton, Cedar Court, 190, 268, *190*
Rome, 29, 31–2, 39–41
    Arch of Titus, 29
    Colonna Palace, 28n.18
    Colosseum, *30*
    Corsini Chapel, 39, 119, *39*
    English Coffee House, 29
    Forum, 29
    Pantheon, 29, *30*
    S. Agnese Fuori le Mura, 29
    S. Maria degli Angeli, 29
    S. Maria Maggiore, 29
    Temple of Minerva Medica, 29
    Temple of Vesta, 29
    Tivoli, Temple of Vesta, 29–30, 157, *30*
    Villa Negroni, 91, 181, *77*
Rose, George, 256

Rothwell, William, 193
Rowley, Admiral Sir Joshua, 124, 242
Royal Academy, 20, 80–1; founding of, 21; School, 21–2; *see also* Soane, Sir John, Royal Academy
Royal Exchange Assurance, 244
Rucker, D. H., 249
Russell, Thomas, smith, 267
Ryston Hall, Norfolk, 76, 131–2, 245, *131*

Salerno, 36
Sandby, Thomas, 22, 65, 70, 96
Sanders, 58, 64, 66, 99, 104n.5
Saunders, Mrs, 266
Savernake Lodge, Wiltshire, 259
Savoir Vivre Club, 24
Saxlingham Rectory, Norfolk, 56, 124, 242, *126*
Scott, David, 257–8
Sealy, 249, *see also* Coade and Sealy
Sebright, Sir John, 267, 268
Segesta, 37, 38
Selby, Mr, 74
Selinunte, 38
Shadwell Lodge, Norfolk, 247
Shaftesbury, 5th Earl of, 255
Sharland, —, foreman, 134
Shee, Mrs, 100
Shee, Martin Arthur, 100
Sheerness, Kent, 255
Shelburne, Earl of, 250
Shotesham Hall, Norfolk, 58, 129–30, 138, 243, *128–9*
Sicily, 37–8
Sillitoe, Purney, 214, 278
Simeon, Edward, 267
Simeon, Sir John, 267
Simonds, William Blackall, 143, 249, 257, 267
Skelton Castle, Yorkshire, 64, 246
Smirke, Robert, 65–6, 80–1, 98, 107
Smith, George, 54, 58, 138, 241, 244; his wife, 54
Smith, Joseph, 253
Smith, Robert, later 1st Baron Carrington, 252
Smith, Sarah, 89, 96, 99, 100, 102–3, 109; her mother, 100
Snaresbrook, Greater London, 275
Soan, Elizabeth (née Toby), wife of Francis, 17
Soan, Francis, 17
Soan, John, senior, 17–18
Soane, Agnes (née Boaden), wife of George, 86, 98, 116n.18
Soane, Elizabeth (née Smith), wife of Sir John, 56–8, 61n.20, 62, 65, 81–6, 88–9, 92, 94, 96–100; death, 100, 204; her dog Fanny, 99, 104n.20; notebooks, 27n.8, 79–80; at Pitzhanger, 74, 79–80, 81; portraits of, 65, 104n.20, *67*, *79*, *101*;

tomb, 102, *see also* Soane tomb
Soane, Frederick, son of George, 109, 116n.18
Soane, George, son of Sir John, 58, 65, 81–2, 84, 85–6, 88, 109, 111, 116n.18, *79*; article in the *Champion*, 100, 105n.23; imprisonment, 98
Soane, George Manfred, son of above, 109
Soane, Sir John
  account books, *see below* notebooks
  appearance, 110
  Bank of England, architect and surveyor, 59, 60, 64, 111–12, *see also* Bank of England
  character, 7, 49, 50
  childhood, 17–18
  Dance's pupil, 18–20
  death, 115, *see also* Soane tomb
  Designs, 1778 and 1797, 26, *26*
  in Holland's office, 21–2
  illness, 97, 109, 113
  in Italy, 29–47, 113, 115; Italian notebooks and sketch books, 29, 36, 42, 43–4, 47n.2; journey home, 44–5
  marriage and children, 57–8
  Memoirs, 17, 112, 113
  notebooks, account books and Journals, 24–5, 50–1, 58, *see also above*, in Italy
  Office of Works: attached architect, 98–9, 106–8, 111, *see also* Office of Works; clerk of the works, 64, 68, 254
  place of birth, 17
  Plans, 1788, 60–1
  portraits of, 28n.14, *frontispiece*, *19*, 115; bust, 113, *95*
  Royal Academy: exhibition drawings, 21–2, 25, 31, 53, 54, 66, 280–7; professor of architecture, 35, 38, 80–1, 84, 99, 102, 111
  Royal Academy School, 22; medals, 22, 23, 45
  Royal Hospital, Chelsea, clerk of works, 81, 111, *see also* London, Chelsea
  'Soane style', 62–3, 78, 91–2, 204
  spelling of his name, 17, 32, 54
  will, 104n.16, 115, 116n.18
  Woods and Forests, deputy surveyor, 69–70
  works: List of, 239–79; Major Commissions, 119–238; composite painting of, *238*; *see also individual place names*
Soane, John, son of Sir John, 58, 65, 81–5, 88, 96, 97, 100, 116n.5, *79*; death, 108, 207; drawings exhibited, 287
Soane, John, grandson of Sir John, 104n.16, 108
Soane, Maria (née Preston), wife of John (son of Sir John), 84–5, 100, 108
Soane, Martha (née Marcy), mother of Sir John Soane, 17, 56; portrait of, *19*
Soane, William, brother of Sir John Soane, 18, 56,

99, 100, 109, 116n.8
Soane tomb, 102, 108, 207, 275, *103*, *114*
Soane's Museum, Sir John, 7, 111, 115; *Description of the House*, 113
Solihull, Warwickshire, 122–3, 243, 261, *122*
Sotheby, William, 239
South Hill Park, Berkshire, 265
Southgate, Middlesex, 258
Sowerby, John, 274
Sparrow, Robert, 244
Spencerwood, Berkshire, 239
Spiller, James, 100, 200, 260, 264, 271
Stanmore, Middlesex, Church of St John, 250
Steephill, Isle of Wight, 250
Stephenson, Colonel (Sir) Benjamin, 98–9
Steuart, George, 71, 150
Stevens, Edward, 27
Storace, Anna Selina, 42, 48n.35, 78, 270, *55*; memorial, 275
Storace, Elizabeth, 275
Storace, Stephano, 42
Stowe, Buckinghamshire, 25, 191–3, 253, 268, 276, *192–3*
Strange, John, 40
Strawberry Hill, Twickenham, 25, 78
Streater, Roberts, 233
Stuart, James, 60
Stuart, John, later 4th baronet, 37, 47–51, 239, 240
Sturt, Mrs, 246
Sudeley Castle, Gloucestershire, 275, 276
Sulby Lodge, Northamptonshire, 254
Sunbury House, Middlesex, 257
Sunderland, Co. Durham, bridge, 256
Sussex, Augustus Frederick, Duke of, 96, 113, 234
Swan, William, bricklayer, 122
Swinnerton, Thomas, 206, 207, 271, 274
Sydney Lodge, Hamble, Hampshire, 140, 249, *141*
Syracuse, 38

Taormina, 38
Taplow, Buckinghamshire, 253
Tarring, John, 109
Taverham Hall, Norfolk, 56, 58, 242
Tawstock, Devonshire, 141, 249
Taylor, Isaac and Josiah, 26, 61
Taylor, John, 100
Taylor, Sir Robert, 60, 72, 152
Taymouth Castle, Perthshire, 266–7
Teighe, Dr, 242
Tendring Hall, Suffolk, 124, 242, *127*
Terracina, 34, 53
Thellusson, Charles, 251, 254
Thellusson, G. W., 264
Thellusson, P. I., 251, 253

Thomas Bros., 276

Thomson, John, 190, 268

Thornton, Bayley & Amyand, 263

Thornton, Claude George, 209, 276

Thornton, Godfrey, 194, 252, 271

Thornton, Samuel, 263, 264; and his wife, 78

Thornton, Stephen, 263

Throckmorton, Sir John, 253

Tofts, Norfolk, 244

Tollemache, Hon. Wilbraham, 48n.19, 122, 240, 250

Trapani, 37

Turner, J. M. W., 56, 79, 100–1, 116n.5

Tyndale, George Booth, 88, 104n.1, 116n.5, 175, 203

Tyringham, Buckinghamshire, 62, 66, 149, 169, 174, 253, *169–72*

Church, 264, *173*

Tyrrell, Timothy, Remembrancer of the City of London, 18, 58

Tyttenhanger, Hertfordshire, 241, 249

Underwood and Doyle, metalworkers, 193

Upper Clapton, Greater London, 276

Valentia, Viscount, 274

Van Assen, Antonio B., works by, 104n.20, *79*

Vardy, John, 108, 221

Venice, 39–40

Verona, 40, 42

Versailles, 29

Vesuvius, Mount, 35, 36

Vicenza, 40, 42

Victoria, Princess, 113

Vignola, Jacopo Barozzi, 111, 236

Waddington, Revd Mr, 246

Wall Hall, Hertfordshire, 264

Walmer, Kent

St Mary's Church, 273

Walmer Cottage, 273

Walpole, Horatio (Horace), later 4th Earl of Orford, 25, 58, 78

Walthamstow

Grove Lane, 53, 239

Rectory Manor, 240

St Mary's Church, 243

Wandsworth

Clapham Common, 261

Common, 253

Westhill, 249

Ward, James, 104n.20

Wardour Castle, Wiltshire, 134, 247

Watson, Hon. Lewis Thomas, 130, 244

Watson, William, painter and glazier, 203

Way, John Raymond, 76

Wegg, Samuel, 76

Wellington, Duke of, 97; design for memorial, 279

Westmacott, Richard, 207

Westminster Insurance, 258

Weston, Hampshire, 260

Westwood, Captain, 109

Wettingen, 45, 48n.42

Weyland, John, 250

Wharton, John, *see* Hall, John

Wheatley, Clara Maria, *see* Pope

Whetton, Mr, 74

Whichcotes, Hendon, 251

Whitley Abbey, Warwickshire, 269

Wicks, Mr, 81–2

Wightwick, George, 109–10

Wildman, Mr, 59

Wildman, Thomas, 245

Wilford, General, 265

Wilkins, James, plasterer, 139, 248

Wilkins, William, 139, 248

Willes, Revd Mr, 268

William IV, 111; as Duke of Clarence, 70, 176, 261

Williams, Thomas, 64, 65

Williams, William, MP, 108, 222

Williamstrip, Gloucestershire, 251

Willis, Richard, 250

Wimborne, Dorset, St Giles House, 255

Wimpole Hall, Cambridgeshire, 62, 63–4, 147, 149, 251, *147–9*

Winchester, Hampshire

Hyde Close, 175, 258, *175*

The King's House, 253

Windham, William, 124, 243

Windsor, Berkshire

Castle, 107

Royal Lodge, 106

Winter, John, 74, 261

Winter, Ralph, 245

Wiston Hall, Suffolk, 251

Wodehouse, Revd P., 244

Wokefield, Berkshire, 248

Wood, Henry, stone-carver, 31

Woodeaton Manor House, Oxfordshire, 250

Woodgate, Robert, 64, 73n.4, *150–1*

Wootton, Somerset, 277

Worlingham Hall, Suffolk, 244

Wotton House, Buckinghamshire, 106, 174, 210, 277, *211–12*

Wreatham Hall, Norfolk, 249

Wrey, Sir Bourchier, 141, 249

Wyatt, George, 55–6, 57, 61n.15, 62, *55*
Wyatt, George, joiner, 122
Wyatt, James, 56, 61, 69, 70–2, 98, 107, 259
Wyatt, Samuel, 56, 81
Wyatville (Wyatt), Sir Jeffry, 107, 113
Wycombe Abbey, Buckinghamshire, 250
Wydiall, Hertfordshire, 253
Wynn, Charlotte, Lady, 253
Wynyard, Miss, 66

York and Albany, Frederick Augustus, Duke of, 107
Yorke, Hon. Mrs, 140, 241, 249, 255
Yorke, Admiral Sir Joseph, 277
Yorke, Philip, later 3rd Earl of Hardwicke, 39, 51, 60, 119, 239, 242, 255, 276; in Italy, 36–7; work at Wimpole Hall, 63–4, 147, 149, 251
Yorke Place, 242

Zurich, 45